# The 6:20 Man

David Baldacci is one of the world's bestselling and favourite thriller writers. A former trial lawyer with a keen interest in world politics, he has specialist knowledge in the US political system and intelligence services, and his first book, *Absolute Power*, became an instant international bestseller, with the movie starring Clint Eastwood a major box office hit. He has since written more than forty bestsellers featuring, most recently, Amos Decker, Aloysius Archer, Atlee Pine and John Puller. David is also the co-founder, along with his wife, of the Wish You Well Foundation, a non-profit organization dedicated to supporting literacy efforts across the US.

**Trust him to take you to the action.**

BY DAVID BALDACCI

**Aloysius Archer series**

*One Good Deed • A Gambling Man • Dream Town*

**Amos Decker series**

*Memory Man • The Last Mile • The Fix • The Fallen*
*Redemption • Walk the Wire*

**Atlee Pine series**

*Long Road to Mercy • A Minute to Midnight • Daylight • Mercy*

**Will Robie series**

*The Innocent • The Hit • The Target • The Guilty • End Game*

**John Puller series**

*Zero Day • The Forgotten • The Escape • No Man's Land • Daylight*

**King and Maxwell series**

*Split Second • Hour Game • Simple Genius • First Family*
*The Sixth Man • King and Maxwell*

**The Camel Club series**

*The Camel Club • The Collectors • Stone Cold • Divine Justice*
*Hell's Corner*

**Shaw series**

*The Whole Truth • Deliver Us From Evil*

**Vega Jane series**

*The Finisher • The Keeper • The Width of the World*
*The Stars Below*

**Other novels**

*True Blue • Absolute Power • Total Control • The Winner*
*The Simple Truth • Saving Faith • Wish You Well*
*Last Man Standing • The Christmas Train • One Summer • The 6:20 Man*

**Short stories**

*Waiting for Santa • No Time Left • Bullseye • The Final Play*

DAVID BALDACCI

# The 6:20 Man

MACMILLAN

First published 2022 by Grand Central Publishing, USA

First published in the UK in paperback 2022 by Macmillan
an imprint of Pan Macmillan
The Smithson, 6 Briset Street, London EC1M 5NR
*EU representative:* Macmillan Publishers Ireland Ltd, 1st Floor,
The Liffey Trust Centre, 117–126 Sheriff Street Upper,
Dublin 1, D01 YC43
Associated companies throughout the world
www.panmacmillan.com

ISBN 978-1-5290-6196-3



1 3 5 7 9 8 6 4 2

A CIP catalogue record for this book is available from the British Library.

Printed and bound by CPI Group (UK) Ltd, Croydon, CR0 4YY

*To Anthony Forbes Watson, my brilliant UK publisher and dear friend. You taught me a lot during our time together, and not just about books and publishing, but about great French wines and important moral philosophies. Wherever your future path takes you, I will be cheering you on. And our friendship will endure, as all true friendships do.*

# The 6:20 Man

# CHAPTER

# I

Travis Devine took a shallow breath, ignored the heat and humidity that was rising fast along with the sun, and rushed to board the 6:20 train, like it was the last flight out of Saigon. He was wearing an off-the-rack pearl-gray suit, a wrinkled white shirt that needed laundering, and a muted dark tie. He would rather be in jeans and a T-shirt, or cammies and Army jump boots. But that couldn't happen, not on this ride.

He was freshly showered although already starting to perspire; his thick hodgepodge of hair was as neatly combed as he could manage it. His face was shaved and mildly scented with a nondescript cologne. He wore cheap tasseled loafers shined fore and aft. The imitation leather briefcase held his company-issued laptop with special encryption and no personal use permitted thereon, along with breath mints and a packet of Pepcid AC. He no longer took the neat little power pills he'd popped when suited up to fight for his country. The Army used to give them out like gummy bears so the grunts would battle longer and harder on less sleep and less to eat.

Now they cost money.

His primary weapons, instead of the Army-issued M4 carbine and M9 sidearm of yesteryear, were twin Apple Mac twenty-seven-inch screens, connected by digital tethers to mighty, encrypted clouds seeded with all the data he would ever need. It was all bullshit, really, and, strangely enough, more important to him than anything else on earth right now.

What they taught you in the world of high finance was simple really: win or lose. Eat or starve. It was a binary choice. No Taliban or Afghan soldier pretending to be your ally before banging a round into the back of your head. Here, his chief concerns were quarterly earnings projections, liquidity, free and closed markets, monopolies and oligarchies, in-house lawyers who wanted you to stick to the rules, and bosses who insisted that you didn't. And most significant of all, the persons sitting right next to Devine at the office. They were mortal foes. It was him or them in Wall Street's version of mixed martial arts.

Devine was commuting south to the big city on Metro North's Harlem Line. At age thirty-two, his entire life had changed. And he wasn't sure how he felt about it. No, he was sure. He hated it. That meant things were working according to plan.

He sat where he always did when commuting into the city—third row, window seat on the starboard side. He switched to the port side on the way back. The train puttered along with no real ambition, unlike the humans it carried. Sleek trains ran like cheetahs in Europe and Asia, but here they were snails. Yet they were faster than the cars stuck in the murderous traffic that piled in and out of the city morning, noon, and night.

Generations before him had ridden this very same route to make their living in the sweatshop spires of Manhattan. Many had died along the way from the usual suspects: widowmaker heart attacks, strokes, aneurysms, the slow death of neurological disorders and cancers, a liver painfully scuttled by too much alcohol, or self-inflicted deaths among those who could take the strain no longer.

Devine lived in Mount Kisco in a saggy town house shared with three twentysomethings trying to forge their futures in various ways. He had left them all asleep as he tried to shape his future day by day. The train would continue to fill as it wended its way along to Manhattan. It was summer, the sun was well on its way up, and the heat was building. He could have lived in the city, and paid a lot more money for the easier commute. But he liked trees and open spaces, and being surrounded by skyscrapers and concrete at all times was not his preference. He had actually been mulling over where to live when a Realtor who knew a friend of his had called out of the blue and told him she had found him a room at the town house. It was cheap enough that he was able to save a bit. And lots of people commuted into the city, even though it made for long days and nights. But that philosophy had been beaten into his psyche for most of his life.

"You work till you drop, Travis," his father had told him over and over. "Nobody in this world gives you a damn thing. You have to take it, and you take it by working harder than anybody else. Look at your sister and brother. You think they had it easy?"

Yes, his older brother and sister, Danny and Claire. Board-certified neurosurgeon at the Mayo Clinic, and CFO of a Fortune 100, respectively. They were eight and nine years older than he was, and already minted superstars. They had reached heights he never would. He had been told this so often, nothing could persuade him not to believe it.

Devine's birth had clearly been a mistake. Whether his father forgot the condom or his mother didn't realize she was ovulating and failed to keep her lustful man at bay, out he had popped and pissed off everybody in his family. His mother went back to work immediately at his father's thriving dental practice in Connecticut, where she was a hygienist. He'd learned this later, of course, but maybe he'd also sensed his parents' indifference to him as an infant. That indifference had turned to fury when Devine was a senior in high school.

That was when he'd been accepted into West Point.

His father had roared, "Playing soldier instead of going out into the world and earning a living? Well, boy, you are off the family payroll starting now. Your mother and I don't deserve this crap."

However, he'd found his place in the world of the military. After graduating from West Point he'd gone through the arduous Ranger School, passing the crawl, walk, and run tests, which was how the three phases were described. By far the hardest part had been sleep deprivation. He and his comrades had literally fallen unconscious while standing up. He'd later qualified to become a member of the elite Seventy-Fifth Ranger Regiment. That had even been tougher than Ranger School, but he had loved the special forces and the dangerous and demanding quick-strike missions that came with being a member.

These were serious accomplishments and he had written to his parents about them, hoping for some praise. He had never heard back from his mother. His father had sent an email asking him what national park he would be assigned to now that he was a *ranger*. He had signed the email, "Proud father of Smokey the Bear." He might have assumed his dad was utilizing his sense of humor, only he knew his father didn't have one.

Devine had earned twin Purples, a Silver Star, and a slew of other bits of metal and ribbons. In the world of the Army, he was known as a combat stud. He would only term himself a *survivor*.

He had gone into uniform as a boy and come out as a war machine. Six foot one and one-quarter inches, as the Army had precisely measured him, he had entered West Point a lanky 180 pounds of average physique. Then the Army, and his own determination, had transformed him into 225 pounds of bone, muscle, and gristle. His grip was like the jaws of a croc; his stamina was off the charts; his skills at killing and not being killed placed him at the top of the food chain with orcas and great whites.

He'd risen to Captain right on schedule and had worn the twin silver bars proudly, but then Devine had called it quits because he had to. It had torn him up back then. It still tore him up. He was an Army man through and through, until he could be one no longer. Yet it was a decision he had to make.

After that he had sat in an apartment for a month wondering what to do, while old comrades phoned, emailed, and texted, asking him what the hell was he doing leaving the uniform. He had not gotten back to any of them. He had nothing he could say to them. A leader who had never had an issue giving orders and being in command, he couldn't find the words to explain what he had done.

He did have the Post-9/11 GI Bill to help him. It paid for a full ride to an in-state public university. It seemed a fair trade-off for nearly dying for his country. He'd gotten his MBA that way.

He was the oldest person in his class at Cowl and Comely, the minted powerhouse investment firm where he worked at an entry-level analyst position. When he'd applied at Cowl, he knew they had looked upon him with suspicion because of his age and unusual background. They had outwardly thanked him for his military service, because that was always automatic. But they probably had to fill a veterans quota, and he was it. He didn't care why they had picked him so long as he got a shot to make himself as miserable as possible.

*Yes,* he thought, as he stared out the window. *As miserable as possible.*

He had tried later trains into the city, but there were too many suits on board just like him, heading to work, heading to war. He needed to get there first, because whoever got there first, with the most, often was victorious. The military had also taught him that.

And so he stepped onto the 6:20 train every morning, and traveled to the city as punishment. And as much as he hated the work and the life that came with it, that penance would never manage to match his crime.

# CHAPTER

# 2

THE 6:20 TRAIN PASSED THROUGH bucolic countryside lurking outside a metropolis of unequaled breadth and complexity. Along the way, it picked up people at stations set in affluent small towns that existed mostly to serve the hungry beast due south. It finally chugged past an enclave of homes that were some of the most expensive in the country. It seemed unfair to call them mere homes. A place nearly as large as a shopping center should have a grander name, even *mansion* or *estate* didn't cut it, Devine thought. *Palace*, maybe, yeah, *palace* seemed to work.

He lifted his gaze from his laptop, as he did every morning when passing by this area. Every time he looked out, another structure was going up, or an existing one was being made even more lavish. The cement trucks drove in with wet loads for larger and more elaborate pools, the houses went higher or wider, or a guesthouse was being built or a putting green added. It kept the working class employed, so there was some good in the greed and pretentiousness, he supposed.

The train slowed as it approached a bend and lazily snaked upward over a lumpy knoll. It slowed some more, coming nearly to a stop. There was a signal-switching hitch here that the train people either couldn't or wouldn't do anything about. To say they had a monopoly was to say the earth revolved around the sun, so why would they give a damn?

And as they came to a complete halt, Devine *saw* her. He had seen her only a few times before, and only when the weather turned warm. He had no idea why she was up so early, but he was glad she was.

The privacy wall was high, but not high enough to block the sight line of those on the train at this point on the knoll. He knew who the owner of this particular palace was, and he also knew that there were height limits on perimeter walls and fences here. The owner had planted trees along the rear wall to compensate for this, but because of the space between the bottom of the tree canopy and the top of the wall, there was a fairly large gap that one could see through.

It was an oversight, he knew, that the owner would no doubt rectify one day, though Devine hoped not, at least while he was riding the 6:20. He felt a bit like Jimmy Stewart in *Rear Window*, the champion voyeur movie of all time. But he wasn't looking out the window because his leg was broken and he was bored, as was the case with Stewart's character. He was looking out the window because of *her*.

The woman had sauntered out from the rear door of the largest palace in this enclave. *Sauntered* was the only word that worked for how she moved. It was a smooth, leisurely pace, like a panther just getting warmed up before breaking into a sprint. The hips and glutes and thighs and shoulders all moved in the most gloriously primal choreography.

The place looming behind her was all modernistic, with glass and metal and concrete whipped into odd geometric shapes. Only the mind of an architectural savant snorting nostrils of coke could have conceived it.

She had on a short, white terry cloth robe that clung to her tanned thighs. When she took it off, revealed was an emerald-green string bikini and a body that seemed too flawless to be genuine. Her hair was all blond highlights with intricate cuts and waves that had probably cost more than his suit.

Devine looked around to see who else was watching. All the guys were, of course. One of the women had glanced up from her computer, seen the lady in question, looked at the gents with their faces burned to the glass, and turned back to her screen in disgust. Two other women, one in her forties and dressed like a hippie, and one in her seventies, didn't look up. The former was on her phone. The latter was diligently reading her Bible, which had plenty of warnings about sins of the flesh.

The woman placed her painted toenails in the water, shivered slightly, and then in she dove. She did a graceful arc under the water, pushed off the other side, and came back up to where she had started. She hoisted herself out and sat on the pool surround facing his way. She didn't seem to notice the train or anyone staring from inside it. Devine could imagine at this distance all she might see was the train's glass reflecting the sunlight.

With her body wet, the tiny bikini seemed to have shrunk. She looked to the left and right and then behind her at the house. Next, she slipped off her top and then her bottom. She sat there for a long moment totally naked; Devine could glimpse comingled white and tanned skin. Then she jumped once more into the water and vanished.

It was about this time that the train started up again, and the next palace in the enclave appeared, only it didn't have a beautiful woman skinny-dipping in its pool. In fact, this homeowner had planted not trees but tall, thick Leland cypresses that left no gaps through which one could peer.

Pretty much every other man on the train car groaned under his breath and slumped back with a mix of ecstasy and disappointment. Devine eyed some of them. They looked back at him, smiled, shook their heads, and mouthed things that sounded basically like, *Dude, WTF was* that?

Devine had never seen her strip down before. He wondered what had caused her to do it beyond some sort of playful impulse. He wondered about many things in that particular palace. It was fascinating to him what people did with all that money. Some were philanthropic; others just kept buying bigger toys. Devine told himself that if he ever got to be that rich, he would not buy the toys. He would give it all away.

*Yeah, sure you would.*

At the next station more people got on. And then at the next station still more.

As he looked around at the mostly twentysomethings on the train, who were already on their fired-up laptops and yanking down data clouds, and scanning documents and fine-tuning presentations and excelling at Excel, Devine knew that the enemy was everywhere. He was completely surrounded. And that should have panicked the former soldier.

And yet this morning, all Devine could think about was the naked woman in the water. And it wasn't for the obvious reasons.

To the former Ranger and Army scout, something about the lovely woman just seemed off.

# CHAPTER

# 3

WHEN HE HEARD THE DING while he was sitting at his desk at Cowl and Comely, Devine checked the message on his phone's personal email. He looked at it for a long moment, wondering whether it was a joke or he had simply lost the ability to read.

She is dead.

It was the shortest of declarative sentences, its noun, verb, and predicate adjective filled with ominous potency.

Then he checked out the rest of the email.

Apparently, Sara Ewes had been found hanging in a storage room on the fifty-second floor of the very building Devine was in, the message told him. She had been found by a janitor, her high heels lying on the floor beneath her. The woman's neck was elongated, her spine cracked, her life over. Or so the mysterious note said.

She had just turned twenty-eight, Devine knew, and had been at Cowl and Comely a little over six years. Ewes was tall and lean, with a long-distance runner's build. No slouch academically, she'd earned her MBA from Columbia while toiling here, and had obviously made the cut. Normally, the weed-out was complete after one year. Devine had been here six months, which meant he had another six to go before he was either shown the door or elevated to the next level.

He looked at the missive again. *Sara dead? It can't be.*

Devine had secretly dated Ewes while they both worked at Cowl. They had slept together, but only once. He had wanted more, maybe much more, in the way of a relationship with her. But then it was over. And now she was dead?

He focused on the sender. He didn't recognize the email address at all. In fact, he suddenly realized, it didn't look like any email address he'd ever seen. It didn't have a domain name, or a suffix like dot-com or dot-gov. It wasn't a Gmail. It was just a series of numbers. Who had sent it? And how? And why to him?

He looked around at the other cubicles where fingers rat-a-tatted keys and commerce moved on and fortunes were won or given back. This email hadn't gone out to his company email account. The compliance folks would be able to see all of that. This had come directly to his personal email. And no one around him was reacting like they had gotten a similar message.

*Am I the only one that got it? Is it for real? Is it a hoax? Is Sara really dead?*

He wrote a reply to the email: Who is this? And sent it off. Then he looked at his screen and saw that his reply had failed to go. He tried again with the same result.

*Okay, this seems to be a one-way message stream.*

Devine rose and headed for the door. Not one head lifted to see him leaving. Their battle was won on the screens in front of them and by the amount of time their butts stayed in these chairs. The pie just got one slice bigger, some of them were doubtless thinking, as they heard Devine walk out.

He stepped onto the elevator and headed to the fifty-second floor. As he approached the fifty-first, on impulse, he hit the button for that floor. But even with his security card, the floor button did not light up. In his six months at the firm, Devine had never met anyone who had access to that floor. It was known, informally, as Area 51. He had heard rumors that no one worked on that floor. He had been on the sidewalk and counted the floors from the top down to the fifty-first, and wondered what was really going on there. Then again, it might just be the firm's high-frequency trading platform. All the major investment houses had them.

As soon as the elevator doors opened, a uniformed policeman stationed there came forward and put his hand out to stop Devine.

*Something's happened*, thought Devine. *The email wasn't a sick joke*. He felt a wave of dread spill over his body.

"Floor's closed, sir."

Devine lied and said, "But I work on this floor."

"Not today you don't," said the cop, and he looked like he meant it. "Nobody does."

Devine caught the eye of Wanda Simms, a senior member of staff who had been assigned as the admin liaison for his incoming class of Burners, as the group of interns was known—as in burning the candle at both ends. She hurried over to him, looking gray and haggard.

He hit the button to hold the doors open.

"Oh, it's terrible, Travis, just terrible. They're keeping everyone off the floor. I just had to go around and check to make sure no one was here."

She was around fifty and dressed diplomatically in the preapproved black dress and black hose and black shoes attire of Cowl and Comely, but it could have been Goldman Sachs, BlackRock, JP Morgan, Merrill Lynch, or any of the other usual suspects. Glasses dangled from a chain around her neck, along with her security RFID card on a lanyard.

"Why, what's happened? What's going on, Wanda?"

She seemed flustered enough to not wonder why he was on this floor during the workday.

"You haven't heard? It's Sara Ewes. Did you know her? I remember she was a mentor to your class of interns."

"No, not very well," he lied. "What happened to her?"

"She's dead."

He didn't have to pretend to be surprised. The realization

that the message was accurate hit him like an IED. "Dead! What happened?"

"She killed herself, or so I overheard the police saying. Hanged herself."

*Oh my God.*

"Folks, if you don't mind, thanks," butted in the cop.

Simms took Devine's arm. "Come on, I can talk on the way."

She swiped her card through the reader in the elevator car and pushed the button for the ground floor.

"Wait, what floor are you?" she asked. "I can never keep track."

"I'll go all the way. I have an errand to run."

She made a show of hiking her eyebrows. As a rule, death in the building or not, Burners didn't leave their desks until it was time to slink home and fall asleep for a few pitiful hours before the hamster wheel started to crank again.

"So, about Sara?"

The doors closed and Simms said, "One of the custodians found her in the supply closet this morning hanging from the ceiling. Apparently, she lifted one of the panels, hung a cord around a metal pipe there, and jumped off a chair."

*The person who sent me that note knew all of this. How? And why tell me?* "When was she supposed to have done this?"

"Late last night or very, very early this morning. It seems she had on her same clothes from yesterday. I guess they can tell from the condition of the body how long she'd been dead," she added, turning pale.

"Meaning she never went home?"

"Apparently not."

He thought about the email. "Did she leave a note?"

"Not that I've heard. And she seemed so levelheaded. You probably know she worked in the M and A Division," she added, referring to Mergers and Acquisitions. "She was really going places. The sky was the limit. Mr. Cowl was her personal mentor."

"I can't believe she's dead."

"I've never even seen a dead body, I mean, not unless it was in a coffin. Have you?"

Devine eyed her and said truthfully, "Never in an office building."

"Her parents will be an absolute wreck. They live out of the country, so it will take a bit of time for them to get here. And it certainly won't be a good look for the firm." She put a hand to her mouth. "Oh, I shouldn't have said that. I mean, someone *has* died."

They reached the ground floor and Simms stepped off. "Aren't you coming?"

"I forgot I have something to finish up," said Devine. "I'll see you later."

Devine swiped his card in the reader and pushed the button for his floor. He imagined Sara Ewes doing this yesterday and perhaps not knowing it would be the last time she ever would. Or maybe she did know. Suicides were often planned. It certainly sounded like this one had been.

As he shot skyward in the elevator shaft, Devine reflected on the fact that he had not told Simms the truth, since he *did* know Sara Ewes very well. Given time, they perhaps could have grown to love each other. But it hadn't turned out that way.

And now Sara Ewes was no more. And he needed to know why.

# CHAPTER

# 4

A CLOUDLESS, STARRY NIGHT AND Travis Devine was mostly unaware of it. He hadn't really looked at the sky since going to work for Cowl and Comely. He had gone from the office to the subway, taken it to Grand Central, and was now on the evening train heading home. From there he would walk from the station.

On leaving the Cowl Building he had nodded at the night security guard, as he always did. For obvious reasons, he related to men who carried guns. The bulky man usually glanced at the clock behind his desk, nodded back, and gave him a patronizing look as if to say, *Really? Seriously? Is this shit really worth it, dude? Come on. How much damn money do you* need*?*

But not tonight. Not after Ewes's death. They just exchanged somber looks.

On the train Devine had his AirPods in and was half listening to a financial news channel on his phone. Money was already being made and lost overseas in Asian markets that would be officially up and running in about an hour. He would rather be listening to Janis Joplin or AC/DC, but he was now a budding financial whiz with a job to do and a career to build. He had no moments to waste on "Me and Bobby McGee" or "Highway to Hell." And with the latter, he was probably already on it.

The train car was packed with weary, sweat-logged warriors, some of whom would have the next two days off to lick their wounds and get ready for another week's slog on Monday. He was nearly cheek to jowl with the man seated next to him.

Devine's mother was a first-generation American of Greek extraction, and he had taken after her in looks, while his siblings had favored their Irish father. Devine had dark, wavy hair, olive skin, a thickened nose, rugged chin, square jawline, and deep-set eyes that seemed to automatically broadcast "brooding" regardless of what he was actually thinking. Some people just thought he always looked pissed off. And maybe he was. And his five o'clock shadow seemed to sneak up on him at noon. It didn't look exotic or cool; it just looked grungy.

He leaned toward the window when they reached the knoll and the commuter train slowed even more. The rear lights were on in the palace of the skinny-dipping woman. He knew she had taken a chance earlier that morning by stripping down in public. These days everybody had a camera in their phone, which put her in danger of being plastered across social media platforms for all of eternity. But maybe she didn't care. Which intrigued him even more.

Party lights were strung up around the outdoor area now, resembling tiny stars that had lost their buoyancy. The pool surround was littered with guests in chic dress that managed to be both casual and, he was sure, costly. It took Devine a few moments to find her in the crowd as the train ground to a stop when the mysterious signal problem reared its head once more.

She had on a white, clingy dress that slid to midthigh and, like the bikini, accented the woman's tan. Her shoes were golden stilettos. She had a drink in hand and was talking to another woman of nearly equal beauty. He watched her laugh and the other woman followed suit. Devine wondered what they were talking about. He also wondered what made women like that laugh, or be happy.

Then Devine started to feel guilty and also stupid for maybe wishing he could be part of that world, especially after learning of Sara Ewes's death.

# CHAPTER

# 5

MR. DEVINE? TRAVIS DEVINE?"

He looked over as the man got out of the car parked in front of the station, which also housed an Italian restaurant.

"Yeah?"

The man walked over. He was Black, about Devine's height and lean, maybe forty-five or a bit older, bald head, and furrowed skin on his brow. He wore a dark blue suit that looked good on his athletic frame. His shoes were black and rubber soled. He flashed a badge and an official ID housed in a cred pack, like he was a magician doing a card trick. "Detective Karl Hancock, NYPD."

Devine grew rigid. "What can I do for you?"

"You mind coming over to the car where we can talk?"

"What about?"

"Come on, what do you think? Sara Ewes. She's dead, didn't you know that?"

Devine didn't like the guy's manner. It was blunt and seemed to leap to lots of conclusions. The brown eyes, clearly visible under the streetlight, scrutinized Devine and came away suspicious.

"I heard about it, along with everyone else."

"Right. This way, sir, if you don't mind. Won't take long."

*That's what they always say. And before you know it, years have gone by.*

He sat in the passenger seat of the car, where the smell of spilled coffee and the vapory veil of cigarette smoke was suffocating.

Hancock rolled down a window and said, "Sorry about that. Fact is, I don't smoke and I don't drink coffee and this isn't my ride. And they ain't supposed to smoke in here, but they do. Motor pool checkout. Serious budget cuts. Don't think they've bought new wheels for ten years or so. Gotta dry-clean my clothes every time I pull duty in one."

"No problem, I've smelled a lot worse."

"That would be first in Afghanistan and then in Iraq, correct? Captain Devine?"

He didn't like that the NYPD knew this about him. That showed they had already investigated him and sent a detective all the way out here on the very day Sara's body was found.

"*Former* Captain. And I've been to bars in the city that smelled worse than those places."

"You were wounded, twice. But you look all there."

"Yeah, in all the places you can see."

Hancock's demeanor changed. "Is that right? You got problems up here?" He tapped his temple.

"No, I'm just fine up there." Devine slid up his pants leg to reveal a thick, hardened scar that wrapped both ways around his calf like the tentacles of an octopus. "If you ever wanted to see the bomb pattern of an IED, there it is."

Hancock glanced at the old wound and said, "Damn, looks like it hurt."

"I didn't have time to feel it. The blast knocked me ass-over-heels unconscious. But when I woke up, I did. Thank God for morphine." He let his trouser leg drop. "But I thought you wanted to ask about Sara Ewes."

The official notebook came out. "You knew her?"

"Yes."

"How?" asked Hancock.

"We worked at the same firm, Cowl and Comely. But you knew that."

"So how *exactly* did you know her?"

"We met at some company mixers. We went out in groups for drinks, some dinners before the recruitment BS was over and our noses got pressed to the grindstone. She was sort of a mentor to my intern class."

"How did she strike you?"

"Talented and hard-charging. But why did you come all the way out here to ask me questions? I was there all day. I'll be there tomorrow. And my understanding was she died by suicide, so why are the police involved?"

"It's *speculated* that she killed herself. My job is to rule out all other manners of death. And you work on Saturdays?"

"In my world, Detective, it's only the day after Friday. And I don't see how I can help. I didn't work directly with her. I haven't seen her in months, in fact. Last time was a group dinner at Per Se, Columbus Circle. Over fifty people, with wine included. Must have cost the firm a small fortune. But it's only money."

"Impressive memory. I can't remember what I had for lunch yesterday." His words were flippant, his stare was not. "And the only time I'll ever be inside Per Se is if someone croaks there."

"In my line of work, you tend to remember things pretty exactly."

"You work hard at that place, I take it?"

"Let's put it this way—I have but one set of balls to give for Cowl and Comely, and that might not be enough."

"You're funny for an investment type."

"I just crunch numbers and give them to the *real* investment bankers, and they make all the money and get all the girls."

"How much money are we talking about?"

Devine knew the man didn't really need to know this for his investigation. It was very American to be nosy about the wealth of the very rich. Whole industries were built around disseminating that information to the fascinated masses.

"The firm has various divisions, and the comp and profit sharing are split differently depending on which camp you fall into.

Partners on the very low end get mid–seven figures. People like Bradley Cowl? Maybe a quarter of a billion or more per year in official comp and stock options. He also gets percentages of all the profit streams, so that goes on top of his base."

Hancock was shaking his head this whole time. "I make a hundred and ten grand a year. And I thought I was doing great till you laid that shit on me."

"How do you think I feel? I don't even make what you make, and I see all those dollars on the screen every day and they just pass right by me."

The man's eyes glittered once more, like a dog picking up a scent. "And so you resent that? Them getting all the girls and the dough?"

"I resent no one about anything. You work hard, you earn it, it's yours. I hope to do the same."

"And the girls? Like Sara Ewes?"

"Give me a break, okay? I can get girls if I want to. And Cowl has a strict rule against employees dating."

*If he finds out we were seeing each other, I'm screwed.*

"Okay. Anything else about Ewes?"

"Like what?"

"The usual. Depressed? Ever spoke to you about suicide?"

"Probably everyone who works on Wall Street at one time or another has contemplated suicide, either in pitiful jest or for real."

"That include you?" asked Hancock.

"Look, I saw guys shot up, blown up, and cut up right in front of me. I'm not taking my own life because a Wall Street firm busts my chops."

"So, nothing else you can tell me?"

Devine glanced out the car window and seemed truly amazed to see the stars in the sky.

His next words were said in a calm, even tone, because that was how he was suddenly feeling. "Sara was a nice person. She never talked to me about killing herself. She never seemed depressed, quite the opposite. She used to pep us up when we were getting ground down. But like I said, it's been a while. And even a day at Cowl and Comely is like a lifetime, Detective Hancock."

"So why stay?"

Devine assumed a stoic look and hit the Play button in his head. "It's the American dream. I'm trying to create my own."

"You don't strike me as the type to give a shit about making truckloads of money."

"You must have me confused with someone else. I *do* want the money and everything that comes with it. But there are a lot of things you can do with that money. You can use it to help other people."

"So you're busting your ass to help others?" Hancock said with a shit-eating grin.

"I did it in the Army. Any reason I can't do it on Wall Street?"

"Come on. Just tell me the truth. It can't be *that* bad."

But Devine didn't open his mouth, because he had nothing more to say.

And it *was* that bad.

# CHAPTER

# 6

Hancock had offered to drive Devine home, probably just to see where he lived. Devine accepted and a few minutes later he climbed out of the car in front of the white two-story brick town house with a one-car detached garage that was part of a small community of like structures. It was not poor, it was not rich. And neither was it just right.

"Nice place," said Hancock.

"It's the only thing I could really afford this close in that had trees and some grass."

"You think *this* is close in?"

"Where do *you* commute in from?"

Hancock smiled and said, "Trenton."

"I rest my case, and I'm not even a lawyer."

"If I need to follow up on stuff?"

"You know where I live and work. I'm easy to find. I'm not going anywhere unless Cowl and Comely decides to pull my plug. If so, you can catch me at the unemployment office."

Hancock drove off in his ratty motor pool coffee-and-nicotine ride. Black smoke poured out of the tailpipe and coated the white brick, and Devine, with a nice, cozy blanket of carcinogens.

Coughing, he unlocked the door and walked in. The front room held one of his three roommates, the big-bellied Will Valentine. He worked from home and was employed as a white-hatter, a person hired by tech firms and banks and other industries to try to hack through their security systems. They had become friends, and Valentine had even taught Devine some ingenious ways to electronically sneak into various databases.

He was also Russian, but had changed his name to something very American. He had shown Devine his passport. His real name was long and unpronounceable, at least for Devine. Lots of consonants strung together had never been his thing.

"I get many more girls with American name," Valentine had explained. "But I tell clients truth, that I am Russian. They know we are best at hacking. You wait and see; I will get rich. I fuckin' lo-o-ove capitalism. And I love your women."

Devine never could tell if the guy knew he was playing a Hollywood version of a Russian now free in America, or if he really was like that.

Valentine was now snoring softly on the sofa, mumbling in his native language. To Devine, spoken Russian always sounded menacing. As though the spoken words were uniformly *And now, you will die horribly, comrade.*

Valentine's laptop was perched on his substantial gut and was being lifted into the air with each inhale and dipping with every exhale. The TV was on but muted. It looked to be one of those limited series that moved at the speed of light, just begging to be binged. An open and empty Domino's pizza box was on the carpet next to the couch. Twin empty bottles of Michelob rested next to it. The Russian was definitely an American in diet now.

Devine went over and touched the open laptop. Its screen came to life, but didn't reveal its treasure box of data. A large dragon came on instead and breathed a wall of fire at the attempted digital trespassing.

*Cute*, thought Devine. He peered into the dining room, which held not a stick of furniture but only a human being. Another roommate, a Black woman named Helen Speers, was on a mat in the middle of the green carpet doing yoga. She was barefoot and performing a downward dog pose in a tight-fitting Lycra one-piece. Speers had just graduated from law school at NYU and was almost never home before Devine was. She was petite and lithe and lovely. And one day she would be in court righteously carving people up with the law.

"Early night?" he said.

Speers had AirPods in. She nodded and said between deep yoga breaths, "Got stood up on a drink in SoHo, if you can believe that. I'm releasing endorphins in retaliation."

"No, I *can't* believe that," he replied, but she had moved on to child's pose and wasn't listening.

He walked up the stairs to the second floor. His third and final roommate, Jill Tapshaw, was a truly brilliant person who had started her own online dating company, known as Hummingbird. He marveled at her guts and drive and brain operating on a different plane from the rest of the world. While Valentine and Speers had come to live here about the same time Devine had, Tapshaw had been here only a little over four months, but she was friendly and outgoing, and he had gotten to know her.

Her company was a true start-up because she ran it from her bedroom and also from a two-room office in a strip mall in downtown Mount Kisco, about a half mile from here. She had five full-time employees other than herself and about three dozen independent contractors working remotely, she'd told him. They specialized in bringing together people fearful of reaching out on their own, or of enduring the usual online dating experience. It was a need and she had filled it. Tapshaw had told Devine the site already had millions of users and over a hundred thousand paid subscribers from all over the world.

"And we're now adding tens of thousands of new users a day. We raised half a million in our Round A and five million in our B a year later. I'm projecting a home run for a Round C, at five times that, at a great valuation. Next, we tack on some tasteful piggyback ads and banner bucks for peripheral revenue streams. With enough capital I can dominate my space. And then we execute different but compatible product silos under separate corporate entities, all under Hummingbird's umbrella brand, to provide a sort of dating-to-grave experience. You want to invest? It's still relatively cheap. Last chance. Friends and family and *roommate* discount."

Cowl and Comely paid shit to the Burners. They just did their eighty- to ninety-hour grunt workweeks in the hopes of the payoff at the end. Most of Devine's money went for rent and the ride in and out. And then there was that other thing called food.

But nevertheless, though he legally wasn't a *qualified investor* under the securities laws, he'd bought a thousand bucks' worth of stock in the little bird that flitted around flowers sucking up nectar and paying it forward. Which was where she had gotten the name, Tapshaw had told him. "You can spend a hundred grand on a branding firm to come up with horseshit and then focus-group the hell out of it for another hundred grand, or you can do it on your own for free."

He tapped on her bedroom door and called out her name.

"Getting ready to Zoom with a Taiwanese venture capital group," Tapshaw's voice barked. "Their birth rate is plummeting. Is it urgent? Is the place on fire? Are you bleeding to death, Travis?"

"No," he called through the door. "All good. Just don't forget to eat." She kept a jar of peanut butter and a stack of celery sticks in a glass with water in her room. She was thinner than a rake and seemed to prefer it that way. She'd told Devine she hadn't been on a single date in over a year, not even digitally.

"Do as I say, not as I *don't* do," Tapshaw had quipped.

Restless and edgy and not wanting to sleep despite being tired, Devine went to his room, changed into athletic shorts and a T-shirt and Saucony running shoes.

He left the house and had just started his run when a black sedan pulled up beside him.

There were two men inside. Serious-looking men. Suits and shades, even in the gathering darkness.

"Mr. Devine? Travis Devine?" a strange man said for the second time tonight.

He stopped running and said, "Yeah?"

The man flashed a badge, a federal one with an agency Devine instantly recognized. "Your presence is requested, please get in."

"Requested by who?"

The man moved just enough so Devine could see the pistol in the shoulder holster.

"Get in."

Devine looked around, and, like the soldier he had once been, he followed orders and got in.

# CHAPTER

# 7

THE RIDE TOOK THIRTY MINUTES. They were heading south, toward the city. Neither man spoke, and Devine knew better than to ask questions. First the NYPD and now the feds; he didn't like all this personal attention.

They pulled off into a small town much like Mount Kisco, extremely affluent in some parts, just as extremely working-class in others. They drove to the very back of a nondescript office park where there was a single brick building. There were no cars parked out front and no signs on the building. The windows were blacked out and it looked abandoned.

The man parked and got out along with his colleague. He held the car door open for Devine and they walked up to the front of the building. The man flashed an RF card in the face of a reader port and Devine heard the door click open.

This was looking both way too official and far too clandestine. He figured neither boded well for him.

*I shot the sheriff, but I did not shoot the deputy.*

The driver led the way inside, Devine in the middle, the other guy bringing up the rear. Devine would have expected nothing less. It was the way you transported either prisoners or soon-to-be prisoners.

Automatic lights came on as they walked through an open space.

Devine was led to an interior door. The man knocked and a voice said, "Come."

The door was opened and the man motioned Devine in. He closed the door and Devine looked around the small space and then at the man sitting behind the desk.

"Sit down, Devine," said the man. "We have a lot to go over, so pay attention. There is no time to waste."

Devine sat.

The fellow looked like a well-worn slab of granite. His gray hair was bristly and cut short. His features were chiseled and fierce. The salt-and-pepper eyebrows swooped in all directions. The decades-old suit never had been expensive or of good quality when brand-new, but it was so unremarkable as to still be serviceable now. The red-and-blue-striped tie was too wide for the times, the collared button-down shirt a bit worn around the edges. He couldn't see the man's shoes from here, but if he had to guess, Devine would speculate they were black, and pedestrian, and shined to spit-polish perfection.

There was something about him, his bearing, the way he gave commands, because they were commands, the breadth of the shoulders, the ominous thickness of the hands.

He was now a suit who was once a soldier. Devine could just tell. And really still a soldier because it gets into your DNA and there is no way to separate it from you. It becomes you.

The man silently studied him.

*Gauging the size of my balls.*

Devine stared back, waiting. He had done this so many times with military superiors that it was second nature.

"Exemplary record at West Point. Then Infantry Officer Basic, Ranger School, Jump School, Stryker Battalion out of Fort Lewis. Line platoon company commander for a year and a half with a string of commendations. Made First Lieutenant right on schedule. Company XO for six months. Next up, line platoon commander, Ranger Battalion, so you're Ranger tabbed *and* scrolled," added the man, referring to the fact that Devine had graduated from Ranger School and been assigned to the Seventy-Fifth Ranger

Regiment. "Promoted to Captain and got your silver bars right at the four-year mark. Bradley company commander out of Fort Stewart for eighteen months. Then Ranger Battalion out of Hunter Army Airfield. Ranger company commander, then staff officer. All along the way, tours of combat duty in Afghanistan and then Iraq, and special ops missions in ten other shitstorm countries, where if you messed up you get a flag on your coffin and a Dignified Transfer at Dover Air Force Base."

Devine was impressed that the man had recited his military CV from memory. Some parts of it even Devine had forgotten.

The man leaned back in his chair and studied Devine. "You have shrapnel in your shoulder and leg, and they'll stay with you until the day you die. You were picked up for 0-4 Major at the eight-year mark below the zone," he added, referring to the Army's esoteric promotion vernacular. "In due time you would have had the golden oak leaf on your uniform, Devine. And then you *quit*. I wonder why."

The man didn't ask it as a question. He had thrown it out as a statement. But still, Devine decided to try to answer.

"I did my time. I took my shots and pretty much all of them hit the target. They took their shots at me. Some hit, most missed. I moved on. It was time. I didn't relish pressing my luck."

"Don't bullshit me, son. I don't have the patience."

"I'm not—"

"My name is Emerson Campbell. Retired Army two-star. Never got the third or fourth ones because I don't play the political games necessary to do that. And so let me be clear, former Captain Devine, I know *exactly* why you left the service, and it has nothing to do with your luck running out."

He opened a manila folder that was lying in front of him. He took out some photos and arrayed them in front of Devine.

He pointed to one picture. "Lieutenant Roy Blankenship. You knew him. You served together." He pointed to another photo. "Captain Kenneth Hawkins. You knew him, served with him as well."

"So what?"

"Patience, Devine. We've been interested in you for a while now."

"Is that right?"

"Who do you think got you the room at that town house in Mount Kisco?"

Devine's eyes widened at this. "A Realtor who was a friend—"

"Right. A friend of a friend. We have lots of friends, Devine, who do what they're told."

"Why did you care where I lived?"

"Let's just say it was a convenient spot for us, considering we have this office nearby. And you take the train in. And you pass a certain house there every day, right?"

The man could only mean one thing. "Brad Cowl's palace, you mean?"

"Palace, eh? You're right. And I'm glad you pick things up fast. Maybe our time won't be wasted."

He took out another picture, clearly a morgue shot of the now deceased Roy Blankenship with ligature marks around his neck.

"He was killed, murdered, you also know that. Even though Army CID ruled it a suicide. The guy was cremated, evidence lost, a total clusterfuck. But you know who killed him. Kenneth Hawkins, his superior officer, his comrade in arms, did the honors. And you know exactly why he did it."

"Says who?" muttered Devine. He was feeling sullen and trapped, because he was. And he also knew exactly where this was headed.

"Says the evidence. Hawkins murdered Blankenship and made it look like a suicide. He got away with it. Until he didn't. As you know. But, to refresh your memory."

He took out another photo of a very dead Kenneth Hawkins.

"And you know who killed Hawkins."

"Do I?" Devine felt every muscle in his body tense. The nightmare had finally come home to roost. He could feel the walls of the small space close in around him.

*Hey, it was a nice, if short, ride. But you've got to pay the piper. I guess I did shoot the deputy after all.*

"You do, because *you* killed him," replied Campbell.

"I didn't kill him."

"You two fought, out in the moonscape mountains of Afghanistan. He was badly injured from that fight. You walked away and left him. He died there. You could have saved him. You chose not to. How would you describe that?"

"You have no proof of—"

"We have proof of *everything*. Enough to take years of your life away. With that said, I'm going to make you an offer that is akin to your winning the goddamn lottery, son. Now, the *choice* for you is astoundingly simple. Those men outside are Army CID special agents. You can either go with them to be charged and thrown in the brig to await a military trial—"

Devine interrupted, "You can't court-martial me. I'm a civilian now."

"Civilian courts have ruled that military retirees *can* be prosecuted under military law for crimes committed *after* they left the service. In your case, the crime was done while you were *in* uniform. So there is no question that the Army will be the one prosecuting your case. And you *will* be convicted and sent to USDB for a very long time," Campbell added, referring to the United States Disciplinary Barracks at Fort Leavenworth, Kansas, the military's max-security prison. "Unless you agree to work with us."

"And who exactly is *us*?"

"The shop I now run. It's a small office within the Department of Homeland Security, and has a joint operation agreement with the Department of Defense. It's aptly called the Office of Special Projects. It has about five hundred operatives, of which I control fifty. I'd like to make you the fifty-first. It has a wide latitude of core interests, with the security of this nation driving all of them. When I took off the uniform I didn't forget my oath—did you?"

"What do you want me to do?"

"A woman died at your place of employment."

"Sara Ewes, yes."

"You knew her."

"I did."

"The fact is, there is something going on at Cowl and Comely, Devine, something seriously not right. We have heard chatter, we have run down a few leads, but we have made no real progress. And we have no grounds to execute a search warrant or bring people in for questioning, and we're light-years from federal prosecutors impaneling a grand jury. We need information, Devine. A lot of it. We need to ferret out whatever the hell is going on there. You are admirably suited to investigate this matter since you are already *there*. That is the reason you're *here*. That is why we've been watching you. That is why you now live in Mount Kisco, and why you pass Cowl's house every day. We want Brad Cowl badly. And we need your help to do it."

"So, I'm to be your plant inside?"

"I don't care what nomenclature you use. I just want results."

"And if I do what you ask and I'm successful?"

"Then you will have accomplished the mission. And I will ask you to serve your country again as a member of the Office of Special Projects."

"And when does this *service* end?" asked Devine.

Campbell glanced down at the photos of the dead men. "You ended Hawkins's life about fifty years early. What is avoiding the consequences of that worth to you?"

"If you know all about it, as you claim to, then maybe you understand why I did what I did. I tried like hell to get CID to take a second look. I went through my chain of command and got stonewalled. Hawkins had friends at high levels, and the Army didn't want the bad optics of one officer's killing another."

"I understand perfectly. I might have done as you did in the same circumstances. However, the law makes no exception. But

I am giving you a chance to avoid the penalty that would befall anyone else in your situation. You might consider yourself the luckiest bastard on earth, hence my reference to your winning the lottery." He paused. "So, what is your decision? Because I need it right now."

"But I can't promise that I'll find out what you want me to. I can only promise to do my best. Will that cut it?"

"When does a soldier ever get a pass on *trying* to complete a mission? You either complete it or you don't. You sure as hell know the United States Army doesn't hand out participation trophies, son."

"If Sara hadn't been killed would you have just arrested me instead of making this offer?"

"I don't answer pointless questions. Are you in, or do I call the CID boys to do their thing?"

It was a choice in name only. "I'm in," said Devine.

Campbell took out a file from a desk drawer. "Excellent. Now, let's get down to basics so you can better understand *exactly* what it is we want you to do."

A good soldier apparently once more, Devine settled back to receive a briefing and his orders going forward.

# CHAPTER

# 8

DEVINE WAS DROPPED OFF BACK at his home. He went to his room, looked up Emerson Campbell online, and saw the same stern face staring back at him. A Vietnam platoon leader involved in some of the most hellish battles of that long, ugly war, Campbell was the recipient of nearly every combat medal under the sun. He was also, like Devine, Ranger tabbed and Ranger scrolled. He had been engaged in pretty much every combat situation the United States had during the intervening years, including the First and Second Gulf Wars. He'd ended up a two-star commanding Fort Benning in Georgia, where Devine had earned his Ranger status, though their paths had not crossed there.

He had the rep of being iron hard but fair, a soldier's soldier. He cared more for his troops than he did for the next star on his shoulder. Then his career had seemed to stall. One article reported that Campbell had been brutally honest during some congressional testimony, and the Army brass hadn't liked that level of candor from one of its senior officers. He'd then been apparently forced into retirement and gone into the private sector. He'd resurfaced a few years later with some civilian position at the Pentagon. After that, he'd dropped off the radar.

Well, the old man was back on the battlefield, it seemed.

Devine stripped off his running clothes and changed into jeans, heavy boots, and a long-sleeved T-shirt, then grabbed his motorcycle helmet and went downstairs and out the back. In the one-car garage was Tapshaw's hunter-green Mini Cooper. She was the only one with a car, for her one-mile jaunt to work. Speers took the train into the city like Devine did, and Valentine performed his heavenly hacking remotely from his room. Or the couch.

Next to the Mini was Devine's BMW motorcycle. It was the only thing he had ever splurged on. He'd bought it used with money saved up from his Army pay.

He fired up the motorcycle and soared off into the night. He had been given a mission, and as a soldier, he had never liked to let time lapse between an order given and its execution. The problem was the file that Campbell had on Cowl and Comely was very thin. But there was enough there that Devine could understand someone like Campbell being deployed to see what was up.

*And now I'm right in the middle of it, sink or swim.*

He zipped along curvy roads going faster than he should have at night, but he didn't really care. At least he was finally flying along with a purpose beyond making money for Brad Cowl, a man who already had far too much wealth.

Ten minutes later he arrived at Cowl's private enclave, the rear of which he saw from his train every morning. It was ablaze with lights, like a movie premiere, for all to see. High-dollar showroom-level cars were parked in the palace's motor court. Wrought iron gates kept out the uninvited, of which Devine was assuredly one. He took off his helmet and watched.

The people he had seen from the train earlier were filtering out now. No doubt they had to get back to their fabulous homes and do fabulous things before getting up the next day to continue being fabulous. But maybe he was just being fabulously cynical and envious.

As he continued to watch, his focus suddenly centered on one man. It was the thick-chested and skinny-legged Bradley Cowl in the flesh. He slid clumsily into the driver's seat of a deep blue Bugatti Chiron that probably cost more than Devine would earn in ten years, even if he did make it at the firm.

Cowl fired up the engine, and it sounded like a Boeing 777 powering up to takeoff thrust.

He slid it into gear and in two seconds made it to the gates, which barely had time to open on the motion sensor before the muscle car blew past. He turned right and headed south. Devine knew Cowl had a penthouse on the top of the building where Devine labored every day. He might be going there tonight, swapping a palace in the burbs for sleeping closer to the sky.

Devine kicked the bike into gear and raced after the Bugatti.

He had a second job now. It was called serving his country once more *and* keeping out of prison.

# CHAPTER

# 9

THE BUGATTI AND THE MOTORCYCLE breached the island of Manhattan from the north and wended their way south like synchronized swimmers. Traffic was light at this hour, and Devine had no trouble following the super-car. The damn thing seemed to glow in the dark. It would have made the Dark Knight's ride look like a drab Ford Escort puttering along.

Devine had met Brad Cowl exactly one time. Well, he hadn't really met the man, but it was the closest he was ever likely to get. It was Devine's recruiting class's official first day, and the company's leadership and the "great man" had been rolled out to greet them. They were gathered in one of the conference rooms where huge deals were routinely closed and enormous amounts of wealth changed hands. Devine could almost smell the money in the air.

Forty-five strong, the incoming class was looking spit-and-polished and serious and focused and grateful for this amazing, once-in-a-lifetime opportunity with a world-class organization, blah, blah, blah.

Then in came the man himself followed by an eight-person platoon of anal-looking people dressed in corporate armor right down to the slash of pocket squares, precisely knotted ties, and, for the sole woman in the group, a black business suit, black stockings, black pumps, and a rigid face heavily lined from years of toil in this place. She was just like the buzz-sawed male lieutenants on that score.

Cowl's pocket square seemed to have been mitered to an impossibly perfect angle with the horizontal line of his breast pocket on his twenty-thousand-dollar custom-made suit. Devine wasn't guessing about the cost, because the man told all of them that was what the Italian tailor had charged him when Cowl had him flown in from Milan on his private wings to mold twenty of these suits to the investment king's stocky frame. And he made sure to share with them that the talented *paesano* charged Robert De Niro and George Clooney and Brad Pitt the same price.

The magnate's hair was parted seemingly with a laser's precision. His teeth gleamed so white and straight that Devine found himself running his tongue over his own in an attempt to remove the grime of his breakfast. The shoes were unlike any he had ever seen, the softest of probably Italian leather, triple-strapped, polished to a sheen that was possible only by a practiced human hand. Cowl's gray shirt seemed grafted to him like a second skin of liquid chrome.

"I came from nothing," Cowl began in his address to the class of newbies. "And built everything you see here entirely on my own."

And it was true, or so the official business press had always dutifully reported. A string of Cowl's ancestors *had* inherited great wealth, but his grandfather apparently had been a lousy businessman and lost half the fortune. Cowl's worthless father had sponged off his inheritance, and what he didn't lose in gambling, he squandered in bad investments. When Brad Cowl had come along, there was little if anything left. But he had worked hard and graduated summa cum laude from his Ivy League college. After that the man had, in around two decades, built his eponymous firm up into the same league as Goldman Sachs and JP Morgan and Merrill Lynch.

No one spoke much of the other name partner, Anne Comely. She was reportedly in her seventies and lived primarily in Palm Beach, or was it Palm Springs? No one that Devine knew had ever seen the woman. She had never come to the office, at least that

Devine was aware. It was rumored that she was a reclusive heiress who had provided Cowl with the initial stake he needed to build his empire, and one of her rewards had been her name on the firm, and even more money in her already deep pocket.

However one kept score, Cowl was one of the hottest commodities in the most important financial center in the world.

"There are forty-five of you here now," Cowl had said, looking around the room and lingering on just a few. Devine had a feeling this was all scripted and that these minions had already been preordained to be passed on up the chain. He hadn't been one of them.

"Only ten percent of you will make it to the next round. They will have a shot at getting to the *next* level, which will come with ample financial and professional reward. The losers, well..." He didn't have to finish this part. Everyone in the room knew what happened to losers. They got flushed down the toilet and went to work at places that didn't have arrogant billionaires at the helm.

Cowl stared them all down. "I *would* wish you all luck." The smirk came back. "But luck, I can assure you, will have nothing to do with it."

Then he had made an impressive leap and landed upright on the table, causing one already tightly wound young woman he had flown past on this maneuver to cry out and nearly fall out of her chair. Devine guessed she would not be one of the ten percent to move on to a financial mecca.

Cowl glowered at them all from his now-high perch. "This place, this space, this world, isn't about luck. It's about brains and talent and belly fire. You have to want it more than the next guy."

He eyed the seven women in the group—one Black, one brown, two Asian, three white, strictly adhering to the firm's diversity program—along with the thirty-eight men, thirty-seven of whom were white and the other Latino.

That summed up diversity in the ranks of the high finance world, Devine mused.

"Excuse me, the next *person*."

The suit platoon clapped, and Cowl cried out, "So, what are you waiting for? Get your asses to work. And may the best *people* win."

Prompted by this voice command, they had all stood like obedient dogs and filed from the room, while Cowl watched them from his intimidating perch.

The guy just seemed to bask in this shit, Devine had thought at the time. His opinion had not changed.

The Bugatti kept blasting south, through Midtown and next Downtown and then straight to the Financial District. There it turned onto Exchange Place, one block south of Wall Street, to the building where Sara Ewes had died. It turned into the parking garage at Cowl and Comely.

The Bugatti's window came down, Cowl held up his phone to the reader, and the garage door cranked up. The $3,000,000 muscle car pulled in and the door closed behind it. The man had not only his own parking space but also his own private elevator, right to the penthouse. Devine knew this, because Wanda Simms had told him.

Devine imagined the man going up in his silver tube. As he continued to watch, lights came on, but on the fifty-second floor, because Devine took a minute to count down from the top.

The penthouse was four floors higher.

So why was he on *that* floor, where Ewes had died?

The next moment he saw someone else he recognized walking down the street. She reached the front doors of the Cowl Building, swiped her card, and entered. He watched as she hurried across to the elevator bank. Devine couldn't see the security guard. He might be making his rounds.

With this interesting development, Devine parked his bike on the street, locked down the front tire, and walked over to the building. He used his security card to get in. He took the elevator up to the forty-fourth floor, where he knew the woman he'd seen had her office. He looked all around, but she wasn't there, and the only lights on were the security ones.

Then he thought about the lights on the fifty-second floor, or the "death floor," as he now imagined it to be. If Cowl was there, was the woman meeting him for some reason? He took the elevator up to that floor, poked his head out, didn't see anyone, and got off.

The place was apparently no longer an active investigation scene. He imagined Ewes's parents were frantically traveling here from out of the country. All that way to look at your daughter on a morgue slab.

He could hear nothing other than the sparse traffic from down on the street and the occasional plane going by. He tried to figure out in which direction the light he'd seen come on was located.

He started down a corridor and then turned to the left. And stopped.

The blue-and-yellow police tape was strung across the doorway.

The storage room where Sara Ewes had died.

Devine decided he needed to see it for himself. This didn't tie directly into what Emerson Campbell had tasked him to do, but if something nefarious was going on at Cowl's business, Ewes's death might be connected somehow. At least he couldn't rule it out at this point.

And Devine had cared greatly for Sara Ewes. He needed to understand why she had taken her own life. Looking at the place where she had drawn her final, tortured breaths seemed like a good start.

# CHAPTER

# 10

HE FIRST NOTED THE CHALKY white fingerprint powder on the lock. He used his shirtsleeve to cover his hand and tried the knob. The door swung open. He was looking at a dark room until he flicked on the light with his elbow.

There was the chair she'd likely stood on, still lying on its side, like it was dead, too. The cord she had used was no longer there, though the ceiling panel was still removed and sitting on the floor, like a tooth missing from a mouth. It had powder on it, as did the chair. Floating through his mind was the image of Sara Ewes standing on the chair, slipping the cord around her neck, and then pushing the chair away.

He wondered if Ewes had had second thoughts, regretted her decision, and pulled and pulled against the cord around her neck that was killing her. At what point did she realize it was useless? That she was going to die? Did she scream for help that never came? And then just...? He closed his eyes and shook his head with the absolute misery of this tragic image.

She had been a wonderful, caring person. But everyone had their dark, unspoken side, of which no one else, not even close friends and family, was aware.

*And I'm the poster boy for that.*

He looked around the space and observed things one would expect to encounter in a storage room. Cleaning supplies, cardboard boxes, a vacuum, boxes of file folders, reams of copy paper, printer ink cartridges, an old fax machine, Christmas decorations, a whiteboard on a stand. She would have seen all these things while dying. It didn't seem…fair. Staring bug-eyed at Christmas decorations knowing you wouldn't live to celebrate the next one.

He punched off the light and closed the door, then he heard the noise to his left, down the hall.

Halfway there, he already knew what he would find. It wasn't hard.

Moaning and groaning and lustful whimpers.

He stopped, looked around, and spotted a door with the necessary sight line. The office in question was in the corner. The lights inside were off and he could well understand why. You would take no chances doing what they were doing, even with the blinds drawn.

He stood behind the door, but left it open a crack so he could see clearly.

Ten minutes went by and the moans and groans stopped. A few mumbled words. Feminine to his ear. Perhaps of praise, or relief that it was over.

Another minute passed, a light came on inside the office, and then the door was jerked open. Out staggered Brad Cowl, smoothing his hair down and putting his costly shirttail back in his very expensive pants and notching his crocodile leather belt closed. He took a moment to slowly zip up his pants like he was reholstering his gun. He looked sweaty and triumphant.

Devine took out his phone and snapped several shots of Cowl, as well as the woman who was clearly visible in the room behind him. Her head was turned to the side, and she was staring at Cowl, seemingly surprised that he was leaving her so abruptly. She was the same one he had seen going into the building earlier. Only now she was naked and lying on the desk on her back, with her thighs still akimbo. Cowl must have finished, jumped up, and headed on his way.

He took three more pictures of what he was seeing. Then he

turned the video function on and held the camera up. He did not like spying on people, particularly at a moment like this. But if something dirty with national security implications was going on here, he instinctively knew having this stick to hold over Cowl's head might come in handy.

The woman called out, "Where the hell are you going, Brad?"

Cowl turned back and said, "Early morning. Need some shut-eye. And thanks, sweet cheeks. It was great. Next week, same time, but I'll let you know where. Don't know what came over me tonight, except you are so hot it makes me lose my damn mind." He laughed.

The woman, Devine noted, did not.

Cowl passed by Devine's hiding spot, no doubt heading for the elevator. If he were a betting man, Devine would say the Bugatti was done for the night and Cowl was going to sleep, this time for real and not on a desk.

A couple minutes later, Devine glanced back in the direction of the office, from which the woman stepped out, now dressed.

Her name was Jennifer Stamos. She was twenty-eight and had been at Cowl for six years. In fact, she had been in Sara Ewes's class. Devine knew this because she was in the firm's employee directory, which was accessible to all at Cowl. It did not contain addresses, like an old phone book did, or other personal information. This was strictly business-related. It was known, firm-wide, without a shred of originality, as "the Book." It contained all the things each person had done while at Cowl: every deal, every triumph, every failure, every screwup. Cowl kept score like no one else. Everyone had a numeric and alphabetical grade that, combined, served to define their firm-wide ranking for all to see, and, to ratchet the pressure up even more, that ranking was updated daily.

Devine knew this glorified digital pissing contest was designed to make the competition even more intense. To see how far you were falling behind, or racing ahead, all you needed to do was check the Book. And then you ran harder and harder to catch up and then pass the front-runners. Or else you ran harder and harder to get further ahead. Or you worked your ass off and still fell behind and got depressed as hell. It was cruel and inhumane, and it was also just the way things worked in this world.

Stamos, he knew from the Book, had been a clear second in her class. But that was not the case now, because Sara Ewes was no longer in the race. Stamos had just taken over the lead by default.

She was beautiful. Long, dark hair that fell straight to her shoulders. Olive skin, full lips, lovely features, green eyes that Devine had watched seemingly spike with electrical current when she was animated. She had been to several of the mixers. He had watched her dance and joke and drink, and even do a stupid line of coke in a back room, and not like it. In off-hours her choice of dress had been sexy and chic. At leisure, she possessed a flippant, playful style that made her appear vulnerable and approachable. Coupled with her prodigious brains and sheer business talent, it was a truly potent combination that had captivated Devine and many others at the firm.

She looked nothing like that right now. She appeared shrunken and depressed. Her hair was tangled, her blouse was untucked from her jeans, and her painful-looking stiletto heels, which cranked her five-three stature to five-seven, were in her hand.

Devine knew that Ewes and Stamos had not been friends. There was no room for that within the same class, or even outside classes. The women knew that it was unlikely both would make the long haul at Cowl, because things simply did not work that way in this arena. But Devine wondered if Stamos felt badly for having sex in an office with the head of the firm on the same day that her chief competitor had been found dead only a few feet away. He at least hoped she did.

Stamos stopped at the women's restroom for a few minutes. When she came back out, Devine followed her, but waited for the elevator doors to close behind her before he rushed forward and pushed a button to summon his own elevator car.

Stamos was heading out of the glass doors when Devine's elevator reached the ground floor. He nodded to the guard, who was back behind the desk and watching him curiously. Then the guard glanced at the departing woman and his eyebrows went up, and a knowing grin spread over his face.

Stamos was walking down the street and looking at her phone. Devine thought he knew what she was doing, and he headed over and unlocked his bike and slipped on his helmet.

The Uber appeared three minutes later and she got in.

Devine followed.

The Uber dropped the woman off at a bar in Greenwich Village that, on Friday night at midnight, was just starting to rock.

CHAPTER

# II

SHE WAS STANDING AT THE far end of the beer-slopped bar. The place was full of young people and the occasional person over fifty trying and failing to fit in. Devine looked to be the only thirty-something there, but maybe his math was off. And he looked older than he actually was; mortal combat just did that to you.

He threaded his way through sweaty, drunk, and getting-drunk bodies that were coiling and uncoiling around him like snakes before copulation. Then he pulled up and did a swift observation.

Next to Stamos was a man holding a half-empty glass of beer. He didn't know if the guy had arranged to meet her here, but he didn't think so. To Devine's mind, you didn't have sex with your boss and then meet your boyfriend for drinks minutes later.

The guy was around six-three or so, and lean, about forty pounds lighter than the more muscular and stockier-built Devine. He was lanky, coordinated, seemed light on his feet. He looked like he had maybe played D-2 basketball or D-1 lacrosse. He was handsome in the traditional way, though he had the kind of thin blond hair that would start to disappear around age thirty and be totally gone except for a scalp rim of white or gray by fifty.

He had handsome, and haughty, patrician features, so, in his mind, Devine nicknamed him WASP.

He was dressed in stylish, expensive jeans and a white untucked shirt that hit at about his waist because of his long torso. Moccasins were on his feet. They looked warm in the heat of the room. He was inching up to Stamos, who had just ordered her drink and was waiting for it to arrive, keeping her eyes on the wooden bar.

*So maybe he's about to make his move.*

Devine picked up his threading-through-the-crowd maneuver once more and arrived in the close-quarter combat space about the time WASP touched Stamos on the arm.

"Haven't seen you here before," he said.

She didn't look at him. "Well, I *have* been here before."

"Well, then that's *my* fault for not noticing. How can I make it up to you?"

Stamos looked to the side and saw Devine shaking his head and rolling his eyes at these pathetic pickup lines. She smiled. WASP thought it was for him.

"Now there you go, *that's* the smile I was hoping for."

"Hey, Jenn," said Devine.

WASP swiveled around and eyed him. "Hey, buddy, do you mind?"

"I *do* mind. Because I came here for a drink with my friend."

WASP looked at Stamos. "Is that true, or is that a line?"

Stamos looked intrigued by this development. "It's true."

WASP kept his eye on her, obviously not believing this. He turned to Devine, looked him over the way guys did one another. The *Can I kick the shit out of him or not?* sort of dance that young men undertook, particularly when booze and women were involved.

Devine said, "My friend has had a rough day. So if you'll excuse us?"

WASP did not look like he wanted to excuse anyone, least of all Devine. But he and his beer moved a few stools down where Devine could see more WASPs greet him, listen for a few moments, and then glare Devine's way. It was all guy-testosterone stuff, and it could mean nothing or a lot. Only time would tell.

Devine took all this in, and then turned to Stamos as her drink came. A gin and tonic with extra lime slices, and a deuce of olives.

"I know I've seen you at work. You're...?" she began, picking an olive out with her fingers and biting it in half. She added sheepishly, "I'm sorry, I don't remember."

"No reason for you to. Travis Devine. Thirty-fourth floor. Newbie class. Still trying to cut it to the next level."

She took this in, licked the gin and olive juice off her fingers. "What did you mean I was having a rough day?" she said.

"Sara Ewes? Weren't you in the same class?"

He fingered the phone in his pocket, where the pictures and video were. Maybe more valuable than Apple and Amazon stock combined. At least to Devine.

"Yes, yes, that was awful." She looked at his sleeve. "You got something on you."

She pointed to the white chalk marks he'd gotten from the fingerprint powder.

*Shit.*

He dusted them off, watching the white particles drop to the bar floor.

"What are you doing here?" she asked.

"Having a drink, same as you." Devine held up a hand to the harried man behind the bar. "Can of Sapporo. Thanks."

She sipped her drink. "Did you know Sara well?"

Devine said, "Not well. She was our class liaison. Funny, though."

"What?"

"When I passed by our office building a little while ago, I saw Bradley Cowl's Bugatti heading into the firm's garage. Dude must never sleep."

She looked alarmed when the name Cowl had come up, but Devine was intentionally not looking at her. He was instead staring at her reflection in the mirror behind the bar. It was just as informative as observing the real thing.

"Why is that funny? It *is* his business. And he has a penthouse apartment there."

"I get that, but you wouldn't think the guy would want to go back there tonight of all nights. I mean, with Sara's having died there today."

Stamos appraised him for a moment. "So, you think you'll make the cut?"

"Not sure. But you're good as gold. Six years in and the Book said Sara was the only one ranked ahead of you. But obviously no more."

As soon as he said this, Devine regretted it. As a newbie operative in the Office of Special Projects, he was showing how ill-trained he was at eliciting intelligence from a target, at least in this setting. He had done okay at it in the Middle East.

"You are such an asshole!" Stamos cried out.

WASP heard this and looked up from his beer. He glanced at his buddies, and seemed to be contemplating something. Devine saw all this in the mirror as well. It was easy enough to read: The man was pondering whether to retake Hamburger Hill from Devine.

"I didn't mean it like that. But that's the way things are at Cowl," Devine said, easing off the gas pedal. "You know it and I know it." His beer came and he took a healthy swallow. It felt good against the rising heat in here.

"Doesn't mean I have to like it," she said in a pouty tone.

"No, you don't."

Devine thought quickly. He was making little progress and he had to turn that around. Campbell didn't strike him as a patient man. His mind flitted over several possible lines of inquiry with Stamos, each fraught with complications. And then, like the soldier he had once been, he decided to cut through the bullshit and try a direct assault.

"Getting back to Sara, did you know her well?"

The answer to this query seemed harder than it should have been for Stamos. "No, not really." She wouldn't meet his eyes when she said it.

He decided to up the ante.

"You have any inkling she might kill herself?"

This question seemed to shake Stamos even more. Her eyes bugged out for a moment and her body tensed. However, she quickly regrouped and shook her head, with the mouthed word *No* tacked on.

"So, no warning signs? Nothing on the grapevine?" he persisted.

"I really didn't see that much of her. She…she was working on other things."

"Did you get an email about her death?"

"What?"

"An email with details about Sara's suicide?"

"No. You mean from the firm?"

"I don't know."

*Maybe it just went to me, then. But why?* "Wanda Simms told me Cowl was her mentor. Did you know that?"

Her face got puffy and her manner grew subdued. She looked down at her gin like she wanted to jump into it and pass through to a fresh new world. "He mentors lots of people."

"So is he mentoring *you*?"

She glowered at him, and in that look Devine knew he had blown it. "I don't have to answer that. I don't have to talk to you at all."

He felt a hand on his shoulder and Devine turned to see WASP and two of his comrades in beers standing there. The other two were at least six-four and built like the college athletes they no doubt had once been.

"Is he bothering you?" WASP asked.

Stamos gave Devine a look with eyebrows raised as if to say, *Should I sacrifice you or not? It's up to you. So start begging.*

But she sure as hell wasn't going to get that from him. Her lovely face once more turned nasty when confronted with his stony, unrepentant look.

"Yes. Can you do something about it?" she said, not taking her gaze off Devine.

"Hell yes we can. Let's go, buddy. There's a little spot around the corner where they keep the trash. We can go there and settle things."

"Or we can just go our separate ways, no harm, no foul," said Devine as he made a move to do just this, until WASP clenched his shoulder harder.

"That's what I thought as soon as I saw you—you're a chickenshit," said WASP. "But if you want to pussy out, feel free."

"Don't go there, buddy," said Devine.

Stamos interjected, "Hey, just everybody cool it. Let him go."

WASP ignored this and said in a louder voice, "I know what, we'll all give a toast to the chickenshit as you walk out the door with your tail between your legs." He pushed Devine away. "Go on, run away before you get hurt."

Devine laid down cash for the beer, finished it in two more gulps, crushed the empty can in his hand, turned to WASP, and said in a low, menacing voice, "I'm leaving now, but consider yourself really, really lucky, prick."

He rammed his way through the crowd and out the door.

And then the three men made a big mistake.

They followed him.

# CHAPTER

# 12

DEVINE TURNED THE CORNER AND neared a sliver of an opening between two buildings where a Dumpster and lines of trash and recycling bins were kept. This must be the place the asshole had been referring to. Beyond these articles, a brick wall faced him.

He looked behind him. WASP and his two pals were moving fast.

*Okay, here we go.*

Devine stepped into the opening, because with the brick wall behind him no one could sneak up on him. He then turned back around as the three men caught up to him. They were shoulder to shoulder as though intending to block his escape.

They could be Iraqis or Afghans, Taliban or Al-Qaeda or ISIS. It had gotten hard to tell the difference, actually. Those desert guys were all tall, and bone and muscle and lethal and muttering shit in a language he had come to learn but never mastered. Their eyes were all the same. Crazy, fanatical, but also cagey, smart. You got plopped in a flag-draped coffin for underestimating those sons of bitches.

WASP was a bit ahead of his pals, but starting to look a little nervous because Devine wasn't looking nervous at all.

He pointed to the man on his left. "Rick played defensive end at Cornell." He jerked a thumb at the other guy. "And Doug was NCAA heavyweight wrestling champ from Iowa. And I was All-American in lacrosse at Princeton."

Devine didn't waste an ounce of breath replying to this babble, because that was all it was. There were guys who could talk a good fight, and there were those who remained quiet and just put your lights out.

As they walked forward he walked forward. Like two trains on the same track, the crash would be inevitable.

His attention was diverted for only a moment as he saw Stamos peer around the corner, her eyes wide and her face tense. This had gone far past what she had intended, he could read that in her nervous features. And she was wondering how she could defuse things.

She gave him a pleading look. It affected him more than he would have thought.

"Okay, last chance, guys," he said. "Walk away now or I can guarantee it will not end well for any of you."

"One against three, and we're all bigger than you," said WASP. "So what exactly are you smoking?"

"I was Army. A Ranger. Just so you know."

"Big shit," said Rick. "I eat fucking Rangers for breakfast."

*Okay, that was the wrong thing to say*, thought Devine. *Really wrong.*

WASP charged forward, his fists held high, *too* high. Devine landed a sharp punch to his gut, which doubled him over, and then that blow was followed up with a fully stretched-out kick by Devine to his opponent's downward-looking face. The force lifted WASP off the ground, revealing that the rough and rugged motorcycle boot had battered the man's delicately handsome features. Then Devine grabbed him by the shirt front and hurled him at the Dumpster. He hit the metal side and dropped to the asphalt unconscious.

Doug the wrestler roared and punched Devine twice in the head. They were damn hard shots, but that was all. He felt some blood on his skin and in his mouth, some snot on his face, but his senses were intact. The guy tried to pin his arms to his sides, but Devine broke that hold by slamming the top of his head into Doug's chin and gouging him in the eye with his thumb. Then he hooked him around the ankle with his foot and laid a thunderous elbow into the man's oblique. This caused the man to stagger back, breathing hard, and bloody from the chin and mouth. Devine pivoted, went behind Doug in a flash of choreographed movement that he had done a thousand times in close-quarter drills, and for real in combat, and came up behind the far larger man. A vicious elbow strike to the left kidney, a rock-hard fist to the right one, and Doug dropped to his knees, howling in pain, because that area of the body was unprotected and sensitive as shit, which made it the perfect target.

Devine planted his left foot firmly on the ground as his fulcrum. Doug's head was lined up like a ball on a stand for an eager T-baller to bang a home run off. He let loose a ferocious roundhouse kick that impacted the left side of Doug's head with both power and velocity. The man's head kissed his right shoulder and his eyes rolled back in his head, as his brain checked out. A moment later he joined WASP on the ground for a long sleep and a painful awakening. This had all taken seconds.

Rick grabbed Devine from behind, lifted him off the ground, and threw him face-first against the brick wall. He struck it hard, painfully so. His shoulder howled, and his face bled and swelled with the impact with the rough brick. Then Rick slammed against him, driving him into the brick wall another centimeter, and cutting his skin below both eyes. Then he landed a trio of hard punches to Devine's back, which was stupid. Head shots would have been far more effective, particularly against unyielding brick. That was what Devine would have done. You couldn't fight back if you were unconscious.

The man stepped back to view his handiwork. However, if Rick thought his opponent was down and done, he was seriously mistaken. That might cut it in college football, but not in Devine's world. And poor Rick was about to realize the consequences of his misjudgment. Devine levered off the wall and used that momentum to boomerang back on the former Ivy League lineman.

He gripped the man's throat with one hand while he hit him with two uppercuts straight into the diaphragm with the other. Then he landed a bruising hook into the oblique. And one more on top of it. Rick moaned and staggered back, with Devine still holding on to his throat. In combat, with a serrated Ranger knife in hand, Devine would have gutted the guy in the midsection area, upward slash and then side to side, to get to the intestines and aorta, and the fight would be over.

Devine once more glanced at Stamos, who was looking terrified and stunned into silence at what she was seeing. In response, Devine let go of his neck grip and pushed Rick violently back against the wall, where he slumped down holding his gut and his throat. Devine had never not finished a fight, and he was unsure about this time. Maybe he was mellowing in his early thirties.

Still looking at Stamos, Devine turned and started to walk toward her.

"Look out!" she screamed.

He pivoted and put up a blocking arm. The trash can lid wielded by Rick hit him on the forearm. It hurt like a bitch, but broke nothing, only bending the flimsy metal nearly in half. But if it had hit him in the head, it would have been a different story. Devine planted a fist into Rick's chest right at the heart, which fired off messages of cardiac panic to his brain. He then leapt forward and used the crown of his head to deliver a staggering blow to the man's chin. Rick's lower teeth jammed into his upper teeth and blood shot out as gums and hardened calcium collided violently.

Rick screamed and slumped to the ground sobbing, his hands pressed against his mangled mouth.

Devine glanced over at Stamos, who looked stunned in the face of this carnage.

He turned and walked toward her. She backed away, looking fearful.

He wiped the blood and snot off his face and onto his sleeve. "Thanks for the warning. And call an ambulance for those guys." He paused and added, "And I'll see you at the office, *sweet cheeks*."

He walked down the street, put on his helmet, cranked his bike, and blew past as she stood outside an alley where three large and disappointed young men lay with the city's trash.

# CHAPTER 13

Devine slept for a couple hours, with an ice pack around his arm and another on his shoulder and a third bag on his face. He'd applied ointment to the cuts and brick rash. He rose, put on his workout clothes, jogged over to the high school football field that was right behind his neighborhood, and started his daily workout.

A tractor tire lay on the football field. The football players used it to build up the thrust strength of their arms and legs. Devine flipped it down to one end, turned around and flipped it back to the other, until he was drenched in sweat. With every flip he had a new thought about Sara Ewes and her death, and Cowl and Comely. Then there were regular car tires that he threw like discuses to build up his obliques. As he did so, Devine thought about his new gig with Emerson Campbell.

Next, Devine ran the bleacher steps until he was soaked in even more sweat. He did pull-ups and chin-ups on a pull-up bar. One hundred of each. Twenty at a time followed by twenty seconds of rest. Two hundred push-ups, fifty at a time. With each rep he imagined Sara swinging on the end of that cord.

Ab crunches followed, both flat on his back and then hanging from the pull-up bar. Squats, lunges, army crawls, high-kickers, then plyometric jumps on and off wooden boxes of varying heights the school kept here for the athletic teams. Followed by burpees. Every one he performed was now accompanied by images of the battle in the alley. His wounds howled in protest of the workout, which made him push himself even harder. When the going got tough, you just kicked your own ass even harder. That was the Army way.

Sprints down the field, and, on the return, he did the run backward. He went faster each time, working off his frustration at the hard left turn off a cliff his life had taken.

Lieutenant Roy Blankenship and Captain Kenneth Hawkins. Names he had heard every day for years, and then no more. Both men dead. Both struck down violently. One with an assist by him.

How many times had he seen those faces in his sleep? It was always the same. They were staring at him, waiting for him to say something. To Blankenship, maybe something about avenging him. To Hawkins, maybe angry words, venting. But Devine never said a damn thing back. Not one damn thing while two dead men stared at him.

He finished off with a series of isometric routines, holding the poses until his body shook violently with the effort of simply standing still.

He jogged back to his place, cooling down and stretching along the way. He showered, shaved, dressed, and left his room. Valentine was on the couch dead asleep, having failed to make it up to his room the previous night. Apparently tapping keys on a laptop could be exhausting. He had heard Tapshaw softly snoring and probably dreaming of new deals and happy couples from the Hummingbird empire she'd created.

He had seen the light on in Helen Speers's room. She was no doubt studying. She had the belly fire, that was for sure. Being Black and a woman were two strikes against you already, Devine knew. It sure as hell had been that way in the Army.

Quite a few of his comrades in uniform resented women being in the ranks. Sure, the guys said all the right things in public so their records and promotion trajectories wouldn't get ripped, but the private mutterings among the men were a whole different story. This pattern of misogyny came from some of the enlisted grunts all the way up to a number of the bars and stars. And the petty shit these men would do to screw with the women was legendary in its cruelty. Nothing wounded a female soldier more than knowing the guy in uniform next to her didn't have her back, and, more insulting, didn't even want her there. Didn't think she would ever be good enough. When all the ladies wanted was to simply be allowed to do their jobs and serve their country. And maybe Devine would have looked down on the ladies in uniform too, except a newbie enlisted had saved his life near Kandahar, losing a hand in the process.

The soldier's name was Alice.

He got to the station and boarded the train. One more working day until his only day off.

The train was empty except for Devine until a woman in a warm-up suit and carrying a large canvas bag got on four stations later. She eyed his mangled face and immediately sat far away from him.

By the time they got to Brad Cowl's palace the train was barely a quarter full. All the others, except the warm-up suit lady, were dressed as he was. But it was Saturday and the numbers were going to be lower. Not every business in New York worked the Wall Street way. Some people did get *two* days off out of seven.

Devine stretched out his arm and shoulder, touched his injured face, and tensed a bit as the train slowed. There it was. The pool, the backyard with the string of lights still up and still on; some servant must have forgotten to pull the plug. Cowl would probably ding their paycheck.

He had looked up the property online. The place was twenty-seven thousand square feet, a dozen bedrooms, seventeen baths, two kitchens, servant quarters in an adjacent cottage, a large guest-house in case the twelve bedrooms weren't enough, along with the resort-sized pool and eight exquisitely landscaped and private acres. There were no pictures of the interior online, which told Devine the place had been built by Cowl and had never been on the market for resale. It was tax-assessed at a figure that was less than half of what it would cost to buy or build.

But the bikini princess of the palace was not there today.

The train picked that moment to hurry up its pace and the landscape changed.

He took out his phone and brought up the pics of Cowl and Stamos. And then he watched the video with the sound turned off. He held the phone in his lap and sat hunched over so that no one around him could possibly see the screen.

Yet something was nagging at him. Like he'd screwed up somehow.

He looked out the window as the train chugged along, taking him to where he needed to go, and where he now didn't want to go. Unfortunately for Devine, they were the exact same place.

# CHAPTER

# 14

Devine sat in his sliver of a cubicle with his twin big-ass Mac screens. The somehow jarring sound of intense silence except for the quickened breaths of the highly intelligent and intensely motivated sitting all around him. It was a humbling experience to be in the presence of that much brainpower and drive to succeed. And it didn't help that Devine's arm ached and so did his shoulder where the brick wall had said hello. And his back from where Rick had popped him. But what the hell was pain anyway? It was life; you had to deal with it. He couldn't do anything about it except swallow some Aleve.

No one had noticed his facial injuries or how stiff he held his arm and shoulder because no one bothered to look at him when they walked in. This was purposeful, because he was almost always the first one to arrive at work, and he knew that pissed them off. Their response was to ignore the early interloper. And then grind him into the dust with their own inspired labor. And all to make Brad Cowl even more money than he already had. But hey, when you had two jets and two yachts, another one of each certainly couldn't hurt.

He hadn't seen Stamos today, though he didn't expect to. They were on different floors. He had her business email, though, and his finger had hovered over it on his computer, wondering if he should send her some message. Only he wasn't sure what he would say.

He decided to just let it rest for now.

Devine had scanned the news but had seen nothing about three young men being found in an alley with the proverbial shit beaten out of them. WASP and his friends might have called the police and concocted some story about his having mugged them at gunpoint or something. Only they didn't know who he was, unless Stamos had hung around and told them.

He crunched numbers and composed reports and sent them to bits and pieces of the Cowl universe so other people could tear them apart and send them back and tell him what a moron he was, and to do a better job if he wanted to really dance with the big boys. And these salvos would go back and forth seemingly forever until the deal was done, or the market had closed, or the deal was scrapped, or someone important wet their pants and wanted to redo everything, or a better offer came in the door.

*It's not like it's my money.*

He looked at his watch. One o'clock. There was a dining hall on the third floor. It had great food, everything from tofu, plant-based burgers, sushi, couscous of every flavor and description, to grilled fish, all varieties of pasta, and veggie, vegan, and pescatarian offerings, along with meats for carnivores, and delectable desserts, all free, with cooks and eager servers just waiting to help you. And none of the Burners ever went there, because, one, they were afraid to get out of their seats, and, two, they were even more afraid that some executive would see them on the third floor in a place meant for people to eat, actually placing food in their mouths.

Almost all brought their lunch and ate it at their desks, getting crumbs in their keyboards and crap smeared over their screens. That could be disastrous if a smudge made a decimal point disappear, or turned a dollar sign into the mark of the euro, or the pound sterling. But they were apparently less afraid of that than appearing in the dining hall and losing a shot at the big time simply because they were hungry. And that was good news for the people who had cleared newbie status. They had the food all to themselves.

And before yesterday Devine would never have even thought about going to eat there. But yesterday had changed pretty much everything for him. His job was to act as a scout and to find important things. And to do that scouts had to keep on the move and go to places other people never would.

Devine rose and called out, "Anybody want to grab some chow with me on the third floor?"

They all looked up at him as though he had just suffered a stroke. Then they eyed each other to see if perhaps other people thought he was joking. Then they finally noted his facial injuries and several men and women stiffened. Perhaps they thought he had been in a car accident and was now hallucinating.

With no takers, Devine left the room and headed to the elevator.

*I'm going to have a nice meal, while you wipe your candy bar and Cheez-It fingers over the whole of the NASDAQ futures.*

He rode the car down to three, turned left, and entered the dining hall that looked one narrow step down from the Ritz, or the Plaza, or whatever was to die for these days. He didn't know because that was not his world. He was just a workingman in the pay of the feudal lord.

He got his piled-up plate and his glass of fancy seltzer water and found an empty table, keenly aware that people were staring at him. Devine knew he was the only Burner in here. It usually took people four years to work up the courage to eat in here unless escorted by a superior. *What an effed-up world.*

He sat down, his back to the wall, and suddenly noticed that none other than Brad Cowl and part of his entourage were here. The boss was dressed in a sharp suit, white shirt, and no tie, a nod, Devine supposed, to it being the weekend. He said something and everyone at the table laughed like the guy was the greatest comedian ever. This audience clearly wanted to keep their place in the inner circle, and that meant busting a gut at the boss's lame jokes.

Cowl's gaze roamed the room. As it did so, he was waving,

nodding, grinning, scowling, growing serious, then laughing and waving again.

It was as if to say, *Look everybody, your king is here on a Saturday in the summer instead of on my yacht or at my country club playing golf... or banging my employee on a cheap desk, while I have an even better-looking lady skinny-dipping in my Olympic-size pool.*

And then Cowl's X-ray beam came lurching over to Devine. And the man's features became unreadable. He lingered, one, two, three beats. He took in the injuries and the man himself. Probing, digging, creeping into unopened pathways that Devine might unknowingly have, like back doors on firewalls. Cowl had built a serious empire. To do that, you had to be smart and ruthless, more of the latter than the former, actually, because you essentially had to take what someone else had and not give a crap when they financially croaked.

And then Cowl's gaze moved on, as he was laughing, scowling, grinning, waving, and even playfully flipping one man off. But he didn't come back to Devine. And Devine wondered two things: why the look had landed in the first place, and what would come of it. Or maybe Cowl was seeing right through Devine and wondering about some problem in the Japanese bond market, or whether a tax audit was going funny, or whether the blond princess would find out he was screwing young, nubile financial whizzes on the fifty-second floor.

But, no, Devine had seen enough assholes in the world to know that Cowl was staring at *him* and seeing *him*, and there was a good reason for it.

And it was then that he realized his mistake, the one that had been nagging at him the whole ride in.

*Sweet cheeks.* He had called Stamos that.

The same term Cowl had used after screwing her barely a half hour before. Heat-of-the-moment thing on Devine's part, bravado. And stupid, which bravado almost always was.

Stamos had told Cowl all of this, and Cowl, smart and paranoid asshole that he was, had put two and two together and decided that Devine had seen things last night he should not have seen.

Thus the stare. And in that stare, he read decisive action coming.

So Devine went back for seconds because this actually might be his last decent meal.

Retired General Campbell would probably have to recruit a new spy.

# CHAPTER

# 15

TRAVIS?"

He had just left work when the person had called out to him. He turned to his left and there was Jennifer Stamos.

"Yeah?"

She drew closer. She was dressed more casually than he was. Newbies struggling not to drown had no latitude in their professional appearance. But her casual was not *that* casual. Black jacket and skirt, white blouse with a bit of cleavage exposed. No stockings because of the heat, revealing smooth skin. Sensible low-ride pumps instead of the jacked heels from the previous night.

"About what happened last night?" She eyed his facial injuries, but made no comment.

He didn't know which "about what happened last night" event she was referring to, so he kept silent. You learned more by listening, and by speaking less your words tended not to come back to bite you. He had already made one error on that score. He just stared at her blankly.

"The *fight*?" she prompted.

"What about it?"

"How did you do that to those guys? They were all bigger than you."

"I was in the Army. They teach you how to fight."

"That's right, you told them you were in the military. A Ranger."

"Those guys got their shots in on me, for sure. But they knew nothing about really hurting another guy. I do. And I did, last night. But it was their choice, not mine. I walked out, they came after me. I gave them another chance to back off and they didn't take it. So I had no choice."

"I... I feel a little guilty. I could have deescalated things."

"And I chose to defend myself and walk out of that alley with my brain still intact."

"I... I couldn't believe what was happening."

"So what *happened* to them?"

"I called an ambulance, like you told me to."

"And the police?"

"I didn't say I called the cops."

"Someone sure as hell would have."

"Okay, the cops *did* show up, but I sort of snuck away before that."

"Before you 'snuck' away, are you sure you didn't tell anybody *my* name?"

She looked surprised at the inquiry. "No, I wouldn't do that."

"Why not? What does it matter to you?"

"Boy, you sure don't make it easy for someone to like you."

He composed himself and reloaded. *Just dial it down, Travis. You need info and she can provide it.*

"I *do* appreciate you not giving my name away and for warning me about the sneak attack by *Rick*. But when those guys' egos act up on them and they get all pissy, they could go to the cops with a whole different angle, where they were the victims instead of being merely stupid and alcohol fueled."

"I guess they might."

He stared down at her. She looked very small in her two-inch satin pumps. And he looked very big in his cheap suit.

"Why were you asking all those questions about Sara?"

"Because she's dead and I was curious," he replied.

"Curious about what? She killed herself."

Devine said, "Curious about *why* she did it. It's happened before at Cowl. Four years ago. The guy had just been fired via the ever-so-personal email torpedo. And his fiancée gave him the ring back when she found out. So the guy ate a round from a gun he bought illegally two hours later."

"How did you find all that out?" she said, looking both puzzled and worried.

"Come on, these days can anyone actually have a secret that someone else can't find out about with a few computer clicks?"

"And do *you* have secrets?" she said aggressively.

"A ton of them. And at some point, they'll come back to bury me."

*They may already have.*

This statement seemed to take her aback. He decided to change tactics and show he actually had some empathy.

"Look, Jennifer, I'm not proud of what happened at that bar. While I was trained by the Army to do it, I don't like wrecking guys. I gave them multiple chances to walk away and they just wouldn't do it. But I would have much preferred it never happened."

"Why were you at the bar?"

"If you want the truth, I saw you go in. I wanted to talk to you about Sara. She was really nice to me, and I'm beyond bewildered that she would have killed herself. I mean, she had everything to live for, unless I'm missing something."

Stamos was quiet for a few moments. "Are you going straight home, or can we get a bite to eat and maybe have a drink? I thought we could talk. You know. About Sara...and stuff."

He looked at his watch. It was not yet 6 p.m. They let you off early on Saturday, or so they said. Actually, he'd just walked out. There were other newbies up there still analyzing away, writing reports to later be trashed, terrified to leave their seats until the coast was truly clear. Which would, in truth, be never.

"I'm always game for a beer. And talking about Sara might be good for both of us."

"There's a place I know down by the water."

He loosened the skinny tie he'd bought online for three bucks. Then he held out his hand in the direction of the harbor. "After you."

# CHAPTER 16

THEY SAT OUTSIDE AND TOOK in views of the Statue of Liberty and Ellis Island set over churning, brackish water. The weather was nice, if humid. A storm might be rolling in as storms often did this time of year after the day's buildup of heat. It was Mother Nature's way of venting. They were sitting under an umbrella, but the sun had long since passed over them and was starting its drop into the western horizon, where it would later flame the sky into an alchemy of red and gold. When Devine was in the Middle East he never tired of that sight for one reason: He wasn't sure he'd be alive to see it again.

Stamos ordered chips and guac and a margarita. Devine had a Budweiser.

"They have a lot of good IPAs here," she pointed out, eyeing his can of beer.

He drank his drink and said, "Bud is fine with me right now."

"You had a Sapporo last night."

"That was because last night I was fine with Sapporo."

"Have you been to Japan?" she asked.

He nodded. "And Korea and Germany and all the other usual stops for Army guys."

"But you were mostly in the Middle East?"

"Yeah, mostly there."

"And you fought in combat?" she said.

"That was pretty much all there was there. You wanted to talk about Sara?"

Stamos stared down at her hands. "She always seemed so put together. I... I actually looked up to her. I had pegged a few people there as possible suicide material, but never her."

He nodded and said, "She never seemed that way to me either. But you said you didn't really see that much of her and didn't know her that well."

She wouldn't meet his eye. "That wasn't exactly true. I know because of the rankings in the Book everyone thought we were bitter rivals." She paused and drank her drink, looking out at the Statue of Liberty. "But there's more to life than work."

"As my old Army buddies used to say, 'You're preaching to the choir, Devine.'"

She ran her gaze over him. "Devine? Isn't that Irish? You don't look Irish."

"My father's definitely Irish, with fair skin and reddish hair. But I'm Greek on my mother's side. My grandparents came over from Mykonos."

"You definitely take after your mother, then."

"You Greek on both sides?"

"Through and through," she replied.

"Siblings?"

"Four sisters. All older."

"That must have been a fun household," he said jokingly.

"It was, actually," she said firmly.

"Stupid remark, sorry."

"You have siblings?" she asked.

"Yeah, they're wonderfully perfect and smarter than me and have great lives."

"Come on," she said skeptically.

Devine said, "I'm being serious. That's exactly who and what they are. Both a lot older than me. Both have hit the very top in their chosen professions."

"Oh. You must be proud of them."

"I'm glad they're happy." He thirstily drank his beer down and waved to the waitress for another. "So, back to Sara. When was the last time you saw her?"

"About a week before they found her. She came to my office."

He looked puzzled. "Why? Last night you said you two were working on different things."

"That's right."

She drank her margarita after gumming the salty edges, then squeezed the lime wedge over the chips and dug into the guac. He watched her do this, and then looked out to the water for a moment before glancing back at her.

"Then why did she come to see you?" he persisted.

"What, are you playing detective or something?"

"I'm just playing a human being. So what did she say?"

"She was asking about some play or other. Whether I'd seen it."

His interest perked up. "What was the play? Did she want a recommendation?"

Stamos fingered the drink and now she looked out toward the water, as though the answers would all be there. "*Waiting for Godot*. Have you seen it? I don't know anything about it."

Devine nodded. "I actually saw it here in New York, before I shipped out to West Point."

"Really? I thought you'd be out binge-drinking or...you know...the girls."

"I had a high school English teacher, Harold Simpson. I told him I was going the officer route at the Point. He told me to go see the play before I did. It happened to be on Broadway back then."

"Why did he want you to see it? Did he not want you to join the Army?" she asked.

"I don't think that was it. He'd served in the Army during Vietnam. He wasn't West Point. He got drafted. He came back pissed off and against the war. But he fought. He did his job. And the country treated those vets like shit. Not fair to fight your heart out, survive, and come back to that."

"But why would he want you to see that play in particular?"

Devine sipped his fresh beer. "I really can't explain it for you. It's just that sort of a play. You have to see it for yourself."

"Did you like it?"

"I'm not sure it's a play you either like or don't like. I'm not sure that's the purpose."

"Then what *is* the purpose?"

He took his gaze from the Statue of Liberty and placed it on her. "What to make of your own life, maybe. But if you ever see it, arrive at your own conclusion. So, you told her you hadn't seen it. What did Sara say about that?"

"She said it might be worth going to see. That I might want to check it out."

"So she *had* seen it. Which theater was it?"

"I forget. Somewhere on Broadway. And recently. But you really can't believe that a stupid play had something to do with her killing herself?"

"It's not a stupid play. Samuel Beckett wrote it, and he later won the Nobel Prize for literature. Are you sure she didn't tell you more than that about her interest in it?"

Stamos looked uncertain. "I think she wanted to, but...she never came around to telling me. I...tried to get her to fill me in. But..."

"But what?"

"I don't know, she seemed...scared." She looked up at him. "Does that make any sense?"

"Maybe it did to her," he said thoughtfully. "Why exactly did you want to talk to me?"

"About Sara, like I said."

"I think you have something else on your mind."

She looked nervously at him. "You were at the office late last night."

"Why do you say that?"

"I asked the security guard later after you left and I slipped away from the ambulance guys. I went back to the building. He said you had come inside earlier, right after I did."

"I didn't see him."

"He was just coming back from making his rounds. He saw you, but you didn't see him."

"Okay, so?"

"He told me you left right after I did. He thought... I mean he didn't say it, but I believe he thought you and I had... you know, gone up there to..."

Devine sat back. *Okay, here we go.*

"I left my phone in my cubicle and went back to get it. Is that a crime?"

Her response was immediate and direct. "I was in there a lot longer than it took for you to get your phone."

*Yes you were.* "And while I was there I logged on and did some work. I didn't even know you were there, but that's what you were doing, right? Catching up on some work?"

"Y-yes, that's right. A report I was working on."

"Well, good for the goose, good for the gander, right?"

She gave him a searching look and he hoped he had passed the test. Or rather Cowl's test. Because this further explained the look Brad Cowl had given him in the dining hall earlier. And it also was the reason she had wanted to meet with him.

"When you left last night, you called me 'sweet cheeks.'"

*Here we go. Round two.*

"It was shitty and degrading. I guess the adrenaline was pumping after the fight and I turned into a stupid punk trying to act big. I used to call the girls in high school that, and I wasn't referring to their faces. Thought it was cool. I was a jerk. I'm really sorry."

Her searching look faded and she looked down. "Apology accepted."

Devine rose, opened his wallet, and said, "I need to grab the train home, and then catch up on some sleep and ice my aches and pains. What do I owe you for the beers?"

She looked up at him. “I invited you for drinks. So I got it.” As he put his wallet away she said, “So, *did* you kill anybody over there?”

“That was sort of the point,” answered Devine.

He headed to the subway, leaving the woman alone with her margarita, chips, and guac.

And doubts.

*About me.*

*And maybe about herself, too.*

CHAPTER

# 17

THE SMOKE-AND-COFFEE CAR was parked out in front of Devine's place, and Detective Hancock had the driver's door open. He was sitting sideways in the seat with his feet on the pavement. He looked up as Devine walked into view.

Hancock stood. As he did, his jacket swung open, revealing a gun in a belt clip holster.

"You prefer the Glock to the Sig?" asked Devine as he drew nearer.

Hancock glanced down in surprise. "You can tell just from the butt of the gun?"

"I can tell from a lot of things."

"Army stuff coming through again, huh?"

"Army green pours through every *pore* I have. What's up?"

Hancock focused on his face. "Whoa, what the hell happened there?"

"Playing pickup basketball at the high school over there and fell flat on my face trying to do stuff I don't have the skill to do against kids half my age and a lot better than I'll ever be. Looks worse than it is."

"Right. Leave that shit to the youngsters. I have some follow-ups. Got a minute?"

"And if I said I'd rather get some shut-eye?" said Devine.

"Won't take long. Let's take a walk. You good with that? Nice night."

Devine started walking and Hancock fell in beside him.

"How's the investigation coming? Have you found out why she killed herself?"

"She didn't kill herself. That's why I'm here with more questions."

Devine stopped walking; so did Hancock.

"Come again?"

"She didn't take her own life. This is now a *homicide* investigation."

Devine held on to that game-changing word for an eternal moment. "*Homicide*, as opposed to *suicide*?"

"This is not for official distribution, you understand," said Hancock.

"So why tell me?"

"I hope being straight with you will make you straight with me, that's why."

"I *have* been straight with you."

"Don't think so."

"But you guys said suicide," countered Devine.

"That was the prelim. Things have changed. Homicide can be made to look like suicide, especially for victims who were found hanging."

"I know," said Devine, looking off now.

"How?" said Hancock quickly. "How do you know?"

Devine started walking again. "We had a case over in Afghanistan. Guy was found hanging just like Sara. All evidence pointed to suicide. He was depressed. His wife was having an affair with some unidentified asshole. He'd missed out on his next promotion. He was drinking heavily, screwing up. He'd had multiple warnings from the brass, and the hammer was about to come down on his career."

*And his name was Lieutenant Roy Blankenship*, thought Devine.

"Damn, a lot to deal with."

"Yeah. But he didn't kill himself. He was murdered."

Hancock eyed him. "Who killed the guy? And why? And how'd they find out?"

"The guy was his comrade in arms. He'd just come back from stateside. Turns out *he* was the one banging the dead guy's wife. His motivation was as old as time: He wanted the hubby out of the picture so he could fill that slot and live happily ever after with the missus."

*And his name was Captain Ken Hawkins.*

"Shit, talk about betrayal. How'd they figure out it wasn't suicide?"

"Probably the same way NYPD did." Devine ran a finger in a vertical line over his neck. "Straight-line ligature mark versus an inverted mark is the key telltale sign. Strangulation always has the first, hanging always has the second, because of gravity's force on the body. And the dead guy's fingernails also had rope hemp in them. So what happened was the killer strangled him with a rope from behind and the victim fought back, digging into the rope and getting fibers under his fingernails. That also made for the straight-line ligature because no gravity at work. Then the killer strung him up with the same rope to make it look like suicide. But the Army CID agents found the straight-line under the inverted ligature mark. And the inverted was made postmortem, because the guy was already dead. They can tell when something happens postmortem, but then you know that already."

"How come you know so much about the details?" Hancock said suspiciously.

Devine knew all this because he had gone over every molecule of the case and spoken with the CID agents multiple times. He knew it wasn't suicide and had wondered why the CID hadn't concluded the same thing. He had come to find out it was more military politics than any sort of search for the truth. And Campbell had pretty much confirmed that.

"Like I said, they were part of my unit. I made sure I was informed."

"What happened to the guy who killed him?"

"He's dead. Killed himself when Army CID started closing in. So his really *was* a suicide."

And that, Devine knew, was a lie.

*Hawkins is dead because I left him out there to die.*

"And the wife?"

"No proof she knew anything about the plan to kill her husband. She's remarried and doing fine," added Devine, who didn't look fine with this at all. "And why is Sara's case now a homicide instead of a suicide?"

"For reasons very similar to what you just said," replied Hancock.

"So the killer was sloppy," observed Devine.

"And the killer is still out there. And it's my job to find him."

"Or her."

"Would've taken some strength to string the woman up like that. Dead weight, no pun intended."

"And what do you want from me?" asked Devine.

"Where were you between roughly midnight and four a.m. on the day she was found?"

"Is that the window on the time of death?" Devine asked.

"Roughly. AC was on high in the building so it screwed with the TOD a bit. They're doing a more thorough calculation right now to get a tighter window, if they can."

"Well, I was home in bed. At four o'clock I was just getting up and going to do my workout."

"Anybody vouch for that?" asked Hancock.

"Probably one of my roommates. But the Cowl Building has cameras and a security guard on duty and you need a security card to get in after hours. You don't have to play gumshoe peeking through keyholes, Detective."

Hancock said jokingly, only clearly he wasn't, "Oh, hey, thanks, man, I didn't realize any of that shit. This sucker is basically solved."

"I'm not trying to tell you how to do your job, okay?"

"Sure sounded like it to me. And you really work out at four a.m.?"

"Yeah, at the high school football field over there. Only time I've really got to do it."

"Okay, and FYI, the guard makes rounds. He's not in the lobby all the time."

*Yeah, that I know*, thought Devine. "And the security card and cameras?"

"Killer could have stayed in the building all night."

"You can do a head count on the video of people coming and going."

"Too many people and too much confusion and bad camera angles to rule everybody out. And that includes *you*."

"I came home the night before. My roommates can tell you that." At least he hoped they could. "And to get back in the building, my security card would be needed. There'd be a record. And I'd be on film."

"Like you were last night. Around eleven or so?"

"I forgot my phone. I went back for it. The guard saw me leave."

"Yes, he did."

"And?" said Devine.

"And nothing, unless you want to add to it."

"I don't."

"You knew Sara Ewes?" asked Hancock.

"I already told you I did!"

"Don't get all worked up, Devine. See, the thing is, I think you knew her better than you let on."

Devine stopped walking again. "Based on what?"

"Did you?" asked Hancock.

"Depends on what you mean by 'better than you let on.'"

"Were you dating her? Did you have sex with her?"

"Should I get a lawyer?" asked Devine.

"Do you think you need one?"

"This is America. Everybody needs a lawyer at some point."

Hancock looked displeased by the response. "If you won't answer the question, it makes me suspicious and it makes you look guilty."

"Even if I was dating her or had sex with her, why would that be a motive for murder?"

"Oldest motive in the book. Spurned lover."

"So now I'm a spurned lover? You should write novels."

"Were you one?" asked Hancock. "A spurned lover?"

"I think we're done here."

"You know, the Army cops got the guy. We will, too."

"I hope you find the person. Only it won't be me, because I didn't do it."

"Oh, okay, I'll just take your word for it. Cross you right off the suspect list."

"You talk to any other *suspects*?" asked Devine.

"No need for you to know that."

Devine turned around and walked home.

Tomorrow was Sunday, a day of rest. For God.

But not for Travis Devine. Tomorrow might just outdo everything else he'd done the entire week. Maybe his whole time at Cowl and Comely.

But then again, why wait until tomorrow? After all, the night was still young.

# CHAPTER

# 18

THERE WAS THE RUSSIAN, WILL Valentine, on the couch, but this time he was awake. A brand-spanking-new pizza box was next to him and one of his Coors Light beers was unopened, but Devine doubted it would be for long. The Russian's appetite for American junk food and beer was apparently insatiable.

Devine sat next to him, eyed the pizza and beer, and said, "You know, there are other kinds of food and drink in this country. And this stuff will kill you if that's all you put inside yourself."

"You like little joke." Valentine grinned, tore off a big chunk of a pepperoni slice with his teeth, and then clacked away on his computer with one dexterous hand.

Devine watched this and shrugged. "Okay, that's my advice for healthy living for the week. Got a problem you might help with. It's a weird email I got, but I don't know who sent it. Maybe you can figure it out."

Valentine glanced sharply at him. "Forward me email."

Devine did so and said, "Whenever you can get to it, but the sooner the better. Lives may depend on it."

Valentine casually waved this off, though his full attention was on the message now resting in his computer email inbox. "You Americans, you get too caught up in stuff like that. In Russia, people die all the time. Usually by government. Or too much vodka. But is good way to go, no?"

"No."

"You want pizza?"

Devine looked down at the box and snagged a piece. "Hey, you remember me being here all of Thursday night, right?"

"Thursday? Sure, sure. All the time. Why?"

"No reason." Devine remembered that Valentine had been dead asleep in his room. Even if he misremembered and told the cops differently, they wouldn't believe him. He was Russian after all. Valentine had not commented on his facial injuries. He might have assumed Americans got the shit kicked out of them on a frequent basis. Maybe the same was true for Russians.

Valentine looked up. "Whoa, dude, this does not look like email address."

"I know, that's the problem. And I can't reply to it."

"You sure you got this over internet?"

"I'm sure."

Valentine didn't look convinced, but then his expression changed as he read the message again. "Wait. Sara Ewes? Didn't you tell me you dated her, dude? And now she's dead."

*Shit, I forgot I told him about Sara.* Devine eyed the man, sizing up the situation and what his response would be. "Just try to track the email, Will. It's important."

He went up to his room eating the pizza and changed his clothes. Jeans and a black T-shirt were his go-to casual attire. His arm and shoulder were still sore, and he went to the bathroom to reapply the ointment on his face. As he was coming out, Helen Speers was standing there in cut-off jean short-shorts with the bottoms of the white pockets exposed next to her muscled thighs, and a red crop top. Her long hair was piled on top of her head and held there by assorted hairclips.

God, she was a knockout, he thought admiringly.

"What the hell happened to you?" she said.

"Cut myself shaving."

That got him an eye roll. "You're not as funny as you think you are. But you share that with most guys."

"I plead guilty to that, Your Honor." The light banter ended right there.

"A woman died in your building."

Devine tensed. "Yeah, she did. Sara Ewes."

"You know her?" she asked.

"A little."

"The news said it was a suicide."

"NYPD may be rethinking that," noted Devine.

"Was that *NYPD* outside talking to you? I was looking out my window. He seemed like a cop." She seemed more intent and into this than was warranted. He wasn't sure how that made him feel.

"Yes, he is."

"What did he want with you?"

"Asking questions, just like they're doing with everybody else."

She folded her arms over her chest and looked alarmingly judicial. "Do you need a lawyer, Travis? I know some good ones."

"I had nothing to do with her death."

"Doesn't matter. Innocent people get sent to prison all the time."

This set him back on his heels, although Devine knew what she said was true. "I'll let you know. Thanks for the offer. Hey, you remember me being here Thursday night, right?"

"Why? Am I your alibi?" she quickly added.

"You can call it that if you want."

"I think so. But then again, I got in late. I remember seeing you last night for sure. I was doing yoga in the dining room."

"Last night is irrelevant to the police investigation."

"I get that. Let me think about it."

"Thanks. How's your studying going for the bar?"

"New York's is really hard, but I feel good about it."

"What kind of law are you going to practice?"

"Criminal."

"Which side?"

She gave him a look that he couldn't readily interpret. "The side that needs me the most, of course."

She walked off downstairs and he heard the front door open and close. He crossed the hall and knocked on Tapshaw's door, after he heard her tapping away inside.

She opened the door and stood there in what looked to be her pajamas.

"Yeah?" she said brightly. She had dirty blond hair that spooled around her narrow shoulders. Her face was button cute and her eyes danced with both focus and merriment. She was in her late twenties, she had told him, but sometimes, like now, the woman still looked to be in her teens. She was too skinny, but otherwise appeared healthy to his eye. She had bunny slippers on her feet. Her room was a wreck. Devine had seen more orderly spaces after he'd tossed a grenade inside them.

The walls were covered in yellow and green Post-it notes. She had three large computer screens on her desk. There was a whiteboard that had revenue and profit projections, and a business flow chart along with a corporate organizational schematic.

He knew that Tapshaw had gone to MIT. Her undergrad degree had been in computer science. He'd also learned that she was a world-class gamer; in fact, she had used her winnings to start her company, she'd told him. She'd also won some prestigious international awards for her out-of-this-world computer skills and overall brilliance. Then she'd tacked on a fast-tracked MBA from Harvard. The burly, beer-chugging Russian downstairs knew his way around computers, Devine knew, but this shiny-faced skinny young woman trying to build an empire in the love and dating space might be in a totally different league.

"How you doing, Jill? Ever come up for air, or food?"

He really liked her. She was ambitious, but nice, and didn't think too highly of herself. He didn't run into too many people like that. And she had a tender smile and a kind, if naïve, manner.

"Oh yeah, I had... breakfast, I think." She looked unsure, and gazed back into her room, as though searching for evidence to back up her statement.

"It's dinnertime."

She looked stunned. "Wow. That went by fast. When I go to the office I usually at least have soup and some coffee, but I've been working here all day." She fixed on his injuries. "My gosh, what happened to you? Did you fall off your motorcycle?"

"Slipped in the shower. Valentine has pizza downstairs. You might want to hurry before he finishes it."

"Good idea. Hey, are *you* doing all right?"

She obviously knew nothing about his dilemma. Her entire world revolved around Hummingbird. But it was nice that she had asked.

"No complaints. Look, if you ever take a break, there's a place nearby that has good tequila."

"I *love* tequila."

"Well, then."

"How about next weekend? I know you work long hours."

"Thanks for noticing." He grinned. "I know you keep kind of busy, too."

She looked at her note-clad walls. "It's crazy, isn't it? But it feels cool to be, I don't know, building something. Particularly something that people need and could help them."

"Beats what I do for a living. Now, go get the pizza. If he puts up a fight come get me."

"Thanks."

She fled down the stairs. A few moments later Devine heard Valentine cry out, "Hey, no, that's...oh well, you already bite into it. So America. But hey, I am American now, so is all cool."

Devine snagged his bike helmet and went out the back door.

## CHAPTER

# 19

COWL'S SUBURBAN PALACE WAS QUIET tonight. Or so Devine thought as he sat on his bike and surveyed the place with a pair of night optics he'd brought back from the war. He figured the Army owed him that. Lights were on, people were moving around inside, and there were a couple of normal cars in the front, meaning a BMW Eight Series and a Maserati convertible. You could have bought at least ten of them each for the cash Cowl had dropped on the Bugatti.

Devine jogged across the road and took up position in the hook of a tree in a stand of oaks, which had been allowed to live when they had otherwise clear-cut this area. He could see into a fresh set of rooms from this vantage point. He hadn't seen the bikini blonde yet and there was no sign of Cowl. But the place had eight garage bays, so the Bugatti could be in one of them.

Devine sat there for a few minutes. Remaining motionless for long periods seemed to be counterintuitive when thinking about what a soldier spent time doing. But the more intelligence you had beforehand, the better the eventual fight would go.

He shifted out of the tree, hustled over some open ground, and jumped up on the perimeter wall. Then, keeping his upper arms and elbows planted firmly against the wall, he slowly lifted the optics up to his eyes, adjusting the focus.

That was when he hit pay dirt.

The bikini blonde was out back at a table beside the pool. She had on white slacks and a pale blue sleeveless blouse. Blue backless casual shoes completed the fashion pool-sitting ensemble. She looked like she could step right onto a magazine cover.

Yet the man sitting opposite her was even more intriguing.

His face was bandaged, but Devine had little trouble recognizing WASP from the Greenwich Village alley. As he looked at them together, sitting close and speaking earnestly, Devine wondered two things: First, was WASP's car the big-ass BMW or the Maserati? Second, were they brother and sister? Because they sure looked like they could be.

Then he also wondered about something else. WASP's being here was one hell of a coincidence. And not one Devine cared for at all. But then again the bar in the Village was popular with folks who worked in the Financial District. He'd been there before on some official Cowl and Comely outings with his fellow Burners. So if WASP was there and he was in the financial field as well, he could very well know Brad Cowl.

Devine couldn't hear what either was saying, so he dropped back to the ground, returned to his bike, and waited.

He didn't have to wait long.

WASP came out and climbed into the BMW. Devine had gotten that wrong. He'd figured the guy for the Maserati. The BMW pulled out through the gates and WASP hit the afterburners. The car roared off, and Devine took up the chase once more.

He was not completely surprised when the route took them to Manhattan. The BMW finally stopped in front of a brownstone on the Upper East Side after sliding into a permit-only space. WASP walked up to the door, unlocked it, and went inside.

Devine pulled in across the street and took pictures of the BMW's plate and the home and its address, which were detailed by brass numbers attached to the stone next to the front door. Every window in the place had coverings, rendering his optics useless. He eyed the homes on either side. They were dark. Cars were parked up and down the street.

He figured the brownstone was worth twenty mil or more. And the WASP looked to be no more than thirty. Maybe he'd inherited the place. There was a lot of that going on in this town.

Devine drove off and headed to Broadway. He'd looked up the address where *Waiting for Godot* was playing for another two weeks. It was on Forty-Fifth in the heart of the Theater District.

*The Lombard.*

He bought a ticket at the box office for the Sunday matinee. After that he turned toward Downtown and soon pulled up to the place in the Village where he had fought the three men. He parked diagonally behind a car at the curb and looked around. There was no police tape up, and he saw no other evidence of this being any type of crime scene. Maybe Stamos had been telling the truth. He next drove farther south to the Cowl Building and stopped in front. He could see the security guard through the glass.

Devine craned his neck back to look up to the fifty-second floor, where it seemed now that someone had *killed* Sara Ewes. And since he had to find out what was happening at Cowl that might be illegal, he figured he also had to find out who had killed Ewes, because they had to be connected. And that connection might stem from a Broadway play.

*And if I don't solve this thing, even with my best efforts, why do I think Emerson Campbell will send my ass right to USDB?*

He headed to Brooklyn, crossing over the East River via the Brooklyn Bridge. The dark water looked sulky and uninterested in its surroundings, at least to him. A few minutes later he reached a street in Park Slope a block over from Prospect Park. It was a quiet and tree-lined neighborhood of upscale homes, many of which had been renovated.

Sara Ewes had lived in one of them, and there were two police cars parked in front of it. A cop was standing guard by the front door and the lights were on inside.

A man in a suit came out of the place and looked around. A slender redheaded woman hurried over to him and they met at the bottom of the front steps. She had a microphone and a power pack under the back of her blouse, and was trailed by a burly cameraman.

*So the media has gotten wind that something is up.*

The suit engaged with the reporter and they spoke briefly, though the cameraman did no filming. This appointment must have been prearranged, thought Devine. When the man turned and walked back to the house, the woman trailed him, ostensibly asking more questions and perhaps wanting to get something on film. Devine couldn't hear exactly what they were, but the reporter obviously had not gotten her fill; however, the man had. He closed the door in her face, and she clearly wasn't happy about that.

The uniform stepped forward and motioned for them to leave. She gave him an earful and then turned away to jabber with her cameraman, who had lowered his piece of equipment. They walked back to a van parked farther down the narrow street and emblazoned with the station's logo. A minute later they pulled off. Devine saw the woman close up as the van sped past. The dented and grimy vehicle said they were with Channel 44, which he didn't even know was a thing. She was around Devine's age. Her expression was determined, and she looked like the type who lived only to be in the middle of all the biggest news stories of the day.

Devine's attention was then drawn to a cab that pulled slowly down the street and stopped in front of the house. Two people got out, a man and a woman. They looked to be in their fifties. The man was bald and dressed in slacks and a white dress shirt. He looked like death itself. The woman's face held the anguish of the recently bereaved. The man pulled out a large roller suitcase from the cab's trunk and then the cab drove off.

The man put his arm around the woman, supporting her, and they slowly headed up the steps, where they were met by the cop. After each of them showed him something, probably ID, the cop spoke into the mic Velcroed to his shoulder pad. The door opened a few seconds later and the same suit appeared. He ushered the couple inside and closed the door.

Devine took all this in. Obviously, Ewes's parents had just shown up from wherever they lived outside of the country. He wondered if they knew that the official verdict had changed to homicide. If they didn't, things were about to get far more difficult for the couple. There was guilt in thinking your child had killed herself. You would find yourself in *What signals did I miss?*, *What could I have done?* sorts of mind games.

But with murder came horror. Knowing that someone out there had killed your kid. Your first instinct was to avenge your child. Then, when that emotion died down, things would be looked at more rationally. At that point, the understanding that someone had violently taken your child's life could make you delve into all sorts of personal spaces where most parents would probably rather not go.

But if Ewes indeed had been murdered, it was someone at Cowl and Comely who had done it. And that meant everyone there, including Devine, was now a suspect.

# CHAPTER

# 20

DEVINE GOT UP A LITTLE late since it was Sunday. By 6 a.m. his workout was complete, and he went back to bed for more sleep. He listened to his body, and it was telling him to slow down and catch up on some rest. He woke at eleven, showered off the remnants of his sweaty workout, and then prepared breakfast: veggie omelet, toast, protein shake, coffee, and a chocolate chip cookie thrown in just for the hell of it.

After that, he went back to his room, fired up his laptop, and did some digging. The deeded owner of the Upper East Side property the WASP had gone into was listed as the Locust Group. He googled *Locust Group* and came up with a ton of results, including variations thereof. Some looked legit, with office addresses and websites and lots of info about what they did. But there were simply too many for him to run them all down.

As a little diversion he looked up the term *locust* online. They were defined as short-horned grasshoppers belonging to the Acrididae family. They were not known to be harmful to humans.

Devine rubbed his sore shoulder and injured face.

*They may have to rethink that part.*

But if the sole purpose of *this* Locust Group was to own the New York brownstone, it was reasonable to have no business address and no website. And he knew it was common practice for the ultrawealthy and/or famous to use shell companies to buy property for privacy reasons. Maybe that was all this was.

He next ran the license plate on the BMW. Valentine had earlier shown him a nifty and pretty straightforward way of accessing this information. When he'd asked him about it, the Russian had waved a slice of meatball pizza around and snorted, "The New York DMV? Please. They suck. My nephew can hack DMV and your FBI and your fuckin' CIA and other letter people. And he is still little bay-bee."

The guy really was a pill.

The car was registered to a Christian Fullerton Chilton, with the address being the brownstone. Devine looked Chilton up online. There was more than one, but he quickly narrowed it down by the middle name and the fact that he knew what the man looked like.

He had a Facebook page, but it was private, and thus restricted regarding what he had access to.

But there were ways around that. And he hadn't needed the Russian to show him how.

He checked the HTML source code, got the Numeric ID off that, plugged it in, did a few more steps of "URL manipulation," as it was known in the trade—because of Facebook's nonstop battles with nosy jerks like him—like copying profile attributes of some of Chilton's actual friends listed on the page and then injecting them into his own profile, and Christian Chilton's page was fooled into thinking Devine was his best "friend." And since Devine was using a fake online identity of his own to do this, it was highly doubtful that Chilton would be able to reverse engineer to the real Devine. At least he hoped he couldn't.

He quickly looked through the photos and posts. He saw some very famous young people and some very famous old people. Chilton apparently got around. He was in a dream car, or on a mega-yacht in the Med, or striding confidently onto a Gulfstream 650. Devine wasn't guessing; Chilton helpfully provided the type of plane in large cap letters. Devine had never ridden on a set of wings like that. For him, an ass-buster seat on a C-130 or C-17 transport plane was the way Army grunts traveled. You could tell your perch was first class if it actually had a seat *and* a harness to keep you there.

Chilton was also, he proudly claimed, a direct descendant of one Edward Chilton, who had sailed over on the *Mayflower*. As though that really meant something today. And yet it would for some, Devine knew.

Chilton listed his occupation as "entrepreneur and investor." He had a company named, what else, Mayflower Enterprises. There was a link to that on the Facebook account. Devine went there and poked around. It looked legit. They had done a ton of investments in all sorts of different business spaces. Chilton was the head guy, and he had lots of smiling faces on the website who made up the rest of his team.

Devine changed into khaki slacks, a blue short-sleeved shirt, and light brown canvas shoes, and was leaving for the play when Helen Speers approached him, frowning.

"I don't think I can provide you an alibi, Travis. I've wracked my brain, but I honestly can't remember seeing you all of Thursday night. You're sure you were here?"

"Yeah, but that's okay. If you don't remember, you don't remember. I'd never ask you to do something you're not comfortable with."

She drew nearer and touched his arm. "I am sorry, Travis. And if you ever need to talk? I'm here for you."

"Thanks."

As she walked off he closed his eyes, took a deep breath, and told himself to not go there. He had too much on his plate as it was.

He eyed Jill Tapshaw's door, and knocked, but there was no answer. She might have gone into the office. For her, Sunday was just another day to build her empire of shared love.

He left and went outside. He wasn't taking his bike this time. He'd opt for the train.

As he walked to the station, he wondered if there was something more to Speers's words. But that might just be wishful thinking. Sure, he had a mild crush on the woman, and she might have one on him. But he didn't think it was that. She seemed genuinely worried about him, and he wasn't sure why. It wasn't like they were close friends, and she probably had a dozen prospects a lot better suited for her than he was.

He broke out of these thoughts when a vehicle pulled up next to him.

"How about a ride to wherever you're going in exchange for an interview?"

He looked into the face of the smiling but determined reporter from Channel Nosebleed who wanted to know every damn thing in the world.

## CHAPTER

# 21

EXCUSE ME?" SAID DEVINE, BECAUSE he wanted a little time to process what she was even doing here.

"You're Travis Devine? You work at Cowl and Comely? Where a woman was found dead?"

"And you are?"

"Rachel Potter. Channel Forty-Four, but I'm working my way up to the single-digit stations and you might just be my ticket." She eyed her beefy cameraman, who was driving. "We have room in the front seat."

"What do you want to know?"

"Whatever you can tell me about Sara Ewes."

"I don't have a lot of time. I have a train to catch."

"Then jump in—it's faster driving."

Devine looked around, and then he climbed in as Potter scooched over to allow room. The cameraman took off at a sedate pace, something Devine could tell was prearranged.

She took out her phone and hit the Record button. "You're Travis Devine, employed by Cowl and Comely?"

"I am. Look, I—"

"And you knew Sara Ewes?"

"I did. I think—"

"And do you know anything about the circumstances of her death?"

"No, I don't."

"What can you tell me about her?" Potter asked.

"She was nice. She worked hard. She was moving up at the firm."

"Did you and Sara see each other, I mean other than at work?" she asked.

Devine eyed her for a moment. This question kept coming up. Hancock had already been sniffing around about it, intimating that Devine had not been entirely truthful. They knew something. They had to. And maybe this Potter woman did, too. Maybe she'd been told last night in fact. And not by the cops.

He put a hand on the door latch. "I think we're done here."

The driver sped up.

Devine eyed Potter. "So what are you doing here? Holding me against my will? Should I be concerned for my safety?"

She eyed him coyly. "Big, strong Army Ranger with a chest full of combat medals? You could probably kill us both with your pinkie."

The woman was right about that, but it wouldn't be much of a challenge. Potter was around five four and one-ten in all her clothes. The driver was in his sixties and about fifty pounds overweight, and every breath he exhaled was full of cigarette smoke. Devine probably *could* take him out with his pinkie.

"Have you killed anyone, Mr. Devine? I mean in war, not in New York City."

"I've always wondered why people find that so fascinating."

"Okay, let's focus on Sara Ewes. Do you know why anyone would want to *murder* her?"

So now that cat was out of the bag. If Potter knew, then it was all over the news. Devine hadn't checked his feed today. He would have to remedy that on the train ride in.

"Murdered?" he said, looking, he hoped, appropriately dumbfounded. "Last I heard it was suicide."

"Then you're behind the curve. I broke that story last night," she said triumphantly. "Before any of the single-digit stations. My scoop."

"How'd you manage that?" he asked, thinking that he had learned that it was murder before she had, from Detective Hancock.

"I'm really good at my job and I have great sources. *Confidential* sources."

*Yeah, I saw your confidential source outside of Ewes's house*, thought Devine. He hoped the loose-lipped cop had told the woman's parents before they found out on the news.

"So, getting back to Ewes. Did she have any enemies?"

"How exactly did you decide to pick on me? A lot of other people work at the firm. And a lot of them knew Sara better than me."

"That's not what I heard."

"Then what you heard was wrong. And where did you hear that?"

"Confidential, sorry."

"Stop the van," he said.

"Oh, come on."

Devine reached a long arm across and slammed the gearshift into Park, jolting them to a stop and causing Potter, who was not wearing a seat belt, to end up facedown in Devine's lap. He looked down at her thick red hair planted in his crotch.

He said, "Hey, don't you want to buy me a drink first before you do that?"

This line actually got a guffaw from the cameraman-driver.

But not from Potter.

She sat up and looked at him furiously. "You *don't* want to make an enemy of me."

"You're right, I don't. Which is why I'm getting out now, but I won't be pressing charges for false imprisonment."

"You sound like a lawyer."

"No, but I know a really good one. So depending on how you end up playing this, you might be hearing from her."

"The First Amendment is pretty broad."

"And it cuts both ways."

He got out of the van and hustled toward the station.

The van zoomed past him, blaring its horn all the way. And he knew it was Potter with her hand on it, her fury still fully engaged.

He reached the station and climbed on board just as the doors of the inbound train opened for passengers.

He sat down at a window, checked his phone, and saw that the media was indeed now reporting Sara Ewes's death as a homicide.

As the train moved out of the station and toward the city, Devine assessed his current situation. The cops were coming from one end, the press from another. Suicide had turned to murder. The NYPD was no doubt under a lot of pressure to solve the homicide of an upstanding young woman at an upstanding white-glove investment firm.

And ex-Army alpha male Travis Devine might just make a fetching target.

It was clear that his roommates could not provide him with a viable alibi. Valentine had been asleep, Speers could not confirm his whereabouts, and he recalled that Tapshaw had been out that night. And thus he would remain on the suspect list, red meat for Hancock and company.

But he had a couple of aces in the hole.

Security at Cowl and Comely was very tight. During nonbusiness hours you needed a security card to get into the building. Even during business hours your card was required to access the elevators. Visitors had to present ID and were photographed and signed in at the security desk after whoever they were visiting was contacted and the okay given. Then they were escorted to the elevator by security, and only the floor they were authorized to visit was made accessible. When they were done, the only floor they could punch in and access without a security card would be the lobby. All of the coming-and-going information on guests and employees was electronically recorded.

Devine knew that he and his security card had been nowhere near Cowl and Comely when Sara Ewes was being killed. They would not be able to overcome that.

But on the ride in to see *Waiting for Godot*, he thought about all the ways he still might be screwed.

He assumed the play might have a whole new meaning for him after all this.

*Out of the frying pan and right into the pits of hell.*

# CHAPTER 22

It wasn't the 6:20, but it still passed by Brad Cowl's humble digs.

Before Devine had rented his room at the town house, he had done some investigating and knew that Cowl lived there and that this commuter train would pass by it. So he had had his eye on Mount Kisco even without Campbell using a Realtor to get him his current home.

Devine had thought, however unrealistically, that seeing how and where Cowl lived could be used as an advantage. He might be able to take an observation he made from the train and then use it in conversation with the man to impress him, to help Devine move up the rungs at the firm. None of that had happened. His only meeting with Cowl had been in that large conference room that day with all the other newbies. So now he was stuck every single day seeing how ungodly rich the man was.

*So much for my grand plan.*

As he thought about that, he started thinking about his last few months in the Army.

Roy Blankenship had confided in Devine about his wife's affair. And Blankenship knew that Ken Hawkins was the one screwing his wife; he had told Devine about it. After Blankenship's death, Devine had gotten access to the forensic records via a buddy of his in CID. That was when he had learned a lot about vertical versus inverted ligature marks. It was clear even to Devine, not a trained investigator, that it was murder and not suicide, and he had questioned his CID contact as to why the verdict had come down as Blankenship's killing himself.

His friend told him, "The brass doesn't like rocking boats, Travis. The war is turning against us, and the last thing they need is an officer-on-officer murder investigation in the mix."

When Devine had told him that was all bullshit, his friend had added, "Welcome to the politics of the United States Army."

But after Hawkins had been found dead—his body had shown telltale signs of having been attacked by animals—Devine had gone into a deep depression. He had hated Hawkins for what he had done. He had managed to get the man alone out in the mountains. And then he had unleashed on him, telling him everything he knew, the centerpiece of which was Hawkins's having killed Blankenship.

At first Hawkins had denied it, but after Devine laid fact on top of fact the man admitted his guilt. And then he had come at Devine with a knife. The men had fought. But Devine was younger, stronger, and his inner motor just couldn't be beat by the likes of Hawkins. He had left him there, unconscious. But he had never expected the man to die out there.

The official cause of death was internal hemorrhaging brought on by repeated blows to the head and body, blows provided by Devine. However, the official report was that Hawkins had died at the hands of the *Taliban*. And Devine had never corrected the record. But he also could not remain in the Army with the guilt of what he had done.

Thus the exit from the one organization where he had felt he truly belonged.

And his subsequent exile to the financial world in New York, where his old man was so, so proud of him.

*My own personal prison. With no way out.*

But maybe Campbell had given him a way. Now he just had to perform.

No one was by the pool at Cowl's place. There was a gardener pruning a bush. A cardinal landed on top of a table umbrella and performed the short, jerky motions of the head that birds did. The water looked cool and inviting but for some reason made Devine slightly nauseous. He turned away as the train jolted and picked up speed, and the palace was gone.

Devine closed his eyes and sat back in his seat the rest of the way to New York. The city was tough for many natives in the summer. It was crowded with tourists who often had no idea where they were going. But assistance by accommodating locals proud of their city was usually provided and any confusion rectified.

The pavements and buildings absorbed every molecule of heat and threw it violently back at walkers and bikers and drivers. Foul air, driven by funneled winds, could almost burn your nostrils out or lift you off your feet. The subway would blow past underneath, and its thrust would come through the pavement grates with velocity, providing a surprise gust of hot air.

Yet he liked the city in the summer more than in the winter. He could sit on a rock in Central Park, or perch on a bench or take a stroll and pretend there was no one else around. And, somehow, in a metropolis of eight million, it worked. At least for him.

He walked to Broadway from Grand Central. When Devine got to the theater his phone buzzed. He looked down at the screen, where a message appeared. Emerson Campbell wanted to meet with him for a progress report. Devine knew why. Suicide had just changed to homicide. He looked around. It was a typical Sunday on a warm summer's day in Manhattan, meaning the streets were packed and people were either leisurely walking along or rushing on their way to get somewhere.

Devine moved over to a corner of the street out of the way of passing pedestrians and called the number on the screen. A voice answered, giving him a time later that day and an address. Luckily, it was in the city. For a moment he wondered if they knew where he was. He looked at his phone. *Idiot.* If Apple knew where he was, of course Campbell did.

He took his seat inside the Lombard Theater, in the back and on the left. The interior had been redone with taste and quality. The place was full and there was a nice mix of young and old, more women than men. There was a heightened sense of anticipation.

The lights went down and the curtain rose, and Devine forgot about most everything else as two performers, who had achieved dazzling heights on both stage and screen and were now in the twilight of their careers, waited for, well, Godot. Although Devine already knew Godot would not be coming. That was the point, after all.

Devine was riveted, just as he was the first time he'd seen a different production fifteen years ago. Back then, the teenaged Devine had just made a momentous decision that had resulted in a bad relationship with his father becoming even worse. Consequently, Devine had seen a bit of himself in the portrayals onstage. The waiting, the creeping doubt, the revitalization of spirit, and the creeping doubt once more. Coupled with all that heaviness was another question: Was there really any real meaning in the lives being led by people? *Were we all just waiting for... nothing?*

He had come out of the theater back then both sure and uncertain of his decision to join the Army, if such things could coexist. And in the complexity of the human mind he knew they easily could. As could the rationale to take the life of another. He knew that better than most.

Now, as a mature man, Devine had a deeper appreciation for Samuel Beckett's tale of two men desperately waiting for something that they could not even begin to define.

Devine had thought he would be in the military for the full ride and then muster out and maybe go work for a defense contractor. Or hell, maybe find an island far away and lie on the beach with stacks of good books. But none of that had worked out. He had gotten his MBA and gone to work for Cowl to appease his father, to be more like his siblings, to be a success in the way that success was normally defined, at least in America.

But mostly to make himself pay for having essentially killed another soldier, regardless of whether the man deserved it.

When the lights came up and the curtain came down for the final time after the actors had performed their bows and filed off the stage, Devine remained where he was sitting and looked around the theater. The seats and the trimmings and the carpet and all the other hundreds of details clearly showed the place had been given some serious TLC. It was good they kept these old structures around instead of knocking them down. Some people would knock down everything given the chance. Including other people.

But with respect to the reason he had come here, the results were disappointing. Why Ewes had mentioned the play to Stamos, he still didn't know. He knew that Ewes had walked into Stamos's office and told her about *Waiting for Godot*, encouraging her to check it out. Well, Devine *had* checked it out. And he still understood not one damn thing about why it was important to Ewes, or whether it was connected to her death or whatever was going on at Cowl and Comely.

But the more he thought about his conversation with Stamos, the more he homed in on her vague response and her reluctance to go into detail about what Ewes had told her about the play.

*Maybe she does know, but just didn't want to tell me the truth? She said Sara was scared. Maybe Stamos is scared, too.*

Something dawned on him. *Maybe she thinks I'm spying on her for Cowl for some reason. And if Cowl had something to do with Sara's death, that would be a reason for Stamos to be afraid, and also not reveal the truth to me.*

But if she was scared of Cowl, why sleep with him?

*To keep on his good side? To avoid ending up like Sara?*

With these troubling thoughts in mind, he rose and left, taking his official program with him, hoping that there might be a clue in there as to why Ewes was so interested in the play. He stood in the lobby and read through it twice. But it was simply a program for a play. This wasn't some obtuse code-breaking movie where the villain intent on global domination conveniently left a trail of inscrutable clues behind so the forces of good could figure them out and vanquish him.

He left the air-conditioning and walked out into the heat.

He had one hour before his meeting with Campbell. He got a Coke and a hot dog with ketchup, mustard, and onions from a street cart and ate while sitting on a raised wall along with a million other sunseekers. After he finished, he checked his watch and gauged the time to get there. When that deadline hit, he rose and headed off.

He was no longer waiting for Godot. He was going right to the source, in a manner of speaking.

And Emerson Campbell sure as hell *would* be there.

# CHAPTER 23

DEVINE VENTURED UP INTO THE land of the Fifties now and headed crosstown between Sixth and Seventh. It was a long, narrow, pothole-riddled street full of construction equipment and ripped-up asphalt and exposed trenches, and plywood and steel-plate pathways with warning signs everywhere. The construction work was thankfully silent on the Sabbath, but the people, heat, food carts, trash, and everything else one would expect in the big city were in full and sometimes malodorous splendor.

He made sure no one was tailing him, and then he reached the door of the Italian restaurant with the single green awning, situated precisely at midblock. It was too late for lunch, too early for dinner, and thus the timing was perfect for Devine's visit.

Someone had been watching, because the door swung open before he could touch the knob. He walked through and was hit immediately with chilly air from the AC. The door was closed behind him. The person didn't look at him and he didn't glance in their direction either. There was no need to.

He walked right down the short hall. There was no one else visible. Chianti bottles with wicker bottoms were lined up behind the tiny bar, and some metal pizza platters were stacked on an old wooden credenza along with a mess of laminated menus. The mingled scents of garlic and basil and Parmesan and pasta sauce were readily apparent. The stained carpet was cheap and coming up in places. The walls were dotted with photos of long-dead celebrities, and the usual cheap prints of Napoli, Roma, and the Amalfi Coast. Bottles of olive oil and single droopy flowers in chipped porcelain vases were on every cloth-draped table. It looked like pretty much every standard Italian restaurant he'd ever eaten at in New York City.

He opened the one door at the end of the corridor, just beyond the single bathroom. He closed it behind him and looked at the man seated on the far side of the small table in the room, which seemed instantly claustrophobic from where Devine was standing.

Emerson Campbell looked at Devine and Devine looked back at him.

"Sit down."

Devine sat.

The older man's voice was low, monotone, and still managed to raise every hair on Devine's thick neck.

"Report, Devine. There have been significant developments."

Devine did so. Short, succinct, each sentence packed with meat and no emotion, though he was feeling a great deal. But Emerson did not care about such things, Devine knew. To him, it was all about the mission. He finished, eased forward, and said what he really wanted to say.

"The cops are bearing down on me. I can feel it. They've been fed info. This will be a problem. And a reporter came to see me. Someone's talked to her. They're trying to tie me to what is now a murder investigation. And I had nothing to do with Sara's death."

"If you're innocent you have nothing to worry about."

Devine looked at him closely. "Lots of innocent people go to prison."

"And I would venture to say that far more guilty people do not."

"What's that supposed to mean? I did not kill her. I'm not a killer." He paused and added quietly, his gaze downcast, "At least not that kind. But who knows, maybe there's no difference."

Campbell steepled his hands and looked at Devine like a judge about to impose a death sentence. "Your actions *and* inactions led to a fellow soldier's death. But this only happened when it became clear that Captain Hawkins was going to get away with the murder of a fellow officer after having an affair with the man's wife. You went through your chain of command. You tried to do the right thing for the fallen Blankenship. In my time I stood up to the brass, too, and got my ass handed to me for my troubles. In that way we are kindred spirits, you and I. Which was one reason I recruited you for this mission."

"I always wondered if Blankenship's wife knew about what Hawkins did."

"Stop wondering. She did, though we can't prove it. And Blankenship had a million-dollar life insurance policy. Combat death was not covered, but suicide was after two years. She got it all and is living fat and happy. Now, you texted me before about *Waiting for Godot*. Theories?"

"I just saw it. Nothing clicked."

"What will you do now?"

"Keep digging. When we first met, it was believed that Sara killed herself. Now the police think she was murdered. That changes everything, including my mission for you."

Campbell said, "When we first met, my assumption was that Ewes hadn't killed herself. I believed she *had* been murdered."

"Why? I didn't think she would kill herself, but I knew her, you didn't."

"Yes, but I know something about Brad Cowl and what's going on there. So if she had found out something illegal was occurring? That is plenty of motive to kill the woman."

"You really didn't get into it at our first meeting, but do you have anything definite you can tell me about Cowl, and why you suspect something criminal is going on there?"

"We believe it started when Cowl was gone from the country over twenty years ago for a considerable period of time, and no one seems to know where he went. He then returned and skyrocketed up the financial ranks right after that. There is also little known about where his seed money came from."

"Most accounts I've heard think it came from his partner, Anne Comely."

"There is even less known about her."

"Look, why would Homeland Security and the Defense Department even be interested in financial crimes? Isn't that for local prosecutors and the DOJ?"

Campbell looked over Devine's shoulder at the closed door. "My job is to worry about enemies both foreign and domestic. And right now we might have both."

Devine tensed. "Wait a minute, are you saying Cowl is some sort of, what, spy? For who?"

"The man had nothing when he left the country over two decades ago, and then when he comes back, he's top of the mountain in less than two years? Doesn't that strike you as suspicious?"

"You sound like a conspiracy theorist now."

"Conspiracies do happen, Devine. More than you probably think. And it's not just the dollars that Cowl is making. I really couldn't care less about that. But if there's something behind the dollars that attacks the national security of this country? Then I care a great deal."

"So can you help with the cops and the reporter?"

"The cops, yes. The reporter, I doubt it. But a reporter can't arrest you, either."

"Maybe she can do worse."

Campbell looked at him thoughtfully and for such a long period that Devine finally said, "What?"

"Why Wall Street and Cowl and Comely? Strange career path for an Army Ranger."

"Why not?"

"That's not an answer."

"Yeah, Detective Hancock didn't buy it either."

"Well then?"

"I can make some money. My old man can be proud of me."

"And that's it?"

"Isn't it enough?"

"Would you like to hear what I think?"

"Does it matter if I do or not?"

"I think you picked an occupation that you loathe. And you did it because you knew your father, a man whom you also loathe, would approve."

"And why would I do that?"

"It's your self-imposed penance, Devine. You let a fellow soldier die. You were never punished for that, and it bothers the hell out of you, because you, unlike Captain Hawkins, actually have principles and a conscience. So you left an organization that had allowed you to reach your full potential. You left an organization that you never wanted to leave. And now you're actually in a prison...of your own making."

"You're wrong! My father *was* proud of me for the decision I made, and I was *happy* about his reaction. In fact, we went to dinner in celebration and got drunk together."

"You joined the Army in *spite* of your father's wishes, Devine. In fact, you put on the uniform to spite *him*."

"You can't possibly know that."

Campbell picked up a file that lay in front of him. "This is your psych eval when you were trying to get into Ranger School. You were quite candid with those folks, as you had to be. You spoke about how your father had been riding you your entire life. Never good enough, never enough like your brother and sister. A disappointment of epic proportions in his mind. You had the well-deserved rep of being stoic about everything, Devine, but not that time, no, not that time."

Devine started to say something but then didn't.

"And do you want me to read the letter the Army got from your father? The Army keeps every scrap of paper, as you know, and this one was quite unusual. Most parents are proud of their children for entering the service, but not your father. He was also quite candid, when he"—Campbell picked up another piece of paper and glanced down it—"called it 'a spit in his face,' your going to West Point to serve your country. That you were only doing it to defy him. While his other two children were shining examples of the American dream, you were the poster boy of his personal nightmare." He laid the paper aside. "His words, not mine. So don't tell me you and your old man were celebrating and getting drunk together, okay? That's bullshit and we both know it."

Devine looked away.

"You left the Army, an institution you served proudly and with great loyalty. That was your first act of penance. A career on Wall Street was your second."

"And is my work for you my third act of penance?"

"That's up to you. But the question becomes for you: Where does it end?"

"According to you I have the rest of my life to give in service to make up for what I did."

"So you concede my theory on the matter is correct?"

"I concede nothing. And what does it matter now?"

"It only matters, Devine, to *you*. But I would say this: Life is a long enough journey without having only *negative* motivations to get your ass out of bed every day. What I'm offering you is, once again, something positive to do with your life in serving your country. And it's not just moneymaking that's going on at Cowl, Devine. I'm not sure exactly what is going on there, but it's more than the dollars. Now, I think it's time we both got back to work." Campbell inclined his head toward the door.

Devine didn't leave the way he came. The door to the rear was standing open. He breathed in the garlic and Parmesan, and the next moment emerged into the heat.

In his recurring dream there was Lieutenant Blankenship on a morgue slab with his throat destroyed. The other person he always saw was Captain Hawkins lying in the Afghanistan mountains unconscious after the battle between the two. It hadn't been much of a fight, actually. Hawkins had allowed himself to grow too soft. And maybe his guilt was a bit too much for him to put up a spirited defense against Devine's ferocious attack. The thing was, Devine thought the man would wake up and limp back to camp. If he had tried to file charges against Devine, he was going to raise the whole murder scenario to anyone he could. Only the man didn't wake up.

*I hit him harder than I thought.*

He walked to the corner, turned, and headed downtown.

The cops were going to be coming after him, too. And he needed to do something about that despite Campbell's assurances of assistance.

So Devine had somewhere to go and someone to see.

One misstep now and it was all over.

# CHAPTER

# 24

He had surveyed the quiet street in Park Slope for an hour and not seen a sign of any squad cars or cops. Ewes's house was evidentiary, he knew, but it was also not the crime scene. They might have gotten everything already. If so, he might be screwed.

He tensed when he saw a cab pull up and the same couple from the previous night got out. They were dressed formally for an early Sunday evening in the summer. Him in a navy blazer, her in a skirt and heels. He wondered if they had dressed up to go and formally identify their daughter's remains. Or maybe they had gone to a church to pray. Perhaps they had done both.

They walked up the short flight of steps. He unlocked the door, and they passed through. Devine gave it more time. He wanted to let them have a chance to settle, if they *had* just come back from the police morgue. And he wanted to make sure no cops showed up to meet with them on either a prearranged basis or a spontaneous one.

Twenty minutes later he eased out of his surveillance spot and walked across the street. He smoothed down his shirt and knocked on the door. It was answered a few moments later by the man.

He was around five eight, with glasses fronting periwinkle-blue eyes that were rimmed with red from crying. Devine could see hints of Sara in him. He had discarded the blazer and the cream shirt under it. He was in a white T-shirt and holding a cup of something.

"Yes?" he said, his tone and look surprised. He probably knew no one in the area and was not expecting visitors other than the police.

"Mr. Ewes?"

"Yes? Who are you?" He stared up at Devine with a bit of anxiety.

Devine knew he could look intimidating as hell to certain people, particularly with his damaged face, and he moved to quickly defuse any rising apprehension.

"My name is Travis Devine. I worked at Cowl and Comely with your daughter." From his pocket he pulled out the lanyard with the photo security card attached and showed Ewes. "I'm so very sorry about what happened."

"Did you…did you know Sara w-well?" His voice cracked before the end.

"She was the liaison with my group of interns. Everyone thought she was terrific."

"Fred? Who is it?"

The woman appeared there. She was as thin as her husband, but paler. Her hair was blond with white roots. Her face was puckered, her bloodshot eyes wandering aimlessly at first but then holding on Devine.

She had on the same skirt but had shed the pumps. She was around five four in stocking feet. Sara had been nearly five nine. Since Fred wasn't tall, there must be height somewhere else in the family tree, thought Devine.

"This young man knew Sara," said Fred. "He worked with her at that *place*."

"Well, please come in, Mr.…?"

"Travis, Travis Devine. Thank you."

"I'm Ellen, this is Fred."

He stepped inside and Fred shut the door.

Ellen motioned him to a chair and the couple sat on the couch across from him.

The place was decorated with a blend of Wayfair buys mingled with original creations from the unique shops that littered the area.

It was colorful and bright and optimistic, right down to the throw pillows and the rugs over the wooden plank floors. The brick fireplace held pinecones, which was a nice touch, he thought, in the heat of summer.

Devine had seen it all before, but when he had, Sara Ewes was alive.

"Excuse me," said Ellen. "Would you like anything to drink? Fred just made some coffee. Or iced tea?"

"No, I'm fine, thank you."

"So, you worked with Sara?"

"Not directly. Different division. And she was about six years ahead of me." He caught their looks and said, "I went to West Point and then served in the Army for a number of years before leaving. Then I got my MBA."

"Well, thank you for your service, Travis," said Fred.

"I know this must be quite a shock to you both. The whole firm is reeling."

"Was...was there any inkling of a problem?" asked Ellen, her voice small, but her hopeful look looming large.

*Do they not know it was a homicide?*

"None. She was doing great. I still can't believe that she...took her own life." He paused, waiting for them to respond to what he now knew was incorrect information.

Fred spoke in a trembling voice. "I know that's what the police initially thought, Travis, but their thinking has changed."

He looked between them. "What? I don't understand."

Ellen glanced down at her lap. She looked like she wanted to leap up and run from the room.

Fred said, "The police now believe that Sara was...that someone...killed her." He put a hand to his mouth even as Ellen let out a sob.

"Oh my God, I'm so...sorry. This...is stunning." And even though he knew all of this, now it *was* stunning to him. Like it was the first he was hearing of it, because he was seeing it through their eyes, their grief.

Seconds passed with nothing but elevated breathing among the three.

"So, you two were friends?" said Ellen.

"She had a lot of friends. She was very outgoing."

"She mentioned that she was seeing someone," said Ellen. "This was a while back. But she never gave a name."

"I don't know about that," he said quickly.

"Do you live nearby?" asked Fred.

"No, I live way out in the northern suburbs. Mount Kisco. I take the train in. This is a beautiful place. She did a nice job decorating it."

"Had you never been here before?" said Ellen, watching him closely.

He met her gaze. "No. Whenever we met it was in a group, mixers, company functions. Things like that."

He glanced to the left where he knew Ewes's bedroom was located.

Then he looked up to see Ellen's eyes still on him. "But you knew where she lived, Travis."

"I walked her home once from a bar near here. We'd been drinking. I just wanted to make sure she got home all right. But this is my first time being inside."

"Oh, I see. I hope you didn't come all this way to see us. But I suppose you didn't even know we were here."

"I didn't. I came into town to see a play. Then I thought I'd come over here just to look at the place. I was thinking about Sara, you see. Then I saw you two get out of a cab and come in here. I didn't want to bother you, so I went away for a while. But the more I thought about it, I just wanted to let you know how sorry I was. I didn't know how long you were staying and didn't know if I would have another chance. I was told you were coming in from another country."

"New Zealand," answered Fred. "I was transferred there. A very long trip."

"A horrible trip," Ellen added. "Nothing but hours and hours of having to think about—"

"I'm sure," said Devine in a small voice. "What sort of business are you involved in?"

"We're missionaries," said Ellen, "spreading the word of Christ. Fred is actually an ordained minister."

"That's great. So, New Zealand?"

She said, "It may seem like an odd choice, but nearly half the people there follow no religion at all. Particularly the young people, which means their children will grow up without God in their lives. And while most Australians who practice a religion follow Christianity, the fastest-growing faiths down there are Hinduism and Sikhism." She frowned at this.

Devine looked at Fred, who was staring at his wife. "Now, those are fine religions, Ellen. Lots of people believe that way. I'm just glad they're practicing a faith. They have their god and we have ours."

"My husband and I disagree on some things," said Ellen graciously. "But we find common ground where we can."

"I hear that most successful marriages do," opined Devine, glancing at Fred before looking back at Ellen.

"We just came back from..." She eyed her husband.

He finished for her. "The...morgue."

"I can't imagine how hard that must have been."

"I suppose you just assumed we were her parents?" said Fred, obviously trying to move on from certain images probably gripping all of them.

"Partly, but I see some of Sara in each of you. Though she was taller."

"My father and brother," said Ellen with a sad smile. "They're both six four. Sara took after them in the height department."

He hunched forward, deciding to just go for it. "Have the police been by? Are they keeping you informed of everything?"

"They were here when we arrived last night," said Fred. "They were already searching her things. I guess they'd do that with anyone, regardless of how she... But now, but now that they know she didn't... That somebody..."

"Right. Sure. I guess they have to do all that. Get her electronic devices, diaries, whatever might help them find out who did this."

Fred nodded in agreement. "Yes, they took all of those things. At least the ones that were here. And they looked everywhere, very thorough, dusted for fingerprints, that sort of thing. They were pretty much done when we arrived, so they said we could stay here while we're in town." He looked around. "She didn't have this place when we moved to New Zealand. She had that little apartment... where again, Ellen?"

"Tribeca."

"Right, Tribeca. Now she's out here in Brooklyn. I thought that used to be a bad area."

Devine said, "It's a lot better than it was decades ago. And consequently the real estate has gotten really pricey."

"Anyway, this is the first time we've seen Sara's house. We haven't been back until now, you see." He paused, gumming his lips. "And now we are."

Ellen just stared at the pinecones in the fireplace. She looked like she was puzzled as to why her daughter had not yet appeared and offered her coffee or tea or a hug.

"What play did you go see?" asked Ellen suddenly, her gaze back on him—unnervingly so, Devine thought.

"*Waiting for Godot*. Sara actually recommended it to a mutual friend of ours."

"I've never heard of it," said Ellen.

Fred said, "Any good?" He seemed to latch on to this line of conversation to escape, for at least a few seconds, what was crushing him.

"It definitely makes you think," said Devine, who was also thinking that Ellen Ewes would hate it. "So I guess she never mentioned it to you?"

Fred shook his head. "We hadn't heard from her in a while. When was it last, Ellen?"

"The problem is the time difference. Her night, our day thing. But it had been over a week. She's our only child. *Was* our only child."

She stopped talking and commenced quietly weeping.

Devine started to think all this had been a very bad idea. He rose and said, "I don't want to intrude anymore. Again, I'm so sorry. And if there's anything I can do while you're in town." He pulled out one of his cards with his direct business and cell phone numbers on it and handed it to Fred, who took it without looking at it.

Devine glanced at Ellen, who was once more staring at him with an intensity he couldn't quite understand. "Sara *did* keep a diary, as you mentioned. But it's not on the list the police gave us. They couldn't find one. Yet she'd been keeping them since she was young."

"That's odd," said Devine. And it did seem odd. "Maybe she started keeping everything in her personal cloud. Lots of people do now."

"I think Sara was a very good friend of yours."

Devine felt his gut tighten under her stare. "I liked her. Everyone did."

Ellen took the business card from her husband and gazed down at it for a tense moment. "You're wrong there, Mr. Devine," she said.

"What's that, honey?" said Fred sharply.

Ellen turned the card over and over in her hands, like it was hot to the touch. "Someone clearly didn't like Sara at all," she said.

# CHAPTER 25

WHEN DEVINE GOT BACK TO the house, Valentine was waiting for him in the living room, excitement and concern competing for equal time on his features.

"What's up, Will?"

"Dude, the email?"

"What about it? Did you find out who sent it?"

"No. It's untraceable."

"Well, thanks for trying. It's the weirdest thing I've ever seen. I mean, it doesn't even look like an email address."

"No, Travis, is not that easy. I mean, *I* could not trace it. People I work with, *they* cannot trace it, either. At first, I think it is some kind of weird spoofing email or maybe hexadecimal."

"What?" exclaimed Devine.

"Hexadecimal. A base system to simplify binary language computers use. But I dig deeper and it is not that either."

"Okay, but people send anonymous emails all the time," said Devine. "Don't they?"

"There are many ways to sending such messages on internet," said Valentine. "Cheap, not so cheap, hard, not so hard."

Devine leaned against the wall. "You're going to need to explain that."

"New phone number, preferably burner or prepaid with cash or cloned credit card, fake name and info, new email account,

Hotmail, Gmail. Different browser, use incognito mode, and off goes mail. Russia has Yandex webmail, no phone verification needed. Hotmail and Gmail require phone number, but that is bypassed with burner phone. Incognito mode still has location IP address sent with email. But this email has none of that."

"So then it's untraceable, you mean?"

"Not if person you send it to has resources. And by being cheap you create big problem."

"What are the more expensive and better ways?"

"Use special service to do just what you want, send anonymous email. Built-in premier encryption, spoofed IP address, auto deletion from whatever server is used, password protect, no personal info required. Good shit like that."

"Who does that?" asked Devine.

"Many platforms do proxy email. Some legit and reputable, others not so much. They all do that and do it good. Or you can jump over them and use VPN platform. But don't do free service, they sell data to third party. Use premium service and your IP address goes poof."

"Well, whoever sent that email must have used one of those services or the VPN method."

When Devine eyed the Russian, the man seemed more serious than Devine had ever seen him. Gone was the pizza-and-beer caricature of a Russian hacker.

"Even with that, you can't hide the computer's MAC address. Every device has MAC address attached to network card. Is like fingerprint."

"But this one doesn't?"

"I think maybe they spoof address, make it invisible."

"I thought you said it wasn't a spoofing email?"

"Does not matter. We can break those systems, no matter which method used," he said quite confidently. "No matter if MAC address spoofed. That is what we do! But this email was not sent on one of those platforms. It could not be. It has none of protocols required to send message over broadband, including an IP, or Internet Protocol, address."

"So I guess it has to have all that stuff?"

"Of course, Travis, get with fuckin' program." Valentine sighed and sat back on the couch. "When you send email, sender and recipient IP addresses are in packet. Then it is directed to gateway or router. Then on to higher-level network. It does this over and over, until it gets to destination email address."

"So then how did the email manage to show up in *my* inbox?" asked Devine, before answering his own question: "Someone had to have my email address."

"Yes, this is true. But that is easy to get. The big thing, Travis, is we do not know who send it or *how* they manage to send it. I mean, we can't even trace message to *any* portal on internet."

"This is getting a little beyond my depth," conceded Devine.

"There are basically *five* IP classes. Classes A, B, and C are used for public and private use. Class D for things like video streaming, TV networks, and such."

"That's only *four* classes. What's the fifth?" asked Devine.

"Class E, not reserved for public. Mainly used for research. Is *experimental* IP class. If I had to guess, I say your email sent somehow using Class E, but I can't figure out how."

"It came in at nine twenty-two a.m. It said that a custodian found Sara's body at around eight thirty that morning and the police were called. So less than an hour later someone knew she was dead and had details about how she died and where the crime scene was and what she looked like hanging there. And then they sent out a message only to me, as far as I know, that you guys can't trace. That's pretty damn fast."

"You have to find out about this, dude. People I work for are freaking out over this. I mean seriously freaking out."

"How can I find out about it if you guys can't? I'm not a world-class hacker."

"I mean talk to people. Talk to this dude that found body."

"Is not being able to trace an email really that catastrophic?"

"For me, it is end of world. It means what I do...goes poof. And it means that bad people on internet, they get away with anything, because they are *invisible*. Get with program."

When he said it like that, Devine began to understand the importance of the situation.

"And you knew this girl, Travis. You told me you dated her. Don't you want to find who killed her?"

"Of course I do. But if I'm going to be snooping around there, I need your help." Devine was thinking about the security database at Cowl and Comely. He told Valentine what he wanted done.

"Give me your log-in and password," the Russian said.

Devine hesitated. "I'm not sure I should do that, Will."

Valentine smiled. "I can find out in about one minute, dude. But if you don't want my help?"

"You screw me, I'll kick your ass," said Devine.

"Dude," Valentine said with a smile.

Devine emailed it to him and the Russian's fingers began flying over the keyboard.

"How long do you think it will take?" asked Devine.

"Is done."

"What!"

"Your employer has bullshit encryption. I email you what you need to get into database." Valentine did so and said, "And you Americans wonder why you get hacked all the time. Is bullshit."

As Devine walked off he knew one thing. There was really only one way the sender of the "invisible" email could have known those details at that point in time.

*I think whoever sent me the email also killed Sara.*

# CHAPTER 26

6:20.

The train slid free from the station and Devine dutifully looked out the window. Sunday had hardly been a day of rest. He felt like he'd already worked a full week at Cowl, not simply starting another one.

The nosy journalist, Rachel Potter, *Waiting for Godot*, the meeting with Emerson Campbell, Ewes's parents, particularly the suspicious mother, whatever the police had found there, the missing diary that might have him in it, and, finally, Valentine and the apparently earth-shattering invisible email revelation. It exhausted him just thinking about all of it.

The train stopped and picked up passengers, then chugged up to the knoll and stopped. It was so regular it was almost funny. Almost.

And there she was through the gap between the bottoms of the tree canopies and the top of the wall. She was already sitting by the pool. Her terry cloth robe was off, and her string bikini was once again shiny emerald. The color looked good on her.

"She's an exhibitionist, you know. Least that's what I figure. Why else would she be out here this early in pretty much her birthday suit for all of us to see? She can't miss spotting a stopped train, can she?"

Devine turned to the man sitting next to him. He was around fifty and dressed in a stylishly cut dark blue suit, slim tie, and white shirt with matching pocket square. His hair was a wavy brown heavily laced with gray, his brow was lined, and saggy pouches undergirded his eyes. Devine thought he might be staring into a futuristic mirror and seeing himself in less than two decades. The man looked woeful and lustful in a hollowed-out, pathetic way, Devine thought. He eyed the man's wedding band.

"What do you know about her?" asked Devine.

"Nothing other than she's got one of the hottest bodies I've ever seen. And she's probably a nymphomaniac. Women who are exhibitionists are usually nymphos, too."

"Is that so?" asked Devine.

The man sniffed, eyed the woman, and in a wishful tone said, "Well, on the streaming shows they almost always are. And the woman before her was just as hot."

Devine started. "The woman *before* her?"

"Yeah. I've been riding this train for a long time. I remember them building that house. That's Brad Cowl's place, in case you didn't know. Anyway, that chick would come out in a bikini, too, from time to time. She was a stunner, just like that one. Cowl obviously likes them young, beautiful, and nearly naked."

"What happened to the other woman?"

"I don't know. One day she was just gone."

"When was this?"

"Oh, a little over a year ago, I think. It was during the summer."

"What did she look like?"

"Pretty much the same as this one, only brunette."

Devine turned to look back at the woman. She just sat there, her legs crossed one over the other. She didn't appear to even realize a body of water was there. She lifted her gaze and it appeared for an unsettling moment that she was staring right at him. But that wasn't possible. Not with the distance and the angle and the glass in between.

*Right?*

She rose, picked up her robe, and walked into the house. He and every guy on the starboard side, and probably a bunch on the port side, watched her every step of the way, their focus so intense it was like the last minute of their lives.

*Maybe she does get off on that stuff*, thought Devine. She knew the train was there, with people on it, watching her. He wondered how Brad Cowl felt about it. But then again, he was having sex with his employees on desktops.

The train picked up speed and headed on.

Later, he walked out of the subway station in the Financial District and into the heat of the morning. It was early enough for the city to still be waking up. Delivery trucks were parked illegally, and cabs, cars, and Ubers were hammering their horns, besmirching the only quiet time of the day the city had. Birds pecked at pavement trash, street sweepers were sweeping, yawning suits and nonsuits were shuffling to their jobs looking like they were heading to their graves.

Food carts serving breakfast items were opening for business. Later, for lunch, there would be offerings of grilled halal, cheong fun, rice noodles, and Indian king biryani, and traditional fare like pretzels, hot dogs, falafel, Tex-Mex, steak, BBQ, and sushi. If you couldn't find a food here it was because it didn't exist.

Construction crews were muscling pipe and wheelbarrows and gripping shovels and lunch pails and smoking their Camels and drinking their non-Starbucks morning eye-openers.

The sky was clear, the heat already percolating over the fingertips of the skyscrapers. At lunchtime the funneled warmth between buildings, coupled with billions of tons and thousands of acres of reflective concrete and glass, respectively, would spike the temperature on the ground to near volcanic proportions, or so it would seem to the clothed inhabitants just trying to earn a buck or enjoy their holiday.

And while he thought about all of this, Devine also mulled over his very serious problems: He had paid a visit to, and raised the suspicions of, a grieving mother. He, and apparently only he, had received an untraceable email about a murder.

And the email had not stated that Sara had died by suicide. Devine realized he had just assumed that was what the email had implied. Yet it had only said that she was dead. And then it had gone on to describe the hanging body. It was Wanda Simms who had mentioned suicide. She said she'd overheard the police. And Detective Hancock had confirmed that initial opinion during their first meeting.

He had to talk to people to find the sender of the weird-ass email, because it apparently could not be done with computer keys and a server. For Devine, it was actually refreshing to see that not every single problem today was solvable by technology alone. Sometimes a little shoe leather and the semblance of a personality and a few well-formed questions might just do what artificially intelligent thinking and petabytes of data hovering in fake clouds couldn't. But the email was tied to Ewes's murder, which had to be tied to whatever nefarious things were going on at Cowl. And this was exactly what Emerson Campbell had told him to work on in order to stay out of a military prison. His marching orders couldn't be clearer.

He knew the guard currently on duty at Cowl. His name was Sam. He was around sixty, grizzled hair, pale skin, sloped shoulders, big gut that stretched his shirt's fabric to near its breaking point, and a pleasing smile to top it all. He seemed like a favorite uncle or grandfather who would get down on the floor and play with the little ones, a beer in hand.

Devine walked up to the granite-topped reception console and placed his leather briefcase on it, rubbing a few sweat bubbles off his forehead.

"Hey, Sam."

"Hey right back, Devine."

"Pretty crazy shit happening around here."

"Got that right. Police have been in and out. New developments."

"Right, I heard. Murder instead of suicide. Pretty damn big difference."

"Hell yes it is. You knew the woman?" asked Sam.

"A little. You ever see her?"

"Oh yeah. Always a smile and a wave. Nice young lady, damn shame."

"Understand one of the custodial staff found her."

Sam shook his head and grimaced, as though something foul had entered his mouth. "Jerry Myers. Thought the poor guy was going to stroke out. He come running in here screaming about this gal hanging in the storage closet. I thought he'd lost his marbles. I mean, in *this* building, what the hell, right?"

Devine stiffened. "Wait, he came all the way down here to tell you? He didn't call you or the cops from up there?"

"No, he didn't, the knucklehead, but he was upset. Poor guy had never seen anything like that. He went into the storage room to get something and bam, there she is. Would've shocked anybody. So I cut him some slack on not phoning from up there. I called the cops and then me and Jerry both went up there. I was really hoping the guy was drunk or having hallucinations or something. But nope, there she was. Poor lady. I used to be with the Newark Police Department, but I have to tell you, I felt my breakfast coming back up on me, too."

"I bet. By that time of the morning there must have been a full house up on the fifty-second."

"That's why I hustled up there as soon as I made the 911 call, and had another guy cover the front, to let the cops up when they arrived. I mean, it was a potential crime scene and there are protocols and all. See, at that point I didn't know *how* she died, nobody did. But you got to preserve the evidence."

"Lucky you got up there so fast before anyone knew what had happened."

Sam eyed him closely. "Well, fact is, I can't vouch for that."

"What?"

"Jerry left the door partially open. Least that's how we found it."

"Did he say that's how he left it?" asked Devine.

"Hell, he was so shaken up he could barely remember his own name. The cops got there about five minutes later. I didn't want that responsibility any longer than I had to."

"And what'd you do after that?" asked Devine.

"Hung around up there in case they needed anything."

"Talk to anybody?"

"Just Jerry and one of the cops."

"None of the office staff or people like me?"

"By the time the staff started trickling in, the cops wouldn't let them get off the elevator. I didn't see anybody else."

"Never mind the admin folks, there must have been the crew like me up there by then. It was going on nine."

"What can I tell you. I didn't see any."

*What the hell.* He thought about Wanda Simms up there getting people out of their offices. That did not mesh with what he had just been told.

"So I guess Jerry probably quit after finding the body? Or took some time off at least?"

Sam waved this off and sipped on coffee in a mug emblazoned with the New York Giants football logo. "Nah. He's a single guy with no kids whose job pays real good with benefits and all. You can't just throw that away. He's here now, in fact. Up on the thirty-fourth changing light bulbs. Least that's what he told me a few minutes ago."

"Okay. Hey, hang in there."

Sam smiled. "I got it easy, Devine. You're the one busting your hump. And for what, I ask you? All you need is some food, a roof over your head, a few brewskies a day, baseball in the summer and football in the fall, a missus to watch over you, and you can be a happy man."

Thinking that Sam was more right about that than wrong, Devine got on the elevator and headed to the thirty-fourth floor.

# CHAPTER

# 27

THE ADMIN CUBICLES UP HERE were not occupied. These folks simply earned a salary, no more and no less, regardless of how hard they worked. So unless there was some sort of apocalypse, they came in at nine and left at five or close to it.

Jerry Myers was up a ladder down one of the halls. The suits hadn't arrived en masse yet here either, Devine knew. He would have heard fingers clacking on computer keyboards behind the closed doors. Most of his kind got in around eight but didn't leave until around nine at night. And there were no watercooler breaks at Cowl and Comely. It was pedal to the metal until lights out.

"Mr. Myers?"

The man turned on the ladder and looked down at him. He was about Devine's height, barrel-chested and strongly built, around forty-five with a thick head of dark hair.

"Yeah?"

"I'm Travis Devine. I work here. I was a friend of Sara Ewes."

Myers finished with the lights, clipped the cover shut, and climbed down. "That was the worst damn day of my life," he muttered.

"I bet. It must have been traumatic as hell."

Myers folded up the ladder and picked up a box of light tubes. He looked at Devine and said, "You want something?"

"Sam told me about you finding her and then mentioned you were up here replacing some lights."

"Okay, so?"

Devine thought quickly, realizing he was close to blowing this whole thing. "Like I said, I was a friend of hers. I still can't believe she's dead. First they said suicide, and now it's murder. I mean, what the hell, right?"

Myers looked sympathetically at him now. "Yeah, it was a gut punch for everybody. It sure as hell looked like a suicide to me, but what do I know? I never found a dead body before."

Devine picked up on this. "You found her around eight thirty or so?"

"Something like that, yeah. Told the cops that."

He started to walk down the hall and Devine kept pace with him as he thought of his next question.

"Sam said you came to the lobby to tell him and that he called the police."

"That's right. I was shaking like a baby. Could barely hit the elevator button or swipe my card through."

"What'd you go in the room for?" asked Devine.

"Look, I already told the cops all this."

"I know," said Devine quickly. "It's…it's just that we were friends and this has really shaken me to my core. I just want to know some of what you know. It might help me process all this."

Myers studied him curiously for a moment and then nodded. "Okay, I can understand that. The fact is, I went in there to get a damn printer cartridge, if you can believe that. Got a message that one of the big printers in the business center on that floor was low and needed to be replaced. Opened the door and there she was. My ticker must be strong, otherwise I'd be dead."

"I bet. So is that room normally kept locked?"

"I don't know about *normally*. I know I had to use my key to unlock it that morning."

The ladder banged against Myers's leg.

"Here, I'll take that," said Devine. He relieved the man of the piece of equipment.

"Thanks."

"Was it a Detective Hancock who told you that Sara had been murdered? Black guy in his forties?"

"No. I heard it on the news, I guess along with everybody else."

He stopped at a point in the hall and he and Devine set up his ladder. Devine held the ladder steady for him, took the old light from him when he handed it down, and passed him a new light. Myers put it in, clambered back down, and they moved on.

"Was there anyone around when you found her? I mean, in the other offices near the storage room?"

"None of the secretaries were in, least that I saw. Little bit too early for them. I can't say one way or another for anybody in their offices. Can't remember hearing or seeing anybody. Told the cops that, too." He shook his head. "Stupid me, I coulda called down to the security desk from my phone, or any of the other phones up there. But I was so..." He shook his head again and glanced up at Devine. "You ever find a dead body?"

"No," Devine lied.

"Well, I hope you never do."

"So you came back up here with Sam, and then what?"

"He took a look-see in the room, probably just to make sure I was telling the truth."

"And did you notice anyone around then?"

Myers stopped and looked suspiciously at him. "Come on, I know you said you were friends, but why all these questions, buddy? You sound like a cop."

Devine was now ready for this. "I was in the military. Army Ranger. I have experience with the Army CID."

"Oh, okay. Hey, thank you for your service."

"You look like you might have worn the uniform."

"Wanted to, but my eyesight and hearing weren't good enough. Failed the physical. Wear a hearing aid and contacts, but they got minimums even with that."

"Yeah, I know. So anyone else around?"

"Not that I could see. Quiet as a..."

"...tomb?" said Devine.

Myers visibly shuddered. "Yeah. About the time the cops got here some of the secretaries were arriving."

"How about the suits, meaning nonadmin people?"

"Nope, don't remember seeing any of them."

"But isn't that strange? They all get in before the staff."

"Don't know what to tell you." He glanced at Devine. "Is that what you do here?"

"Yeah. But I work on another floor. Then the cops secured the room and started clearing the space?"

"Yeah, but only *after* the detectives showed up, you know, *those* guys in suits. Until then, they wouldn't let anyone *off* the floor, including me. Later, they took folks down to a conference room on another floor. I guess to take statements and such. That's where the cops took my statement and then cut me loose. I went outside and just walked around. I couldn't get her image out of my head."

"How long do you think it was between the time you left the body and then returned?"

Myers knitted his brows and then said, "I had to explain things to Sam, and I was all tongue-tied, so that took a bit. Then he had to call the cops, then he had to get another guy to cover the lobby. Mighta been like six, eight minutes, something like that. Maybe a little longer. I wasn't looking at my watch. I *do* know after we got back up no one went near that door other than me and Sam."

"Okay, look, I appreciate your time."

Myers studied him for an uncomfortably long moment. "You two must've been *really* good friends."

"We were."

He left Myers and walked back out into one of the main areas for the secretarial staff. Grunts like him were sequestered in large interior, windowless offices separated into cubicles, so their focus would be total. The company executives had the corner offices with views outside. He walked through the staff slots until he spied an empty space. No photos, flowers, other personal touches. But it did have a computer. With the log-in information for the computer helpfully printed on a Post-it note stuck to the screen. Decent security defeated by a tiny slip of yellow paper and a lazy or forgetful employee.

He sat down and used the information Valentine had sent him to get into the security logging database.

He typed in the search. Who had accessed the fifty-second floor on Friday morning? Because it would all be in there, and at least that would tell him who was around. It was likely that whoever had sent him the email had killed Ewes. And the person would have been in the building the previous night between midnight and four. But there was still a chance that someone else had killed Ewes, and the email sender had simply seen Ewes's body between the time Myers had found it and when he and Sam had returned to the fifty-second floor. If so, Devine wanted to find that person. And ask them why Devine had been sent the email.

*Did they know about me and Sara?*

He waited for the names associated with the swipe cards to cascade down the screen. At that time in the morning, the floor should have been filled with stiffs like him.

He was thus stunned when not a single name, other than Jerry Myers, appeared on the screen as having accessed that floor on Friday morning. How was that possible? He did another search and then popped his head up for a moment to make sure the coast was still clear. He checked his watch. He still had time.

Okay, now he was going for the big fish as he put in his search parameters. Who had *not* left the building the night Ewes was killed? Before he hit the Return key to initiate the search he recognized there was a flaw in this methodology. If people had left in a *group* at night, which they often did, it would only take one of their security swipe cards to send all of them down to the lobby. And you didn't need your card to leave the building after hours;

you just hit an exit button set next to the doors. You also didn't need your card to enter the building during normal business hours, but you did need it to access the elevators. So the electronic count of the people coming and going really wouldn't be accurate. But the record of anyone's coming into the building within the time frame the cops were looking at would clearly be relevant, since no *group* would be coming in between midnight and four o'clock.

He also checked the log and saw that Ewes had used her security card and arrived on *Thursday* morning at seven thirty. However, there was no record of her taking the elevator down that evening. That could have been because she left with a group, so he checked to see if Ewes had returned later that night. But there was no record of that, either. She had probably never left because someone had prevented her from doing so by killing her. But why had she been there that late in the first place? Was she working, or maybe meeting someone? *Like Brad Cowl? Like Jennifer Stamos had?*

He modified his search and hit the Return key. And waited.

It didn't take long. Only one name came up. Logged in at midnight and logged out at one ten on Friday morning. Perfect window to kill Sara Ewes.

He looked at the name, both seeing it and trying to unsee it.

*Travis R. Devine.*

# CHAPTER

# 28

DEVINE LEFT THE FLOOR AND headed to another using his security card. Right now he needed to answer a question, and he thought he knew who might be able to help him. When the cops saw that entry log, things were going to go from bad to infinitely worse for him. He was surprised they hadn't already seen it and arrested him.

He got off on the forty-first floor and found Wanda Simms about a minute later. She normally got in early, he knew, and she had her office on this floor. She was striding through the halls making sure that everything in her domain was ready to go for when everyone arrived. He imagined her home would be spotless and well organized right down to the kitchen cutlery drawers and the kitty litter box.

"Hey, Wanda."

She saw him, and her expression changed to a look of terror, all professionalism ripped right from the woman. She rushed forward and gripped his arm.

"Did you hear about Sara?"

"Yeah, I did," he said grimly.

"I can't believe it. There's a killer somewhere around here."

"I'm sure the police are doing all they can."

"I just wish they'd do it faster."

"I had a question about something here at the office."

"What?" she said, all efficiency again.

"I talked to some folks who said there was no one on the fifty-second floor the morning Sara was found. You said you were up there looking for people, but I don't think anyone was there. At least that's what I heard."

She was already nodding. "There was a seminar for the M and A Division that morning. They were all over at the Ritz, well, all except the support staff, of course. The police found me and asked me to make sure the floor was clear. I told them about the seminar, but they still insisted I go office to office with two police officers. But I wasn't surprised when no one was there. It was an all-hands seminar, you see, no exceptions." Her expression grew sad. "Sara didn't deserve to be killed like that."

"No one does," said Devine.

* * *

The cascade of financial data washed across his computer screen, but Devine wasn't really focused on it. He was just treading water in a shark tank. It couldn't be long now, could it?

He still flinched when the knock came. The door opened and a woman's face appeared. She was one of the staff here. He couldn't recall her name at the moment. His mind was already moving past her.

He started to rise even before she spoke. "Mr. Devine? Someone wants to speak to you."

He slipped past the other cubicles. Several heads lifted to glimpse him for a moment before falling back to their screens and the pursuit of vast wealth thereon.

He followed her down the hall toward the elevators. There were two men there, both in suits that looked more like his than most of the other suits here, meaning rumpled and cheap.

One was a little taller than him, about six two, beefy, around fifty with grayish hair parted on the side. His partner was in his forties, balding, five ten and lean, with an expression that gave away nothing. The woman didn't make introductions. She just scurried off while the men showed Devine their badges and identified themselves.

The tall one was Ralph Shoemaker, the shorter one Paul Ekman. They were assigned to the NYPD's Homicide Squad and were investigating Sara Ewes's death, Shoemaker said. His voice was low but sharp. Ekman's was even sharper, with a helping of falsetto on certain words. Whether that was for effect or had something to do with his vocal cords, Devine didn't know or care.

"We'd like to talk to you, Mr. Devine," said Ekman.

"Okay. Seems like lots of people want to talk to me lately."

"We have a room. This way."

He followed them down the hall and into a space not much larger than the storage closet Ewes had been found hanging in. There were three chairs. Ekman told Devine to sit and he did. Both men sat across from him. There was no table separating them. They were nearly knee to knee. Devine knew this was intentional. Take away personal space and you got your target on edge from the get-go. He had done this very same thing interrogating Taliban and Al-Qaeda fighters they had captured. Even with a translator present, you could still put the screws to people. And they were doing it to Devine right now, or at least trying to.

Ekman took out a notebook, while Shoemaker leveled his gaze at Devine.

Shoemaker said, "Ranger, huh? My son's in the Army. Infantry. He's in South Korea."

"Yeah, I did a stint there, too."

"You earned lots of medals. Wounded. Twice. Served your country well. Helluva soldier."

"I did my job."

"You were friends with Sara Ewes?"

"I knew her."

"That's not what I asked." The man's expression didn't change, though the tone of his words had. It was neatly done, thought

Devine. He had sat through these sorts of interrogations before, when he was having his security clearances updated, and was being grilled on whether he'd ever had sex with animals. He could appreciate skill when he saw it.

"We went out to mixers. I saw her at group events. I liked her. I think she liked me. If that's being her friend, then I was her friend. But so were other people."

"You went to her place. Visited with her parents. Out of all the people here, you're the only one who did *that*." Shoemaker sat back and unbuttoned his jacket. Clipped on his belt was a holster with a Glock riding in it and his shiny badge on the other side of the belt clasp. He looked like he was ready to stay here all day, if need be, and just let Devine stare at that gun and that badge, two powerful symbols for sure.

"I was walking past her place and saw them—"

"How'd you know where she lived?" interjected Ekman, the falsetto notes boomeranging around Devine's head.

"As I told her parents, I walked her home one night from a nearby bar to make sure she got there safe."

"Go on," said Shoemaker.

"I saw them, figured they were her parents. She took after them in appearance, and on the spur of the moment I knocked on the door and things went from there. I just wanted them to know I was sorry about what had happened and if they needed anything to call me. I left them my card."

Shoemaker reached in his pocket and pulled a card out. "Mrs. Ewes gave this to us this morning when we saw her. She called and told us about your visit. That's why we're here to talk to you."

"Why did she do that?" asked Devine, who was relieved they weren't here because of the electronic log showing him entering the building in time to kill Ewes.

Ekman leaned forward. "Let's just say that she felt you weren't being entirely forthcoming about your relationship with her daughter."

"In what way?"

"Why don't you tell us?" replied Ekman.

"How? I can't read minds."

"Just read your own, then."

"I knew Sara and liked her, just like other people here did. Have you talked to any of them?"

"Quite a few," replied Shoemaker. "But now we're talking to *you*."

"Okay, and I'm answering your questions."

"Ewes kept a diary, did you know that?"

"Her mother told me she kept one ever since she was young, but that the police apparently didn't find one at her house. Were her phone and laptop at the office or her home?"

Shoemaker said, "We've gone through her emails and other communications and calendar entries on her electronics. And do you know what we found?"

"I have no idea."

"Ms. Ewes had had an abortion."

Devine sat up straighter and leaned forward. "What? Sara was pregnant?"

"Abortions are not performed on women who *aren't* pregnant," pointed out Ekman sarcastically.

"Where did she have it done?"

"It was a calendar entry with the procedure listed. We'll run down who performed it."

"Did she say who the father was?"

Shoemaker crossed one leg over the other and tapped his wingtips with his index finger. "Was it you?" he said, staring off before swinging his gaze around to Devine's. It was clearly done for dramatic effect, and Devine had to admit the cop pulled it off nicely.

"I know nothing about any of this."

"Again, not really my question. Did you have sex with Sara Ewes?"

"I don't have to answer that."

Ekman interjected, "No, but your refusal comes with consequences. And she *did* name you as the father, just so you know."

Devine now swiveled his gaze in the man's direction. "And it's totally legal for cops to lie to suspects to trick them into saying something. So that could be a load of bullshit. Show me where she says that."

Shoemaker said, "Paul, this guy sounds like a lawyer. Who woulda thought that about a fine Army lad."

Devine knew all about this because the CID had interrogated him after Hawkins's death, tried to screw with his head, lied to him, tried to get him to confess, pounded him with everything they had. Only the body had been so torn up by animals that the forensics were of no use in assigning legal blame to Devine, and the injuries he had incurred in his fight with Hawkins were minimal and inconclusive. All soldiers had bumps and bruises and cuts. And any DNA of one man found on the other was also inconclusive, since they served in close proximity to one another. No witnesses, no other evidence, and a time of death that was all over the place allowed Devine to reasonably argue that he had an alibi for the broad time window in question. The CID had finally given up. Devine also assumed that they didn't want to pursue it more thoroughly because doing so might open up for scrutiny the whitewash investigation they had done of Blankenship's supposed suicide.

"You can take my prints and my DNA. I did not kill her."

"How about a polygraph? Will you take one of those?"

Devine sat back. "Which means you found no DNA and no prints at the murder scene. Or maybe you just didn't find any of *mine*. And you're trying to railroad me into a confession so you can clear this one off your list and make your boss happy and Wall Street rest easy. Only if you did pin it on me, the killer would still be out there. But I'll make a deal with you."

"I don't remember *asking* for a deal," said Ekman.

"I'll take a polygraph if you show me where Sara names me as the father and you swear in an affidavit that it's legit and not made up to get me to confess to something I didn't do."

"You watch too many cop shows," said Shoemaker. "But while we *can* make deceptive statements to you in an interrogation, we can't manufacture evidence. *That* would be a crime."

"Do I take that as a no-go on my offer, then?"

"Where were you between the hours of midnight and four a.m. on Friday?"

Devine grimaced impatiently. "Come on, I already told the other guy all that."

"What other guy?" said Shoemaker sharply.

"Hancock."

"Hancock?" parroted Ekman.

"Detective Karl Hancock with NYPD. I guess he's working the case with you two."

The two men exchanged a glance that Devine couldn't really read, but didn't like.

"When did this *Hancock* talk to you?" asked Ekman.

"He was waiting for me at the train station near my place in Mount Kisco, this was on Friday. And he was waiting for me at my house the next day when I got home from work."

"And you told him where you were that night?"

"Yes, and he wrote it down."

"Describe him," said Shoemaker.

"Black guy, around six one, bald, athletic build, in his forties. Dressed like you guys, and he said he was driving a coffee-and-cigarette motor pool piece of crap, at least in so many words. Because NYPD hadn't bought new cars in ten years, at least that's what he said. He also told me he lived in Trenton, New Jersey." He looked between the two men. "Don't you know him? How many homicide detectives are there in the city?"

"Manhattan South Homicide, where we're from, has *ten* of them, down from twenty-six in 2001. And you're looking at two of them."

"He had a badge that looked real. And he talked like a cop. He was the one who told me that Sara hadn't killed herself. That she was murdered."

"He said that?" exclaimed Ekman. "On *Saturday*?"

"Yeah. And he knew all about my background in the Army."

"Exactly what about the *crime* did he know?" asked Ekman.

Devine told them everything, including the straight-line ligature versus the inverted. But he didn't tell them about the similar case in the Army that he had mentioned to Hancock. "He said that proved it was a murder and not a suicide."

Shoemaker gave his partner a nervous glance, one that showed he was no longer fully in control of the situation. His partner seemed to read this like a cue card.

"Okay, let's move on for now. Where were you between those times?" asked Ekman.

"At home in bed until four. Then I was doing my workout at the high school next to where I live. Then I showered, dressed, and took the six twenty train just like always. Must be cameras in the station to show me coming in. Not that many people are there at that hour."

Shoemaker said, "You could have killed her that night, taken the train home, and come back into town on the six twenty."

"But again, the train station may have cameras, and the office building has a security guard."

"You didn't have to take the train," Ekman pointed out. "And the guard makes rounds."

"But you need a security card to get in the building. There's a record of coming and going because of that."

*And it shows me coming and me going at the critical time in question, so why are you jerking my chain on all this other crap?* wondered Devine.

"We're checking all that," said Shoemaker. "It's taking a little time to pull the records."

*And I won't be happy with what you find.*

"You get up at four a.m. to work out?" said Ekman.

"Doesn't everybody?"

"Anybody corroborate this?"

"No. I slept alone and I worked out alone. Nobody else around."

"No roommates?"

"Yeah. Three. But they were asleep at that hour, like most normal people. They can't alibi me."

"How do you know?" asked Ekman.

"Because I asked them if they could when this Hancock guy showed up and seemed to be trying to pin all this on me. But they couldn't. And I wouldn't ask them to lie."

Shoemaker studied him so closely that Devine was sure the man was going to read him his rights and cuff him. "What a nice guy you are," he said, but there didn't seem to be much acid behind it. The big cop just looked truly confused.

"If you saw this Hancock again, would you recognize him?" asked Ekman.

"Hell yes I would. I don't like getting played. And why pick on me in the first place? That's what I don't get."

"Well, maybe there's something special about you, Devine, at least when it comes to Sara Ewes," said Shoemaker.

Devine didn't like any bit of that remark.

The two men rose as though connected by string. "You don't leave the area," warned Shoemaker.

"I have no intention of doing that. I have a job to do."

Shoemaker looked around. "Yeah, making dough at this place."

"That's not the job I'm referring to."

And it wasn't. He was thinking about Emerson Campbell and the mission. He was also thinking about dead Sara Ewes.

Shoemaker and Ekman exchanged curious glances and then left.

Devine sat there for a few minutes digesting everything that had just happened and trying to place it neatly into certain boxes in his mind that would make the most sense. Some of it did, much of it didn't.

*Sara was pregnant and then had an abortion?* This news was staggering to him.

He ran a hand through his hair and closed his eyes for a moment, trying to process all this: *Was I the father? We slept together once. I didn't use protection because she said she was on the pill, but maybe she wasn't. They didn't say when she had the abortion. Did I lose a child and not even know about it?*

He rose and looked out the small window. Staring back at him was another building of equal height. He felt boxed in, trapped, blindsided beyond all reason.

*And they're going to look at the entry log and they're going to see my name as the only one. And then they're going to be back. With an arrest warrant. And who the hell is Karl Hancock?*

But now it made sense why the guy had approached Devine away from the office both times. If he wasn't a real cop, it was much safer that way.

He lifted his lanyard from around his neck and looked at his security badge. He had not been in the building when Ewes had been murdered. So maybe someone had stolen his badge and then returned it before he woke up at his home in the suburbs, which he did not think was likely at all because the timing was just too tight. *Or maybe someone hacked into the system and set me up as the fall guy.* That was also not easy to do. But for the person who had sent an email that could not be traced by the best in the business, it might be a piece of cake.

He shuffled back to work, with what felt like a knife sticking right in his gut.

# CHAPTER

# 29

When Devine returned to his office, he found several of the other Burners staring daggers at him as he walked in. He retook his seat. Something was up. Somebody knew what was going on and had shared it with others. Emails and texts must have been flying since he'd been gone.

Devine had a few people here he'd gone out with on occasion for beers or meals and a couple of concerts, and he counted Wanda Simms as a friend. His direct supervisor had lots of newbies just like Devine to oversee, and the unwritten rule at Cowl and Comely was you never got close to any Burner because chances were very good they would be gone in less than a year. And the competition here was so fierce that close friendships were just not possible, at least that was the perennial vibe around here.

But he knew what his fellow associates were thinking.

*Devine has the cops all over him. Devine killed Sara. I knew he looked creepy. Maybe PTSD. Asshole. Hope they fry him.*

Maybe that was overkill on his part, but he was still feeling it.

He lumbered through his tasks. His job right now was to help analyze a slice of risk on a deal between two corporate titans, on which Cowl and Comely was advising the buyer. On the other side was the mobilized army of venerable Morgan Stanley. Both clients wanted this spin-off of a subsidiary in a management-led buyout to be completed, so the dealmaking was fairly amicable. It was what was known in the business as a "shit sandwich."

The management was buying the company on the cheap because that was part of the plan. It was all front- and back-end-loaded with fees for the M and A boys. The sub would then issue debt that it never intended to repay. They would use the proceeds from the debt offering to pay management a huge dividend. Then they would go back to the bankers, wrap the junk debt with some decently rated stuff into a CBO, or collateralized bond obligation, and then sell it off to pension funds, police unions, and grandmas. Management would next bleed the company dry, sell whatever of the assets it could make money off of, fire a quarter of the workers, raid the pension plan in such a complicated way prosecutors would never be able to prove anything, and eventually leave the remaining workers hanging without paychecks or health care. When the debt went bad, which it was designed to do, they would go back in, peel off the good stuff, and make even more money off that, while the grandmas and the workers went to the poorhouse. They had no recourse because to have recourse you needed to hire lawyers. And even if the grandmas had any money left, folks like Cowl already had the best attorneys in the business. The litigation would take years and by the time appeals were done, the deep pockets would have vanished under a wall of legalese and there was no money left to pay off any judgment.

*Heads I win, tails I win even bigger. And you, Grandma, you lose every single damn time.*

He hated every tap of the keys. He despised every dollar moving across his screen. He loathed the fact that the rich were getting unbelievably richer by pitting everyone in this room against one another. And in twenty years the ones who survived would be at the top looking down at a new crop of suckers and doing the very same damn thing. It was a hamster wheel of plutocratic proportions, aiming straight for something maybe even worse.

The man next to him got up abruptly, holding his stomach and looking a bit green.

Devine knew he was from Connecticut and had gone to Yale.

His father was the CEO of a Fortune 100. The guy really wanted to be a full-time gamer, he had told Devine. But the old man had threatened to cut him off if he did. So here he was, looking ready to puke.

When Devine gazed up at him, he stammered in an embarrassed manner, "S-stomach b-bug. Had it all night." Then the man rushed out of the room.

*Thanks, bud, you've only been sitting next to me all morning.*

He glanced over at the guy's screen, which had not gone blank yet. Streams of numbers flew across it. He didn't know what his fellow Burner was working on, so the data lines didn't make much sense to him. Actually, nothing made much sense to Devine now.

At lunchtime he swam against the current once again and rode the elevator down to the third-floor dining hall. He got his food and was going to sit by himself. Until he saw her.

Jennifer Stamos, looking stricken and lost, was sitting alone at a table with a nice view of the East River. However, from her expression, the woman didn't appear to even be seeing it.

He carried his tray over to her and said, "Want some company?"

She looked up at him in a daze. "Um, okay."

He sat, sipped his iced tea, and looked her over. Her makeup had hidden some of the dark circles under her eyes, but not every fragment of them. Her face was pinched and her normally luxuriant hair seemed thinner, less robust.

"You doing okay?" he asked.

"No, I'm not." She glanced at him. "I heard the cops talked to you earlier."

"They were asking about me and Sara. Did you know she was pregnant?"

Stamos tensed for an instant. "How do you know she was?"

"Because the cops told me she'd had an abortion."

She said aggressively, "Did they want to know if you were the father?"

"They did, actually."

"And were you?"

"No."

"How would you really know whether or not you're the father, if you had sex with her?"

"Who says I had sex with her? And I didn't kill her."

"Some guys kill women who are pregnant by them."

"But she had already terminated the pregnancy. So where's the motive to kill her?"

Stamos looked at him funny. "I... You... I guess you're right about that."

He looked out the window and bit into a celery stick.

"What else did the cops want to talk about?" she asked.

"The usual stuff. Alibis, polygraphs. They lied to me to try to get me to confess."

"How did they even know to talk to you?" asked Stamos.

"I'm sure they're talking to lots of people."

"I wouldn't be too sure about that."

"Did you get a strange email the day they found Sara's body?"

She sat forward, tense once more. "Strange email? No, I didn't. You asked me that before. Did you get one? You mentioned it talked about details of Sara's death. What exactly did it say?"

"I think it was just somebody trolling or something," he said vaguely. "I couldn't really understand it. It was all over the place. And I have no idea who sent it."

Stamos didn't look like she believed him. He decided to change the subject before she pushed him further on it.

"Someone I talked to said there were no suits on the fifty-second floor that morning."

She stared at him, puzzled. "There should have been."

"I know. Sara's office was on that floor. But there was a seminar at the Ritz that morning for the M and A Division. All hands on deck. And the support staff don't show until nine."

"What are you saying?" she asked.

"Just that it's either a coincidence that there was a seminar that morning. Or it wasn't."

She processed this and came away looking even more stricken.

He said, "I was in here having lunch on Saturday. Brad Cowl was here with some of his usual posse."

"I'm surprised you would do that. I'm surprised you're here now."

"Hell, I'm probably not going to make the cut. So why not enjoy a few good free meals until they give me the boot?"

"You sound like a prisoner awaiting execution," she noted.

"And maybe some people would be fine with that."

She didn't comment on this jarring statement. "Why did you mention Cowl?"

"Because he gave me a look that I can't explain. I mean, why would the guy even know who I am?"

"You're a rookie, Travis. And he knows it, even if you think the guy doesn't notice the newbies. Brad Cowl lives and breathes this place. And he was probably pissed to see you in here. You're supposed to be eating crackers at your desk and busting your ass to make him more money. So you got the *look*."

"What's he really like?"

"How should I know?" she said.

"Come on. You're a star, Jennifer. Don't sell yourself short. And Cowl is a smart guy. He takes care of his stars. So you must know him better than most at this place."

Her response was unexpected and chilling. In a lowered voice she said, "You saw us, didn't you?"

"What!"

"That bullshit explanation about calling me 'sweet cheeks.'" She leaned forward and spoke in an even lower voice. "You were in the building that night. You didn't leave your phone behind. You went up to the fifty-second floor. And saw us. And you're here trying to, I don't know, blackmail me? Or make me feel like shit. Or both."

"If I knew what the hell you were talking about, I'd answer you. But I don't."

She gave him a patronizing look and he answered it with one of bewilderment. He didn't know if it carried the day or not. He sort of doubted it. Stamos hadn't gotten to where she was by being thick-headed.

*But maybe I'm thicker than a log, since my security card would not only show I entered the building that night at a certain time, it also would show I went to the fifty-second floor at the same time they were doing their thing on the desk. Cowl must have found that out and told Stamos. And she would have told him about my "sweet cheeks" comment. That explains the evil eye from the guy* and *this confrontation with her.*

She stood. "You know, you might want to try the truth for a change."

Devine felt like saying, *Look who's talking*. But what would have been the point?

She walked out, leaving him staring moodily out the window at the bright sky.

Who knew there could be so much resolute darkness in the middle of the day?

# CHAPTER

# 30

As Devine was leaving that evening a man in a dark suit and a blood-red tie and sporting a self-important demeanor approached him in the lobby of the building.

"Mr. Devine. I'm Willard Paulson, special assistant to Mr. Cowl."

"Okay." Devine recognized the man as being part of Cowl's official harem. He was thin, narrow-shouldered, and in his late thirties, already balding, and as bland and innocuous as Cowl was showy and pretentious.

"Mr. Cowl would like to meet with you."

"Okay, but I'm surprised you're conveying the message. There's a chain of command here that rivals what we had in the Army."

"Normally this would go through your immediate supervisor, but Mr. Cowl preferred to go outside the normal channels."

"And why is that?"

Paulson bristled at this response, obviously not expecting any reply other than *Yes sir, thank you, sir, for this gift from Heaven to meet with Emperor Cowl.* "He didn't say."

"Where and when?"

"At ten this evening. Here's the address." He handed him a slip of paper.

Devine took it but didn't look at it. "Is this really necessary?"

"You must be joking. It's Mr. *Cowl.* Do you like working here?"

"Best job I've ever had," he said with as much sincerity as he could muster, which, granted, wasn't much.

He headed to the subway, unfolding the piece of paper and reading off the address.

*Well, this could be instructive. Or maybe disastrous.*

Devine took the train to Mount Kisco and walked quickly home, sucking in the heat and humidity. His mind was going a million miles an hour and still getting him nowhere fast.

Valentine, with his gamer headphones on, was lying on the couch working on his laptop, as always. A beer was on the floor next to him. He looked up as Devine came in, his expression anxious. He had apparently been awaiting Devine's return.

"So?" said Valentine in a prompting manner as he took off his headphones.

"I talked to the security guard and the guy who found the body. That room was unguarded for maybe a max of ten minutes. But there was no one on the floor because there was a seminar for people like me at an off-site location. And the support staff weren't in yet."

"So how did whoever send message get all that info?"

"I don't know. The killer would have known some of those details when he murdered her. But the person could not have known that Sara had been found hanging in that room by a *custodian* unless they were around at the time, and either saw it for themselves, which is doubtful, or someone told them shortly thereafter. And that just isn't likely. And I don't think anyone else got the message that I got, or if they did, they're not saying anything."

"So during those ten minutes maybe person sending email saw the body and stuff?"

"*And* saw the custodian finding the body. But that's not certain and I'm still working on it. By the way, I used the info you gave me to access the security logging database, and I've got a question."

Valentine closed his laptop and looked up. "Shoot, dude."

Devine explained to Valentine about the security logging system at Cowl using the RFID cards. "Can that be manipulated to show that someone was there who really wasn't there?"

Valentine nodded before Devine was finished. "Sure. Clone card. Then, it like electronic twin walking in place. Easy-peasy. Do it in seconds, depending on what protection they have on card. Let me see yours."

Devine handed over his security card. Valentine pulled a device out of his backpack on the floor and held it up to the card. "This is one twenty-five. Is bullshit. I have app on phone. I can clone card right now by writing what's on your card onto clean one I get from Amazon. Is big bullshit just like encryption on your 'security' database."

"'One twenty-five'?"

"One hundred twenty-five kilohertz. Is radio frequency. Open twenty-six-bit format. Card is just simple LC circuit, capacitor, and integrated circuit working in combo. Card number transmitted is key, is what reader reads. But one twenty-five not encrypted. You get that key, you tell reader 'Let me in' and it does. Ten-buck RFID reader/writer, bam, you got card number. Most 'security' cards are one twenty-fives. My little bay-bee cousin can hack that shit."

"Your little *bay-bee* cousin really gets around. So what else is out there you can use that's better?"

He said promptly, "Thirteen point fifty-six megahertz. SOS technology. Encrypted. Hard to clone, hard to hack, but not impossible, for someone like me."

"In the Army we would use protection shields over our RFID cards to prevent any electronic skimming."

"That is good. That works, mostly. Unless hackers really good. Two-factor authentication is very good. Need two things to get in door."

"I use that on my phone."

Valentine took a swig of beer. "Good for you, Travis. You kickass champ."

"But we don't have two-factor authentication at Cowl, and it looks like all the cards are one twenty-fives. And everyone wears them around their necks with no shields."

"Is bad. Is bullshit."

"Can that be proved? I mean that someone cloned a card?"

"Depend on card and depend on how good cloning is. Pretty technical." He held up his phone. "Use this as security card. Mobile cards too easy to loan out. You don't do that with phone. With newer Apple phone models they have NFC chip. Activate Bluetooth, engage NFC chip, and you can use with door reader to open door if reader is programmed to recognize Apple phone. And if you lose phone, still has security feature before you can get in. Cards don't have that. Readers read card, not person with card. That takes biometrics. That is good too. Better than phone. You need eyes or thumb. In Russia they have to be *living* eyes and thumbs, you know. In Russia they used to take fingers and eyes from people to open doors. But dead fingers and eyes not work anymore. Need pulse. I can tell you that."

"Yeah, I bet." Devine thought back to the night Cowl had accessed the garage entrance. "Cowl used his phone to get into the building's garage. And I've never seen him with one of these cards around his neck."

"That is because he is not messing around. He uses NFC chip. He just lets guys like you have bullshit one twenty-five security."

"But it's *his* building. And we can get in with these *bullshit* cards."

Valentine handed the card back. "Does this let you go everywhere in building?"

Devine thought about this. "No. There's an off-limits space on the fifty-first floor. We call it Area 51 as a joke." He watched Valentine closely, to see if he got the reference.

"What is special about it?" said Valentine in a way that made Devine unsure whether he had gotten the cultural allusion or not.

"I'm not sure. I don't think anyone works on the floor. I think it's just computers."

"Not so weird. It might be supercomputer trading space. They get millisecond head start on trading at volume. They make millions every day on head start over others who not do this."

"I know. It's called high-frequency trading. Buy it a millisecond before the shares or bonds rise a penny, which in the course of a day they all do, and sell it a millisecond later before the shares or bond prices drop a penny. It's like being just ahead of a wave rising and falling. You have to have expensive and specially designed software and infrastructure. The institutions have that, plus, because they're licensed brokers, they're hardwired into the exchanges; it's called naked access. And it's not just brokers, but hedge funds and specialty firms."

"Is smart and is stupid at same time."

"Why is it stupid if they make so much money off it?" asked Devine.

"First reason, you have flash crash, when computer make mistake because of bad line of code or something. Then it sells when it should buy, or vice versa. You lose billions in snap of finger."

"That *has* happened," conceded Devine. "And what's the second reason?"

"All eggs in one basket, dude," replied Valentine. "Ransomware? You hit that one target, what will they pay to get back up and running? Huh? I tell you what they pay. Shitloads. And nobody will know because company will tell no one because they are afraid clients will not trust them and run to other guy. So, a few computer clicks and you are fuckin' billionaire. They pay in bitcoin now. Cryptocurrency."

"How do you know that?" said Devine, staring at him suspiciously.

Valentine caught this look and held up his hands in mock surrender. "I hear on street. I do not do this. I am good guy now. I do not fill up my bank account."

"But with ransomware you have some countries filling up their treasuries," amended Devine.

"Is true. But for ransomware, North Koreans have nothing to eat and then they throw out little leader in glasses. Others do it, too."

"Russia?"

Valentine pointed his finger at him. "Ha-ha. Putin loves his money. He buys big horses and rides them without shirt on. He is crazy-ass stud."

"Can you see if Cowl is doing their high-frequency trading from Area 51?"

"I can see trades if buying and selling is on public markets. I can't see if they buy and sell through darkpool, not till sale complete. Is how high-frequency traders operate for so long without being found out."

"But can you tell if it is high-speed trading going on? Based on the activity in the pipe?"

"Will take time. I have other things to do."

"I thought you liked a challenge. And you couldn't trace the message. I thought I'd give you a shot at redemption."

"What is this redemption bullshit?" he asked, frowning.

"It means a second chance to prove that you are a world-class hacker."

"I *am* world-class hacker. I know this already."

"But *I* don't, not based on the email fail."

"You are funny man. Let me think. I get back to you."

"Just don't take too long. I have a feeling knowing sooner is better than knowing later."

Valentine put his headphones on, flipped open his laptop, and went back to work.

Devine climbed the stairs, rinsed off the day's grime in the shower, and changed into a pair of light brown slacks and a short-sleeved white shirt that he wore untucked. He put his dress shoes back on.

As he was heading back down, he met Helen Speers coming up the stairs. She'd obviously been doing yoga in the dining room again because the woman had on another set of colorful duds and was sweating. And he felt his heart start to race as she approached.

"Going out?" she said.

"Got a meeting."

She gave him an odd look. "How's the police investigation going?"

"It's going. In some pretty odd directions."

"Need that lawyer yet?"

"Probably any minute now."

She looked at him severely, then headed off to her room where she would slide out of her yoga clothes and step into the shower...And he had to stop thinking about that.

Devine knocked on Tapshaw's door. "Hey, it's Travis. Did you eat today, Jill? The dating world of Hummingbird wants to know."

She opened her door and stood there in red athletic shorts, a white tank top, and crew socks with pink Converse tennis shoes. Her hair was done up with an assortment of bobby pins. "I had lunch," she said brightly. "And I *might* have dinner."

"How's the fund-raising going?"

"Hey, you work on Wall Street, right?"

"Yeah. Cowl and Comely. Why?"

"Let me show you something."

She led him into her room and over to one of her giant computer screens. He had been to her office in the strip mall, and it looked like a cyberwarfare command center.

*All in the name of love.*

She brushed some of the sticky notes off the glass and hit a few keys. Her LinkedIn page came up. Tapshaw scrolled down and pointed to a message.

"I got this ping. It's from an investment group looking to *fully* fund my next round. I mean the whole twenty-five million, Travis. They want to Zoom-meet and then start doing due diligence. They said if things go well, they could have a term sheet to me in two weeks and the money days after agreement on the deal points and the lawyers papering it all."

"That's great." He looked at her. "So why the long face?"

"I've been beating the bushes trying to get this round filled for a while. It's been tougher than I thought. You heard me on with the Taiwanese VC group the other night. They were interested, but said the process would take about six months, and our cash flow is tight. I've heard that same song over and over. And *I* reached out to *them*. I've done the same with all the other potential investors for this round. I've run out of friends and family and angel sources. This round is with the pros. But then these guys ping me and say it could all be done in a little over two weeks? I don't know. It just seems weird. What do you think?"

"It *does* seem off. What's the name of the investment group?"

She hit another key and a second screen came up. She pointed to it.

"Mayflower Enterprises. Ever heard of them? I've done some digging on them but there's not much. Some guy named—"

Devine didn't hear her because he was looking at the name of the gent who had pinged her with the proposal.

*Yep, old Christian F. Chilton. That is no coincidence. He clearly knows who I am and that Jill is my roommate.*

He pulled his gaze away. "Look, don't do anything with these guys right now, okay? Just executive-lag it for a bit."

She said doubtfully, "Okay, but twenty-five million is twenty-five million, Travis."

"Just play it cool and that might become fifty mil or even more."

"Wait a minute, I don't want to *sell* the company. I want to build it. It's my *baby*."

"I'm not asking you to sell anything. Just trust me, Jill. And go get some dinner."

He left her there and rode out into the night on his motorcycle for his appointment with Brad Cowl.

# CHAPTER

# 31

DEVINE PULLED TO A STOP across the street from Cowl's palace, locked his bike and his helmet up, and jogged across the street. This was the address on the note Paulson had handed him. The place was lit up like a Christmas tree, and there were exotic cars parked in front, including an old but perfectly restored cherry-red Duesenberg Phaeton. There seemed to be a party going on. Devine had envisioned a private confrontation on Cowl's home turf. The investment magnate had scored the first surprise of the night.

There was a call button at the gate and a video camera. He waved to it and told them who he was. The gates parted and in he walked.

At the front door were beefy guys Devine's size or bigger who gave him a methodical pat-down, made him lift his shirt, and then wanded his torso and arms and legs for good measure.

"The ladies must love that almost as much as you guys do," he said to one of them. That didn't even score him a grin in return.

Inside, the place was as modern-looking and fantastic as the outside. Soaring ceilings, lots of oddly shaped windows, expensive woods and shiny metals in interesting configurations. Textured tiles on the floor interspersed with bursts of colorful rugs. Minimalist furnishings, one-of-a-kind lighting fixtures, some small and intimate, others the size of small satellites, with customized features in wood, metal, and even fabric. The paintings on the walls were more Picasso and Pollock than da Vinci or Degas.

Devine counted about twenty people, at least in this area. It was a nice night and he figured there would certainly be people out by the pool. He looked around for the bikini lady but didn't see her. He wasn't really sure what to do. Did he ask for Cowl? Would the man find him? Was he to stand here like a schoolboy awaiting his punishment from the principal?

Instead, he decided to go in search of a drink.

Devine found it in the next room, where there was a full bar set up. A few people were in line ahead of him. They turned and stared at him for a few moments. Devine figured he didn't look important enough or wasn't stylishly dressed enough, because they turned back around without speaking.

He took his glass of beer and started wandering from room to room. There were a few people scattered here and there, but they seemed dwarfed by the space. Devine figured you could cloister an entire Army battalion in here, no problem.

Everyone looked tanned and relaxed and outfitted casually in clothes that he was pretty sure had cost a small fortune. He walked into another room and stiffened as the bikini lady appeared out of nowhere and walked up to him. A man should have a little warning before she glided in from stage right, he thought.

She had on an ultra-tight lime-green strappy Lycra minidress that accentuated her figure and tan to a stunning degree. Remarkable blue eyes, flashing white teeth, blond hair dancing around her elegantly chiseled features. Gold sandals completed the picture, and he caught himself gazing at her turquoise-painted toes.

All Devine could think of was Christie Brinkley in the red Ferrari driving that sucker Chevy Chase to the gates of horny Hell. While that movie had been made before he was even born, it was a classic and still brought a shit-eating grin to Devine's face.

"I'm Michelle Montgomery."

"Travis Devine."

They shook hands.

"Mr. Devine, nice to meet you."

"It's Travis, please."

In the back of his head was the image of her and a bandaged Christian F. Chilton chatting by the pool.

*Maybe about me?*

And next he wondered if Chilton was here tonight. If so, the gig would be up. He hadn't seen the BMW Eight in the courtyard, but a guy like Chilton would have multiple cars. And maybe someone who drove him places when he so desired. Maybe the punk owned the Duesenberg.

Montgomery said, "Hey, were you in an accident or something? Your face is all scraped up."

"Fell off a ladder and landed on a brick path, pretty much face-first."

"That must have hurt."

*Not as much as the other guys*, thought Devine. He glanced at Montgomery. *Not as much as your guy.*

"Are you here to see someone?" she asked.

"Brad Cowl. He invited me."

"Brad's around here somewhere. He'll find you. Let's go get a drink. Your glass is empty and I'm *thirsty*."

She hooked his arm and led him away.

# CHAPTER

# 32

As they walked along, he breathed in her scent. Equal parts vanilla, coconut suntan spray, lavender, and part something else he couldn't readily identify. It was all heady stuff, and he fought against it because he needed to keep his head straight tonight.

"Nice place," he said.

"Brad had it built a few years ago, before we met. He's into things like this. He has homes everywhere. Two jets, a yacht he uses like one month out of the year, his own chopper. It's too much for me. I like things simple."

"Doesn't sound like you're going to get *simple* with the guy."

She led him to the bar and he got another beer and she had a Cosmo. She held up the glass.

"I was only four when *Sex and the City* ended its run, but I later binged all the seasons. What a fun fantasy. But really, no one can live like that in New York on their salaries. Same with *Friends*."

"Like you said, a fun fantasy. So how did you and Cowl meet?"

"He was in Italy and I was in Italy and we hit it off. I know he's a lot older than me, but he doesn't seem it. Some days *I* feel like the older one. He's still very much a little boy in many ways, with all his toys."

"He's made a ton of money in business."

"He never talks business with me. I'm not into that."

"So, do you live here?"

"Not all the time. Brad and I are just, I don't know, boyfriend and girlfriend, to use an old-fashioned term."

"And what are you *into* when you're not hanging out with him?"

"Travel. I went to college for a year, didn't like it, and decided to see some of the world. That's how I met Brad. I was staying at a student hostel in Tuscany, and he had rented like *three* villas on a hillside. We met at a restaurant, bonded over some really great Brunello di Montalcino wine, and suddenly I was in one of the villas."

"Hey, good for you. How long ago was this?"

"Nearly a year now. Time goes by. How do you know Brad?"

"I work for his firm. Just a low-level newbie. I got a late start."

"What were you doing before that?"

"Did some time in the Army."

"Why?"

He had expected her to thank him for his service like everyone else, so this threw Devine a little. He answered more truthfully than he probably intended. "To piss off my old man."

She laughed and it was a nice, throaty laugh. She sipped her Cosmo and gave him a look that he couldn't quite decipher.

"Do you like working for Brad?"

"Just chasing the money, like everybody else."

She wrinkled up her nose and looked around. "I watched you when you came in. You looked very uncomfortable. You got a beer instead of something expensive and hip. You don't really want to be here."

"And yet here I am, summoned by the man."

She looked disappointed in this response. "Like a dog on a leash, you mean?"

He took a mouthful of his beer and worked this around in his head. He decided to take control of the conversation.

"A woman at my firm was found dead. Suicide, they thought. Now it looks like murder."

"I heard about that. What was her name again?"

"Sara Ewes."

"Is that why you're here to talk to Brad?"

"I don't know."

"Did you know her?"

"I did," he replied.

"Why would anyone want to kill her?"

"That's what the cops are trying to find out."

She shivered. "There are so many creeps in this world."

He looked past her, out to the pool area.

"My train comes through here early every morning. It stops right behind this place, for reasons unknown to anyone other than some systems engineer."

She glanced where he was looking. "I'm in the pool sometimes in the morning."

"I *know* you are."

He let that hang out there.

She looked back at him, her manner unapologetic and her eyes wide and seeing...everything. "So you're trying to tell me, in a painfully roundabout way, that you've checked me out?"

"Me and every other guy on board. I think the popularity of the six twenty is spiking. Word gets around."

Now her face flushed, and not in a good way.

"I didn't say that to embarrass you," he said hastily. "I'm just amazed you're up that early."

She composed herself. "I like to have time to myself. Meditate, swim."

"That's a good thing."

She sharpened her look at him. "Don't patronize me."

He said, "Not my intent. Before I catch the train, I do a full workout starting at four a.m. I guess that's a form of meditation for me. Endorphins, fresh start to the day."

"You look very fit," she said, running her gaze over him so slowly and provocatively that he felt like he was naked.

"Army sort of required it. And I've kept it up because I like to be able to take care of myself." *Like I did in that alley.*

"I wasn't aware that people on the train could see the pool area. There're trees back there."

"Right, but there's also a gap."

She gave him an enigmatic look. "I'll have to keep that in mind."

"Okay."

"Six twenty? Why do you go in to work so early?" she asked.

"In my world, if you want to make it to the next round, you have to work your ass off and beat the other guys."

"Sounds like a fast track to a heart attack."

"Maybe. I guess you know pretty much everybody here?"

"No, not everybody. There are always new faces. Brad knows lots of people."

"So, when you're not here, where do you go?"

"I have a little walk-up apartment in SoHo," she said.

He didn't ask if Cowl had arranged it for her. He didn't have to. She hadn't mentioned having a job, and it didn't sound like she came from money since she had been staying in a hostel in Italy. And even *little* walk-ups in New York were not cheap, particularly in SoHo.

"Do you work around there?"

She ignored the query and said, "Maybe I'll see you sometime. Or you could come by here and go for a swim with me, maybe late at night when Brad's not here. He stays at his penthouse a lot."

This one caught him like a left hook. "I'm not sure how my boss would feel about my swimming with you alone at night. No, I *am* sure how he'd feel about it. He'd fire me."

"Why? I'm his *girlfriend*, not his wife."

"Who knows, you might end up *being* his wife."

"Not in the cards. I don't want that, and neither does he. He'll trade me in for a younger model at some point."

"And how do you feel about that?"

"I *don't* feel anything about it."

"So what's in it for you?" he asked.

"Just something…different. So, how about that swim? You game?"

Devine was having a hard time keeping up with her. "I imagine a place like this is loaded with help, servants, whatever you want to call them. Lots of wandering eyes to tell on us."

"Like they would care. Brad treats them like crap."

"If he's that kind of a guy, why do you stay with him?"

"You assume I have a choice."

"Don't you?"

"Give me your phone number. I can text you my address if coming here makes you nervous."

For some reason that was not entirely clear to him, Devine told her his number and Montgomery put it in her phone.

"Now I see Brad coming. So I'll say goodbye." She added, "I'll be at my place tomorrow night. I'll text you the address. Just in case you're interested."

She walked off as Devine turned to see Cowl bearing down on him like an Abrams tank.

CHAPTER

# 33

DEVINE, RIGHT?" SAID COWL.

He had on jeans, a black shirt open enough to reveal dark, curly chest hair, and loafers. His hair wasn't slicked back, like he wore it at the office. He was less Gordon Gekko and more tousled-hair man-child, but with something definite and important on his mind.

"I'm Travis Devine."

"Come with me."

He headed off and Devine followed. He glanced around and saw Michelle Montgomery staring at them. She raised her Cosmo and added a supportive look.

Devine thought they would head to a private room. Instead, Cowl led him outside, to the pool area. There wasn't anyone else around, so it *was* private, and maybe prearranged. Devine spotted a beefy security guard hovering at the rear door, probably to make sure no one else came out here. The lights were lit, and fancy tiki torches kept the bugs away, though crickets sounded off all around them and the smell of freshly mown grass dominated. Cowl sat at a table next to the pool and motioned for Devine to sit across from him. Devine did and put his beer down.

Cowl didn't look at him. He stared at the pool and then the wall beyond it.

Devine followed his gaze and saw the outbound train slowly passing by. The lights were on in the train, and through the gap he was used to looking at from the other side he could see a collection of weary New Yorkers. Their heads were bent and shoulders slumped, some half dozing, as they returned from battle to catch some sleep and get up the next morning to do it all over again.

"Poor assholes," said Cowl.

"Why's that?"

"Schlepping on a train in and out every day like mice on a treadmill. But on the other hand, I need them to do exactly that to keep *my* dream going. But I'm not a total dick, despite what some say about me. I was born into money, and then by the time I could count, it was all gone, because my father and grandfather were morons. So I know what it's like to have zip. I could have grown up a legacy kid, gotten into all the Ivy Leagues I needed through those connections. And then I could have become an entitled prick all nice and polite and holding my fork and cup just so, while I stab you in the back. Instead, I'm a street fighter who chooses to stab you in the front, which you have to admit is a lot fairer." He eyed Devine, as though to make sure he was listening, *really* listening, to all this. "So, I know what it's like to ride that train, but it's partly a gravy train. They're not doing it for free, and the lowest paid on there who work in my world make a shitload more money than most folks."

"Okay. I get that." Now Devine wondered if Cowl had allowed the gap to be there so those poor suckers on the train could see how opulently he lived. He was just that kind of a jerk.

"You live somewhere around here, right?" asked Cowl.

"But not this neighborhood. Out of my price range. I share a town house with three other people."

"Uh-huh." He drummed his fingers on the teak tabletop. "You knew Sara Ewes, I understand."

"I did." He hesitated, mulling over how best to play this. He decided to slide a stack of chips forward on the pass line and roll the dice. "Did *you* know her?"

Cowl knifed him with a glare. "I'm asking the questions, Devine, not you."

Devine took a breath and rolled his neck from one side to the other, letting the tension ease.

"You want to throw a punch, throw it," said Cowl, who was watching him closely. "Then I bury you under legal bills *and* you go to jail for assault." He paused and made his own play. "And maybe for more than that."

Devine didn't take the bait. He reverted back to his military training. When in doubt, say nothing. When not in doubt, double down on that advice.

The train moved on with its beaten-down riders, and still Cowl did not speak. He was now staring at the dark pool waters so intently, Devine wanted to check to see if there was a body floating in there.

"I'm trying to come up with the best way of handling this, Devine."

"Handling what?"

"The cops are interested in you; I hope you're smart enough to know that. Otherwise, you have no business working for me."

"They've talked to me. They know certain things. They've talked to other people. They have no proof I had anything to do with Sara's death, because I didn't."

"Except for one thing, and it's a big one."

Devine knew exactly what that one thing was. The entry log, showing him in the building and on the fifty-second floor in the time window necessary to kill Ewes. "Then why haven't they arrested me?"

"You can thank me for that" was Cowl's surprising reply.

Devine tensed more than a bit. "You'll have to walk me through that one."

"It's delicate. It's all delicate, Devine." He abruptly sat up straight from his slouched position. "A dead body in a building invites all sorts of attention. Unwanted scrutiny for a firm like mine."

"Why?"

"It's obvious, Devine. Shit, are you that stupid?"

"Maybe."

He held up one stubby finger, even as Devine's mind wandered to the image of him walking out of that office zipping up his pants, not far from where Ewes had been strung up, while Jennifer Stamos was lying naked with her thighs still spread on a metal desk with a laminated top. Cheap on cheap.

Cowl said, "The one major asset I have isn't money or talent, it's respectability. People pay us enormous amounts of money because we are respectable. No scandal. No dirt. No Ponzi Bernie Madoffs, no bloodsucking Enrons, no dickhead Ivan Boeskys. They are the kiss of death."

"A murder is not the same thing as financial crimes," noted Devine.

"You have to go deeper than that, Devine. No one is implying that we're stealing their money by Sara's body being found there. But in the backs of their heads, clients will think, *Do I risk it? Why go with them when I could go with Morgan Stanley or Merrill Lynch or one of their other competitors?* And it doesn't take much to move the needle, because we all do basically the same thing."

"You can't make the murder go away, Mr. Cowl. The cops are not going to stop investigating because you're afraid it will cost you clients and business."

"Which brings me back to you. Did you kill her?"

"No."

"Did you hire someone to do it?"

"And give them my security card?"

"Why do you say that?"

Devine wasn't about to give away his hacking game on that one. "How else could they have gotten in the building and accessed the floor Sara was found on?"

"Uh-huh." And then Cowl unloaded a shocker. "And maybe there's security video of someone who looks a lot like you coming in and out at the required time." He glanced at Devine for his reaction to this.

Devine had looked down at his drink for precisely this reason. When he looked up, he was composed. "I'm no computer genius, but give me the right equipment and a little time, and I could put your face on somebody else's body and walk it anywhere I wanted."

"Is that right?"

"You just bought a company two months ago that does that very thing."

"Cyber-Surgeon, yeah, I know. We're going to flip that sucker in a year and make a killing, because, like you said, they can do that very thing. Which means truth becomes meaningless because you can invent your own. Not that people don't already do that all the time. Only with this technology the lie becomes very convincing."

"And there goes any proof of anything," said Devine.

"Maybe, or maybe not, if the cops believe what they *think* they see? And then a jury does, too? You got about a million bucks to spend on the best lawyers? And that's probably the *minimum* you're going to need."

"No, I don't. Nowhere close."

"Then I don't care if you didn't kill the woman, you're screwed," replied Cowl.

"Justice in America?"

"Reality in America. And for your information, we don't have a 'justice' system in this country. We have a *legal* system. I got a whole platoon of in-house lawyers and fifteen more on the outside on retainer. All top of the heap in talent and connections. And I still don't think it's enough. Just the cost of doing business. Courthouse is open to every son of a bitch who wants to play the legal lottery. And I am one big target."

"So why am I here?"

"I wanted to see what kind of guy you are, Devine. Military, combat guy, medals, blah, blah, blah, yeah, I got all that. But I wanted to talk to you, feel you out, poke inside your head." He looked at the facial injuries. "Hurt much?"

Devine could tell the man knew what had happened from Stamos. "Not even a little bit."

Cowl gave a sneering smile. "Right."

Devine decided to attempt a draw to an inside straight. He pulled out his phone and laid it down in front of him. "I've spoken to Jennifer Stamos a couple times. Saw her at a bar, too."

"Oh yeah? Why do I care?" Cowl didn't even look at the phone.

Devine glanced down at it. "I heard you were mentoring her, like you were Sara."

"I mentor dozens."

"But they're not all like Jennifer. They're not all . . . *sweet cheeks*."

Cowl now looked at the phone. "Maybe you *are* smart enough to work for me."

"Maybe I am."

"And maybe I need to think about this some more, rather than bring the hammer down, like I thought I was going to."

"Maybe you should. Like you said, it's *delicate*." He paused and chose his next words carefully. "But then again, you can always just fire me."

The man shook his head. "Friends close and enemies closer, Devine. That's the way I do business. And thanks for confirming for me which one you are."

He rose and walked away, leaving Devine to stare down at his phone and let out a tight, uncomfortable breath. Funny, when you'd been in a war and had killed others and been nearly killed yourself, you wouldn't think a battle of words could stress you all that much. But getting fingered for a murder charge and spending the rest of your life in prison did give a man pause.

*At least it does this man.*

He rose and walked right through the palace, not making eye contact with anyone.

And outside, he ran right into Christian Chilton.

# CHAPTER 34

WHAT IN THE HELL ARE you doing here?" Chilton snapped. He instinctively took a step away from Devine, his fists made and held at the ready. But the fear in the man's eyes told Devine that Chilton would haul ass before fighting him again.

Devine studied him. The bandages were gone, but the bruises and cuts were still there.

"Just visiting a friend."

"What? In there? Bullshit!"

"You never know where you might find one."

"Rick needs major dental work. And Doug has a fractured jaw."

"I know you were lights out and didn't see, but I let *Rick* walk with only a sore gut. Then *Rick* decided to try and crack my skull while my back was turned. He's lucky it's not worse."

Chilton looked over Devine's injured face. "At least my buddies got their whacks in. And you sucker-punched me, you asshole."

"While I was standing right in front of you and you were coming at me with fists raised?"

"You know what I mean. I was trying—"

"You were running your mouth. It wasn't a duel where you count to three. You wanted to fight, so I fought. It was three against one. What the hell did you expect, Marquess of Queensberry Rules? And I gave you lots of chances to walk away, but you wouldn't take them. But if it makes you feel any better, I couldn't raise my arms over my shoulders for a whole day, and my back still aches like a son of a bitch." He touched his face. "And I'm not getting any better-looking with brick face."

The two men glared at each other for a few seconds.

Chilton finally said, "Yeah, I guess fighting over that woman was pretty stupid."

"Fights over girls usually are," said Devine, who was still suspicious of why Chilton had even been at the bar that night. "So, you frequent that place?"

"Sometimes. Did you really know her?"

"We work in the same office. A friend of ours died there."

"Shit, I read about that. Suicide, right?"

"That's what they initially thought. Now it looks like someone killed her."

Chilton went all wide-eyed on this, which made Devine even more suspicious. "Damn. Do they know who did it?"

"Not yet. One more thing."

"What?" asked Chilton.

"You were at that bar in Greenwich Village hitting on a girl who works at Cowl and Comely. Now you're here."

"So what?"

"Did you follow the woman to the bar and pretend to hit on her? Otherwise, I'm feeling a bit of a coincidence here."

"In case you didn't know, the New York financial world is pretty small and that bar is popular with our crowd. So piss off."

As Chilton started to turn away, Devine said, "Hummingbird?"

Chilton turned back. "What?"

"Word on the street is your firm is interested in funding Hummingbird's next investment round."

"How do you know anything about that?"

"I work in that 'little' financial world you just referred to. And I keep my ears open."

"How do you even know about me or my firm?"

"Your family came over on the *Mayflower*. Everybody knows you."

"You're really starting to tick me off."

"Not really my intent. And we already did that dance. Actually a friend of mine told me. How can you do the Hummingbird deal so fast?"

"I don't have to explain my business to you."

"You're right, you don't. But if you want my two cents, Hummingbird is a great company. It's going be worth a shitload really soon. Your investment will be worth a hundred mil in a year."

Chilton's aggressive attitude faded. "Based on what?"

"Based on the CEO. She's the smartest person I've ever met in my life. MIT grad. Harvard MBA. World-class gamer. There's nothing she can't do with a computer. And she lives and breathes Hummingbird. Her subscription base is soaring, she's got positive cash flow, her business strategy is sound, and all she needs is the capital to be the preeminent platform out there. And it's a big market and only getting bigger."

"You sound like her CMO," said Chilton, referring to a chief marketing officer. "You got skin in the game?"

"About one-millionth of one percent. But I believe in her. I've been around a lot of business types. Some good, some terrible. She's really in a league of her own."

Chilton looked away for a moment. When he glanced back at Devine, his entire demeanor had changed. "Everything you just said comports with what we've found in our preliminary due diligence."

"So can you really do the deal that fast? She's got other suitors, but nobody who can pull the trigger as quick as you guys."

Chilton smiled. "We've heard that before. Fact is, we've got a ton of capital to deploy, and I've been looking at the online dating space for a while now. Tapshaw's coming at it from a whole other angle. Not just dating, but a whole other array of services and benefits. It shows in the sophistication and thoroughness of the business product she's put together. I think she really wants to bring people together. Most of the other platforms are clearly in it just for the bucks, at least that's my opinion."

"So, where did you hear about her?"

"We have spies everywhere. She talked to a Taiwanese VC firm recently. The Taiwanese don't screw around. If they're interested, we need to be interested."

"So you haven't met Tapshaw yet?"

"No, but we have officially reached out to her. We hope to have a face-to-face with her very soon."

This was all sounding legit to Devine. Maybe Chilton wasn't targeting Tapshaw because she was Devine's roommate. Maybe he didn't even know they were roommates.

"So where does all your money come from? Just professional curiosity," he added.

Chilton looked for a moment like he might lash out again. He shrugged. "I can't give out names. But from all over. Family offices to institutional investors. My grandfather started Mayflower. I'm no wunderkind who built something from scratch. I'm just this generation's rep. Been groomed for it from first grade. We have ties to everybody."

"Brad Cowl?"

Chilton looked up at the house. "You must know him, since you're here."

"He's my boss. He invited me here to meet."

Chilton looked at Devine in a different light. "How'd your meeting go with him?"

"Too soon to tell. So, you're friends with Cowl, then?"

"We do business together. He did the same with my father before he died."

"Good luck with Hummingbird. Treat her right, and you won't regret it. But you're not the only game in town, so be prepared to pay a premium valuation. Oh, I met Michelle Montgomery, too. Very nice. You know her?"

"Yeah, she's actually a family friend. I was over here the other night visiting her."

*I know.* "Funny that you know her, and she knows Cowl, and you work with Cowl, too. Another coincidence."

"No coincidence about it. I was the one who introduced Michelle to Brad. This was over in Italy."

"Really? You had no interest yourself?"

"We grew up together. And I thought it would be good for Michelle."

*Rich boy and a girl who stays in student hostels grew up together? Curious.*

"Well, have a fun time in there."

Devine watched him walk inside and then he left, got on his bike, and sped off.

He couldn't believe that he'd threatened the head of one of the biggest investment firms in the world. If Cowl got the cops involved? If he said Devine had tried to blackmail him? The guy could probably make it stick, and Devine didn't have enough money to hire the legal firepower to fight back, just like Cowl had intimated.

*So basically I'm SOL. And what else is new?*

And if he got swept out to sea there was no way in hell Emerson Campbell was throwing him a rope. Unlike being in the Army, now it was sink or swim all by his lonesome.

CHAPTER

# 35

Dude?"

Devine walked into the house and saw Valentine on the couch.

"Yeah?"

"Cowl is *not* doing high-frequency trading from your building."

Devine sat down next to him. "How do you know that already? I thought you were still *thinking* about whether to look into it or not."

"So I change mind, kill me. Anyway, I track flow over pipe, and confirm on both ends. Is very unique stream of data. Like a river that is green." He laughed. "Green. You get my little joke?"

"Yeah, very little."

"There aren't many that do trading like that. Easy to check."

"Okay, you say Cowl isn't doing high-frequency trading, but I know that they *do* have a division that does that. And you said you confirmed that data flow, so I'm a little confused."

"That is what I am talking about, dude. You are right. They *have* high-frequency trading platform, only it operates out of building in *Queens*. That is pipe I trace."

"You're sure?"

He looked at Devine with his head cocked and his features full of incredulity. "Dude? Digital signature is unique, okay? I'm no amateur."

"Okay, so what is Area 51 in my building, then? Did you manage to hack in there?"

Valentine looked down at his screen. "It is...well protected. Take a lot of time to get in. And maybe not even then."

Devine had a thought. "Could they be doing crypto-mining in my building?"

"Is possible. Takes lots of energy and computational power. Lots of people doing it. But in the end, I think it is bad thing."

"Why?"

"Is perfect for ransomware. You can trace money wire. But very difficult to do with something like *Monero,* a decentralized crypto, very private. You can negotiate terms, and the really professional hackers always keep their word and unlock the encrypted files. Only way they stay in business. But is still bad because you can't find where money went."

"Then I have to find another way to see what they're doing on that floor."

"Why?"

"It might have something to do with Sara Ewes's death."

"You mean, she might have found out what is going on there?"

"Prime motive for murder, don't you think, depending on what's there?"

"Maybe. But, dude, crypto-mining is not illegal."

"But it might not *be* crypto-mining. And Sara might have heard or seen something she shouldn't have. And maybe *that's* where the untraceable email came from."

This got Valentine's interest. "How will you get in there?"

"I can't access the floor with my card." Something occurred to Devine. "But maybe I can find another way."

Devine climbed the stairs and knocked on Tapshaw's door.

She opened it, dressed in pale blue capri pants and a white blouse. He smiled and she returned it. "Got some news on Mayflower. I know it's not the weekend, but how about having that tequila now, before the bar closes? I can fill you in."

She slipped on flip-flops and put her arm through his. "Let's go."

The bar was within walking distance, a few blocks off the main street. The Mount Kisco area was an interesting mix of working-class and mega wealth. The bar they were going to would have no such mix. It was all folks living paycheck to paycheck.

They sat outside, a shot of tequila and a bowl of nuts in front of each of them.

"Well?" she said curiously. "Mayflower?"

He told her about his meeting with Chilton. "So when they come in with an offer, triple the valuation. They'll still bite. So long as you have the numbers to back it up, and I know you do."

"Can I kiss you?"

He grinned like a schoolboy. "I have no problem with that."

She leaned over and pecked him lightly on the cheek, then sat back. "I really appreciate this, Travis. It was so nice of you."

He lifted his shot glass. "Hey, I'm a shareholder too, right?"

They tapped glasses and drank their tequila. "So, after you take over the world, what's next?" asked Devine.

"You think way too highly of me," she said.

"Not from where I'm sitting."

"It's ironic that I founded a dating service, because I haven't been too lucky in that regard."

"Sometimes luck has nothing to do with it. Sometimes it just happens when you least expect it to."

"I'm still waiting for that to happen to me. Maybe I work too hard."

"There's no maybe about it. You *do* work too hard. But you clearly love it, so maybe you don't really work a day in your life. Isn't that how the old saying goes?"

She smiled and then her expression turned serious. "You haven't seemed yourself lately, Travis. Is everything okay?"

"A woman was killed at my office."

"What!"

"They thought it was a suicide, but turns out someone murdered her."

"Oh my God. Why would someone do that?"

"I don't know. Yet."

"Helen told me the police were questioning you but she didn't say what about."

"I think they believe I had something to do with it."

"Did you know the woman?"

"I did."

"What was her name?"

"Sara Ewes."

Tapshaw slowly put down her shot glass, looking like she might be ill. "Sara Ewes? *That's* her name?"

"Yeah. Wait a minute, did you know her?"

"No, but I know the name."

"How?"

"A woman named Sara Ewes was one of my very first subscribers on Hummingbird."

# CHAPTER 36

It *WAS* the same Sara Ewes. Devine was in his room staring at her picture on Hummingbird. He'd gone over her dating file. She'd had matches with three men. All had been right around the time she had signed up on the site, years earlier.

Ewes looked younger and carefree, though she would have already pulled time at the max prison otherwise known as Cowl and Comely. She had obviously been looking for someone to share her life with. And hadn't found him. And perhaps she had grown disenchanted, because, after these three tries, there had been no more activity on the site for her.

She was smiling, her hair was set just so, grazing her shoulders. He knew she had a nice laugh, an easygoing manner. Nothing pretentious about the woman.

He had liked her. He could have maybe come to love her, given time.

And now her body had been autopsied, with the remains to be handed over to her crushed parents. At age twenty-eight. Nothing could be more tragic.

He looked up at his open doorway as Tapshaw appeared there. "Is... is it her?"

He nodded slowly.

"I'm so sorry."

"You have a good memory for names."

She walked over and stood beside him. "My first hundred

subscribers were the only ones I had for a long time. I studied them every minute of every day, figuring out how to get more just like them. I knew them in some ways better than I knew my own family."

"I can see that."

She glanced at the image. "Was she nice? I mean, in person?"

"Yeah, she was very nice."

"Did you two... were you dating?"

He looked away for a moment. "Maybe I would have wanted that."

"I sense a *but* coming."

"But she apparently didn't."

"Did you two... ?"

"TMI, Jill."

"Right, sorry," she said, her face reddening. "It's just the matchmaker in me." She looked at the screen again. "Will this help find who hurt her?"

"Maybe. I looked at her profile. There were three men she had matches with. But I don't know more than that." He glanced at her. "Can you help?"

"Get up."

Tapshaw sat in the chair in front of the screen, cracked her knuckles, and her long, slender fingers flew over the keyboard so fast he could barely follow the movements.

"Here are the three men," she said.

Devine looked at the photos of a trio of handsome gents with refined features. They all looked remarkably similar.

"And here are their backgrounds."

More key slashes and another screen came up with the bios.

"One in the theater, one in finance, and one in medicine," he said, reading off the information. "Do you know what happened to them?"

Her fingers flashed again and multiple screens came up.

"Okay, the one in the theater posted that he's in London working in the West End. I guess that can be verified. The businessman met his beloved on Hummingbird and is married with a newborn in Boston. Again, that can be checked. Now, the doctor." She studied the screen, brought up still more screens, studied them, shook her head and said, "Let me try something."

The keyboard rattled again as she attacked it. Then an obituary popped up with a picture.

"That's him!" said Devine. "He's dead? What happened? He was around my age."

Tapshaw ran her eye down the page. "He was working in Chicago in a COVID ward near the beginning of the pandemic. He caught the virus and died. No wife and no kids."

"Damn, when you think you're having a bad day, think about people like that."

She straightened and looked at him. "When I founded Hummingbird, I have to admit, I did it really for myself. It's so hard to meet people and develop a relationship. But then I started thinking beyond myself." She looked at the screen. "To people like them."

"So, do you have a profile on Hummingbird?"

"I used to. And I got some matches. But none that really went anywhere. I think I'm resigned to building my business and then looking for someone."

"Well, thanks for all this info," he said. "You are a true artist with computers."

"I got my first Apple MacBook when I was eight and never looked back."

"I remember you telling me about your parents. Did they encourage you?"

"Oh yeah. My dad has a slew of patents he developed for companies like Microsoft and Intel. He also lectures all around the world. My mom teaches physics at Caltech."

"Well, you clearly didn't inherit any brains from them," he joked. "You told me before that you had a brother?"

"Dennis. We're twins. He's a scholar-athlete, sort of the perfect sibling. It can be intimidating. But I love him to death."

"Yeah, I've got the perfect-sibling thing going, too. It can be tough. But I don't see how anyone can hold a candle to what you've accomplished." He looked at the keyboard. "Hey, Jill, can I ask a favor?"

"Sure."

He pulled out his phone. "I got a weird email from someone who I think might be involved with Sara's death."

"What?" she gasped. "Have the police traced it?"

"That's the thing. It seems to be untraceable. I've had people try, including Will, but no go."

She looked intrigued. "Will is very good."

"But you might be better."

"Send me the email and I'll see what I can do."

"Thanks, Jill."

After she left, he forwarded her the email. Then Devine took the two remaining names from Ewes's match list and found them online. The actor was indeed in London's West End. He was an understudy in a play there, and had actually performed in the lead role on the night Sara had died, so he was obviously out. The businessman was employed at Fidelity in Boston. Devine accessed his Facebook page by using the same skullduggery he had with Christian Chilton.

On the night Sara had been killed, the businessman and his family had been in the Netherlands on vacation, with pictures to prove it.

A total dead end.

Devine grabbed a beer, walked outside, and sat on the front porch of the town house. The air had turned cool, the sky was threaded with stars, and the quiet of the night was immensely soothing.

He looked over as Helen Speers walked up to him, dressed in a dark jacket and matching skirt, a briefcase in hand.

"You're getting in really late. And it's not safe to walk from the station at this hour," he admonished.

"*You* do it all the time," she retorted.

"Yeah, well, I outweigh you by over a hundred pounds and I'm a badass Army Ranger. What were you doing?"

"Working at a firm in town. Part-time until I pass the bar."

She sat next to him and took off her high heels, rubbing her stockinged feet. "Why the sad face?"

"Just a long, shitty day, no other reason."

"Yeah, I had one of those, too."

"Then you could use this." He held up the beer.

Speers took two swigs and let them go down slow. She handed the bottle back. "Need that lawyer yet?"

"Getting *really* close, I think."

"NYPD any closer to nailing whoever killed that woman?"

He took another drink and passed the bottle back and told Speers to finish it. "I don't know about that. I *do* know that the guy here asking me questions lied about being with NYPD. There apparently is no Detective Karl Hancock, or at least that's my take from the reactions of the real detectives who questioned me."

"A fake detective? What the hell is that about?"

"I wish I knew. I seem to be right in the middle of a little conspiracy."

She shot him a look. "Are any conspiracies actually little?"

He eyed her. "Not when you're in the middle of one, *actually*. You gonna do your yoga?"

"Thinking of bagging it, *actually*. Why?"

He gave her a look up and down, taking the woman all in; she was just mesmerizing to him right now. "I don't know," he lied as he looked away.

"Don't you, Travis?"

He shot her a glance. "What?"

"You ever see me reading Braille? No. Because I'm not blind."

She stood, put on her heels, and said, "Give me a few minutes to freshen up."

He glanced up at her, thoroughly taken aback by this abrupt development. "You sure about this, Helen? I mean..." To Devine it all seemed sudden, but also a long time in coming, with lots of glances and sneaked looks and innuendos that danced around probably the most natural, and difficult, phenomena between two people.

"I'm attracted to you, and you to me. We're consenting adults, are we not?"

Devine didn't answer; he didn't think he had to.

He gave her ten minutes and then headed up.

She was lying on the bed when he walked into her room. She had on a loose-fitting top and a pair of pajama shorts. As he slipped next to her, Speers met him with her mouth. After five minutes of feeling each other out in both familiar and unfamiliar ways, they slowly undressed one another. She pushed him flat on his back and climbed on top.

She looked at his shoulder where the shrapnel had torn through, with some of the metal still in there. She next glanced down at his damaged calf.

"Still hurt?"

"Not right now, no."

Her lips curled into a smile. "Thank you for your service, soldier."

He grinned back. "Fuck me, legal eagle."

"Your wish is my command."

Twenty breathless minutes later, she toppled off her perch and nestled beside him.

"Been a while," she said, nicking his chest with her nails.

"For you or me?"

"Both, I think."

"Yeah."

Speers closed her eyes, her hand gripping his, and fell asleep.

He lay there with her for about an hour before quietly disengaging and heading to his room.

Later, when four o'clock came and his phone alarm went off, Devine didn't budge.

The rain was pouring outside and he heard a crack of thunder. A moment later the accompanying lightning brightened his room briefly.

No workout this morning. He needed to sleep anyway. But he stared at the ceiling.

And on its surface Devine saw the image of a dead Sara Ewes. And his heart felt like it was about to break.

# CHAPTER

# 37

DEVINE HAD ARRIVED AT THE train station a little early and had a chat with a man who worked there. The security cameras were often not working, he was told. And the police had not been by to check them. That information had cost Devine ten bucks.

He had a mobile ticketing app on his iPhone and paid for his train passage that way. The conductor would simply zap the screen with his reader. So there would be a record for when he had used it. The only problem was you could still buy single tickets at the machine using cash. There would be no record attached to that, or so the police would argue. And he could have driven his motorcycle into the city. If he took the Henry Hudson Bridge on the way in there would be a toll and record thereof. But there were alternate routes he could take that did not include toll roads. So that would not be conclusive, again, as far as the cops were concerned.

*But you didn't use your card to get into the building that night, and your name still showed up on the entry and exit log. Someone cloned your card—the only question is who.*

As he waited for the train, he thought about Cowl. The man must have somehow delayed giving the electronic log to the cops. How he had managed to do that in a murder investigation, Devine didn't know. The guy was rich and influential and probably had a direct line to the mayor's office. But at some point he would have to turn it over.

*And Cowl intimated my picture was on the security video. Will the police think I'm stupid enough to have left that kind of trail?*

But criminals *were* stupid. You heard such stories all the time. But what would his motive be? Not the pregnancy. Ewes had already terminated it. Then something occurred to him.

*If I knew she was pregnant with my child, and I wanted the kid and found out she* had *terminated it?*

That was a clear motive.

The train opened its door and he climbed on board. With these perilous thoughts running through his head, he was mentally exhausted before he'd even gotten to work.

The storm had spent its fury, and the 6:20 ran dry all the way to the palace pool.

And there she was. Now he knew her name at least.

Michelle Montgomery was staring into the pool water. This time her bathing suit was—shocker—not a bikini. It was a one-piece the color of the sky. After Devine had met the woman and intimated that there were lots of guys watching her, maybe Montgomery had decided to show some modesty.

Devine thought that right up until the moment she turned, revealing that the one-piece had a thong backside showing off her tanned buttocks. Montgomery catwalk-stepped away and then raised both her hands overhead and flipped off the morning Harlem Line riders with both barrels.

He had to smile. The lady had a certain style, he had to admit. Along with a pair of brass balls.

The train rode on while Devine thought about the previous night, with Helen Speers. It *had* been a while since he had been with a woman. He knew the exact date, in fact. And that might cause him problems down the road, because that woman had been Sara Ewes. They had had sex at her place in Brooklyn. It had been a wonderful experience and Devine had thought there would be many more. But it was not to be. And it had not been his decision. It had been hers.

His phone buzzed. By the string of weird digits, he could tell it was an international number.

"Hello?"

"Mr. Devine?"

"Yes?"

"This is Ellen Ewes. I apologize for the early call."

That explained it. The phone number was from New Zealand.

The mother sounded eerily like Sara on the phone. And he felt immensely uncomfortable hearing her voice when he had just been thinking about having had sex with her deceased daughter.

"No problem, Mrs. Ewes."

"Please make it Ellen. I understand the police have been by to see you."

"They *have* been. I told them what I knew and it was left at that."

"Did they tell you why they came by?"

"Yes, that you had contacted them."

"Can you come by the house later? We'd like to talk to you."

"I can come by after work. Say around eight?"

"Eight will be fine. We'll see you then."

He put his phone away and thought about this all the way into the city.

* * *

Devine was sitting at his cubicle when a message dropped into his business email box.

> 5:00 top floor. I'll have someone escort you. BC

He fingered his phone, very glad that all of his "evidence" from that night was safely on his personal cloud. But even with that, Cowl could have something up his sleeve.

He looked around the room and noticed several people staring at him before quickly looking away. This had happened so frequently throughout the day that Devine finally stood and walked over to one woman who had done this multiple times.

"Is there a problem?"

Her name was Lydia White. She had dark hair and was heavy-set and was probably going to make it to the finish line at Cowl because she was smart, worked like a dray horse, and knew what she wanted. He hadn't spoken fifty words to her, and she had never given him the evil eye like this before.

"I don't know. Why don't you tell me?"

"And that's supposed to mean what, exactly?"

All tapping had ceased, and the rest of the Burners stopped working to listen.

"The detectives talked to you," said White.

"They talked to a lot of people," replied Devine.

"No, I asked around. It seems they really just talked to you, at least more than once. And you knew Sara."

"We all knew Sara, everybody in this room."

"Maybe you knew her better than the rest of us," said White in an accusatory tone.

"And you're basing this on what?" he said.

"I don't have to base it on anything." She looked him over. "You were in the Army. You know how to kill people."

"Yeah, I was killing the enemies of this country. And don't bother thanking me for my service. I think we're past that."

White flushed at his words and looked away.

He glanced around at the others. "Anybody else have a problem they'd like to bring to my attention?"

The keys started tapping again, soon turning into an avalanche of sound. That was why most people here wore headphones or AirPods.

Devine sat back down. And put in his AirPods. They did nothing to quell all the noise in his head.

He worked until 4:58. Then the door opened and there appeared

Willard Paulson, Cowl's lapdog. He caught Devine's eye and motioned him to come.

Devine left with the Burners' gazes on him the whole way.

Paulson said nothing, and Devine had nothing he wanted to say to the dweeb. Paulson used his card to access the elevator bank. It looked just like Devine's, a 125, as Valentine had described it. Easily cloneable *bullshit*.

"I didn't think this elevator went to the penthouse," said Devine. "Only Mr. Cowl has access."

Paulson shot him a glance. "We'll get off at the floor below and someone will meet you and take you to Mr. Cowl."

As they approached the fifty-first floor, Devine eyed Paulson, who was looking at his phone. Devine leaned against the wall and used his elbow to nudge the button for that floor. It didn't light up, and they whizzed right past it.

*That's interesting. Not even the inner circle can get in there.*

The doors opened and Devine got off, where he was met by her smiling face.

"Hello, *Mr.* Devine," said Michelle Montgomery.

# CHAPTER 38

THE DOORS CLOSED BEHIND PAULSON, leaving Devine and Montgomery all alone. She was dressed for the office, not the pool. Dark pinstriped jacket and slacks, white blouse, no hint of cleavage, two-inch pumps, hair parted and a little slicked back on the sides. Her tan wasn't as vivid under artificial light.

He followed her down a long hall.

"So, why did you get picked for this assignment?" he asked.

"Because I don't think Brad trusts anyone who works here."

"By the way, I loved your act this morning. Both finger barrels to the whole train."

She smiled. "Did you also like the *view*?"

He involuntarily glanced at her bottom.

"I thought so," she said impishly.

When they arrived at another elevator, she held a phone up in front of a reader there.

*Cowl's phone?*

The doors opened, they entered, and she hit the button.

"So, can I be allowed to hold a billionaire's phone for a second?"

She looked over at him, smiled, and passed it across.

The phone was one of those new, big Apples. The cover was gold and shiny. And the screen saver was a Bugatti Chiron.

*Of course it is.*

He took out his phone and snapped a photo of Cowl's screen.

"Why'd you do that?" she asked.

He laughed. "For posterity."

She laughed, too.

He handed back the phone.

She said, "So, how did a billionaire's phone feel?"

"Heavy as a ball and chain. I'm actually surprised Cowl trusts anyone with it."

She shrugged. "What am I going to do with it, make a long-distance call?"

*She obviously doesn't know the possibilities*, thought Devine. *But I do.* "I ran into your family friend last night."

"Christian told me."

"And what else did Christian tell you?"

"That you kicked his ass and the asses of his two large friends."

"And did he tell you why?"

"It was over a girl. He didn't say he was in the right, just in case you were wondering. He's actually a nice guy—a little full of himself, but I've seen far worse from guys with money."

The doors opened directly into the foyer of the large penthouse.

"Nice place," said Devine.

"Yeah, if you like stuffy, overfurnished, and mundane. I like the other house a lot better. Minimalism is my thing." She called out, "Brad? He's here."

"Do you know why *I am* here?"

"I don't get involved in his business. I told you that already. You coming by my place like I asked you to?"

"How late are you up?"

"As late as it takes. I'll text you my address. It's not far from here."

*Maybe farther than you think, at least from my perspective*, he thought.

"Devine," called out Cowl as he rounded a corner. He held out his hand, and Montgomery placed the phone directly in it. "This way. Thanks, Michelle."

Montgomery smiled inscrutably at Devine and disappeared somewhere.

Cowl said, "Follow me."

They entered what looked like a study. Cowl closed the double doors and said, "What do you want to drink?"

"Beer?"

"No. We'll drink brandy."

"Okay." *So much for having a choice with this guy.*

Cowl poured out two snifters from a bar set against a wall and handed one to Devine. Then he took out an electronic wand from inside a cabinet and ran it over Devine.

"Just checking for wires and stuff. Can never be too careful these days. Take out your phone and turn it off."

As Devine turned his phone off Cowl said, "Everybody—and I mean everybody—is spying on everybody else with this electronic shit. I don't like using email or texts. I don't even like calling people, because you never know who's listening. The important stuff? I do it the old-fashioned way. *Analog*. Face-to-face."

They sat across from each in leather club chairs.

"So, I've been thinking about our little discussion."

"And?"

"And I need to see your hand before you see mine."

Devine showed him the pictures and video on his phone.

"What were you doing up there anyway?" asked Cowl, shaking his head.

"Seeing where Sara Ewes died. Then I heard you two going at it."

"So you didn't go up there to catch us in the act?"

"Not my intent, no," said Devine.

"But you *did* take the pics and the little film."

"Wouldn't you?"

Cowl said, "So, let me show you my hand. You killed Ewes."

"No, I didn't."

"Let me rephrase that. The evidence that I've seen is enough to convict your ass of murdering Sara."

"And that evidence is?"

"Video of you entering the building, *and* your security card showing you accessing the building and going up to the fifty-second floor in time to kill her."

"Both can be fudged, as you already conceded. And why haven't you turned that over to the police? Before, you said I had you to thank for that. What does that mean?"

"I haven't turned it over to the cops because we actually had a technical glitch."

Devine sat back. "I'm confused, Mr. Cowl. See, at that point I would have made a perfect patsy for the murder. Leaves Cowl and Comely unaffected. I knew Sara. I was a disgruntled employee, former military with maybe some PTSD baggage, look at the shiny object here and not over there. Police are off the premises. So what gives?"

"What gives is that I do not have to explain myself or my reasoning to you. So, in exchange for what's on your phone, the video of you and your entry log disappears. What do you say?"

"How can I possibly be sure you'll really do that?"

"And how can I know you don't have that stuff stashed in multiple places? At some point we have to trust each other."

"If that's the case, why exchange at all?"

"Mutual assured destruction. I was about to propose it myself. But there is no statute of limitations on murder. The video of me and Jenn shows up somewhere ten years from now, what I got is miraculously discovered and goes right to NYPD. And you go to Sing Sing or whatever place they have going at the time. And you never get out. Are we clear on all that?"

"Why do you care if anyone sees the pictures or video? You're not married. You're both consenting adults."

"It's the optics, Devine. I'm the head of a major investment house. I don't need that crap plastered over the trash press. Clients wouldn't like it. They'll think I'm reckless. They'll think I'm demeaning to women. And ladies run some of our biggest clients." He added in a growl, "And I talked to you before about that. Use your damn brain."

"Okay. Fair enough."

Cowl eyed him. "So, who killed Sara?"

"No clue. Did you have the same relationship with Sara you do with Jennifer?"

"Just like the last time you asked that, I'm not going to answer. But I will say that what Jenn and I have is . . . special."

Devine visualized them on the desk and tried hard not to laugh. "You mean like you have with Michelle Montgomery?"

"Michelle is short-term. She knows that. She's great to look at, great in the sack, and that's the extent of her repertoire. Jenn is different. Gorgeous, with the brains to match."

Devine felt his temper rising with these callous statements about Montgomery. He decided to change the subject. "Sara had an abortion."

He couldn't tell from Cowl's features whether he was aware of this or not.

"Well, I'm not the father," said Cowl.

"How can you know for sure?"

"A certain act has to take place for that to happen. It did not take place between Sara and me." He paused. "Not for lack of trying. She was like Jenn. Brainy, beautiful, but also aloof, played hard to get. She drove me nuts, but I could never land her."

*You really are a dick*, thought Devine.

Cowl finished off his brandy and rose. "Okay, we done here?"

Devine stood. "Done."

"Good, now get your ass back to work and make me some damn money, Devine."

# CHAPTER

# 39

DEVINE WAS LEAVING THE BUILDING for his meeting with Ellen and Fred Ewes when the woman hurried up to him. She had obviously been waiting outside for him to appear.

Rachel Potter looked fired up and itching for battle as she approached him, microphone in hand, while her beefy cameraman hovered behind her filming it all.

"Mr. Devine, Rachel Potter, Channel Forty-Four News. I understand that NYPD is investigating you in connection with the murder of Sara Ewes, a story I previously broke. Do you have a comment, Mr. Devine?"

"No." He pushed past her as people on the street gawked and started whispering.

Potter raced after him, the power pack on the back of her waist jiggling with the movements.

"Are you denying that you are a suspect in Sara Ewes's murder? Are you denying that you had a relationship of a sexual nature with her? Are you denying that you are the father of the child she aborted? Are you denying that you had a motive to kill her?"

It was like machine-gun fire, only with words.

Devine allowed this barrage to go on for a half block as more damaging and lurid statements in the form of questions that the woman never expected answers to rained down on him like explosives from carpet-bombing planes.

"Is this live?" he asked, suddenly whirling around so fast she bumped into him.

"Would it be a problem for you if it were?" she said in a simpering manner. She stuck the mic in his face. "So, talk to our viewers, Mr. Devine. Here's your chance. Tell us your side!"

"Okay, do *you* deny taking me *prisoner* in your news van while attempting to coerce me into giving you a scoop because you said you wanted to get away from shitty Channel Forty-Four and make it to the big-league single-digit stations?"

He stood there, and Potter stood there, her face shedding color like a landing plane did altitude, while the camera shot was jumping due to Beefy's trying hard not to bust a gut.

"How dare you make such an accusation!" she wailed.

"Took the words right out of my mouth, lady."

He turned and stalked off. This time Potter did not follow.

He dialed up an Uber and took it to Ewes's old home in Park Slope.

*Old home. It makes it sound like she's been gone for decades instead of days.*

Ellen Ewes answered his knock. She was dressed in jeans, a sleeveless white blouse, and sandals. The inside of the house was warm. It would be winter in New Zealand now, he thought. Maybe they were trying to take in as much heat as possible before heading back.

Fred Ewes was in the living room drinking what looked to be lemonade. He had on jeans, too, and a lavender polo shirt. He looked up absently at Devine. Ellen and Devine sat across from each other.

Ellen began: "The police have told us some things."

"Really, such as?"

"They traced the clinic that Sara used for the abortion."

"How did they do that?" asked Devine.

"I'm not sure. It was a place outside the city."

"Were the doctors able to provide any information to the police? Do they know who the father was?"

"No, at least not that they've told us."

Devine sat back, looking and feeling disappointed.

"If they had, would your name have come up?"

"Why would you ask that? Is it something Sara mentioned?"

"No, she was not very transparent with me on her relationships."

"I thought you two were close. You said you talked pretty much weekly."

Ellen looked uncomfortable with the question. "The fact is, Sara and I were estranged over the last year or so. She seemed to have changed."

"Changed? How so?"

"She was not the girl that I raised," replied Ellen.

"I don't understand."

"You don't have to. I just want to know if you could have been the father."

"Okay, do they know how far along Sara was?" asked Devine.

"Eight weeks. At least that's what we were told."

"And when did she have the procedure done?"

"In December," Ellen replied.

"Then I was not the father. I hadn't even met her at that point."

"But you had sex with her? Outside of marriage?"

"Is that the reason for the estrangement? Sara was having sex outside of marriage?"

"That is not how we raised her." She glanced at her husband. "Fred?"

He didn't look at her or Devine. He merely said, "Young people sometimes make...poor decisions."

Ellen rolled her eyes at this mild rebuke and shook her head. "Yes, *very* poor. She took the life of our grandchild, which is a mortal sin."

"I'm sure it must have been an incredibly difficult decision for her," said Devine.

"It shouldn't have been *her* decision at all," Ellen said heatedly.

He put up a hand. "I'm not going to get into all that with you right now. But she must have had a good reason. The woman I knew was kind and gentle."

Ellen exclaimed, "Then you obviously didn't know her. But, no, you *did* know her. You slept with her like the *slut* she was."

"How can you say that? She was your child," Devine snapped back. "She was a good person. And she didn't deserve to be murdered!"

"Neither did that poor, innocent baby."

Silence lingered for a few moments until Devine broke it. "Did anyone check Sara's social media accounts? I know she was on Instagram."

Fred said, "The police looked at all that and found nothing helpful. No pictures or references to current or past boyfriends."

"But that could mean nothing, since you weren't on any of it, Travis," noted Ellen sharply.

"Did the police tell you that specifically?"

She looked down and didn't answer.

"Did they ever find her diary?" asked Devine.

"They found nothing like that, as I told you before."

"How about on her electronics? Or in her personal cloud?"

"So were you two dating?" she asked.

"Relationships like that aren't allowed at Cowl and Comely," said Devine. "That gets you fired."

"You kept it secret, then?" persisted Ellen.

He ignored this. "Do you know the name of the doctor who performed the procedure on Sara?"

"Yes, why?"

"Can I have it?"

"You say you're not the father, so what does it matter to you?"

"It matters to me because a friend of mine, someone I cared about, was killed. I'd like to find out why and by whom."

Ellen looked at her husband. He pulled something from his jeans pocket and handed it across. It was a slip of paper. On it was a name and address of a clinic in Westchester.

"Thank you."

"I'll see you out," said Ellen.

They stood on the stoop for a moment. Ellen said, "I can see you do not approve of my beliefs."

"They're *your* beliefs, so I have to respect them."

"But not agree with them?"

"Like I said before, Ellen, this is really not the time or place to have that discussion. You have the absolute right to believe what you want, and so do I."

Her mouth suddenly twisted in disgust, but she wasn't looking at him, Devine observed. He looked over his shoulder to see two women on the pavement holding hands and kissing.

Devine turned back to her. The disgusted look was gone, but she said, "I can't wait to get the hell out of this town."

# CHAPTER

# 40

WELL, TWICE IN ONE DAY. What a lucky girl I am."

Michelle Montgomery had answered Devine's knock on the front door of her walk-up. She had taken off her business suit and wore faded, holey jean short-shorts, a white short-sleeved T-shirt, and no shoes. Her toenails were painted scarlet.

"Depends on how things turn out," he replied.

She ushered him inside, and he took in the space. Clean, uncluttered, minimal furniture, some decent artwork, colorful rugs on the hardwood floors, a couple pieces of what looked to be African sculpture, and the scent of reefer.

"Well, a couple more breaths and I'll be feeling quite mellow after my long day of toil at Cowl and Comely."

"I've got some good weed if you're interested."

"If you have some cold beer, I'd be very interested."

She got the beers and said, "Come on, I know where there's a breeze. The AC here isn't the best."

She led him up to the flat roof, where a couple of deck chairs were set up. He took off his jacket and loosened his tie. They sat and she pointed out a sliver between two buildings and said, "Water view. That apparently costs extra."

"And worth every penny. And so is that breeze." He turned his face and let tendrils of air slide over his skin as he drank his beer.

"How'd it go with Brad?"

"Surprisingly well. We reached a mutual understanding."

"I guess that's good for you, then."

"Good for us both. Hey, were you with Brad last Thursday night?"

"Thursday night?" She thought for a minute. "No. I was at his house, but he wasn't there. He probably was in the city."

*Maybe at the place where Sara died.*

"Do you know a Jennifer Stamos?"

"No."

"Okay. Chilton said you were family friends. Since I know his family dates to the *Mayflower* and his blue-blood family comes from money, I guessed you did, too. But then you mentioned staying in a student hostel in Italy."

"We're not blue bloods and my family's not rich. My father worked on the Chiltons' Rolls-Royces and Bentleys, and my mother cleaned their house and took care of their kids. I was the wild and fun daughter of the hired help who lived on the premises."

"Interesting. You have any siblings?"

"Two sisters. One younger and in college and thriving, and one older and married. To a doctor. And very happily."

"Good for them. Do they look like you?"

"I think my younger sister is better-looking than I am."

"Not what I meant, but that's hard to believe."

"Believe it. My older sister, Beth, is the one with the brains."

He thought back to the disparaging remarks Cowl had made about her. "I don't think you're too shabby in that department, Michelle."

"I couldn't even make it through college."

"You probably didn't want to be bored with all the cookie-cutter courses in return for a boatload of student debt. And you wanted to see the world, like you said. And look where it landed you."

She fingered her beer. "Yeah, I get paid to hang on the arm of a wealthy man and look wonderful. I like to think of it as living by my wits, but it's not really that." She looked down at herself.

"I need this. Brad is not interested in my brain, in case you hadn't noticed."

"Use what you have. Guys do it, why not girls?"

She glanced at him. "Guys do it in a very different way. And I like you more when you're less agreeable." She stared off. "My mother wanted me to be a model. Pushed me from an early age. All the auditions, shooting local commercials when I was six, this pageant, that pageant, teeth fixed, lessons on how to walk a certain way and talk a certain way. I never got to have a normal childhood. She got mad when I tried to do my schoolwork. She told me my strength, unlike my older sister's, was not my mind, but somewhat lower on my body. She was pissed off when I finally walked away from it all. Said I had betrayed her. Yeah, like it wasn't my life, but her little vicarious fantasy."

"My father rode me all the time, too. I was never good enough. Not like my brother and sister."

She said suddenly, "How about giving me a foot rub?" She put her feet up in his lap. A little surprised by this, he put his beer down and started rubbing her feet.

"You have very strong hands. And I can feel the calluses."

"What every guy wants to hear."

"I *am* saving up," she said abruptly. "Brad pays me and invests it for me. My portfolio is going gangbusters."

"Good for you. I've got like ten bucks in my account."

She took a sip of beer. "My goal is to retire when I'm thirty."

He started grinding away at her heels, applying lots of pressure.

"Oh my God, this is like heaven. You should charge for that."

"I just might, Miss Portfolio," he said. "And then what would you do after you *retire*?"

"Maybe go back to college. Learn something that doesn't require me to wear a bikini."

"Sounds like a plan."

"It has to be. When my looks go, it's over."

"Come on, don't sell yourself short. You seem damn astute to me, more than a lot of the so-called brainiacs I work with who can barely pack a lunch or cross the street safely."

"You're lying to make me feel better."

"I don't lie to make anyone feel better, including myself."

She put a hand on his arm. "But you want to have sex with me, right? I am the fantasy train girl, right?"

The further they went in this direction, the less he liked it. Was Cowl paying her to do this, as some sort of chess move in the battle between them?

"I'm not on the train now. I'm rubbing your incredibly tense feet and enjoying the four-inch Hudson River view. And you're flesh and blood, not a fantasy. And we're having a nice conversation that is heading to pretty deep waters for some reason I'm not sure about." He looked over at her. "And why would you want to have sex with *me*?"

She almost coughed up a mouthful of beer. "Okay, *that's* a first. No guy's ever asked me that before, especially when I've made the first move. I usually have to stop them from ripping my clothes off." She eyed him appraisingly. "You're a nice guy, or at least you seem to be. You're certainly different. You don't seem to care about what so many people care about in this city."

"Meaning money? Prestige?"

"All of that. It's a great town for culture and entertainment and I love the vibe, but it's also hypercompetitive. Whatever folks have, it's never enough. I hate that."

"You mean like Brad Cowl?" he said.

She finished her beer and stared dully out at the gap to the water. He picked up his beer and asked, "If you went back to college, what would you get a degree in?"

"People," she said slowly, drawing the two syllables out.

"So psychology, then?"

"No, I want to be a photographer. A picture can capture everything. No matter how much people lie to you, their true selves are always revealed in their pictures."

"Always, even when they know you're taking them?"

She looked at him. "Especially then, because they try so hard to hide who they really are, it comes out in some other way in their body language, their expression." She slipped her phone from her pocket. "Say cheese."

Montgomery took his picture and looked down at it.

"What do you see there?" he asked, mildly curious.

"A troubled man. But a good one. You have a lot on your mind."

"So, you think we'll get through all of it okay?" He didn't know why he was asking, but for some reason he wanted to know her answer.

"I don't know, Travis. I don't think anyone knows for sure. Especially us." She glanced over at him. "What would you do today if you knew tomorrow wasn't coming for you?"

"I'd go and see my father."

"Why? To make peace with him?"

The image of him and his father getting drunk the night they had celebrated Devine's getting the job at Cowl and Comely came into his head.

"No. I'd tell him to stay out of my life and let me run it the way I want to. And that I didn't want or care about his opinion of me anymore."

She stared at him for an uncomfortably long moment.

"What?" he finally said.

"That's pretty much exactly what I said to my mother."

# CHAPTER 41

DEVINE LEFT HER ON THE roof and hit the street once more. He had only gone about ten feet when he had an idea. He used his phone to look up the real estate records to see who owned Montgomery's building.

*Bingo.* It was owned by the good old Locust Group.

He put his phone away and was starting to walk toward the nearest subway station when two men approached from the shadows.

Detectives Shoemaker and Ekman.

They both looked grungier and even more pissed off than the last time. And that was saying something. Shoemaker took the cigarette out of his mouth and tapped it dead on the pavement with the heel of his shoe.

*He'd probably like to do the same to me*, mused Devine.

"So, are you following me now?" he asked. "I feel very special."

Neither man said anything.

"Found Detective Karl Hancock yet?"

"He doesn't exist," said Ekman.

"Tell me something I don't know."

"Because we think you made him up."

"And why would I do that?"

Ekman barked, "To make yourself look innocent. An alleged victim of some nutty conspiracy to throw us off the scent."

"Oh, right. And it worked so well. I mean, you guys spent, what, *minutes*, going down the rabbit hole because of it?"

Shoemaker said darkly, "Shut up with the smart mouth. Who were you visiting in that building?"

"It's got nothing to do with what you're looking into."

"We'll be the judge of that," snapped Ekman.

"No, you won't be."

"You think we're messing around here?" said Ekman, drawing so close Devine could smell his fuggy breath. "You think we screw around with murder investigations?"

"I think you're trying to do all you can to solve it. At least I hope you are. Have you checked the video feed? Examined the electronic entry log for the time in question? You have a time window you can fit your suspects in. I actually pointed all that out to Detective Hancock."

The only response was twin glares.

He looked at each of them. "Please tell me you've at least done that."

"There seems to be a little electronic hiccup," conceded Ekman.

*Oh, it's bigger than a little hiccup, Mr. Homicide Detective.*

"Okay. And in case you talk to her again, Mrs. Ewes asked me to meet with them tonight. I already have. She told me about your finding the abortion clinic." He glanced around, thinking. "But maybe you followed me here from Brooklyn."

"She shouldn't have told you anything."

"Did you explicitly tell her not to? Because I think with that lady, you give her any wiggle room and it's off to the races. Just my two cents."

When they didn't respond, he continued, "Now, here's something really relevant to the investigation. Will there be any DNA left in Sara's womb that you could match to whoever the father of her baby was?"

"Why?" asked Ekman.

"Because if you have any, I'll volunteer my DNA to clear me from the pack."

"You're only offering because you know there's nothing there."

"Are you sure? She *was* pregnant."

Ekman snapped, "And she aborted the fetus months ago. We'd get nothing admissible."

Shoemaker was watching Devine through slitted eyes. "And why do I think Mrs. Ewes told you how far along Sara was, and you knew you were in the clear on the window, even though you'd slept with her?"

"You make that sound like a bad thing."

"And now you're trying to play all innocent by offering up your DNA. You make me sick."

"Well, that was clearly not my intent. But if there's nothing else, I have a train to catch."

Shoemaker put a hand on his shoulder. "Do not, I repeat, do not leave the area."

"I already told you I wouldn't. Since you guys can't seem to catch Sara's killer, I guess I'll have to do the honors."

"If you obstruct this investigation in any way— " began Ekman.

"I was thinking more along the lines of *improving* it."

"You better watch yourself, Devine."

"Right. I hope you guys have a productive rest of the night. In case you want to follow me, I'll be on the Metro North out to Mount Kisco. If you could ever manage to find Karl Hancock, he could tell you all about that."

# CHAPTER

# 42

ON THE TRAIN HOME DEVINE looked out the window as they passed Cowl's place. He knew Montgomery wouldn't be there tonight, but he still found himself staring. Muscle memory, perhaps? Or something else? Part of him had wanted to sleep with her. He was a young, single guy after all, and she was beautiful and sexy and willing, and some things were just that simple. And it wasn't like he had sworn off sex while he was searching for Sara Ewes's killer.

*I hopped right into bed with Helen Speers, didn't I?*

But that one had been a long time building and she had walked up to him on the front porch and shared his beer and words were also exchanged and things came to a head when she made her feelings clear.

But still, he felt guilty for enjoying himself with Speers while Ewes lay dead.

By the time he had left Montgomery's place, the passion of the moment had passed and been replaced with something far more somber and intricate. They both had been lost in thought about their lives, past and future, as he took his leave.

*Whoever said life wasn't complicated had never really lived.*

Later, he walked home from the station and there was Valentine on the couch.

Devine sat down next to him and said, "I want you to see what you can dig up on the Locust Group. There are a lot of them out there, but the one I'm interested in is tied to some specific properties." He took out his phone and texted him the information.

"What is big deal about this Locust thing?" asked the Russian.

"I don't know, but their name keeps showing up. I'd like to know if Brad Cowl has ties to them."

"Okay. I get on it, dude. But at some point, you need to pay for this shit. I am not freebie, I am America capitalist."

"What's your rate?"

"Five hundred an hour. But for you, two-fifty."

Devine gaped. "Shit, if you make five hundred an hour, why are you living in this dump?"

"Is much better than my flat in Vladivostok. That had no door and no windows. Just blanket hung in doorway."

Devine walked upstairs, slipping off his tie and jacket as he did so. As he passed Speers's door it opened and there she was. She was not dressed in an alluring transparent nighty but in an NYU Law T-shirt and sweatpants. Over the woman's shoulder he saw a stack of legal tomes and bar study guides piled on her desk.

"What's up, Helen?"

"You haven't asked about a lawyer yet. Don't wait too long."

"Actually, can we talk about that?"

She held the door open wider and stepped back. "But just *talk*. I'm studying."

He held up his hands. "Don't worry, I won't let you have your way with me again."

She shut the door and sat in her chair while he perched on the bed. He recalled the sexual gymnastics that had taken place right here, the heat, the intensity, her soft skin...

"Travis!" she barked.

He looked up to see she had clearly just read his sorry-ass-guy mind. "Right. The cops have been by to see me again. They really think I'm guilty, but they have no evidence. They can't show I was there at the time in question."

"What about cameras, security card logs?"

"Apparently there was a hiccup, or so they said. There's nothing there."

"Damn, that's incredible."

"I know. But are there other ways for them to come after me?"

"Why? Were you involved in her death?"

"I was not in any way, Helen, I'm telling you the truth. Why would I be out there busting my ass to find out who did kill her, if I'd been the one to do it?"

"Well, to make it appear as if you're innocent."

He knew she was right and it still pissed him off. "Well, I *am* innocent." He hesitated.

"But what?" she said in a prompting manner.

"But I did have a relationship with her. We kept it secret because of the fraternization rules at Cowl."

"Did you sleep with her?"

He took a moment to process this and form a response. "Yes. But only once."

"Could you have been the father of the child she terminated? Because that would be a prime motive."

"How did you know about that?"

"It's all over the news."

"No, I wasn't the father."

"How can you be sure?"

"She had the abortion in December. I started at Cowl in early February. I didn't even meet Sara until then."

"But do you have proof of that?" she said.

"How do you prove a negative?"

"You can't, not in court, which means it's irrelevant as a defense."

Devine flopped back on the bed. "Great."

She sat down next to him and patted his shoulder. "But it sounds like the cops can't tie you to the murder forensically."

He sat up and looked at her. "Not for lack of trying. And they might find another way."

"Has anyone looked at a motive for someone killing her?" she asked.

"Just the pregnancy angle, I think. They seem to believe no one else in the whole world ever had sex with the woman other than me. And there's something else."

"What?"

"You can't tell anybody."

"I'm going to be a lawyer. If I can't keep confidences, I won't have a very long career."

"I hacked into the firm's security log entry system. The only card logged in during the time in question was... mine."

She looked at him stoically, her gaze piercing.

"I wasn't there, Helen. I swear." He held up his security card. "And ask Will, he says it's easy to clone one of these suckers. Even his little *bay-bee* cousin could do it, he says."

"Go on."

"Brad Cowl told me that he knew about my card being on the security log and also that there was video of me entering the lobby at the same time. But that can be faked, too."

"But then this hiccup you mentioned happened?"

"Cowl basically told the cops the system went down. There's no evidence to give them. He made that happen."

"Why would he do that?"

He reluctantly told her about the pictures and video he had taken of Cowl and Stamos after they'd had sex.

"So you basically blackmailed the guy into not throwing the cops enough dirt to arrest you?"

He looked at her with an air of desperation. "I know it doesn't look good, but the evidence was made up. I didn't do it. I had to fight fire with fire."

"No, it *doesn't* look good. But have you considered another possibility?"

"Like what?"

"That Cowl doctored the evidence to incriminate you."

"But then why not use it?" Then it all hit Devine. "Of course. He basically told me why."

"Right. You turned the tables on him with *your* dirt before he could pull the trigger and throw you to the cops, so he had to change plans and stonewall NYPD."

"He bought a company recently that can manipulate any video. Before he knew about the dirt I had on him, he basically said he wanted to get the cops off his case by framing me."

Surprisingly, Speers was shaking her head.

"*What?*" he said.

"Have you considered the possibility that there might be video and entry log evidence of *Cowl* being in the building when the woman was killed? If so, he would definitely take steps to erase it. Then he would have the video doctored, maybe using this company he bought, and there you would be instead."

Devine looked both intrigued by and wary of this theory. "And his motive?"

"*He* might have been the father of her baby. And he might have known about her abortion and decided to use that against you, because he might have found out about you and Sara having had sex. Which means, if I'm right, that he could have ended up playing you *and* the cops."

Devine once more slumped back on the bed. In a hollow tone he said, "Meaning I did a deal with him to avoid being charged with Sara's death, even though I'm innocent? And in putting together that deal, he might have destroyed the real evidence of his guilt and just gotten away with her murder?"

"What a smart boy you are."

# CHAPTER 43

As he was heading to his room, Jill Tapshaw called out to Devine from her doorway. She was dressed up, her hair was styled, and she had on makeup, all a rarity for her.

"You going out?" he asked, walking over to her.

"No, I've already *been* out. I had a meeting with Christian Chilton from Mayflower Enterprises. He came out to Mount Kisco. We met at a fancy restaurant in town. He bought the meal and everything. And he had two associates with him."

"What'd you think?"

"He's very professional, stylish, expensive suit. His haircut cost more than my dress. But his face was bruised and swollen; he must have hit it on something very hard."

*Yes, he did*, thought Devine. "How did it go?"

"They're very interested in Hummingbird. We're sending them our current slide deck and updated financials. I could tell from what he said that they have a ton of capital and not many viable places to put it. That's a problem for a lot of investment firms these days. There are lots of shitty companies out there begging for money."

"Well, you're not a shitty company, you're the real deal. And don't forget what I told you about valuation."

"Don't worry. I'm going to *quadruple* rather than triple it. That way we can back off to look like we're giving something up and still get to three-*x* of what we had hoped for."

"There you go, thinking like a Harvard MBA again."

"But I wanted to thank you for what you did. This could really be the turning point for Hummingbird."

"What I did was nothing compared to what you've done, Jill. If Hummingbird blasts off, it'll be because of you and no one else."

"You know, you might want to register on our platform. There are legions of wonderful ladies looking for someone like you."

"Maybe I will. Hey, any luck with the email I forwarded to you?"

"I'm through about three layers of obstruction. I can see why Will was having trouble, but I'll keep working on it. I see it now as a cool challenge."

"Thanks."

"So, they haven't found out what happened to Sara Ewes?"

"No, not yet. I met her parents. They came in from New Zealand. They're staying at her place for now."

"I'm sure they're devastated."

"Maybe the father is."

Tapshaw frowned. "What do you mean? And her mother's not?"

"She's a piece of work, actually. Turns out Sara was pregnant but she terminated it. Her mother accused her of being a slut and of murdering her child."

"That's awful."

"And no surprise, her mother and Sara were estranged. She said Sara had changed over the last year. So I'm not sure she cares all that much about her daughter's being dead. And they're missionaries, teaching Christianity in New Zealand."

"They should try *teaching* themselves to be nice to other people."

"But you're trying to make the world a happier place," said Devine. "So just keep doing what you're doing."

She pecked him on the cheek and went into her room and closed the door. He was about to go to his room when he heard the doorbell ring. He looked at his watch.

*What now?*

He hustled down the stairs to find Valentine at the open door staring at…Jennifer Stamos.

# CHAPTER 44

VALENTINE TURNED TO LOOK AT Devine. "It's for you, Travis."

"Thanks."

Valentine walked off and Stamos looked nervously at him. "Surprised?"

"Yeah, I am. Everything okay?"

"Can we talk?"

He looked around. "Out on the front porch is the most private. I've got three roommates."

"Okay. But what about the people living in the places next to you?"

"They're empty. Being renovated by the owner."

"Okay."

"You want a beer or something?"

"No, I'm good."

He closed the door behind him, and they sat side by side on the brick steps.

She had on shorts and a sleeveless blouse and sandals. The temperature was still around eighty and humid. She looked at his clothes and said, "Did you just get home?"

"I had a few errands to do after work."

"Is this a bad time?"

"No, it's fine. Did you take the train out here?"

"No, I took that Zipcar parked over there. It's silly to keep a vehicle in the city."

Devine looked at the green Prius. "Agreed. And you got my address from...?"

She looked embarrassed. "From the personnel office."

"Didn't think they gave that info out."

"They normally don't. Look, I'm sorry. I just wanted—"

"It's okay, Jennifer. Fire away."

He knew why she was here. He just wanted her to know this was not going to go all her way, or easily.

"I spoke with...Brad."

"And he told you that we met?"

"Yes. It seems that everything is resolved."

"Nothing is resolved."

She looked startled. "What? But I thought—"

"*That* part is fine. But we still have no idea who killed Sara. It wasn't me. Do you know where Cowl was when Sara was killed?"

Stamos shrank back from the question. "You can't possibly think that—"

"Well, people certainly thought that *I* might have killed her. And he told me he wanted to have sex with her, but it was a no-go on her end and that probably pissed him off. I'm telling you this in good faith. If you run to Cowl and tell him I told you, things will get complicated really fast."

"I won't do that, I swear."

He looked at her, trying to gauge her sincerity. "Did you know that Sara had her abortion back in December? That was before I even got to the firm."

"Why is that important?"

"Because some people were trying to make out that I was the father of her child."

"That's crazy." She paused. "But *did* you sleep with her?"

"I'm not going to answer that. Do you know where Cowl was when Sara was killed?"

"No, I wasn't with him that night." She suddenly scowled at him. "I understand you took pictures of Brad and me..."

"Don't get all pissed off, Jennifer. I needed some leverage. And what the hell were you thinking doing it out in the open like that? He has a damn penthouse with a bed!"

"He... just grabbed me, said it would be exciting. It all happened so fast." Her cheeks flushed. "Will you erase the pictures?"

"No, but I'll never look at them again."

"How can I believe that?"

"Believe it. I did not find it the least bit pleasant. I don't just mean with what happened to Sara. I mean it seemed pretty damn degrading... to you."

She flushed again. "That's *my* business."

"Yes, it is. But why exactly are you screwing the boss? You have the talent to make it on your own. This isn't nineteen eighty."

"Do you really think things have changed that much, Travis?"

"I don't know. I'm not a woman."

"That's right, you're not. So *don't* judge me," she added sharply. "And for your information, there are only three female partners in the entire firm. I know two dozen more who lost out to guys who weren't half as good, according to the damn *Book*. So take your eighties comment and shove it."

"Okay, okay, I guess I deserved that. But the thing is, Sara wouldn't sleep with him, or so Cowl complained to me. Do you think that's a motive for him to kill her?"

"Come on, he could have pretty much any woman he wanted."

"But the woman he apparently wanted was *Sara* and she was having no part of it. That might have pissed him off."

"You just won't let that go, will you?"

"The guy, as far as I know, has no alibi for when she was murdered. And maybe he lied to me. Maybe they *did* sleep together. And she got pregnant and the child was his. And maybe he paid to have it aborted, and she regretted it and was going to expose what had happened. The boss impregnating the help and then paying for her abortion? Do you know how much money Cowl gets from church and state pension funds and teachers' unions and other organizations that would frown on that sort of thing?"

"He wasn't the father."

He stared warily at her. "How do you know that?"

"I just do."

"How?" Devine persisted.

"Sara told me."

"Why would she do that? You weren't close friends."

"We...we were closer than I let on."

"Wait a minute. If that's true, did she tell you the real reason why she was interested in the play *Waiting for Godot*?"

"I don't know."

"What the hell do you mean you don't know? Either you do or you don't."

"She was worried about something. But she wouldn't fully confide in me. I think she was scared. I told you that before. And she didn't want to involve me. I think she was protecting me."

Devine studied her. He said slowly, "It sounds like you and Sara were way more than friends."

"Sara and I—"

"Sara and you what?"

"I...I can't—"

Devine was out of patience. "For God's sake. Sara is dead! Just fucking tell me!"

She drew in a long, tortured breath and then let it go. "We...we were in love. Okay! We were in love. Satisfied, asshole?"

She jumped up, hurried over to the Prius, started it up, and drove off.

Devine just sat there and watched Stamos disappear into the dark.

He finally went back inside, where Valentine said, "Damn, she is so hot. Are you doing her?"

"Just shut up, Will. Just shut the hell up."

Devine, his mind reeling, walked upstairs to his room and slammed the door.

# CHAPTER

# 45

FOUR FIFTEEN A.M.

Ten minutes into his workout at the high school. Warm, muggy, dark, cloudy skies, sprinkles of a predawn summer rain commencing.

Devine was already loosened up, sweaty, into a rhythm, trying to focus on his physical side, while his mental side was all over the place. There was simply too much to process. And whenever that happened to him, he had focused back on the basics. Take one step, figure it out, and go on to the next step. And the one after that. At some point it would start to make sense.

*At least I hope to God it will.*

It was then that the three men stepped from the outer rim of the darkness and blew up all his thoughtful plans. However, Devine had heard them coming and moved forward to confront them.

"Why, if it isn't Detective Karl Hancock of NYPD, where no one knows your name."

He looked at the other two men, carbon copies of Hancock, only white.

Hancock nodded. "Surprised it lasted as long as it did. You talked to them and told them about me and they went batshit, am I right?"

"Something like that."

Devine looked at the other two guys as the rain started to fall. Remorseless bastards paid to do harm. He had seen enough of such men. They all pretty much looked the same. Zombies with guns.

Hancock took some gum from his pocket, popped it into his mouth, and started to chew it. His jacket was open. The Glock was there. They were all armed, Devine was sure of that. All he had was himself and whatever he could find to defend himself. He was pretty sure it would be enough. They had already made one cardinal mistake.

*They didn't kill me right away.*

"Care to explain the subterfuge?" said Devine.

Hancock cracked a smile. "*Subterfuge*. Now there's a word you don't hear every day."

"Seems the only one to fit, at least to me."

Devine moved slowly to his left, an inch at a time, while not appearing to move at all.

"Who are you, Devine, really?"

"I can ask you the same thing."

"You have upset some serious folks. They don't like to be upset. That's why they bring in guys like me."

"I'm not sure what I've done to deserve the attention."

"Not being square with me was part of it. Military dude, now trying to make it in the investment world? What kind of bullshit is that?"

"I can't spend the rest of my life getting shot at."

"But see, you've also been playing detective, asking questions. Getting involved in shit you shouldn't be. That bothers people greatly."

"Well, you've been doing the same. And it bothers me greatly, too. And Sara was my friend. I was naturally curious as to who killed her. But I did a deal with the head guy. It's all good. Your services are no longer needed."

"I seriously doubt that."

That was a slip on Hancock's part. He had just divulged something very important.

*Now if I can just survive this encounter to use it.*

"Care to explain that?"

"We didn't come here to chitchat, Devine. And thanks, by the way, for telling me your workout schedule and where."

"Yeah, I didn't know you were a dirtbag back then."

"Not a dirtbag, just a workingman, like you. And who do you work for, Devine, really? You don't want to be where you are, clear to see. You're there because someone put you there. Tell us who, and we go on our way."

"And leave me for the high school football coach to find on the fifty-yard line with a bullet in my brain?"

"We won't leave you here. We're a class act. We do things right. There's a lake not that far from here. You won't feel a thing, swear to God."

Devine had now moved, in total, nine inches to his right, without, in the poor light, seeming to have moved at all. It was like an optical illusion, and these guys had bought into it, slightly moving along with him to keep their relative positions the same and not even realizing they were doing it. It was like planets revolving around each other; so long as the distance and angle were the same you never focused on the actual movement. He had been taught this in close-quarter combat drills in the Army. And it was as true now as it had been then.

And they were overconfident, cocky because they outnumbered him; that was what separated guys like them from guys like him.

"We need information. If we have to beat it out of you first, we will."

"There's only three of you, so how will you manage that?"

"Army Ranger speaking?" said a grinning Hancock. "All badass, right? If you're faster than a bullet, kudos to you. So, last chance: Who are you and why are you at Cowl and Comely?"

Devine moved another half inch until he felt the tire against his ankle. "I love capitalism, guys, just like you."

"I don't want to kill you, but orders are orders."

"And who's giving the orders?"

Hancock shook his head.

"Come on, Hancock or whatever the hell your name is. It's not like I'll be telling anybody. I'm heading for that nice little lake, right?"

"I can tell you that what this involves goes way beyond anything you can imagine. Sounds like a cliché from some lousy movie, I know. But in this case, it happens to be true. See, actually the real world is way more complicated and dangerous than how the movies and TV make it out to be."

"Thanks for telling me basically squat."

"It's nothing personal. But this is how I put food into my family's mouths. So nobody's messing with that."

"Just be prepared to deal with the consequences," replied Devine as he tensed and bent slightly at the waist.

"Okay, we're done." Hancock looked down and pulled out his pistol just about the time the car tire hit him in the head, knocking him heels over ass.

The second tire flung by Devine slammed into the man next to Hancock and down he went, too.

The third man had his gun pointed right at Devine and was about to fire. The third guy had always been Devine's worry bead.

*Shit.*

Then a loud crack sounded somewhere. The gunman whirled around to see what had caused it, giving Devine time to hit him at gut level. They went tumbling and the gun spun off into the darkness. As the men fought, Devine gripped the man's throat, placed his rebar-strong thumb against the left carotid, and at the same time pressed his index finger dead center of the throat. He crushed the carotid with his thumb and used his index finger to rupture the trachea. The man stopped struggling and went limp.

Next moment, Devine was up and sprinting flat-out. As he passed by Hancock, who was trying to stand, Devine kicked him in the head, sending him hard back to the dirt, grunting in pain.

Devine jumped the waist-high fence and hit the ground running on the other side. As shots rang out, he zigzagged his way over and then in between two buildings, kicked it into high gear, and got free of the men's sight lines. He made it back to his town house and called 911, telling the dispatcher what had happened. It was only then that he noticed he'd been wounded. The guy he killed must have had a knife, too, because Devine had a slash across one arm and a deeper cut in the palm of his hand. The loud noise, probably a car backfiring, had saved his ass. He cleaned and dressed the wounds and changed his clothes by the time the cops showed up.

They had checked out the football field first before heading over, the head cop told him.

"Nobody there now," the cop said. "Dispatch said you thought you'd hurt one of them bad or maybe killed them, but you must've been mistaken. But we found some shell casings and some blood. You're damn lucky, buddy. What the hell were you doing out there alone at that time? I mean, this is a pretty safe area, but you were just asking for it."

*Yeah, I was really asking for it*, thought Devine.

# CHAPTER 46

6:20.

The train bumped out of the station with Devine in his normal seat staring out the same window at the same countryside.

He didn't expect to see Michelle Montgomery, and thus was surprised when she was sitting by the pool in her itty-bitty bikini staring at the water like it was the most mesmerizing thing ever conceived. She didn't look up once at the train. She didn't flip them off, or—to the chagrin of all the guys with their faces pressed to the glass—show her thonged butt, or better yet, strip to her birthday suit and take the plunge.

Only as the train started to gather speed, did the woman look up…and wave.

Pretty much every man on the train car waved back. Except Devine. Ironic, since he was pretty sure he was the one she was waving to.

And then Montgomery was gone from sight as the train sped up.

Devine sat back against his seat. He figured she was appearing more routinely because he was on the train and would be watching her. Devine wasn't sure how he felt about that. He was investigating Cowl and she was Cowl's girl. That was going to get really complicated really fast.

He took out his phone and sent a text to Emerson Campbell to arrange a meeting that day. Next, he looked at the slip of paper that Fred Ewes had given him, with the information on the clinic that had been involved with Sara's abortion. He doubted they would tell him anything over the phone. But they might if he went to the clinic. He had to try. He checked the train schedule on his phone and calculated the logistics.

He next thought about the man he had killed that morning, glancing down at his big, strong fingers, which had done the deed. He rubbed the bandage across his palm and felt the one under his shirtsleeve.

*Don't feel anything, Devine, not remorse, and sure as hell not guilt, because it was either him or me.*

Maybe he had a family who would miss and mourn him when he didn't show up. But he'd made the decision, not Devine.

He made fists with his killer hands and hid them in his pockets.

The 6:20 moved on and took a reluctant rider with it.

* * *

It was lunchtime and Devine didn't head to the dining hall to hobnob with the exalted of Cowl and Comely. He headed north, to the Fifties. To the little Italian restaurant that was apparently never open to the public.

Campbell sat in the same room, in the same chair, but wearing a different set of clothes. A bowl of spaghetti and a bottle of wicker-bottomed Chianti was in front of him next to a half-full glass of wine. A large napkin was tucked into his shirt. He did not look up from his food.

"I had to kill a man this morning," said Devine.

This news did not startle or disturb the old soldier. Campbell took a mouthful of pasta and a sip of wine.

"Explain in fuller detail."

Devine did so and added, "I don't think Cowl is at the top of the pyramid on this."

"I never thought he was. He's a means to an end who is paid a king's ransom."

"Care to elaborate?"

"I wish I could. But I don't really know more than that."

"Hancock also knew I was an Army Ranger. He knew that the first time he saw me."

"Your military service is not a secret."

"I still don't like it."

Campbell finished the wine and pushed his plate of food, only half eaten, away. "I don't actually like pasta." He wiped his mouth.

"They wanted to know who I really was, and why I was at Cowl and Comely. That cuts very close to the bone. You need to be concerned about *that*."

Campbell poured some more Chianti. "I will make inquiries. What else?"

"Sara Ewes and Jennifer Stamos were a couple, at least according to Stamos. And she said she knew Cowl wasn't the father of Ewes's baby, which makes me believe she knows who the father is."

"And that man might be Brad Cowl?"

"He has no alibi for the time she was killed," said Devine.

"Does this tie into what might be going on at the firm? Which *is* your mission, after all."

"Ewes came to Stamos and told her about the *Godot* play. To check it out. I did and found nothing, but now that I know they were more than friends, there has to be something there. And it has to tie into Cowl. And then there's Area 51." Devine quickly explained about the inaccessible floor. "It's not their high-frequency trading center, like I thought. That's in Queens. I had a buddy check that."

"A buddy?" said Campbell, a look of alarm on his face.

"He has no idea about any of this. He's a white-hatter, hacks for a living."

"We had heard of the off-limits floor there from another

source. But we also assumed it was just the high-frequency trading space. But now that we know it's not, you need to get in there."

"I'm working right now on a way to access it."

Campbell leaned forward. "Have you figured out how you can?"

"I think so. But I need your help. That's the other reason I'm here."

# CHAPTER

# 47

After meeting with Campbell, Devine rode the train to Westchester and took a cab to the abortion clinic. There were protestors out front with graphic pictures on posterboards. They were marching and chanting.

One man confronted Devine and wanted to know if he was the father of a baby being butchered inside the "chamber of horrors," as he termed it.

"No," said Devine as he hurried past the man and rang the bell on the front door of the clinic. It was barred and armored and had a surveillance camera mounted in the corner.

A voice coming over a callbox said, "Yes?"

"Travis Devine. I phoned earlier. I spoke with a Dr. Tillis?"

"ID?"

He held up his driver's license.

"Just a moment."

He waited, glancing back at the protestors, who had to keep their distance per the law.

He heard the door buzz, and he pulled it open and shut it firmly behind him.

There was an armed guard in the small foyer, who looked at Devine suspiciously as he told him to walk through a magnetometer, then wanded and patted him down.

A woman in her forties in hospital scrubs met him in the foyer a few moments after that.

"This way," she said.

He was deposited in a tiny, drab room, where he supposed women came to consult about having an abortion. Devine knew that this particular subject would be one in which no general consensus would ever be reached. But he could imagine people sitting here and making perhaps the most momentous and gut-wrenching decision of their lives.

A woman in her fifties walked in. She was in a dark blue dress with a long white lab coat over it; she had let her hair go gray and it hung limply to her shoulders. She had rimless glasses on a chain around her neck. Her eyes were blue and alert, and her manner efficient and professional. She introduced herself as Dr. Cynthia Tillis.

"The police have already been by, as I told you over the phone, Mr. Devine. I conveyed to them what I was legally allowed to tell and nothing more. I believe they will come back with a subpoena to compel more information and I will have to deal with that then."

"I understand."

"But I can't really tell you anything. The police at least are trying to find out who killed Sara. I only agreed to see you because the fact of Sara's abortion has now come out in the press, and you said you were a friend of hers."

"How did she come to this clinic?"

"Sara said she had been referred by someone; she didn't give a name. We went through everything, and the decision was made on the best way to move forward."

"And she never mentioned who the father might be?"

"Even if she did, I could not provide that information."

"Is that what you told the police?"

"Please, Mr. Devine."

"Okay, did she say *why* she was having an abortion?"

"I can't divulge that either."

He looked at some pictures on the wall with accompanying medical terms. "Can you tell me how it was done?"

She began carefully, "I can *generally* tell you our range of procedures. Up to eleven weeks is deemed the embryonic period. Up to that point the abortion can be done by what is called medication abortion."

"A pill, you mean?"

"Yes. And in that event, there may be a follow-up appointment within one to two weeks to ensure the pregnancy is terminated and the patient is well. If the woman's last menstrual cycle was more than eleven weeks ago, an in-clinic abortion may be required. That would have to be performed here."

"I was told she was only eight weeks along, so Sara could have just done it with a pill?"

"She could have," said Tillis vaguely. "About forty percent of clinic-managed pregnancy terminations are done that way."

Devine thought quickly and something occurred to him. "Do you know who her ob-gyn was?"

"I'm afraid that—"

"Look, I know that HIPAA doesn't allow you to tell me anything about her personal medical history, but I'm just asking for the name of her doctor. I don't think there's any law that says you can't tell me that."

"And what will you do with that information? Go and talk to the person?"

"Probably, and they won't tell me anything they're not legally supposed to. I just wanted to know about, well, her pregnancy. Why she ended it. Her ob-gyn might know."

"I take it you knew her well?"

"We worked together. We were friends, as I told you on the phone. I'm very sorry she's gone."

"I can understand that." Tillis tapped her fingernails on the desk and then looked at something on her phone for a few moments. "The name Sara provided was a Dr. John Wyman." She gave him the man's contact information.

"Thank you very much. Was Sara alone when she came here?"

"I won't get into that. But if the person is undergoing a medical procedure they need someone to be with them. With medication abortion, they normally don't. It can be done at home, and often is."

"It must have been a very hard decision for her."

"For every patient I see it is, and Sara was no exception."

"Her parents are in from New Zealand. Have you talked to them?"

"No, I've had no contact from them. Why do you ask?"

"Sara's mother was the one who told me about your clinic. That's how I knew to contact you."

"She must have gotten that from someone else, the police perhaps."

"That's right, she did mention that."

"Do the police have any leads as to who killed Sara?"

"Not that they're sharing with me."

She looked at him closely. "I don't necessarily expect you to answer this, but were you the father?"

"No, I wasn't. But I guess I could have been, if things had turned out differently."

Tillis did not seem to know how to take this. To Devine she seemed a bit alarmed, and he suddenly wondered if he had really stepped in it again. She might call the police the second after he left.

"I didn't even know she was pregnant until after she was killed," he said. "Nobody did, apparently."

"She wouldn't have been visibly showing at that stage. Many women don't even know they're pregnant at that point."

"She was very nice. A good person. When everyone at the firm found out what had happened, we were all rocked. It just didn't seem possible."

"I can see that. Do you have any idea who could have done it?"

"No. But I hope to find out."

She looked alarmed again. "I think that is better left to the police."

"You'd think, wouldn't you? Only it might be more complicated than that."

# CHAPTER 48

ON THE TRAIN BACK TO the city Devine called Dr. Wyman's office with a request to speak to him about Ewes.

However, he was told that Wyman was not available. Devine then left his name and number and asked if the doctor could contact him when he had the chance and that it was important. The receptionist said she would pass along the information and then she hung up.

*Okay, so much for that.*

He got off the subway at Broadway and walked until he reached the Lombard Theater. *Godot* was still playing for the next week or so. He walked around the front of the building and took in the marquee, the ticket office, the stanchions, and the people scurrying around.

Ewes had been interested in this play for some reason. She had walked into Jennifer Stamos's office and told her to go see it. Now that Stamos had told him that she and Ewes were in love, her confiding in Stamos made sense. But the more he thought about it, the more Devine was convinced that Ewes had told Stamos more. He didn't believe Stamos's explanation that Ewes was trying to protect her by keeping her in the dark. If Ewes had told Stamos to check out the Lombard Theater, he was sure she would have told her lover why.

Then something occurred to Devine, and he groaned, chastising himself for not thinking of it earlier. He took out his phone, did a Google search, and found his answer.

The Lombard Theater was owned by...the Locust Group. Ewes's interest had nothing to do with the play. It had everything to do with the property. The nicely rehabbed property.

Christian Chilton's property on the Upper East Side—the Locust Group. Montgomery's walk-up—the Locust Group. The Lombard Theater—the Locust Group.

He looked up and down the street. What else did the Locust Group own? And what was the connection to Cowl and Comely? He had told Campbell that he had thought of a way to get inside Area 51. Maybe the answers to his questions would be found there.

During their meeting at the restaurant, Devine had made a request to Campbell for some equipment he would need. Then he looked on his phone and found the nearest Apple Store for the other item he required.

Later, back at his cubicle, Devine took out his phone and texted a message to the same number from which he had received the summons to meet with Brad Cowl.

A problem has come up. We need to discuss tonight.

His thumb hovered over the Send key, then he pressed it and put his phone away. He spent the rest of the day laboring over work that he couldn't have cared less about. All around him the other Burners were going full bore, analyzing data from all four corners of the earth. Every dollar to be made, every dollar to be paid, every dollar to be lost. That was, ultimately, what it was all about. As he had heard Brad Cowl say in an interview with CNBC once:

"The first billion is the hardest to make. After that, it gets a lot easier."

*I'm sure it does, asshole.*

At seven that evening, when he was looking at his phone clock and thinking about leaving, the text came in:

Same place, same process. Nine o'clock.

*Smart guy*, thought Devine. *He wants me to work overtime just for the honor of meeting him.* But then again, no Burner got paid overtime. The only one who made money off that extra work was the firm of Cowl and Comely. But he was glad it was later, because he hadn't gotten the item he needed from Campbell yet. It was supposed to have arrived by now. Without that, his plan was dead. A bead of sweat appeared on his forehead. Now he had to confirm something else. Again, without it, his plan was useless. Normally he would have all his ducks in a row before executing a strategy. But here it wasn't possible. It was a classic chicken-and-egg problem.

He texted Michelle Montgomery and asked her to let him know if she would be once more escorting him to his meeting with Cowl.

*Come on, come on. Please.*

Ten minutes later he got an affirmative on that from her.

He felt tremendous relief. Without her his plan had no chance of working. It still might not have a chance, depending on how good or bad his powers of persuasion were.

Next, he googled the name Anne Comely. He had done this before and found nothing. The result this time was the same. Even Emerson Campbell and his people could find nothing on the woman.

He then googled Bradley Cowl and found about ten billion results. Maybe one for each dollar the man had.

He sat back and thought about this. Morgan and Stanley. Plenty of stuff on both people, now long dead. Same for Merrill and Lynch. The defunct Lehman Brothers, the same. J. P. Morgan was a real guy. E. F. Hutton as well. Hell, even Harley and Davidson, if you ventured outside the financial world.

But Cowl and Comely, apparently not so much. And he doubted he was the first person to wonder about that. He did another search focused more on that inquiry and found a video from six years ago that Cowl had done with the *Wall Street Journal*. The reporter had asked Cowl about his "partner."

Cowl's response had been interesting. Without directly addressing the question, he had said, "Partnerships can be of many different varieties. It can simply be an idea or a perspective."

When the journalist had asked him point-blank if Anne Comely existed and, if so, where and who she was, Cowl had terminated the interview.

As the video ended, Devine thought he could see just the barest of smiles on Cowl's features.

At seven fifty, Devine finally received a text from Campbell.

*Thank you, Jesus.*

He left the building, walked around the corner, and passed a man who had just left a paper bag on a stone wall. Devine gripped the bag as he walked by and looked inside it. The object was small and wafer thin. He surreptitiously palmed it, then threw the bag in the trash and bent down as if to tie his shoe. He slipped the device into his sock and pushed it down until it rested inside his shoe.

He had no formal training as a spy, but he had spent years as a soldier in the Middle East. And those wars weren't just about carrying guns and shooting at the enemy. They had been about gathering information, getting Afghans and Iraqis in villages and towns and cities and deserts to trust him and provide intelligence. And he had participated in a number of info drops where he knew he was being watched and had to carry it off in a way that would not cause harm to him, or death to his informants.

He returned to work, feeling better about things.

At 8:58, the door opened and there stood Willard Paulson. He motioned to Devine, who put on his jacket, grabbed his briefcase, and waved to the remaining Burners. Two of them, a man and a woman, looked up at him curiously. He'd had beers and meals with them, not many, but a few. They had vented about Cowl and Comely, about the oppressive workload, the ungodly competitiveness abounding in this building, and the insecurities they all possessed about not being good enough to make the cut.

And yet he knew little about their personal lives, and they knew next to nothing about his. It was just that way here. As a soldier, he had known pretty much every personal detail of the men and women with whom he served. It was just a totally different reality on Wall Street, where literal walls were set up everywhere.

*And I hope to breach a big one tonight.*

CHAPTER

# 49

MONTGOMERY MET HIM AT THE elevator and Paulson left them. She was dressed all in black, as though she were in mourning. Devine hoped it wasn't for him, and he suddenly began feeling some nagging doubts about the woman. But he had a mission to perform and he had to get started.

He glanced at the pot of gold in her hand. Here was the whole ball game. He drew a deep breath and said, "Um, Michelle?"

"Yes?"

"Can you help me do something?" He hadn't asked her this in the text. This was something he needed to do face-to-face. Like Cowl had said. *Analog.*

"What?"

He took the iPhone he'd bought that day and held it up. It was the same model as Cowl's, with the same gold cover. And he had made the screen saver the exact same image of the blue Bugatti Chiron. He also had the same icons showing, using the screenshot he'd taken previously of Cowl's phone as a guide. He had also signed up with the same phone carrier so it would have that name and network bars showing.

"I don't understand," she said, glancing at it.

"I need that phone, just for a few minutes. And you can give Cowl this one while I have his."

She paled and drew back. "What the hell! Are you crazy? *No!*"

"I am a little bit crazy, I guess. But some men tried to kill me early this morning. And it had to do with something going on here."

She just gaped. "Someone tried to kill you this morning? Do you really expect me to—"

He took the bandage off his hand and held it up. "I didn't cut that on a soup can." He took off his jacket, rolled up his sleeve, and showed her the wound there.

"Oh my God, did you call the police?"

"Yeah, and the guys were long gone by the time they got there."

"How do you know it has anything to do with Brad's firm?"

"From things the guy said. He might be freelance, I don't know."

"Freelance?"

"*Mercenary* might be a more recognizable term."

"What the hell are you mixed up in, Travis?"

"The question is what the hell is *Brad Cowl* mixed up in. And that's why I need his phone."

She looked down at Cowl's phone like it was a cobra about to strike her.

"Please, Michelle, it might have to do with Sara's murder, too."

She looked visibly distressed. "What are you going to do with it?"

"I'm going to get into a place in this building I can't get into without it. At least I hope it's the golden key. If it's not, there's no harm done."

"And what are you going to do once you get in there?"

"Just look around. I promise. I won't take anything."

"If you're lying to me—"

"I'm not lying to you. I don't want to do this. But I have no choice, not now. Those guys didn't get the job done this morning. They'll be back." He added, "Look, we better get going or he'll be suspicious."

"But he'll know I switched—"

"It's an exact duplicate, complete with screen saver and apps."

"But if he tries to use it?"

"He won't use it while I'm meeting with him. And once I'm

gone, just keep him busy. I won't be long. Then I'll sneak back up and switch them back."

"My God, do you know how many things could go wrong with that plan? And I would be in so much trouble."

"It's the only way to get to the *truth*, Michelle. If there were another way, I'd do it."

"Look, Travis, I don't really know you that well. And I've known Brad much longer. I know he can be a prick, but—"

"The Locust Group."

"What?"

"The Locust Group. It owns your building. It owns the Lombard Theater. And it owns the brownstone where your buddy Christian Chilton lives."

"I don't understand."

"Sara told Jennifer Stamos to check out the Lombard Theater. She was worried. She was scared. Then she ended up murdered. I checked the property records and found it was owned by the Locust Group. Just like your walk-up. I'm pretty sure Cowl *is* the Locust Group."

"It's not a crime to own property."

"It is a crime to kill people, Michelle."

"But you have no proof that Brad—"

"Give me the phone and I'll try to find that proof. The fact is there's an entire floor here that's off-limits. I thought it was the firm's high-frequency trading platform, but it's not. It's something else. And I need to find out what it is. I'm betting Cowl's phone, which he uses like my security card, will get me in there."

"But why are you doing this? Because of Sara Ewes?"

"Partly."

"Were you more than just professional colleagues? And don't lie to me."

"We were more. We... I thought she could be the one, in fact. For me."

"Did you sleep together?"

"Once. And then she broke it off. Now I think I know the reason."

"Which is?"

"She was in love with someone else. A woman."

Montgomery drew a long breath. "What's the other reason you're doing this, besides Sara?"

"You just have to trust me on that, Michelle. I took a big risk telling you all this. You could easily run to Cowl and tell him everything. But I trust you not to. Will you do the same for me? Will you trust me?"

An excruciatingly long moment passed, and Devine held his breath for all of it. Then she slowly held the phone out. He took it and handed her the fake one.

"Thank you," he said quietly.

She didn't look at him.

The security app was already pulled up on the phone screen. Cowl had no doubt done that before handing the phone off to Montgomery. Devine used it to get them on the elevator.

They rode it up, and when the doors opened into the foyer there stood Cowl. He used the wand on Devine, but didn't go below his calves.

"Make this fast, Devine." He nodded curtly at Montgomery and held out his hand. She passed him the fake phone; he didn't even look at it. "Follow me."

They walked into another room, where Cowl set the phone down on a table. "Thanks, Michelle," he said, waving her away.

She walked off down a hall.

He sat on a couch and motioned Devine to join him. "Well?" said Cowl.

Devine sat across from him. "Some men came to see me, really early this morning."

"Men, what about?"

"One of them had earlier pretended to be an NYPD cop assigned to Sara's case. But he was an imposter. They came to make me tell them things about this firm. I refused, so they attacked me." He showed Cowl his wounds.

Cowl barely looked at them. "What sort of things did they want to know about *this* firm?"

Devine had been watching him closely, because it was not outside the realm of possibility that, despite what Hancock had said about other people being out there, he was actually working with Cowl. He would certainly have a motive to get rid of Devine once and for all. But Cowl seemed surprised, and, more important, worried. Not for Devine, of course, but for himself.

"What was Sara really doing here," he lied. "Who had killed her and why. That sort of thing."

"And you told them nothing?"

"What could I tell them? I didn't know anything. And do you think they would have cut me up if I had talked?"

"No, I guess not," said Cowl absently, his mind clearly leaping ahead.

"So, what do I do if they come back?"

"I'll make some inquiries." Then Cowl looked at him closely. "You can tell me, Devine, just between friends, or business partners, I guess is what we are now."

"Tell you what?"

"Why you killed Sara."

"I didn't kill her."

"Come off it already!"

"Look—"

"No, you look!" barked Cowl. "Your card was the only one that showed up on the entry log that night. And your picture was on the video."

"Because *you* put it there!"

"That's what you say."

"You cloned my card and had somebody walk in the door with my face on their body. Come on! You bought a company that can do exactly that."

"I know I bought the company, but the thing is, Devine, I didn't have anybody do what you're accusing me of. I didn't mess with your card or put your face on another body."

Devine's gaze bored into him. "You really expect me to buy that?"

Cowl shook his head, his expression resigned. "Hell, maybe I would have done that manipulation stuff, but the fact is, I didn't think of it, okay? You're right, when I saw the video and the entry log, I was going to send your ass right to the cops and get this problem off my back. But then you hit me with a shot to the gut with the pictures and video of me and Jenn. I just thank God I didn't turn the stuff I had on you over to the cops before you showed me your hand. I'd have had nothing to hit you back with."

Devine, for reasons he could not entirely understand, believed the man, because everything with Cowl was transactional. So if the man hadn't tried to frame him, who had?

Cowl continued to grouse. "I need to get better people advising me. Not one of them even mentioned the possibility of framing you using the technology I had just bought and paid for. Useless pricks." He sat back on the couch and stared off, clearly pissed.

"Let me know what you find out," said Devine.

"Yeah, right. Okay, we're done."

Devine rose, but Cowl said, "Wait a minute, I got to let you on the elevator with my phone." Cowl rose, too, and started to the table to get his phone. Only it was the fake one.

Devine hadn't thought of this and his mind went blank; his panic level hit the top floor.

"I've got it, Brad," said Montgomery, who suddenly appeared from around the corner, where she must have been listening.

She snatched up the phone before Cowl could get there, and led Devine out.

"I owe you," breathed Devine.

"More than you'll ever be able to repay. Don't ever forget that, *Mr.* Devine."

# CHAPTER

# 50

THE ELEVATOR WENT DOWN, AND Devine hit the button for the fifty-first floor and held his breath. It lighted up and stayed that way. He let out the breath and leaned back against the wall. The doors opened on the fifty-first and he cautiously stepped out. He had checked the phone's settings. Cowl wasn't using a time lock right now, probably because he had had to give the phone to Montgomery to get him on the elevator and up to the penthouse, so he was good to go on that score.

The hallway was long and bare of anything. There wasn't even carpet on the floor, only the building's underlying concrete slab. He looked around for signs of video surveillance but saw none.

*They must count on the fact that no one can access this floor except Cowl. And he wouldn't want anyone watching.*

He checked his watch and hurried forward. There was a door at the end of the hall with an electronic reader. He put his ear to the door and all he heard were hums. No footsteps, no snatches of conversation, no one on the phone.

*You're running out of time, Devine. Just do it. Shit, you took less time to go into rooms in the Middle East, where you knew there were guys inside waiting to kill you.*

He held the phone in front of the reader, and the door clicked open. He slipped through. And stopped, again looking around for any sign of video surveillance, but again coming up empty.

The room was vast. All he could see were servers stacked

in cabinets and computer screens set on tables across the entire space.

He rushed over and looked at some of the screens. Data appeared on them, much like they did on his computer in his cubicle. He took out his own phone and started taking pictures and then video. Account numbers, maybe, wire routing data, perhaps. Money moving, almost certainly. Names of companies, properties, and other assets, being bought and sold, surely.

He was thinking the whole time, trying to piece together or envision what sort of business was being done here. Illegal, or just highly confidential, he didn't yet know.

The streams of numbers he was seeing, and the currency symbols attached to them, demonstrated that assets were being moved around the world. If this went on 24/7, the size of the operation, whatever was being *operated* here, was leviathan in scope. At least from what he could glean on the screens, most of the assets being acquired seemed to be in the United States. But from the bank names and other data he saw, a lot of the money pouring in seemed to be emanating from outside the country.

As he watched one screen, he saw the name "The Locust Group" pop up. Four million had just gone into its coffers from somewhere. He took a picture of that. On other screens properties were being purchased. Big, small, in between. Accounts filled up and then accounts were drawn down. And then they were filled back up, in what seemed like an endless cycle. He took video of all that.

He looked at his watch. He had to get back upstairs to the penthouse, without being seen. He couldn't make some excuse to Cowl about returning, because the only way he *could* return alone was if he had a phone he wasn't supposed to have.

From inside his shoe Devine brought out the wafer-thin device, provided by Emerson Campbell, and looked around for a good place to locate it. He quickly found a spot on the wall. After he affixed it there, the device blended right in. This camera was space-age in its capability and had originally been designed by NASA for use in outer space, but then was deployed by American intelligence for surveillance purposes in the most demanding environments. Area 51 had to have pretty significant protections against electronic eavesdropping from the outside. There were no windows in this room, and underneath the walls were probably copper sheathing and other counterintelligence measures. Valentine had been unable to get through them, apparently. Only Devine had an advantage there. Valentine had been outside trying to peek in. Devine was inside, trying to get intelligence out. And this space-observation device turned spy video camera, he believed, could do the job of stealing Area 51's secrets. At least he hoped.

He brought the related camera app up on his phone, engaged it, and on the small screen he saw...Area 51 operating on all cylinders. Now he just needed to see if it would do the same when he left the building.

He exited the room and headed up on the elevator. He said a prayer right before the doors opened. He glanced out, saw no one, pushed the button for the lobby and then for the door to stay open, and darted into the foyer. This was it. This was where it was probably all going to go to hell. Because the chances were very good that as absorbed as the man had been, Cowl was probably still on the couch, thinking, or else had the fake phone with him.

Devine did a turkey peek into the room they had been in minutes earlier.

Cowl wasn't there, and he wondered where the man might be.

He hurried over to the table and breathed a sigh of relief because the phone was still there. He made the switch back after wiping his prints off the case with the sleeve of his jacket. He once more looked around, and that was when he heard it.

*Oh shit.*

He followed the sounds and saw the door where they seemed to be coming from. When he looked down at the floor he had confirmation. There, in a pile, were the clothes Montgomery had been wearing.

He was sorely tempted to go over there and put a stop to it all, to tell Montgomery that—

But what would be the point?

He ran back into the elevator, released the hold, and the elevator shot down to earth.

All the way, the only thing Devine could envision was the door to the bedroom opening and Cowl walking out, zipping up his pants with that triumphant expression that made Devine want to punch his lights out. And Montgomery would be in the room, flat on her back, legs akimbo, like Stamos had been, and wondering what the hell she had just done.

As Devine left the building he couldn't remember feeling more miserable with himself.

*God, let it be worth it.*

Then he engaged the camera app on his phone and said a silent prayer. One... two... three.

Popping up on his screen were real-time images from Area 51. He let out a lungful of air.

*Bingo.*

As he stared back into the building where the night security guard was at the front reception desk, an idea struck him.

He used his card to get back inside and walked over to the man.

It was the same guy as always. He grinned at Devine. "Trying to get a jump on tomorrow so soon?"

Devine smiled back. "No way. I'm done, but I did have a question."

"Shoot."

"You were on duty the night that Sara Ewes was killed?"

The man's smile faded. He shook his head and closed his eyes for a moment. "That was some sick shit, man. Sick."

"Yeah, it was. The cops have been talking to me and others here. Apparently, they said someone came into the lobby at midnight and then left at one ten a.m."

"Nobody came in during that time."

Devine looked startled. "What do you mean?"

"I make my rounds exactly at twenty past the hour. Takes me about twenty minutes. I have to key into certain areas so there's an electronic trail. That means I was in the lobby at midnight *and* at one ten. Nobody came into the lobby that night. I can count on one hand the number of times someone came in that late, and I've been working here six years."

"And you told the cops this?"

"Yes, I did. And I also told them what they needed to look at."

"What was that?"

"The service entrance and elevator in the rear. Same security cards get you in there. And there's a camera back there." He pointed to the console, where there were video feeds on six different screens. "The one on the right over there. Shot of whoever's outside that door. That's one of the places I check every hour, just to make sure it's secure. But you need a security card to get in and there's a phone outside the door. During business hours, contractors have to call and we have someone go and let them in, verify they're supposed to be there and all that."

"Did the police check the feed from that camera to see if anyone came in that way the night Ewes was killed?"

"Since I was the one who suggested it, I did it for them."

"So did anyone come in that way at the time window in question, midnight to four?"

"I figured if the dude didn't come in the front, because I would have seen him, he came in that way. I ran the video feed back to like eleven o'clock, just to be sure." He shook his head. "But there was nothing. Nobody was there."

"Could the video have been manipulated, doctored?"

"I don't know, man. I'm just the security guard. Not a computer whiz. After business hours no contractor rings that bell unless they got some special job and have to come in at night. But that's all arranged beforehand. I don't usually look at that camera during my shift. But the feed was clear, I can tell you that."

"But won't the security card show what entrance the person came through?"

"Not to my knowledge. Front or back door, it's all the same. But the point is you need a *card* to get in. And the cops would have checked the entry log for that time. But I can tell you that the cameras were clear and I saw no one come in during the night. So I think whoever killed the lady was already in the building."

What Devine knew that the guard didn't was that the video had been doctored to make it look like he had come into the building during that time window. And his card had been cloned and the log manipulated to further incriminate him.

*So the entry log and surveillance cameras are basically useless.*

But the guard had suggested an intriguing possibility: Was the killer already in the building? That certainly could be the case, because it was really impossible to confirm that every single person had left Cowl and Comely that night. *Including Brad Cowl.*

The cops had made no mention of Ewes having had sex or being sexually assaulted or raped. Had Cowl tried to have sex with her and she refused? And in a fit of rage he had strangled her and then hoisted her up to cover up his crime? Cowl was physically capable of doing that. And he had clearly been frustrated by her rejection of his advances.

And Speers might have hit it on the head. Despite his denials, Cowl could have erased his own info from the electronic log, put Devine's in, and then had someone at Cyber-Surgeon show Devine coming into the lobby at that time. Only the security guard would have blown that scheme all to hell. So even if the NYPD had gotten the entry log showing Devine coming in and even seeing him on the video camera, they would have been confronted with a real, live person saying that did not happen.

Electronic skullduggery apparently had its limits.

*And maybe I have my limits, too. And I might be just about to reach them.*

Devine walked off into the darkness.

# CHAPTER

# 51

THE NOTEBOOK DEVINE WAS USING was full of scribbles, notes, and thought balloons that had resulted in calculations, lists of entities, dollar and foreign-currency amounts, along with dates of transactions and other data. And lots and lots of question marks.

Devine yawned and drank down another cup of coffee. He was in his room on his bed. He had downloaded the video images he'd taken of Area 51 from his phone onto his laptop and had gone through pretty much all of them. He next looked at the feed on his phone from the camera he had planted. Area 51 was still roaring along. He could clearly make out some of the screens from the surveillance camera he'd planted.

He had seen the Locust Group mentioned many more times. And he had also seen money flowing to Chilton's Mayflower Enterprises. Nearly three million in one night.

He looked at his watch. It was almost four o'clock in the morning.

He decided he needed to work out. He changed and was leaving when he saw the light under Jill Tapshaw's door. He knocked.

"Jill, you're up early. Everything okay?"

She opened the door, fully dressed and beaming. "I'm being interviewed by a magazine in Amsterdam."

"What time does your flight leave?"

"Don't be dumb. It's on Zoom."

"What's the name of the magazine?"

"*The Magazine*. I mean, isn't that clever? Although that's the translated name. It's something else in Dutch. I don't think I could speak Dutch. The words are too long and there are too many consonants."

He smiled and quipped, "But they have great coffee and even better weed."

"They're one of the hottest online publications in Europe, Travis. And their subscription base and Hummingbird's sweet-spot users are a perfect mesh. We've been trying to beef up our international exposure and this will do it."

Her enthusiasm made him feel better, even this early in the morning.

"Go knock 'em dead."

Her smile faded. "I forgot to ask you before. Why were the police here yesterday morning? It was early but I got woken up when I heard them knock on the door, and then I saw the police lights outside. You know my room faces the street."

"Oh, that? It was...nothing."

She looked at him crossly. "Travis, the police don't show up for nothing."

"Okay, I was working out at the high school like I always do and somebody tried to mug me."

"Mug you!"

"I'm fine, Jill, just fine. It was just a couple of punks."

"Did...did they hurt you?" She ran her gaze all over him. Fortunately, he'd had the presence of mind to put his bandaged hand behind his back so she wouldn't see he'd been wounded.

"No, not at all. They saw how big I was and they just took off. But they had a knife and stuff, so I thought I better alert the police. So, not to alarm you or anything, but keep your eyes open, okay? Anything looks suspicious, call the cops. And you're really bad about not locking the back door when you come in from the garage. And lock your car up. Start doing all that, okay? None of us can be too careful."

"Sure, Travis, I will." She looked at his workout clothes. "Should you go back over there after that?"

"I'm not." He held up a flashlight. "I'm just going to go for a run. Now, go get some Dutch people to start dating."

Her smile returned. "I will. Thanks."

As he walked off, Devine thought that if Hancock tried to do anything to Jill or Helen or Will, Devine would hunt the man down and rip him apart.

* * *

Later, showered and changed into his suit, Devine walked off to the station.

On the train he kept checking his phone to make sure the surveillance camera was still working. He still marveled at the amount of money and transactions moving through that digital space.

He didn't expect to see Michelle Montgomery after what had happened the previous night, but he was wrong, because there she was in her bikini. She didn't look at the train or wave. She looked tired; her shoulders slumped. She must have come back here with Cowl. He didn't blame her for getting up early to meditate by the pool after what had happened the previous night.

*I do owe her more than I could ever repay.*

He got to the city and jumped on the subway. He checked his phone again and got a shock.

The entire operation in Area 51 had shut down. The computer screens were black. The servers were no longer humming. It was dead.

When he got to the office building two men were standing out front. For some reason he thought they were waiting for him.

Shoemaker and Ekman looked like they had been up all night.

Devine approached them and said, "I thought *I* looked like crap until I saw you two."

"Stuff the bullshit, Devine. We have a major problem, which means *you* have a major problem."

"What are you talking about?"

"Where were you last night between midnight and three?"

"Home."

"Anybody verify that?"

"At that time people are in bed, including me. And what do I need another alibi for, anyway?"

"Jennifer Stamos was found murdered at her home," said Ekman grimly.

# CHAPTER

# 52

To say Cowl and Comely was like a morgue might have been an understatement, Devine thought.

Everyone looked on edge. Everyone looked like they wanted to be somewhere else.

*Me included.*

The firm had had an all-hands-on-deck meeting at nine o'clock in the largest conference room. Surprisingly, Brad Cowl didn't speak. He wasn't even there. Neither did the mysterious Anne Comely pop out of a cake and give her two cents' worth to the troops. Instead, one of the top executives provided scant information about the crime.

Stamos had been found in her bedroom. The police had not released any information on how she had died. When someone asked who had found her and called the police, the executive said he didn't know. The firm was providing counselors for anyone who wanted them.

And that was about it. Everyone went back to work.

And that included Devine, until a message dropped into his personal mailbox.

> And there goes Jennifer. It was only a matter of time. You can only love one person. After that, you love and lose. And she lost. I will spare you the more intimate details. It wasn't pretty. And it wasn't fun. But it had to be.

Devine stared dully at the message. Again, he didn't recognize the sender. It was just a series of numbers like last time.

Devine texted Montgomery, asking if she could meet him for lunch in the city. She texted back in the affirmative and he ducked out of the office around twelve thirty.

They met roughly halfway between the Cowl Building and her walk-up in SoHo. Montgomery had on white jeans and a blue short-sleeved blouse. Her features were strained and her eyes were puffy.

Devine had a terrible thought. "Wait a minute, he didn't—"

She held up a hand. "No, he didn't force himself on me. I... I let him. I encouraged it, actually."

"You didn't have to do that, Michelle. When I said 'distract him,' I didn't mean—"

"Then what *did* you mean?" she shot back. "For me to read him fucking poetry? As soon as I got back he grabbed the phone and was going to make a call. I had to think fast and that was the only thing I could think of."

"God, I'm an idiot. I'm so sorry."

"Just... just forget it. It's over and done with. It's not like I haven't screwed the guy before. It's the only reason he has me around."

"You're taking this pretty calmly."

"Sex is sometimes just sex, Travis, okay? Men look at it differently than women. So long as I controlled things and it ended on my terms, I can deal with it. So please just deal with it too, okay?"

"Okay," he said quickly.

They went inside a small brick-faced café, sat at a table in the back, and ordered. After they got their drinks Montgomery said, "Did you get what you were looking for on that floor?"

"Yes."

"What's going on?"

"Transfers of money in amounts that are beyond belief. And that money is being distributed to lots of different entities, which, in turn, use it for other purposes."

"But isn't that what Brad's company does? What all those companies do?"

"Not like this." He took a sip of his iced tea. "Something about this has me confused."

"Just one thing? Wow, you're way ahead of me."

Devine continued, "I was sure that Cowl had framed me in connection with Sara's murder, cloning my security card and putting me on the security video around the time of her death."

"What?" she gasped.

"Yeah, that's right, I didn't tell you that before."

She looked at him suspiciously.

He said in an exasperated tone, "I didn't do it, Michelle. I talked to the night security guard at the building, and he told the cops no one came in at the time the video of me was on the security film and my security card showed up on the entry log. So the frame would have been worthless. But Cowl didn't know that."

"Okay."

"But last night I point-blank asked him about trying to frame me. And he denied it."

"Come on, what else did you expect him to do, confess?"

"I know, I keep going back and forth with that, too. Did he or didn't he? But the more I think about it, the more I think he was telling the truth. He is one competitive prick and he always wants value for his money. And he was pissed that he hadn't thought of framing me. He was also ticked off at his highly paid advisers because they didn't think of it either. He said he saw the security log and video later, and *then* he was going to use it to put this problem behind him. In fact, based on that evidence, I think he thought I really had killed Sara. He doesn't want the police snooping around here, and after what I found last night, I can understand why. But then I countered with some dirt I had on him that stopped him from revealing what he thought he had on me."

"What kind of dirt?"

Devine thought of Stamos, now the dead Jennifer Stamos. "Just something that he would never want to see the light of day. But the point is, if he didn't try to set me up, who did?"

"I can't help you there. I have no clue."

He looked over at her, his own suspicions ratcheting up. "When did you leave the penthouse last night? I saw you by the pool from the train."

"Around one in the morning. I couldn't sleep after, well...that. And Brad got woken up by a call from someone. And he said he had to go out. But that I could stay the night if I wanted, which I didn't, not after what happened. We went down together in his private elevator and then he called a car service for me. I decided to go out to his place in the suburbs. I didn't want to be in the city at all last night."

"Did he take his Bugatti?"

"No, he called a car service, too."

"Did he say who called him or where he was going?"

"No, why?"

He eyed her nervously. "Because Jennifer Stamos, a woman he was having a sexual relationship with at the office, was murdered last night at her home between midnight and three."

Montgomery had taken a sip of her Coke and almost spit it out. "What!"

"And we had a big meeting of everyone at the firm this morning. With two people murdered, folks are getting edgy. Only Cowl wasn't there. Some other guy filled in for him."

"You asked me before if I knew Jennifer Stamos."

"I did, yes. Because I knew she and Cowl were a thing." He eyed her closely.

She flinched and said, "Wait a minute, you're not...are you suggesting that Brad...killed her?"

"I don't know. It would make sense that she would call him late at night. Even if he didn't kill her, he might have found the body. The guy this morning didn't say who had notified the police or who had found her."

"Do you think Brad might be dead, too?"

"I think we would have heard about that if he was."

"Unless they haven't found his body," countered Montgomery.

"He also might have called the police anonymously and then run for it. If he found her dead, he'd probably think, like I did, that people would believe that he had killed her. And others might know of their relationship. I gave him a lot to ponder last night—and a murder on top of it, with a woman he was screwing around with? The press would have a field day with that. And the cops would be all over him." He paused and said, "Did you have any idea he was seeing somebody else?"

"With Brad it was pretty much a given. And our relationship wasn't going to be permanent. And I asked you over to swim in the pool. I was ready to go to bed with you the other night. So I have no problem with him sleeping around when I'm willing to do the same. Fair is fair."

"Okay."

She shook her head. "And I thought I had a shitty night. That poor woman."

"I have something else to tell you."

"What?"

"I got a message from her killer."

"Travis!"

He explained about the email he'd gotten that morning, and about the previous one he'd received after Sara Ewes had been killed. And about both messages being untraceable.

"Why would the killer be contacting you?"

"I don't know, Michelle. I knew both women. That's the only connection I see. But so did lots of other people."

"But you and Sara had a thing. You slept together."

"That's true," he conceded.

"And there's no way to find out who sent the messages?"

"I had a world-class hacker try. And fail. I have someone else trying."

"This is beyond bizarre."

"Agreed, but we have to keep pushing forward." He paused, took a sip of his iced tea, and said quietly, "Look, can you contact Cowl and tell him that I want to talk to him about Stamos's murder?"

"That's a little vague, isn't it?" she replied.

"It's meant to be."

She pulled out her phone and texted the message to Cowl. She set her phone down and fingered her Coke. "Where did *you* go after you left there last night?"

"I went home and started going over the stuff I found. Let me know if you hear back from him."

"Do you really think he killed Stamos?" she asked.

"Someone sure as hell did, and it wasn't me."

# CHAPTER

# 53

EIGHT P.M.

Devine was standing across the street from where Jennifer Stamos had lived in Hamilton Heights, near Harlem. And where she had now died. He had found her home address on a database at work. He had read the cryptic message a dozen times. *You can only love one person*. That might be significant. Stamos had loved Ewes. Had Ewes loved someone else before? And because her love had moved on to Stamos, she had lost? And so had Stamos? And what did the sender mean by it not being pretty? Or fun?

Stamos's apartment was on the ground floor of a walk-up like Michelle Montgomery's, only situated in Upper Manhattan. She would have to traverse nearly the entire island north to south to get to work each day. While not as tony as where Sara Ewes had lived, it was a diverse and thriving working-class community. Police cars were parked outside, and he figured detectives and forensics people were inside trying to find out who had killed her.

There were no details in the news on how Stamos had died. The police were holding that back for obvious reasons. He again wondered if Cowl had been the one to report the murder before fleeing. If it hadn't been Stamos who had called Cowl, it was quite a coincidence that he had gone out right around the time she had been killed.

*And did Cowl send me the untraceable emails? With all his resources, he could afford to hire the best IT people around.*

Was Stamos pressuring him somehow? Perhaps Ewes had told Stamos something about Cowl and maybe what was going on in Area 51. Ewes knew about the Locust Group and its ownership of the Lombard Theater. That knowledge had probably gotten Ewes killed, and now maybe the same thing had happened to Stamos.

He texted Campbell and arranged to meet, then took the subway back to Midtown and the little Italian restaurant.

Campbell was in the same room sitting in the same chair with another plate of food in front of him.

"Bronzini," he said in answer to Devine's curious look. "People think of Italy as the land of spaghetti, it's actually the land of fish. You hungry?"

Devine had noted that with each visit the retired general was more informal and friendlier. He didn't know if this was an act, a tactical move, or whether the man was actually beginning to like him.

And since Devine had barely eaten any of his lunch eight hours earlier and no breakfast, he said, "Thank you, sir."

Food was brought and the men began to eat.

Devine took about five minutes filling Campbell in on what he had found on the fifty-first floor and how Michelle Montgomery had helped him.

"Sounds like she would make a good operative," said Campbell.

*Probably better than me*, thought Devine. "There's bad news, though. The camera feed was working great. But on the train ride in this morning, the whole thing shut down."

"What?" said Campbell sharply.

"I was checking the phone constantly, to make sure it was all good. And it was until my ride into the city."

"They must have found the camera."

"I don't think so, sir. If they had, why not remove the camera? I can still see inside the place if it ever starts back up."

"Well, forward what you have to me," said Campbell.

"It's a lot of data. It won't fit in an email."

Campbell made a call. A minute later a man entered the room.

Devine showed him what he had. The man arranged for a secure file transfer onto a laptop and then left.

Campbell said, "I'll get my people working on it immediately. And, by the way, why have you waited this long to report in?" he added gruffly.

"That was the other thing I've yet to tell you." He went on to inform him about the NYPD detectives meeting him outside the office early that morning to tell him that Jennifer Stamos had been murdered.

"I've been preoccupied with that all day," said Devine. "But there's something else." He showed Campbell the untraceable emails he'd received.

Campbell looked at them and said, "If this is the killer, he's targeting you for some reason. Any ideas on that?"

"No, not really."

"Do you need us to try and trace them?"

"I have someone working on it who's making progress."

"Your hacker friend?"

"No, someone even better."

"Still, forward them to me and I'll put my people on it. Another set of eyes never hurts."

Devine did so.

Campbell said, "We'll have our forensic accounting people go over the surveillance footage, of course. But you have your MBA. What do you make of it so far?"

"Enormous amounts of money coming in from what looks to be foreign sources, and enormous amounts of money going out. Locust Group is one recipient. They own the Lombard Theater, on Broadway, and Michelle Montgomery's walk-up in SoHo, and the brownstone on the Upper East Side that Christian Chilton lives in. That's just the tip of the iceberg. There could be thousands, tens of thousands of properties and assets being purchased."

"You said foreign. Can you tell the precise sources of the funds coming in?" asked Campbell.

"Numbered accounts, maybe Swiss, maybe Bahamas, maybe Chad. Offshore platforms, the routing is a labyrinth. It'll take an army of your forensics accountants to unravel it. There were also what looked to be transfers of cryptocurrency of various types. This is definitely a global scenario."

Campbell tapped his fish with his fork. "So what do you think is going on there? Money laundering?"

"The obvious answer, of course, would be yes. But in the world of modern finance, having an automated system like this in place to buy all sorts of assets and transferring money all over the globe could be completely legit. Speed is one's friend in this arena, and lots of firms do things similar to this, although not with near the same velocity and scale."

"Do you really think it's legit?" asked Campbell.

"Except for two things, I would tell you I'm not sure."

"What are those two things?"

"Sara Ewes and Jennifer Stamos being murdered. That is obviously not something that typically happens in connection with big investment firms doing these sorts of transactions. So hopefully it will be enough to take them down, right?"

He looked at Campbell; the man didn't seem overly confident.

"What is it?" asked Devine.

"There's the matter of proof."

"What I got—"

"—is inadmissible, Devine. Fruit of the tainted tree."

"But I'm a civilian."

"Any competent defense lawyer would argue that you had been effectively deputized by the government, and, indeed, used a piece of specialized surveillance equipment provided by the federal government. We won't have a legal leg to stand on."

"I guess not," conceded Devine.

"But there are perhaps ways to work around that."

"I sure as hell hope so. What did you learn about Hancock, the imposter in NYPD detective clothing?"

"We can't confirm this yet, of course, but my sources told me it sounds an awful lot like a chap named Eric Bartlett. He's a former CIA operative. Left government service about eight years ago. He's popped up here and there working for some unsavory types. But he was too slippery to catch and hold. He's previously pulled impersonations like this for different clients."

"Well, hopefully we can put an end to those impersonations, and to him. Because I don't want to run into that guy again if I don't have to."

* * *

When Devine got home later that night, Tapshaw's light was out, but Speers's light was on. He knocked on her door.

"Yes?"

"It's Travis, got a minute?"

She opened the door and eyed him appraisingly. "Jill told me about the mugging and your warnings to her—to all of us. How bad was it?"

"Could have been worse."

"Only it wasn't a mugging, was it?" said Speers.

"It was the guy who was pretending to be NYPD, and a pair of thugs. They had guns and knives. That's how I got this scratch." He held up his hand.

"Impressive you got away alive, then," she said coolly.

"More luck than not."

"I doubt that. The Army taught you well."

He looked over her shoulder at the stack of books. "How's the studying coming?"

"It's coming. Torts are easy. Criminal law is harder."

"That's what all the criminals say," quipped Devine.

"I've seen the news. Jennifer Stamos is dead."

"Yes."

"Was she the one who came here to visit you the other night?"

"Yes."

"And you told me she was having an affair with Brad Cowl and you had proof of it."

"Yes."

"That does not look good, Travis. For you."

"I didn't kill Stamos, Helen. Why would I?"

"You keep lobbing legal softballs at me. Your motive is she decided to call your blackmail bluff and threatened to expose you. So you silenced her. Do you have an alibi?"

"No, but I found out that Cowl got called out at just around the time she died. And now he's pulled a disappearing act. So either he killed her, or else he found the body, called the police, and went into hiding."

Speers said, "Maybe he killed her *and* called the police."

"Why would he do that?"

"Guilt, or thinking it might help him somehow. People under stress do strange things."

He looked over her shoulder at the pile of books again. "Well, I'll let you get back to it."

As he walked off he had a brand-new problem. And that problem was Helen Speers.

Because those books and study guides hadn't been touched since the last time he'd seen them. They were all in the exact same position.

She wasn't studying for the bar. She might not have graduated from law school. Her name might not even be Helen Speers. He had had no reason to check before.

Now he did.

# CHAPTER

# 54

THE 6:20 WAS DELAYED FOR five minutes by some problem at the station; then it lumbered on its way.

Later, the train slowed and then stopped. Devine looked out at Cowl's pool area. It was empty this morning. No meditation for Montgomery in a bathing suit. And Cowl might have already fled the country, if he had indeed killed Stamos.

As the train remained motionless, Devine once more checked the video feed on his phone. Area 51 was still dead as a doornail. What the hell had happened between his looking at the feed the previous morning on the train ride in to find everything firing away, to his checking the feed as he arrived in the city only to find Area 51 shut down?

Devine decided to call Montgomery to check on her.

She answered on the fourth ring, sounding groggy.

"Sorry it's so early," he said apologetically.

"No, it's okay. What's up?"

"I passed by Cowl's house this morning. And you weren't out by the pool. But it made me think of you. Just wanted to touch base with you to make sure everything was okay. And whether you'd heard back from Cowl."

"I haven't heard from Brad. And I'm fine. I stayed in the city last night."

"I was surprised that you were out by the pool yesterday after everything that had happened the night before. I forgot to ask you about that when we had lunch yesterday. But Stamos's murder sucked up all the oxygen."

"Well, that wasn't my call."

"Come again?" Devine said sharply.

"Brad texted me at like three in the morning and told me to be out by the pool before six forty-five. Luckily I wasn't really sleeping and heard the text come in. I texted him back and told him I'd do it."

"Wait a minute, he wanted you out by the pool in time for *my* train to come by?"

"I don't know about that, he just told me the time."

"Michelle, why didn't you tell me about this at lunch yesterday?"

"With everything else going on, it didn't seem important." She yawned. "It still doesn't, at least to me."

"Not important! I told you that he might have murdered Stamos, or at least found her body."

"I know that," she shot back. "But how can that be connected to him texting me about going out by the pool? I mean, what would that matter? And he didn't tell me where he was, so I had nothing to tell you on that score."

"But didn't that make you suspicious? That after maybe finding a body, or killing a woman, he took the time to text and tell you to be out by the pool by a certain time the next morning?"

"Look, if you want the truth, Brad has a voyeur fetish. He wanted guys checking me out. I lied to you about that train. I knew about the gap, that people could see me. Some men get off on that, and Brad is one of them. So I parade around in my bikini when Brad tells me to, and he pays me well for it. And it's not like he asks me to do it all the time. It's actually pretty rare, although it has been more often lately."

"But he wasn't there to see it last time."

"But he has cameras around the property. I figured he was going to watch later, like it's his own little porn video."

Devine shook his head, and then something occurred to him.

Something maybe crazy, and then again maybe not. "Do you pick the bikinis to wear, or does Cowl?"

"I do."

Devine looked deflated. His theory had just gone down in flames.

"But Brad picks the colors."

He tensed once more, his adrenaline racing. "He picks the colors?"

"Yes. I don't like red or emerald green. They're not really my colors. I prefer blue. The only green I wear is lime, and that's only in the summer when I'm tanned. But Brad likes me in those colors."

"And he tells you when to go out by the pool in the bikinis?"

"Yes. Like I said, he has a fetish."

"Is it always by six forty-five?"

"Yeah, it is."

"Okay," he began. "Let's go over the chronology. Last Friday, before they found Sara's body, you were wearing a green bikini. Correct?"

She thought for a moment. "Yes, that's right."

"And you weren't by the pool on Saturday."

"That's right."

"I didn't take the morning train in on Sunday, but were you told to sit out by the pool then?"

"Yes."

"Red bikini?"

"Um, correct."

"I was told on Saturday that Sara's death was due to homicide, not suicide."

"Okay," she said. "But I don't see the connection."

"Then on Monday morning, I saw you wearing a green bikini."

"That's right, I was. Just like Brad told me to. I was surprised because normally it wouldn't be that frequent. Most of the time weeks would go by. And this goes back to last summer. We met in August, and that's when I moved here."

"I think I know why the frequency picked up."

"Why?" she asked curiously.

"Because people started dying. Now, you were by the pool on Tuesday, but you had on a *blue* swimsuit. Why that color?"

"That was all me, not Brad. Like I said, blue is my favorite color."

"But why were you by the pool if Cowl didn't tell you to be?"

She smiled impishly. "I decided to have some fun after you told me about all the guys checking me out. I mean, I knew they were, but I knew you'd be on the train, too. So I decided to put on a show and then flip everybody off."

He shook his head. *That's why it didn't fit the pattern.* "Okay, then on Wednesday you were by the pool with the red bikini?"

"Yes. That was when Brad texted me late and told me to get over there."

"So Stamos was dead, Cowl probably knew about it, and you got the message to be by the pool in your red bikini?"

"I must be pretty dumb, because I don't see where all this is going, Travis."

"I think you got the message from him to wear the red bikini because he had found Stamos's body."

Her face screwed up in confusion. "Why are you so fixated on me and my bikinis? It's just one of Brad's quirks, like I said. He has a lot of them, let me tell you," she added wearily.

Devine sighed and sat back. "You ever heard of Hermes?"

"The people who make the handbags?"

"No, the Greek god."

"What does that have to do with anything?"

"He was the cleverest of the gods. He was their interpreter. And he was also their *messenger.*"

"Again, so what?" said Montgomery in a puzzled tone.

"So, at the most basic level, Michelle, green means go. And red means stop."

# CHAPTER 55

DEVINE FINISHED EXPLAINING EVERYTHING TO Montgomery and then clicked off.

The pattern was now established. Transactions flowed into Area 51 with green, and those same transactions stopped with red. And someone on the 6:20 train was receiving those signals and then doing what needed to be done, namely either putting on the brakes or punching the gas based on the color of a freaking bikini.

And Stamos's murder had made the signal go to red this last time, and led to Area 51 shutting down. But whoever was driving all that money to Cowl and Comely must not like it when those shutdowns happened. It was like a blood vessel with an obstruction, or a rain-swollen dam; at some point the thing was going to burst. Thus, Cowl had to keep opening the valve back up, even if it caused personal peril for him.

Cowl was no doubt afraid, and he had good reason to be. With two murders, the police would dig deep. But there were problems with that theory, too. If they went in there and saw all those silent servers and blank-faced computers, it could easily be explained as being related to Cowl's business, and how could the cops prove otherwise? And without that there would be no warrant issued to search the cloud connected to all that data, particularly not with the legal firepower Cowl had on retainer. Hell, they probably wouldn't have enough probable cause to search anywhere in the building, because Stamos hadn't been killed there.

It occurred to Devine that he was struggling because he didn't know enough about his opponent, Brad Cowl.

Now he had a specific search he was going to employ with a slightly different spin.

He typed it into his phone: *Bradley Cowl negative stories.*

He found that there were more than a few, but they all had the same theme. Big, bad billionaire who only cared about himself. Again, what a shock, Devine thought. Like he built what he had by being a nice guy.

But after a great deal of searching, he found one article that took a different theme. It was by a financial journalist whom Devine had never heard of, but Elaine Nestor had once been a respected reporter and had contributed pieces to the *Wall Street Journal*, the *New York Times*, and *Mother Jones*. She had also been a commentator on numerous business shows. Then she had simply vanished from the radar nearly two years ago. And the story Devine had just pulled up, written by Nestor around that time, must have pissed Cowl off immensely. And maybe that was the reason Nestor no longer had a career.

Nestor was basically arguing that something was very shady in the land of Cowl. Every other name partner of a major Wall Street investment firm was well documented and vetted, even those long dead. Not so Anne Comely, argued Nestor, which was the same thing Devine had previously thought. While others in the financial field waved this off as trivial and unimportant, Nestor said that Comely was a red flag because no one could find out anything about her. And in the financial world, that sort of deception might have been reflected in other areas of the firm's business, Nestor had concluded.

In the matter of Brad Cowl personally, the lady had been even more pointed.

Nestor maintained, based on anonymous sources, that Cowl's elite academic status at college had been bought and paid for. That he was not nearly the amazing businessman he claimed to be. That he had, in fact, inherited large sums of money from both his grandfather and father but had squandered it on partying and lousy investment decisions. Nestor went on to write that the entire foundation of Cowl and Comely could very well be rotten to the core. She had even called for an SEC investigation.

Devine read some related articles and could now understand what had happened to Nestor. The "anonymous" sources had come forward and claimed they hadn't said what she had written about them. That she had offered them money and other types of bribes. Cowl's grandfather was dead and his father was in ill health, but in a prepared statement Cowl Sr. said that his son had gotten nothing from him, and that Brad Cowl had earned every penny of what he had.

Cowl's university had roundly rejected the allegation that anyone could have purchased high academic status, although the president, the provost, and other key figures there at the time Cowl had attended refused to comment.

And on top of all that, Cowl and Comely had been enormously successful for two decades. Inept but slick-mouthed grifters rarely seemed to really pull that off. Although Nestor had countered that almost all the investors who had given their money to the likes of Bernie Madoff and others of his ilk would beg to differ.

Cowl had sued Nestor and buried her under legal bills, another article said.

*It's the same threat he made to me.*

The publication she had written the piece for rolled over under threats from Cowl's lawyers and had hung Nestor out to dry. The matter had been quietly settled on terms that were never disclosed. Devine was surprised that her article was still even available online, but he'd had to dig really deep to find it. Once something was on the internet, it was really difficult to purge it from every platform.

Nestor's last known address, at least that Devine could find, was in rural Connecticut.

He searched to see if she was still there. It seemed that she was. There was no phone number or email, and she had no social media presence. He wondered if that was part of the *settlement*.

He texted Montgomery and asked her if she was up for a motorcycle trip to Connecticut the next morning.

Hell yes, was her response. I can meet you in Westchester, at the train station.

* * *

After another grueling day of work and suspicious looks from his fellow Burners, Devine took the train back to Mount Kisco.

As he walked home from the station, a black sedan pulled up.

"Get in," said the driver.

Devine got in and found himself sitting next to Campbell.

"The chatter we've been relying on died out completely," said the retired general.

"When *exactly*?"

He told Devine the precise time it had happened. "Thoughts?"

Devine explained to Campbell his theory regarding Montgomery's being the unwitting messenger using the color of her bikini to signal someone on the 6:20 train to either halt or start back up the Area 51 operations.

Campbell nodded knowingly. "That's the way they used to do it in the old days. Not bikini colors, mind you, but person-to-person communication using a signal or system that would raise no suspicion whatsoever. A folded newspaper with the below-the-flap part showing, a different-colored flower left in a vase in a window, a light left on or off. In 'Nam we would tie different-colored bandanas around trees, change the meaning frequently, and the Viet Cong never figured it out. But why did they pull out the red bikini and grind Area 51 to a halt?"

"Stamos's murder. Cowl sent the order to Montgomery to wear the bikini before the cops even knew she was dead. So he either killed her or found her body and panicked. But if Stamos did call Cowl that night, the police will be able to tell from her phone records."

"Okay, what's your next move?"

Devine told him about Elaine Nestor and his planned trip.

Campbell nodded. "Make it count, Devine. My old soldier's instincts are telling me that we are running out of time."

# CHAPTER

# 56

THE NEXT MORNING DEVINE CALLED in sick and then met Montgomery at the train station. She was wearing jeans and a long-sleeved shirt and black ankle boots. He passed her his spare helmet, she climbed on, and they set off for Connecticut.

When they arrived at the address, they saw that Elaine Nestor's cottage was small but quaint, with gray cedar shake siding, white trim, and beds filled with colorful summer flowers. Hers was the only house on the macadam rural road.

When they knocked on the door a woman answered. She was in her late forties with graying hair cut short on the sides with one long bang in the front and black-rimmed glasses on a chain around her neck. She looked more like a caricature of a librarian than a hard-charging financial journalist digging up dirt on the wealthy and powerful. But her features were alert and her eyes bright and probing.

"Elaine Nestor?"

"Yes. Who are you?" she said. He saw a phone in one hand and a wooden mallet in the other. But when she saw Montgomery standing next to him, she relaxed just a bit.

"My name is Travis Devine. This is my friend, Michelle. I work at Cowl and Co—"

That got the door slammed right in his face.

*Should've seen that coming, idiot.*

He glanced at Montgomery, whose expression said pretty much the same thing.

He called out, "I read your article on Brad Cowl. The one that got your career torpedoed. I just wanted to tell you that you were *right*."

The door slowly opened, but Nestor's look remained suspicious. "Why are you here? What do you want?"

"Have you read about the murders?"

"Of course I have. And what do you mean I was right?"

Devine had prepared what he was about to say on the ride up. "I think Cowl is running the biggest money-laundering scheme in the history of the world. And would you like your career back?"

Nestor stared at him for an uncomfortably long moment.

"Would you both like some coffee?" she said brightly.

Three cups of coffee later Nestor was still shaking her head. "'Area 51'? Really?"

"Really," said Devine. "As crazy as it sounds."

"It doesn't sound crazy. People will do anything to make money. But you took a huge risk doing what you did."

He looked at Montgomery, who was fingering her coffee cup and looking pensively out the window into the rear garden. "I had incentive enough," Devine said.

Nestor said, "You asked me about Brad Cowl, and I told you what I thought. He's a slick operator and can talk a good game, but if he knows the difference between an LBO and HBO, I'll run naked down the street. And he *did* inherit a lot of money and he blew it on coke and women, and shady investment types who took him to the cleaners, and I have the receipts to prove it. He's a front man, plain and simple, and I wrote all about that in my article. And then I got my ass handed to me and basically run out of town on a rail. It's just history repeating itself. Anyone who had the temerity to question Bernie Madoff's guaranteed returns got the same treatment for decades."

"Nobody wanted to pop the illusion," interjected Montgomery. "It's the Emperor's New Clothes syndrome."

Nestor eyed her. "Nobody likes to admit they were suckered. It's easier on the psyche to keep living the lie."

"But not easier on the wallet," said Devine. "It has to come to a head. Although Cowl is not running a Ponzi scheme. I think what he's doing is actually a lot worse. It goes right to this country's national security interests."

Nestor nodded. "I'm sure you read about the Panama Papers and, more recently, the Pandora Papers. It's no secret to those in the industry that rich people from all over the world have been stashing trillions in opaque trusts that run from generation to generation, in perpetuity, and they don't pay a dime of tax on any of it, ever. A lot of it is illegal money from cartels, terrorist organizations, deposed dictators who have emptied treasuries, ransomware players. Creditors can't touch it, and the people whose money it really is can never recover it."

"I read that South Dakota is sitting on over six hundred billion dollars of that trust money," said Devine. "It creates a few hundred jobs in the state, but it sucked the lifeblood out of the places where that money originated. And Wyoming has something called the 'Cowboy Cocktail' that has even more privacy layers."

Nestor nodded. "You can be the trust's grantor *and* the beneficiary, and the people running the trust have no clue who the real owners are. They just see account numbers. You've got do-nothing descendants who haven't worked a day in their lives and they have their own jets courtesy of these tax-robbing schemes."

Devine added, "And you have some high-and-mighty politicians screaming about working-class joes pulling three jobs getting a few hundred extra bucks a month in government benefits, because they think it'll make them *lazy*."

Nestor said, "From the scale you mentioned, I could imagine it being Russian oligarchs and Saudi princes, dictators who have raided national treasuries, crime syndicates, drug cartels, your run-of-the-mill billionaires with criminal sides to their businesses, or legit ones who just want to offload money to avoid taxes and acquire more wealth surreptitiously and then pass it down from generation to generation without the taxman getting a dime."

Devine said, "But there's more to it than that. This money is *not* sitting in stock and bond portfolios. From what I saw, they're buying huge chunks of this country with it."

Nestor shook her head. "Can you imagine if the Taliban or Iran or North Korea or Russia were getting cash flow from investments in *this* country to fund their terrorist activities? Kim Jong-un a landlord in New York? An Iranian ayatollah owning hog farms in Kansas? Or Putin having oil fields in Texas? That would be the scandal of the century."

"How do you think this all started?" asked Devine. "I know that Cowl left the country over two decades ago and was gone for a while."

"He had burned through all his inheritance by then, and he had some personal scandals he was dealing with. Over twenty years ago, when I'd only been an investigative journalist for a few years, I traced a meeting that Cowl had with some shady people in the Seychelles, but then the trail went cold. Then he dropped off the radar for about a year or so. He might have been in Asia or eastern Europe, at least those were my best guesses. Next, the man waltzes back into New York, buys and rehabs that skyscraper, starts his investment group, hires all sorts of pricey talent, suddenly has a client list that the biggest players on Wall Street would covet, and boom, he's the talk of the town. He wasn't even twenty-five years old."

"And no one really questioned that?" said Montgomery. "That seems crazy."

Nestor said, "The money folks will forgive a lot if the cash keeps rolling in. Same goes for the government. Cowl's operations bring millions to the city and state in taxes. He employs lots of people, and they also pay taxes and spend money there. He greases the palms of politicians he needs to. He gives liberally to charities. Always good for a funny one-liner or an 'expert' diatribe on a business show. Lives life fast and hard but backs up the talk with results, and he can afford an army of lawyers. Who's going after a guy like that? Hell, I'm living proof of that." Nestor looked at Montgomery. "Now, this signaling technique using a bikini is intriguing, and unique."

"Not the words I would use for it," said Montgomery, looking embarrassed.

"I actually thought it was cumbersome," interjected Devine. "It just seems like sending an email would be a lot more efficient."

"I think I can shed some light on that," said Nestor. "About twelve years ago Cowl came really, really close to being indicted by the Justice Department *and* the State of New York for some financial shenanigans. I mean huge fines, delicensing, and possible prison time. They got on to him by electronic eavesdropping. Phone, computer, associates' electronics. He used his money and influence and a fleet of high-priced attorneys and calling in chits from political pals to get out of the jam, but—"

"—but it would make the man paranoid about relying on those types of communications again," interjected Devine. "He actually mentioned to me something along the lines of what you just said. He told me for the important stuff, he always went *analog*."

"And let me tell you something else. Anne Comely? I spent years trying to track her down. She doesn't exist. I'm sure of it."

"I watched an old interview where Cowl said she might just represent an idea or something like that," said Devine.

"Well, maybe now we have our answer: It *represents* a criminal enterprise." She eyed Devine over her coffee cup. "So, what will you do now?"

"Keep following the money. And anything we do find goes right to you for your exclusive. I want to make sure you come out of this with your career and good reputation back."

"I appreciate that very much, Mr. Devine. But what about the murders? Do you think these two women found out what was going on and that's why they were killed?"

"Ewes knew about the Locust Group. Stamos was her lover and was also sleeping with Cowl. He might have let something slip over pillow talk, and Ewes and later Stamos followed up on it. And they were both murdered, maybe as a result."

"Financial crimes are one thing, killing people is totally something else."

"I don't think Cowl is calling the shots here, not really. I've run into some goons who decided my time on earth was up. Luckily, they were wrong. But it was strongly intimated that Cowl is not running this show."

"If Brad Cowl is involved with the sorts of people it looks like he is, this will become even more dangerous," said Nestor.

"I'm actually sort of counting on it," said Devine.

# CHAPTER 57

ON THE WAY BACK TO New York, Devine and Montgomery stopped and had lunch at a restaurant on the water. They sat at an outside table overlooking Long Island Sound. It wasn't too hot; the breeze off the water was pleasant and refreshing and the views were lovely.

Still, Montgomery stared sulkily off before glancing at Devine. "Doesn't sitting here just make you want to chuck it?"

"Chuck what?" he asked.

"You know exactly what I'm talking about, Travis."

He sat back and looked out to the water, where a sailboat was cutting through the waves. "Got to make a living. I'm not rich. I'm not even well-off enough to take a vacation."

"I've got my portfolio."

"Then *you* can chuck it, Michelle."

"Not that much fun alone. You could come along for the ride."

"There are about a million other guys who'd be a lot better for you than me."

"And I can't make that decision for myself?"

"Yes, but I also have to make that decision for *myself*."

She hiked her eyebrows. "And you have no interest?"

"I think you know that I do. But I've got baggage that you don't need to deal with."

"And you think I don't?"

"And you don't believe that'll be a red flag for them to hunt us down if we suddenly disappear together?"

"I suppose it would be." She studied him closely. "Why are you really at Cowl, Travis? You don't strike me as a person interested in that world at all."

He started to tell her the standard line, but then he decided to be more candid. His conversation with Campbell had made him reevaluate things. And Montgomery had stuck her neck out for him. She deserved something close to the truth.

"I left the Army under a sort of cloud. It messed with my head. My old man always wanted me to go for the money, so I decided to do what he wanted."

"Even though you really didn't want to?"

"I guess it was a form of self-punishment. Force myself to do what I hate."

"What the hell happened in the Army to make you want to do that to yourself?"

"I can't talk to you about it. I can barely talk to myself about it."

"Okay, I guess I understand that," she said slowly, but looking disappointed.

"You said your family situation wasn't a ball of fun," he noted.

"I'm the black sheep, I guess. Never lived up to my promise, or so my mother told me."

"Come on, you're only what, twenty-two?"

"Almost twenty-three. I should have graduated from college by now. I'm way behind, Travis. No way to catch up, really. It's like being in the nineteenth century and suddenly realizing you're a washed-up old maid at age eighteen."

"I went back to school after getting out of the Army. It can be done."

"But that's not what I want. I just want to travel to different places, experience different things. I don't want to be tied down to a desk or a computer for the rest of my life. But now I'm arm candy for a rich criminal."

"But you got me into Area 51. You went with me to see Nestor."

She stared off moodily. "Where do you think Brad is now?"

"It's anybody's guess. I don't think they found the surveillance device I put in there, because I can still see the space."

"Maybe and maybe not," replied Montgomery. "They might have found it but didn't remove it so you wouldn't know they had discovered it. Give them time to come up with a counterattack."

"You're getting good at this stuff," noted Devine.

"Not really, but I'm going to need to be."

"What do you mean?"

"The thing is, Travis, they're going to eventually realize how that camera got in there. And when they do, we are *both* going to be in deep shit."

# CHAPTER 58

THEY RODE BACK TO NEW York. Devine pulled in front of the walk-up, and Montgomery climbed off and passed him the spare helmet.

"Can you come up for a little bit? Now that it's fully hit me that I was the unwitting messenger for a criminal syndicate, I don't want to be alone. I might slit my wrists."

"Don't joke about that," said Devine.

"I'm not joking."

They went upstairs, got beers, and returned to the roof and sat in the deck chairs.

"Now, you said you met Cowl about a year ago. But I imagine Area 51 has been going on a lot longer than that."

"So how did they work the signals before me? Did he just use a different method?"

"He built the house that the train overlooks three years ago. And now I guess I understand why he allowed a gap between the tree canopies and the wall. So the person on the train could see. So maybe that method of communication dates to back then."

"You know, one morning while I was there I couldn't sleep and got up early. I looked out the window and Brad was raising the umbrella at one of the tables by the pool."

"Red or green?" asked Devine.

She thought for a moment. "Red. I thought it was odd. I mean, it was so early. And I think the train came by a few minutes later."

Devine looked thoughtful. "There was a guy on the train who said he saw another woman by the pool, before you hooked up with Cowl. She was a brunette and she wore a bikini early in the morning sometimes, too."

"Really?"

"Yeah."

She sat back, looking perplexed at first, and then a look of understanding came into her eyes. "I thought Christian was helping me by introducing me to Brad in Italy. But maybe Brad was looking for a new messenger girl and Christian was really helping *him*."

"I think you might be right. Hey, do you think this 'brunette' might have stayed in this building, too?"

Michelle suddenly became rigid. "When I was moving some things into my bedroom here, I found a credit card slip that had fallen behind a drawer."

Devine perked up at this. "Do you remember the name on the credit card?"

"I do actually because it was so unusual. Dominique Deveraux. Very alliterative. I mean, it sounds fake."

Devine took out his phone and searched the name.

"Okay, Dominique Deveraux was a character on the TV show *Dynasty*. Both in the original series back in the 1980s and then on the reboot on the CW."

"Maybe it was an alias, then."

"Hold on, here's another Dominique Deveraux." He clicked on a link and read down the page. "Age twenty-four, originally from California. And—"

He stopped speaking and stared at the screen, his look troubled.

"And *what*, Travis?"

He glanced up at her. "Deveraux killed herself nearly one year ago, by jumping into the East River."

# CHAPTER

# 59

DEVINE RODE BACK TO THE town house in Mount Kisco.

After they learned about Deveraux's fate, he and Michelle had first talked about her going into hiding. He had even thought about calling up Campbell to have his people protect her. But in the end they had decided that her best protection was to stay put. To not let Cowl or others know that anything was amiss. But he had told her to keep a watch out and call the cops if anything looked off.

He had communicated with Campbell about these latest developments and his meeting with Elaine Nestor, and arranged to meet with the man later.

There was no one at the town house at this time of the day. Valentine wasn't on the couch and the Mini Cooper wasn't in the garage. Tapshaw must be at her office, he thought.

He knocked on Speers's door; there was no answer. He called out, "Helen, you decent?" There was still no answer.

He tried to turn the knob. It was locked. That wasn't unusual. He locked his door, too. He could have picked it, but he didn't want to risk it. If she had a camera in there…

He went to his room, looked up the number for NYU Law School, and placed a call.

He was passed from person to person and department to department until he came to a man who seemed to be the right one.

Devine said, "My daughter, Helen Speers, just graduated from NYU. I haven't been able to reach her and I'm getting concerned.

She still lives in the same apartment. I'm on the West Coast. I wanted someone to go and check on her."

"That might be a matter for the police, Mr. Speers."

"Look, I paid a ton of money for her to go to law school there. Can you at least help me?"

"Please hold for just a moment."

He heard classical music for about thirty seconds before the man came back on. He said in a somewhat snarky tone, "We have no record of any Helen Speers being enrolled at the law school or having just graduated, Mr. Speers. You might want to check with your *daughter* about that. Have a good day."

Devine put down the phone. *Okay, Helen Speers is not who she claims to be. So who is she and why is she here?*

Devine thought back and recalled that Speers had come here just about the time he had. Was she a plant? If so, by whom? She had been very curious about everything, telling him time and again to let her recommend a lawyer for him. Since she hadn't gone to law school, he wondered what she would have done if he had taken the woman up on her offer. And where did she go during the day with her briefcase?

His phone buzzed. It was a number he didn't recognize.

"Hello?"

"Mr. Devine?"

"Yes?"

"This is Dr. John Wyman. You called my office seeking information on Sara Ewes?"

Devine tensed. "Yes, I did. I worked with her. We were friends."

"So you said in your message. What exactly do you want to know?"

"I know that she was pregnant but she ended up aborting the baby."

"I knew about her pregnancy, I didn't know she had terminated it."

"I talked to the doctor who helped with the abortion. Sara wasn't that far along, so it seems no medical procedure was necessary."

"So a medication abortion, then," said Wyman. "Probably done at home."

"Yes. Sara gave your name to the abortion clinic. Are you her ob-gyn?"

"Not exactly."

"I don't understand."

"Can you tell me of your interest in all this?" asked Wyman.

"As I said, I worked with her, and, well, the police and her mother seem to think that I was the father. Even though I didn't meet Sara until after she became pregnant. I'm not sure they believe that. Quite frankly, I think they want to make me out to be her murderer."

"I thought that might be it."

"What?" Devine said sharply.

"I know you're not the father of Sara Ewes's baby."

"How?"

"Because she underwent artificial insemination and utilized a donor in acquiring the sperm. I run a practice pretty much devoted to that. I told the police this when they came by to see me as well, which is why I'm telling you. They mentioned your name, not understanding at that point how Sara became pregnant. When I told them, they were quite surprised. They wanted to know if you had donated the sperm. I told them that you had not. I told them that Sara never mentioned you to me. When I saw your name on the message my receptionist took from you, I put two and two together and decided you needed to know the truth."

"Well, I appreciate that, Dr. Wyman. Do you know who donated the sperm?"

"No, I do not. Sara provided it. I told the police that, too."

"Then how do you know it wasn't me?"

"About six weeks after she became pregnant through insemination, Sara told me that the sperm donor had died. You obviously are very much alive."

"Was it Detectives Shoemaker and Ekman who talked to you?"

"Yes. And they seemed very disappointed to know that you were not the father."

"I'm sure they were. Did Sara have anyone with her when she consulted you, or when she had the insemination done?"

"No. But I got the sense that she was not going through this alone. That there was someone who was partnering with her in this process."

Devine thought of Jennifer Stamos, and then Brad Cowl. Cowl said he hadn't had sex with Ewes. But with artificial insemination, he wouldn't have had to. "She didn't mention any names?"

"She didn't, but from the little she volunteered, I had the impression that she was going to take time off to be with the child." He paused. "Was there someone like that in her life that you knew of?"

"Possibly," said Devine vaguely, and he meant to be very vague.

"Do you know how far along Sara was when she terminated her pregnancy?" asked Wyman.

"I was told about eight weeks. So, shortly after she told you the sperm donor had passed away."

"She seemed so excited about being a mother. I wonder what changed her mind?"

*So do I*, thought Devine.

# CHAPTER 60

DEVINE HEARD TAPSHAW'S CAR PULL into the one-car garage. Shortly thereafter he heard her come up the stairs. He listened to her open and close her bedroom door a few moments later. He sat on his bed and thought about things. The problem was there were too many things to think about.

Later, he heard the front door open and the sound of footsteps came up the stairs. He could tell by the footfalls that it was Speers. Her door closed as well. Then he heard her bedsprings squeak.

He looked at his watch. Six thirty. Speers would not expect him to be home. He walked over to the wall separating their bedrooms and put his ear to it. He heard clicking. She was on her laptop. He stood there, hoping that she might make a call and he could attempt to listen, but that didn't happen. The clicking stopped. A minute or so passed and her door opened and she passed down the hall. He opened his door a crack to see her at the top of the stairs dressed in her yoga clothes. She went down the steps.

He slipped out and quietly moved over to her door. He tried the knob. It turned. She had forgotten to lock it or thought there was no need. He slowly opened it and glanced back at the stairs. Normally Speers would take a good forty-five minutes for her yoga routine.

He stood in the doorway, looking around. The clothes she had obviously been wearing were lying on the floor. He glanced at the bed and thought for a moment of that sex-charged night and then pushed that right out of his head. This woman he'd thought was a friend was a potential enemy. He eased into the room and closed the door softly behind him. He could also hear clicking coming from Tapshaw's room; she was obviously humming away on her monster screens.

He did a quick search of the desk drawers and eyed the pile of law books that were stacked exactly as before. He opened the one on top and riffled through the pages: no marginalia, no highlighting; they were clearly for show. He went through the closet and bureau drawers and found nothing helpful. Her laptop and phone were time-locked and biometric protected, and thus inaccessible. Her purse was there and he took out her wallet. All the cards and driver's license said "Helen Speers," and the picture on the license was her. He put the wallet back and looked under the bed. A suitcase was there with no name tag. It was empty. He lifted the mattress and saw it underneath. A Glock 17 in black matte finish with pebbled grips and a Big Dot tritium night sight.

He put the mattress back in place and left.

As he was closing the door to leave, a voice said, "What are you doing, Travis?"

He turned to see Tapshaw in the doorway of her room holding a large coffee cup with Hummingbird's logo.

He said, "I was looking for Helen. I thought she was in her room. I had given her a book to read that I needed back. But I couldn't find it."

"Oh. I think she's downstairs doing her yoga."

"Thanks, I didn't hear her."

"Why are you home so early? Did you get fired?" she added playfully.

He grinned at her remark. "Some days I wish I had."

"Want some coffee? I'm going to make some."

"No, I'm good, thanks. I'll ask Helen about the book later, no need to bother her if you were going to."

"No problem." She glanced at him. "Are you sure you're okay, Travis? You just seem, I don't know, out of sorts."

He decided to tell her the truth. "Another woman from my office was found dead at her home."

She just stared at him for a moment. Then she shivered, shook her head, and said in a low voice, "Another woman? Was she...?"

"She was killed, yes."

Tears appeared in Tapshaw's large eyes. "Oh, God. I just don't understand how..."

"I...I got another email from that same source. Can I forward it to you to see if it helps you trace the other one?"

She looked at him with determination. "Definitely. I *will* trace it, Travis."

Tapshaw turned, walked back into her room, and closed the door. He heard the lock turn.

*And who could blame her?* he thought.

* * *

At eleven thirty that night Devine was awoken by movement in the hall. He listened for a moment, then rose and opened his door a crack.

Speers was in her nightgown and was peering down the steps leading to the main level. When she turned back around, he eased the door closed. He heard her walk back down the hall and then a door opened.

He looked out again and saw her enter Valentine's room. She closed the door behind her. Devine slipped out into the hall and wondered if Speers was enjoying a sexual encounter with Valentine as she had with him.

*Why should I be special?*

But then he heard snores wafting up from the main floor. He edged down the stairs and saw Valentine sleeping on the couch. Now he understood. That was why she had gone there first, to make sure the Russian wasn't in his bedroom.

Devine went back to his room.

A couple of minutes later there was a knock at his door.

"Yeah?"

"It's Helen."

"Give me a sec."

Devine sat up in his bed, laid his pillow next to his right hand, sat back against the headboard, and slipped his hand under the pillow where it gripped something.

"Come on in."

The door opened and Speers stood there in her nightgown that hit at midthigh. It was transparent enough with the backlight from the hall illumination to get his full attention. She had nothing on underneath.

"What's up?" he said evenly.

"I've missed you," she said.

"I've been here all evening."

"You know what I mean."

*Do I?* thought Devine. "With the way you're dressed, I guess I do, yeah."

She came in and closed the door behind her, locking it.

"I'm not sure Jill and Valentine are asleep," he said.

"I think Jill went out. Will is snoring on the couch. Pizza and beer do it every time. He's gonna have a coronary any day now."

She sat on the bed next to him, drawing her legs under her, and studied him. He made no move to draw closer.

"What? You're no longer interested?" she said.

"I'm just trying to understand why a young, beautiful, newly graduated lawyer needs to knock on my door. You can do a lot better than a thirtysomething Wall Street wannabe like me."

She said, "You undersell yourself, Travis. You're good-looking. And you're working in a field where you can make a lot of money. That's an attractive package. And you were a soldier, too, so you know how to take care of yourself. And me."

*I don't think you'd have any problem taking care of yourself*, thought Devine.

She reached out and put a hand on his thigh. "It's not complicated, Travis."

"It's all complicated, Helen. And for that reason, I think you need to go back to your room."

She eyed where his hand was under the bed and he saw something in her expression he didn't care for.

*She knows.*

"All right, but remember one thing."

"What's that?" he asked.

"I *never* sleep with my enemies."

He heard her feet padding back to her room, where she closed her door.

Devine sat up and pulled the Sig P226 out from under the pillow. He looked down at the gun, which looked similar to Speers's Glock, at least to the untrained eye.

What the hell was she doing searching Valentine's room?

*And was the visit tonight just about showing me she's my ally?*

Then it dawned on him.

*She knows I searched her room. I put everything back just so, but I must have been a millimeter off somewhere. So, the lady is good. Real good. And if she is my ally, that's also really good for me.*

*But if she's lying and she's my enemy?*

# CHAPTER 61

THE 6:20. RIGHT ON TIME. Devine was really starting to hate this commute.

*Actually, there's no* starting *about it.*

He looked, but there was no Michelle Montgomery at the pool. He didn't imagine she would be told to wear the green bikini for a while, if ever.

Later, he walked into the lobby at Cowl and Comely, waved at Sam the guard, and took the elevator up to his floor.

Turning a corner, he nearly tripped over the custodian, Jerry Myers, who was kneeling in front of a door fixing the lock.

"Sorry," said Devine.

The man looked up, and recognition sprang into his features.

"You were the one asking questions that day."

"I was."

Myers stood and put his tools back in the box on the floor. "And now there's another one, they say. Only she wasn't killed here, thank God. Couldn't take finding another body."

"I'm sure."

"The police got any leads?" Myers asked.

"Not that I know of, but they're not keeping me in their confidences."

Myers hefted his toolbox. "You guys slaving away in this place. I mean, you ask me, it's not worth it. No sir."

"Maybe it's not."

"So why do it?"

"When I figure it out I'll let you know. Got a question. I understand that contractors and other service people come in through the rear entrance."

"That's right. There's a phone they have to use. Goes to the security desk. Then they go let the person in, if they're authorized."

"Or if they have a security card, they can get in that way."

"Sure, but contractors don't have security cards. That'd be a problem. Can't just let folks waltz in the back door like that."

"Right. Thanks."

Later, around two in the afternoon, Devine was working away in his cubicle when the door opened.

"Mr. Devine?"

He looked up and saw the same woman who had previously come to retrieve him motioning to him. He rose, looked around at the Burners watching him suspiciously, and made his way out.

Detectives Ekman and Shoemaker were waiting for him.

"Now what?" he said.

"This way," barked Shoemaker.

They led him to the same room as before.

Sitting across from him, Shoemaker said, "We talked to the guard on duty at night. He said that you and Stamos came into the building late on the day Ewes's body was found, and then left at the same time."

"That's not true."

"You saying the guard's lying?" Ekman said sharply.

"No, he just misinterpreted what he saw. I didn't know Stamos was in the building that night. I came back for my phone and did some work. Then I left. Alone. Did the guard say Stamos and I were together?"

The detectives exchanged glances. "Did you meet up with her in the building?" asked Shoemaker.

"No, and I'll take a polygraph on that if you want."

"Did you meet up with her later?"

Now they were getting into dangerous territory. But since he had asked the question, Devine suspected the man already knew the answer.

"It wasn't a meeting. I went to a bar in Greenwich Village. She was there. We talked."

"And you never mentioned this before because...?"

"I saw her in a bar, so did a lot of other people."

"You seem to use that excuse a lot," said Ekman.

"Because it's true."

"We understand that you two argued in that bar. And then you kicked the shit out of three guys in the alley next to the bar. And that she saw the whole thing."

"I did have a fight with three guys, yes."

"Over Stamos?"

"It could be construed that way."

"And again you never mentioned that to us because..."

"What relevance would it have?"

"You've gotta be kidding, right?" said Ekman.

"That all happened *before* she was killed, in case you forgot. And by the way, I found out that Sara's pregnancy was from artificial insemination. Thanks for telling *me* that. You knew I wasn't the father all along."

"Just to get this straight, we don't have to tell you jack shit," barked Ekman.

"And how did you find out about that?" asked Shoemaker, leaning forward and drilling Devine with a hard stare.

"I got the name of the doctor from Mrs. Ewes. I called him. He told me."

"And why would he do that?"

"Because he thought you guys were trying to pin the murder on me."

Shoemaker sat back and said, "And we understand Stamos came

to visit you at your place in Mount Kisco. You two had another argument."

*Shit, how could they have found that out? Helen Speers?*

"She did come out to my place, but we didn't have an argument. We just talked."

"What did you talk about?"

"Sara."

"What about Ewes?"

"Just chitchat."

"Devine, you are one inch from being arrested for obstruction," exclaimed Shoemaker. "So you better consider your next answer really carefully. What did you discuss about Ewes?"

"Stamos said that she also knew I wasn't the father of Ewes's baby. She didn't come out and say it, but reading between the lines she knew that Ewes had gone the artificial insemination route."

Ekman shot his partner a look. "Wait a minute, from all we learned those ladies were rivals at the firm. Why would they be talking about babies and such?"

Devine decided to just tell the truth. He could tell he was close to being put in jail, and he couldn't very well do much from there.

"Stamos told me that she and Ewes... that they were in love."

Devine expected both detectives to blow up at him.

Instead, Shoemaker cracked a smile. "Finally, we get some truth out of you."

"What do you mean by that?" said Devine curiously. "Did you find something to back up what I just told you?"

"Stamos's place has been searched. Electronics all gone. Phone and computer are probably at the bottom of the Hudson by now."

"Did you find something online then? Instagram, Facebook?"

"No, we checked all that. There was nothing."

"Not surprising," said Devine. "There're rules against employees seeing each other."

He thought for a moment about Stamos and Cowl, but *he* really wasn't an employee.

Shoemaker said, "But we talked to one of Stamos's sisters. Apparently she'd confided in her."

"So you know I'm telling the truth, then?"

"Just about *that*, Devine. But there's a lot about you that neither one of us likes."

"Well, when that becomes a crime, be sure to let me know."

# CHAPTER 62

Devine left work around eight and headed to check in with the Eweses. They might go back to New Zealand anytime now. Ellen Ewes had made it clear that she loathed the city. And he wanted to find out if they knew about Stamos and their daughter. Or about Sara's being artificially inseminated. Ellen Ewes hadn't mentioned that fact. She hadn't really said whether she knew her daughter was pregnant before the police had told her. She was just furious about the termination of that pregnancy. Devine wanted to ask her directly. She struck him as the sort that kept a lot back.

He got to the house and knocked, but there was no answer. He looked through the sidelight next to the door, but could see nothing.

"Mr. and Mrs. Ewes?" He knocked again, then tried the knob. It was unlocked.

*Just like in the movies.*

He pushed it open and poked his head in. "Hello, Ellen, Fred? It's Travis Devine. I just wanted to talk to you for a minute."

He went inside and closed the door behind him. "Hello? Anybody here?"

The place was dark, with the dim outside light being the only illumination.

He walked through the front room and peeked into the kitchen.

Nothing, although there were some dirty dishes in the sink and an empty coffee cup was on the table.

He walked toward the bedroom and looked in there. The bed was made and the bathroom was empty. His gaze lingered on the bed for a moment. It was there that he and Ewes had had sex. Once. And then she had broken it off. He thought she had found another guy.

But then to find out she and Stamos were in love? He shook his head. He'd had no inkling that Ewes had been gay or maybe bisexual. Yet she had obviously wanted a child. But then why go through all the steps necessary for artificial insemination and then terminate the pregnancy?

But now that he thought about it, the timing was off. The pregnancy had occurred before Devine had even met Ewes. If she and Stamos were going to have a baby together, why would Ewes sleep with him? They must have gotten together *afterward.*

*Then maybe Sara had a relationship with someone else along with the pregnancy. Then was that relationship broken off and the pregnancy terminated? Was that how she fell into bed with me? A rebound off another guy? Or another woman?*

With Ewes, Devine had thought he might have finally found a woman with whom he could spend the rest of his life. In addition to being beautiful, Ewes had been kind and funny and smart and caring. There had been a spark from their first meeting, which led to other meetings. During firm outings they had ended up spending time together, talking and secretly planning to see each other. Everything had to be kept on the QT because of company rules. And then they had come here and slept together. It had been immensely satisfying to Devine. He had even thought about quitting Cowl and getting another job so that Ewes and he could come out in the open.

But after that night together, she had withdrawn from him, and finally the end had come. Not in an email or a text. Just a look from her in the hallway and a mouthed *I'm sorry, Travis*. And that had been it. And if Ewes was attracted to women instead of men, he could understand her decision. One had to be who one was.

He turned and walked to what he knew was the guest bedroom. Outside in the hall were two large roller suitcases. He looked at the tags. They were the Eweses'. They had flown on United from California to here, after the much longer journey from New Zealand to the Golden State.

He stepped inside the bedroom and flicked on the light.

And Devine stopped right in the doorway.

Ellen and Fred were in bed. They would not be waking back up. There was blood all over the bedcovers and they were staring up at the ceiling with lifeless eyes. Ellen Ewes looked surprised. Fred just looked like he was watching TV.

Devine slipped over and touched the woman's skin. Ice. He tried to bend her arm. Still pretty stiff. He knew that meant rigor was already well established. They'd been dead awhile, he knew. Devine had seen his share of stiff bodies in the Middle East.

He looked for what had killed them. There were slashes in the covers around their chests. A knife, probably. It was a savage attack.

He retreated, wiping off his prints along the way.

He poked his head out the front door and looked all around. The coast right now was reasonably clear, at least he hoped. He stepped out and closed the door with his coat sleeve over his hand. He set off at a rapid pace and called Campbell along the way and told him what he had discovered.

"Get as far away from there as you can," said the old general. "Full retreat, Devine."

"But what about the bodies? The police have to be notified."

"Leave that to us."

Devine clicked off and picked up his pace. He reached the subway on Fulton Street and made his way back to Grand Central, covering the four miles in about twelve minutes. He retraced his train's morning route and eyed Cowl's place closely when they reached it, looking for any sign of activity, but saw none.

He had seen his share of violent death in war. Bodies mangled beyond all recognition. People he knew and fought alongside. He had grieved and moved on because you had to in a war zone.

But the two bodies in the bed? It had sickened him, shaken him right to his core. He was no longer in a war zone, but it felt like he was.

Devine didn't make eye contact with anyone the whole ride home.

He grabbed a cab at the station because his legs were rubbery, took it home, went up to his room, and sat on his bed, trying to make sense of what had just happened.

*Who would want to kill the Eweses? The same people who killed Sara? But Sara was killed because she had found out that Cowl and Comely was a laundering machine. She knew about the Lombard. She probably knew a lot more. Stamos the same.*

But why the parents? Ellen Ewes said she and her daughter were estranged. Why would Sara have told her mother and father anything about Cowl and Comely—and if she hadn't, why would someone kill her parents? Because the killer was afraid she *might* have told her parents something? Or since her mom and dad were staying at Sara's place the killer might have feared the Eweses would find something damaging?

Something felt off about that, but what else could it be?

He went downstairs and grabbed a Coke from the fridge. There was no one here, which was a good thing, because Devine didn't want to deal with any of his roommates right now.

He sat at the small kitchen table and looked out the window. Someone might have seen him enter and leave Sara Ewes's old home, where two butchered bodies lay. Campbell said he would take care of notifying the police. But even with that Devine expected a visit from Shoemaker and Ekman. And as unpleasant as the first few encounters had been, he assumed the next one would be the worst of all. If they could find any reason to arrest him, they would.

He heard the front door open, and a few moments later Will Valentine poked his head into the kitchen.

"Locust Group?" he said.

"What about it?" asked Devine, perking up. "Did you find stuff?"

Valentine sat down next to him and opened his laptop. "They own shitload of stuff. I mean shitload."

"I know of three different places in the city alone."

"Three! Dude, give me fuckin' break." He hit a key on his laptop and screen after screen of line items associated with properties and other assets flashed across it.

"Wait a minute, that's all Locust?" exclaimed Devine.

"I have computer stop count at one hundred forty-one thousand three hundred and twelve different properties, assets, and businesses. In fifty-seven countries, but most of it in America. That is tip of iceberg. It is serious shit. In all fifty states. And they are buried deep, so nobody will find out. I track Locust Group through shell companies, consortiums, SPACs, investment funds, tax shelters, CBOs, derivatives, debt funds. They own whole fuckin' towns in Idaho and Wyoming and Montana and Alabama and Arkansas and other places. And they own whole blocks in New York, Chicago, Los Angeles, Atlanta, Houston, and other big cities. Gold and silver mines, uranium, chemical, and manufacturing plants, oil refineries. They own sports teams and TV and radio stations and newspapers and streaming platforms, social media sites and a whole shitload of other stuff. Never seen anything like it, dude. I mean, not even Putin is this fuckin' big, and never in my life did I think I would ever say that."

"How much asset value are we talking about?"

"Shit, maybe forty trillion."

Devine gaped. "How far back do some of the transactions go?"

"I find slew of them back over fifteen years."

"Okay, that fits with other things I've found out."

"What is going on, Travis?"

"Money laundering, probably. For example, your buddy Putin and his friends have dirty money to get rid of. Money they steal from the Russian people. Right?"

"Shit, yes. Putin is so rich he makes Bezos and Musk look poor. But he say he is not rich, and nobody disagrees with him because they get shot or poisoned or put in prison."

"So, the dirty money comes over here and it's used to buy all sorts of assets. Then instead of dirty money, you own a house or a building or a company or a chunk of the Dow Jones, whatever. That's why they call it money laundering."

Valentine nodded. "I know this! Clean money, dude. That is name of game."

"But it's not just about owning assets. With radio and TV and newspapers and online streaming platforms and social media sites, and owning whole towns and city blocks, they can manipulate and control everything. From cradle to grave."

"Dude, that is not good. That is Russia."

"Can you send me all that stuff? I've got someone I want to show it to."

Valentine looked at him curiously as he did this. "You are not what you want us to think?"

"Are you?"

"Just a hacker, dude."

"A good one."

"Take you long enough to say, asshole." But he tacked on a grin to this. Valentine opened the fridge, grabbed a beer, and walked off, while Devine stared down at his hands, thinking. Something Valentine had said had stuck in his head and had made him think of Cowl's own words from that old interview with the *Journal*: *A partnership can be simply an idea or a perspective.*

He grabbed his laptop from his room and plugged in the name Anne Comely, running it through a popular site on the internet that he had used before, but then only for fun.

There was nothing fun about the exercise this time.

It didn't take long for the program to kick out what Devine knew was the exact right answer.

An anagram for "Anne Comely" was... *CLEAN MONEY.*

# CHAPTER 63

Devine would not be taking the 6:20 in that morning. He knew that as soon as he saw Detectives Shoemaker and Ekman waiting for him at the Mount Kisco train station. Shoemaker tapped out a smoke and both men came forward.

"Pretty early for you guys to be all the way out here."

"Come on, we'll drive you to work this morning, Devine, courtesy of NYPD," said Ekman.

His tone was friendlier, which bothered Devine greatly. Was it just a façade before the hammer came down?

They started off, Devine in the rear seat. He was waiting for the question and it wasn't long in coming. He just needed to pull off the surprised part.

"Fred and Ellen Ewes are dead." Before Devine could reply in a shocked manner, Ekman turned and looked at him. "We know you already know."

Devine nearly swallowed his tongue on that one.

"And we know you got an alibi. We talked to your 'friend' Helen Speers. You were with her at the town house during the time in question."

"You talked to Helen? When?"

"That's none of your concern," pointed out Shoemaker. "I thought you'd be thrilled she'd provided an alibi."

"So is that when they were killed?" he asked.

Ekman nodded. "Between eleven and one that night, yeah. Stabs to the heart. Died pretty quickly. But whoever it was just kept right on stabbing them. It was damn vicious. I've been doing this job a long time. It was one of the worst I've seen."

Shoemaker said, "You have friends in high places. You should have told us."

"I would if I could have."

"So three people dead who were connected to Sara Ewes, who was also murdered. And what was her sin?"

"She was connected to Brad Cowl, who has disappeared."

"So, he killed her?"

"He was probably in the building that night. He got a call that I believe was from Stamos on the night she was killed. He headed out in time to murder her. Her phone records should show that."

"And why would he do that?"

"My friends in high places didn't enlighten you?"

"The only message we got was that you were a good guy on a government mission and to have your back."

Ekman added, "So, what's so special about Cowl?"

"Some things have come to light. But I can't share them with you. Not that I don't want to, but fruit-of-a-tainted-tree sort of thing. If I infect the cops with it, the case is dead and the man walks."

Ekman nodded. "Okay, that makes sense. So, Cowl is a bad guy. Is his money dirty, is that what this is about?"

"It's not *his* money. It belongs to other people. People from outside this country. And that's really all I can say. If the folks above me want to say more, that's up to them."

Ekman and Shoemaker exchanged a look. Ekman said, "Okay, but we're homicide. Financial crimes are another division. We just want whoever killed these people. And it looks like it's Cowl to you?"

"Or someone working for him. Rich guys don't usually do the deed, do they? They hire others to do it. Like that Hancock guy. Speaking of, why would he focus on me out of all people?"

"We don't know," said Ekman.

"And he also knew before it was made public that Sara had not killed herself. That it was murder. Did you give someone a heads-up on that?"

Shoemaker said, "Brad Cowl is a very important guy in this town. He's been very generous with certain people at NYPD and City Hall. I'm not saying any heads-up came from there, but I wouldn't be surprised if it did."

Ekman interjected, "But from what you said, Cowl might have done Stamos himself."

"He might have. There might not have been time to hire a gun. By the way, how did she die?"

Ekman glanced at Shoemaker. "It goes no further, Devine."

"It won't."

"The killer drugged her, then tied her to her bed, and then carved the word *bitch* on her belly. She bled out."

Devine felt the little breakfast he'd eaten start to come back up on him. He bent forward and stared at the floorboard, his breathing short and choppy. After about thirty seconds he sat up straight and looked at the two men.

Shoemaker almost appeared sympathetic. "Yeah, I know," he said quietly. "Pretty sick."

"Was Stamos pregnant?"

"No, that's what we thought, too. ME confirmed that she wasn't," replied Ekman.

"So why do it...that way?"

"It was to send a message, is what I'm thinking. What that message was, who knows."

"And no one saw anything?" asked Devine.

"Nope. We've checked. That late on a weekday in that neighborhood, not surprising. We think the killer got in through a window in the back. Stamos was on the first floor. No signs of a struggle. Same with the Eweses. They were probably dead asleep." Ekman blanched. "Sorry, bad choice of words."

"So, the Ewes family got wiped out," said Shoemaker thoughtfully. "Which seemed to be the killer's intent. But why? Why did they have to die? They just got to the country. What possible beef could someone have with them? Is it just the connection with their daughter?"

"And her connection to Brad Cowl?" added Ekman. "If he is involved in some crooked money scheme, and maybe Sara Ewes found out? They could have been afraid that she had told her parents something."

"I was thinking that, too, but now I seriously doubt that actually happened," said Devine. "She was estranged from her parents. They were Christian missionaries, and I don't think they would have had any interest in or understanding of any part of Sara's world."

"You mean her and Stamos being a thing, like you told us before?"

"Yes. Her mother was not in favor of same-sex couples and made no secret of it."

"But how could someone even know that? They just got to New York."

"Well, I found out just by being around her for a few minutes. And she thought her daughter was a slut sleeping around outside of marriage."

Shoemaker said, "We seem to be going in circles. If all these deaths aren't connected to the Cowl business, what then?"

Devine thought back to the emails he had gotten. The one that not even the likes of Will Valentine could trace, and he didn't know if Campbell's people would have better luck. Although he was hoping Tapshaw, and her magical fingers, could do the trick.

*Was the killer trying to let me know that I'm involved in all this? Do they blame me for what happened to Sara and Jennifer? Who would have that sort of grudge against me? What have I done?*

He debated on whether to share this with the detectives, but decided not to. It would just piss them off that he had withheld such evidence. And they were getting along so well right now.

"You said the Eweses were stabbed in the *heart*?"

"Right through, yeah. Why?" asked Shoemaker.

"The heart symbolizes emotions, beliefs, feelings."

"So?" said Ekman.

"I don't know. Just thinking out loud. Maybe the killer murdered each person in ways to symbolize the *reason* why they were killed."

Ekman and Shoemaker exchanged another, interested glance.

"Sara Ewes was hanged. What does that symbolize?" asked Ekman.

"Well," said Devine, "in the past, they used to hang *traitors*."

*So when does my turn come?*

# CHAPTER 64

It was barely noon and the news of Fred and Ellen Ewes's having been murdered had circulated throughout Cowl and Comely.

Devine abruptly left his office and sought out Wanda Simms.

"Any idea where Mr. Cowl is?" he asked.

"I'm not his keeper, Travis," the woman said sharply, but then her look immediately softened. "I'm sorry, but this is all getting to me. Four people have been murdered. And two of them worked here, and the other victims were the parents of one of them."

"You'd think the head of the company would be around to lead the troops."

She looked at him skeptically. "For all I know he jetted off to some island with a group of swimsuit models. But if you say I told you that I'll deny it."

"Have you spoken to his little group of executives?"

"I have. And they won't say a word about him. Too afraid, I would imagine."

*I would imagine, too.*

"Wanda, do you have any idea what's on the fifty-first floor?"

Her look immediately became guarded. "Why, what's it to you?"

"Four people have been killed, like you said. And that floor is the only one that no one can access."

"Oh come on, Travis. Every investment house has secure areas.

It's probably where the high-frequency trading takes place. Just servers and the like. Did you ever think of that?"

*Yes, I did*, thought Devine. "One more thing. Did you tell anyone that I had come up to the fifty-second floor on the morning Sara's body was found?"

She looked warily at him. "Why?"

"Just trying to figure something out."

"I might have mentioned it to Jenn Stamos, actually. Now she's dead, too. And she was really broken up about Sara's death. I didn't think they were that friendly."

"Well, you just never know. Thanks."

*So that's why Hancock was sicced on me so fast. Stamos might have learned from Sara that we had slept together. And then I show up asking questions. She tells Cowl, and Cowl gives marching orders to Hancock—or Bartlett, rather—to go play detective and find out what he can. And Stamos also told Cowl I had come back to the building that night and that the guard saw me. He checked the security log and there was my security card for the fifty-second floor. And then he sees my security card log-in and my face on the video on the night Sara died and plans to frame me.*

And he also thought that might be why Rachel Potter from Channel 44 had been on his case, too. One of her confidential or probably anonymous sources might have been Hancock/Bartlett using her to put the squeeze on him.

He texted Campbell, asking for a meeting.

He got a nearly instant reply, and location. He left Cowl and headed for the Fifties again.

And on the way he got another email from the untraceable source.

I was surprised I could find Mr. and Mrs. Eweses' hearts to stab. The world is better off without them. I hope you agree.

Devine slowly put the phone away and kept walking. But with every step the dread he was feeling grew like a cancer, creeping to every organ he had.

* * *

The restaurant door opened for Devine and he slipped inside.

Campbell was waiting for him in the same room.

"Thanks for running interference for me last night."

"I take it the detectives assigned to the case have made contact?"

"Early this morning. They're playing nice."

"Good. We have been monitoring Area 51. It's still shut down."

"I had a buddy of mine dig up some things on the Locust Group." He went on to tell the general about how many companies and assets and countries were involved.

"My folks are finding the same thing. And it goes far beyond the Locust Group. We saw a great many entities that appeared regularly on the surveillance feed, even in the short time we had access before it was shut down."

Devine also told him about his theory on the name Anne Comely being an anagram.

"*Clean Money*? I think you must be right."

"Were you able to trace those emails? Because I just got another one." He showed Campbell the latest message.

The general sighed and sat back. "The long and short of it is, no. The general consensus is that none of my IT people have seen anything like this."

Devine said, "I received that first email on the day that Sara's body was found. As you saw, it had intimate details about the murder that only the killer would know. At first I thought someone else had found her body and emailed me because, well, they knew that I liked Sara."

"I think it was more than *liked*, Devine."

He looked at the general with a blank expression.

"I have three sons and two daughters, soldier. I've seen broken hearts before."

Devine looked at the general with a new level of respect. "As far as I know, I'm the only one who got those emails."

"The killer must be someone at the firm. We thought that all along, didn't we?"

"Yes, and there's something else. The way the people were killed. Sara hanged. Stamos... Stamos..."

"Yes, I know all about that, continue."

"And Sara's parents stabbed through the heart. I think each was symbolic."

"What's your take on what each one represents?"

"Sara the traitor. Stamos, well, I'm not sure. But her wounds reflected the killer's anger at maybe losing Sara, and Stamos and Sara were in love. And Sara's parents' hearts were destroyed. And from what I learned of their relationship it might mean the killer knows about Sara and her mother's estrangement, too. The killer intimated that it was difficult for him to find their hearts, and that the world was better off without such people."

"You know what all that adds up to, don't you?"

"Sir?"

"That the reasons these people were killed have nothing to do with Brad Cowl and Area 51, and everything to do with Sara Ewes. Which means the matter is more for the police than it is for me and you. We need to focus on the scheme at Cowl and Comely, Devine. The police can solve the murders."

"But it could still be someone at Cowl's firm who committed the murders," countered Devine. "Sara was pregnant. And even though she had artificial insemination through a donor, we don't know who that donor was."

Campbell looked intrigued by this theory. "You think it might have been Cowl? Because that would put it back in our camp."

Even though Devine had been told the donor had died, there was no proof of that. "It's certainly possible. He said he never slept with her, but he could have donated his sperm. And he had motive, means, and opportunity."

"So, you have *two* different cases to solve, but maybe with a related core element: Brad Cowl. And then there's the question of who might be next," added Campbell.

Devine looked up to see Campbell staring at him and perhaps reading his thoughts.

"And that someone might be you," Campbell said.

# CHAPTER

# 65

DEVINE WAS ON HIS WAY to the subway after leaving work early when his phone rang.

"Michelle?"

"Where are you?" she asked.

"Walking up Broad Street and enjoying the heat, why?"

"Can you meet me at Brad's place later, the one outside the city?"

"Why?"

"I can't get into his penthouse without his phone, but I do have a key to the house. If he's not there, we can make a search. We might find something to nail that son of a bitch. And if he is there we can... well, *strangle* the asshole."

"Sounds good to me."

Devine took the train home, changed, and was heading out when Tapshaw called out to him.

He turned to see her at the top of the stairs. "I got an email this morning. Mayflower is going to pull the trigger and invest. *Fifty million*, Travis, and at a valuation that will leave me with complete control of the company. This will change everything."

He tried to force a smile. Force, because if this *was* dirty money, and it had to be taken back? "That's great, Jill. You must have really wowed them. And that valuation means you are rich!"

She blushed at this. "I've been scrimping and saving for so long, it doesn't feel any different. But I believe they definitely think there's a lot of potential in my platform and business plan. If I close the deal, how about another tequila date? You helped me a lot."

He again forced a smile. "I'm all in. But my turn to buy."

She put her hands on her hips. "Hell, Travis, with all that money I think I can afford to splurge a little. And the thousand dollars *you* put in? It's worth a lot more now."

He watched her walk off. And then his smile faded. *Shit.*

He hopped on his bike and sped off to meet Montgomery.

She was waiting outside the gates for him. She had Ubered out, she told him.

"What about the hired help?" he asked.

"They're used to me being around. And as I said before, they're no fans of Brad's."

They headed into the house and a maid came around the corner and nearly plowed into them.

"Oh my goodness, Miss Michelle, I'm sorry."

"It's okay, Denise. Is Brad here? I've been calling and calling and nothing."

"No, ma'am. I haven't seen him in a few days. But that's not unusual. He's so busy. He might be in China for all I know."

"Right, well, we're going to hang out here for a bit. Travis here works for Brad, and hopefully, he'll show up. Look, why don't you and the rest of the crew take the rest of the night off? There's no reason for you to hang around."

"But if Mr. Cowl—"

"If he shows up, I'll take full responsibility." She smiled impishly. "And I can mix the man a drink myself if he so requires. And fry him an egg."

Denise grinned. "All right, miss, if you're sure."

Ten minutes later the staff had left and gone to their quarters on the other side of the property.

Montgomery closed the door behind them and turned to Devine. "Let's hit it."

She led him into what looked like a home office.

"What exactly are we looking for?" he asked.

"Anything to show the guy is a crook."

"And maybe a killer," he said.

"Two people dead and—"

"It's now *four*, actually."

She whirled around to stare at him. "What!"

"Sara Ewes's parents. They were murdered in their bed at Sara's place two nights ago."

"Oh my God. And you think Brad—?"

"I don't know. I do know someone sent me, and apparently only me, an email detailing Sara's crime scene. They also sent me messages about the murders of Stamos and the Eweses. It has to have been the killer. Which means the person has some beef with me. Only I don't know why."

"You had a thing going with Sara. Maybe the killer knew and was jealous."

"That would explain some things. And Stamos and Sara were apparently a couple but keeping it under wraps. Maybe that's why Stamos was killed."

"And the parents?"

"The mother was outright hostile to Sara's lifestyle. The email shows the killer didn't like that. But I'd like to know how the person knew about it."

"It might have been in a diary or something."

"Which the cops couldn't find."

"Why would the killer care what her mother thought of Sara?"

"I don't know," admitted Devine.

"Hey, maybe she broke up with the guy she was seeing. He was the father and she ended the pregnancy because she didn't want to carry his baby."

"I found out that Sara had artificial insemination. She used a sperm donor."

"But then why terminate the pregnancy?"

Devine shook his head. "No idea."

They began searching the office. They found nothing helpful there and headed upstairs.

"We have separate bedrooms," Montgomery told him. "Brad's is at the end of the hall. It's about as big as my apartment."

They went inside the chamber, which was really a suite with multiple rooms and every rich-guy toy one could hope for: two fireplaces, enormous TVs, a full bar, a sitting area, a spa with steam room, sauna, and whirlpool, a massage room, and a bathtub nearly large enough to do laps in, with a walk-in shower next to it that looked like a Roman grotto. And five classic pinball machines along with a pool table.

"Who could sleep in here?" he said. "Too many distractions." Devine looked at the bed that was about the size of his room. "How do two people find each other on that?"

"Brad never had a problem finding *me*, I can assure you."

"Don't go there, Michelle. I do not want to hear it."

After a fruitless search, they perched on the bed and gazed out the floor-to-ceiling tinted windows.

"So, what now?" asked Montgomery.

"The penthouse is a no-go. Area 51 the same. So I'm not sure what now."

Devine's phone buzzed. It was Campbell.

"We need to talk right away."

"Where are you?" asked Devine.

"The first place we met."

"I can be there in thirty minutes." He glanced at Montgomery. "Mind if I bring along someone?"

"Who?"

Devine told him.

"That is not a good idea, Devine. We have no idea if she's working for Cowl and just stringing you along."

Devine looked at Montgomery. "I've trusted her with my life, and she came through. She's had plenty of opportunities to throw me to the dogs and she hasn't. I've told her a lot. And if she had ratted me out to Cowl, I wouldn't be around."

"This is highly unusual, Devine."

"You recruited me, sir. I'm not a trained spy or intel officer. I'm flying by the seat of my pants. But in the Middle East I spent years reading people, trying to decide if they were trustworthy or would betray me when the opportunity arose. And I got damn good at it. So I'm just asking you to trust me on this. Soldier to soldier."

"See you in thirty."

Montgomery stared at him fearfully. "Y-you…you're a spy?"

"I don't know what I am, really."

"Who the hell was *that*?"

"You're about to find out."

# CHAPTER 66

A RETIRED GENERAL?" SAID MONTGOMERY after Devine finished explaining where they were going as they climbed on the bike and sped off.

"Yeah."

"And you work for him?"

"It's complicated."

"You really *weren't* at Cowl for the money. I knew it," she added in a self-satisfied tone.

"It's complicated," he repeated.

"Not from where I'm sitting." She hugged him more tightly. "I'm so proud of you."

"Okay. And thanks, I guess."

They reached the strip mall and Devine knocked on the door. It opened and they were admitted. A man in a suit led the way and ushered them in to see Campbell. He rose from behind his desk and extended a hand to Montgomery.

"Pleasure to meet you, Ms. Montgomery. Let me get the technicalities out of the way. You breathe one word of this to anyone, you'll be spending the next twenty years in a federal prison, are we clear?"

Montgomery gave Devine a dubious look. "Pretty damn clear," she replied.

"Sit."

"What's so important we had to meet this fast?" asked Devine.

"Certain lawmakers in Washington have gotten wind of what we're doing and are seeking to put the kibosh on our mission."

"Why the hell would they do that?" said Devine. "Enemies of this country are—" He broke off and eyed Campbell.

"Devine, there is one thing that drives our politics. It's simple and out in the open and yet most people never give it a second thought: money. It used to be that the sources of political funding were severely limited, and those sources also had to be disclosed. That is no longer the case." He leaned forward. "So, let me tell both of you why my humble office is really interested in Cowl and Comely." He paused, collecting his thoughts. "We think Cowl is the key link in not just laundering money and buying parts of this country by global players all over the world, but some of the money—billions and billions of it—is going into the coffers of public officials at every level, from local to federal. Now, people do not give that sort of money without expecting something in return. That means that what was revealed in the Pandora Papers and like investigations is just the beginning. The laundered money is being weaponized to really take over this country at all levels."

Montgomery said, "I thought there were, like, laws against that kind of stuff?"

"But if you have enough money, the laws don't apply to you," answered Campbell. "And certain people, some of them in high positions of power, want it to keep going. Certain others don't want this to be uncovered and investigated because they would be directly implicated."

"So, what do we do?" asked Devine.

"Solve this thing before they pull our plug. However, I do have one lead for you."

"What is it?" asked Devine.

"The brownstone on the Upper East Side owned by the Locust Group?"

"The one my good buddy Christian Chilton presumably lives

in," said Devine, glancing at Montgomery, who looked uncomfortable at this change in the conversation's direction.

"We put it under surveillance after you told us about the connection. Two people who are on an Interpol 'keep eyes on' list were seen entering and leaving the premises."

"And you couldn't grab them?" asked Montgomery.

"We had no legal grounds to do so. But these are bad people."

"Do we know if anyone else lives there with Chilton?" asked Devine.

Montgomery answered. "His grandfather, Carroll Chilton, did. We called him Poppy. But I haven't seen him in years."

"Was the brownstone Carroll Chilton's and then he sold it to Locust?" said Devine.

Campbell nodded. "From what we could uncover, yes. For three times what it's worth. And it might have been his grandson who actually sold it."

Devine and Montgomery exchanged glances. He said, "Maybe I should go check the place out."

"Maybe you should."

Devine and Montgomery rose. Devine looked at her and said, "I'll drop you off at your place in town."

"I'm going with you."

"I can't let you do that, Michelle."

Campbell said, "He's right, Ms. Montgomery. That is not possible."

"Either you let me go, or I'll just show up there on my own."

Devine said, "I'm dropping you off. Let's go."

He grabbed her arm and dragged her from the room.

When they were outside, she yanked her arm free and said, "Look, you son of a bitch, you can't tell me what—"

"Shut up and get on the bike. That was for the general's benefit. You're coming."

Montgomery closed her mouth, put on her helmet, and they rode off.

# CHAPTER 67

THEY PARKED ACROSS FROM THE brownstone.

"That's Chilton's BMW in front," observed Devine.

"I've known Christian since we were kids. He's not some criminal."

"He told me he's running Mayflower. His grandfather started it, and he's his generation's representative. What do you remember about his father and grandfather?"

"Mr. Chilton was a decent guy. Always nice to me. Christian's grandfather, Poppy Chilton, was incredibly kind. He would play games with us and read to us. Those were really happy times."

"And they had money?"

"Oh yeah. Lots."

"A ton of it? I mean, like Cowl?"

"No, not like that. They... they actually had to let my parents go when I was sixteen. The cars had dwindled down to just two. My dad didn't just work on the cars, he would chauffeur them around, too. The kids had grown up, of course, and my mother acted as a housekeeper and such. But I guess they couldn't afford her anymore, either."

"So they ran into hard times?"

"The year after we left, the Chiltons had to sell their home. It was a big estate, but old, outside of Boston. Before we left, I remember overhearing Mr. Chilton a couple of times talk about bankruptcy. My older sister was in college by then. My younger sister and me and our parents moved to an apartment in another part of Massachusetts. My parents got other jobs. I did some local modeling gigs and worked as a waitress until I went off to college for a year."

"Surprised your parents could afford that."

"They couldn't. The Chiltons had started college funds for us. I burned through one year and then decided it wasn't for me, and I didn't like wasting money."

"Christian said his dad died."

"In a car accident two years ago. His mother lives in Boston, or she did. I haven't seen her for several years."

"How old is Christian? I had him pegged at thirty."

"No, he's only three years older than me. He was at Princeton when the family money totally ran out. But he had a full lacrosse scholarship. He's very smart. He has two younger brothers. They're on the West Coast and doing their own thing. But Christian stayed on the East Coast."

"And now he's running Mayflower and living in a big brownstone owned by the Locust Group, who paid a lot more for it than it's worth, and he's hanging out with guys on Interpol watch lists. And apparently making a lot of money after the family lost almost everything around six years ago."

"It doesn't look good, I know."

"Not good at all."

"There he is," hissed Montgomery.

Chilton had walked out of the brownstone. He got into his BMW and drove off.

Devine and Montgomery pulled into traffic behind him.

*Let's see where you're going*, thought Devine.

It didn't take long. The BMW turned into a posh assisted living center. It was located in an old brick building that took up half the block.

They waited for Chilton to go inside and then followed.

The place looked like an upscale hotel. As Devine glanced

around, he saw elderly residents in wheelchairs and walkers. Some were reading in what looked to be the library; others were watching TV. Still others were just sitting and gazing off or slowly walking around.

Montgomery caught sight of Chilton walking down a hall and grabbed Devine's arm to alert him, before Chilton disappeared around the corner.

"What do you think is going on?" he asked her. "Why is *he* here?"

"I think Poppy might be here."

"So, what do we do?"

"Act like we belong here. I've actually been doing that my whole life," she added with a weak smile tacked on.

They walked down the hall, passing by staff members. One stopped and asked if they needed help.

Montgomery said, "I was supposed to meet Christian Chilton here."

"Oh, yes, he just came in. He's with his grandfather."

"That's right. He said that Poppy was here now. I haven't seen him in some time. Is he doing okay?"

The woman smiled sadly. "It's not easy getting old. And Mr. Chilton is over eighty. He used to be in the assisted living part of this facility. But now he's in our memory unit."

"Oh, you mean . . . ?" said Montgomery.

"Yes, I'm afraid so. Would you like me to take you to them?"

"You know, I think we'll just catch up with Christian when he's done, if that's okay. I didn't know Poppy was . . . I'll just let them have their visit."

"All right, you can wait in the lobby."

"Thanks again."

Montgomery turned to Devine, her eyes teary. "God, I didn't know that about Poppy. I just remember this wonderful old man who liked to play games with us."

Thirty minutes later Christian Chilton appeared in the lobby. Devine noted he was wiping at his eyes.

When he saw Devine and Montgomery, he jerked back. "What are you doing here?"

"How's Poppy?" asked Montgomery.

Chilton looked flustered. "He's…he's got Alzheimer's."

"Why didn't you tell me that, Christian? I *live* here. I could have come and visited him."

"He wouldn't remember you. He doesn't remember *me*." He glanced at Devine. "And what are you doing here with her?"

"We're friends, Christian, like you and me," answered Montgomery.

Chilton stuffed his hands in his pockets and glanced away.

"This place must be very expensive," said Montgomery.

"Everything in New York is very expensive."

Devine said, "You've come a long way in a very short period of time."

"What is that supposed to mean?" barked Chilton.

"From family bankruptcy to mega bucks in six years?"

Chilton shot Montgomery a look. "You should keep your mouth shut, Michelle."

"Is that why you did it? To pay for Poppy's care? And to support your mom?"

"Did what exactly?"

Devine said in a low voice, "You really want to go down with Brad Cowl?"

Chilton took a step back and said, "I got a meeting to get to."

Montgomery put a hand on his arm. "Christian, we can help you get out of this."

He shook his head, then looked at her and smiled sadly. "No, you can't, Michelle. We're not kids anymore. And this isn't a game."

"It's never too late. You remember Poppy telling us that when we got into trouble."

"Poppy…It's just too late, Michelle. But I appreciate you trying."

"Michelle told me that you set her up with Cowl," interjected Devine. "Why'd you do that?"

Chilton eyed Montgomery. "I told you why. I knew she could use the money. Brad loves beautiful women, and there's no woman more beautiful than Michelle."

"Is that the only reason?"

"Yeah, why?"

"He also pays her to wear red and green bikinis at certain times out by the pool."

Chilton looked at him funny. "A bikini? Why would he pay for that?"

"And the last lady he employed for that purpose ended up dead. They said suicide, but I don't think she jumped into the East River all by her lonesome."

"What 'last lady'?"

"You really don't know, do you?"

"No, I don't."

"How much funding do you get from Cowl?"

"I don't have to tell you anything."

"But you will have to tell the police."

"I have no idea what you're talking about," said Chilton heatedly.

"Your brownstone is owned by the Locust Group, not by you. They're laundering and hiding money, Christian, on a global scale. We're offering you an exit ramp. You just have to work with us."

"Christian," said Michelle, "we're trying to help you."

"I don't need help. Everything will be fine."

"Four people are dead and Cowl has done a runner," said Devine. "He's leaving people like you to hold the bag."

Chilton walked away. They followed him outside.

Devine said, "If you work with us, we can help."

Chilton whirled around. "Who *are* you? I thought you were working for Brad."

"I am. And I'm not."

"That's as clear as mud."

"If you don't jump to the other side, this will not end well for you. Then who'll look after your grandfather?"

"Fuck off."

"Christian!" said Michelle.

He got into his BMW and left tire rubber on the asphalt as he sped off.

Devine looked at Montgomery, who was staring after the car.

"Like he said, you're not little kids anymore, Michelle. You can't save him if he doesn't want to be saved."

"I doubt I can save anybody, not even myself."

"Well, for that, you've got me."

# CHAPTER 68

When Devine returned home it was nearly eleven. He was surprised to see Tapshaw sitting on the couch eating a bag of chips along with a bowl of ice cream. She was almost always in her room, and he had never seen her eating chips and ice cream before.

"Hey, Jill, what's up?"

She looked up at him. Her face was puffy, and it looked like she had been crying.

"What's wrong?" he blurted out.

"Mayflower bagged on me."

*Oh shit.* "What the hell happened?" said Devine automatically, although he knew very well what had happened.

"About an hour ago, Christian Chilton sent me a very curt email and said that their investment plans had changed, and that they were no longer interested in the dating platform sector. I mean, they go from investing fifty million to nothing?"

Devine sat down beside her. "I'm sorry. But maybe it's for the best."

"That money would have launched us into the stratosphere, Travis. I don't think I'll be able to find that good a deal anywhere else. The valuation was sky-high."

"But you've overcome every challenge. You'll get past this one, too."

"But what the hell happened between him emailing me this morning and everything was hunky-dory and an hour ago when he told me to basically eat shit and die?" She looked at him. "Do you have any inkling?"

Devine couldn't even look at her. "I don't know, Jill. Crap happens in business, I guess. Maybe they ran into some funding problems," he added lamely.

She perked up, wiped her eyes, and patted his hand. "It's okay. I've got other irons in the fire. Our cash burn is under control. We can make it until new money comes in. And in two years I'll look that jerk up and he can eat some crow."

He smiled but still couldn't meet her eye. "Now you're talking."

He went up to his room and fell asleep in his clothes.

* * *

The next morning, he took the 6:20 in. He knew Montgomery wouldn't be at Cowl's place, so he almost didn't look out. But when he saw others in the train staring out the windows, he did, too. And his pulse rate spiked.

*Oh God.*

The police and a forensics team were by the pool. And they were pulling something out of the water. It looked like—

The train gave a jolt and picked up speed. Devine craned his neck back, but he couldn't see anything.

The man next to him said, "Damn, man, was that a body in the pool? Please don't tell me it was the bikini gal."

Devine didn't answer. His heart was racing so fast he thought he might be sick.

He took out his phone and punched in Montgomery's number.

*Come on, come on. Shit, please, please answer your phone. Don't be dead, Michelle. Don't—*

It went to voice mail. He tried again. Same thing. He texted her and awaited a reply. Nothing. He went online and scanned the news about a body's being found at Brad Cowl's house.

There was nothing.

When the train pulled into the next station he jumped up and ran out the opening doors. He hoofed it outside the station and grabbed the first cab he saw. He gave the address and tried calling her the whole way.

By the time the cab dropped him off he had no hope left. *Why did she come back here?*

The area was blocked off, so Devine joined a group of other gawkers in front of the house. A black van waited, presumably for the body. Police were everywhere, keeping people away and securing the crime scene.

A sedan pulled up, and Ekman and Shoemaker climbed out. Devine ran over to them. "I saw them pulling a body out of the pool when we passed by on the train. Is it…is it…?"

His phone dinged. He looked down as every bit of breath in his body left him.

Sorry, I was asleep and didn't hear the phone. Everything okay?

It was from Montgomery. She was alive.

He looked up at the detectives.

"Come with us, Devine," said Shoemaker.

They led him through the perimeter by flashing their badges.

People were gathered around the pool surround, where a body lay under a sheet. Activity was swirling everywhere as police personnel looked for clues and collected evidence.

The NYPD detectives and Devine stopped in front of a plainclothes man from the county.

"Figured you guys needed to know because of the connection," the man said.

"Let's see it," said Ekman.

The sheet was lifted, and Devine found himself looking down at a very drowned and very dead Christian Chilton.

# CHAPTER

# 69

Shoemaker gave Devine a ride to the station while his partner stayed behind.

"Did Chilton die by drowning?"

"Yes and no."

Devine looked at him curiously. "You want to try that again?"

"There was water in his lungs, which means he did officially die by drowning. But he had blunt force trauma wounds on his head."

"Which means someone knocked him out and tossed him into the water, where he drowned?"

"Right."

"Anybody see anything?"

"Staff had been given the evening off last night." He looked at Devine. "By the girlfriend, Michelle Montgomery. But you knew that because you were there. Anything you can tell me?"

Devine told them about their seeing Chilton last night. "If I had to speculate, after our encounter, Chilton went to Cowl's to see what the hell was going on. And we saw how Cowl responded."

"But we have no proof Cowl was even there."

"Then we have to keep digging," replied Devine. "Because, by my count, the man is now involved in five murders."

"You and your higher-up friends ever going to come clean on this at some point?"

Devine snapped, "Look, if it was up to me, I already would

have. But even though I'm no longer in uniform, I'm trained to follow orders. So that's how it's going to be. If and when that changes, you'll be the first to know."

Later, Devine took the train into the city after calling Campbell and filling him in on this recent development. He then arranged to meet with Montgomery at a diner around the corner from her walk-up. He figured there was no sense in going in to work today. Not with the firm's founder a probable murderer and on the run.

She was standing outside the diner looking tired, her features puffy and her hair still tousled from sleep. She gave him a warm smile. But when she saw his grim features, she blurted out, "What's happened?"

"Let's go inside," he said quietly.

They got coffees, and he took her hand and told her about Chilton's being found.

She grew pale and slumped forward, the tears sliding down her cheeks. "Oh my God," she gasped.

He rubbed her arm and patted her hand. "I'm so sorry, Michelle. I know you two were friends. I just wish he had listened to us."

She sat up and wiped her eyes. "You think Brad was involved?"

"You saw Chilton last night. We put the fear of God in him. I bet he called Cowl, arranged to meet, and ended up dead for his troubles. For now, you need to move out of the walk-up. Chilton might have told him about us, what we know. That makes both of us a liability. I can help you."

She glanced up. "Where will I go? A hotel?"

Devine thought for a moment. "No, I'll take you to my place. You can stay in my room, at least for tonight."

"*Your* room?"

"I can sleep on the couch. But in the interim, I'll contact Campbell and hopefully he can arrange more secure quarters for you."

"Does this mean Brad *did* kill all those people?"

"Not necessarily. We have to keep the two cases both separate and together, as crazy as that sounds. Cowl is running a global money-laundering scheme. He's in bed with some very dangerous people. But he also had a relationship with Stamos and wanted one with Sara. So if they found out about his scheme, what do you think would happen?"

"They would be killed, like Christian. And they killed Sara's parents because they couldn't risk them knowing something. But what about the emails you got? How do they tie in to Brad? Why would he send you those messages?"

"It doesn't tie in to it, at all. Unless they're trying to muddy the waters. But even that doesn't make much sense."

"Then there could be a separate killer out there?" she said.

"Yes, there could."

She reached out and took his hand. "I'm really scared, Travis."

He gripped her fingers. "There's nothing wrong with being afraid. When people are in danger, they should be afraid. But you can't let fear paralyze you, then you're as good as dead."

"I guess you learned that in the Army while fighting overseas?"

"I've also learned it all over again right here in good old New York."

# CHAPTER

# 70

DUDE?" SAID VALENTINE EARLY THAT afternoon as Devine and Montgomery walked in the front door. Devine was hefting two large suitcases while Montgomery carried a smaller one.

"Hey, Will, this is Michelle."

Valentine eyed Montgomery and smiled. He quickly stood from his usual perch on the couch and put out his hand. Montgomery set her bag down and shook it.

"Hello, Will."

"Hello, *Michelle*," said Valentine, giving Devine a look along with arched eyebrows. "That is lovely name."

"Michelle is going to stay here for a bit, in my room."

"Dude," said Valentine with another shit-eating grin.

"While I sleep on the couch."

"Oh, right," said Valentine. "On *couch*."

"Which means you have to sleep in your bed, at least for tonight," said Devine.

This possibility apparently hadn't occurred to Valentine. "Oh, okay," he said, his smile fading.

If the Russian was aware that Helen Speers had been in his room, he certainly wasn't showing it. For a security expert, he was lax about his own security, thought Devine.

Devine led Montgomery up to his room and they put her things down in the corner.

"I'll just pull out what I need for tonight," she said. "I'm sure I can find a place in the morning."

"I've already texted Campbell. He's on it."

"I still can't believe that Christian is dead."

"You sleep with a cobra, you get bit."

"So, these people are just going to get away with it?"

"I didn't say that."

"But what can you do about it? Your boss said the whole thing might come tumbling down because of a bunch of corrupt politicians."

"But we still have a shot."

"Who's your friend, Travis?"

They turned to see Helen Speers standing in the doorway. She had on a red dress and black pumps. Her hair was done in a French braid. A briefcase was in one hand. She eyed Montgomery inquiringly.

"This is Michelle Montgomery. Michelle, Helen Speers, a recent NYU Law grad."

The women shook hands and eyed each other with what Devine thought were aggressive looks.

"Michelle will be staying here tonight."

"Here, in your room?"

"I'm bunking on the couch."

"Does poor Will know? That's basically his second home."

"He knows."

"Well, I'll leave you to…arrange things. Nice to meet you, Michelle. Let's get together again, Travis, *after* tonight."

She walked off. Hands on hips, Montgomery immediately faced off with Devine and said, "What was all *that* about?"

"What was what all about?"

"Oh, please. You two have a thing going."

Devine went over and closed the door. "No we don't. We're just roommates."

"*Just roommates* don't give women who are moving into a guy's bedroom *that* look. She might as well have peed on the floor to mark her territory."

Devine closed his eyes and ran a hand through his hair. He did not want to get into all that, and he certainly didn't want to tell Montgomery that he and Speers had slept together.

"All I can say is there is nothing between us." *Except for a pair of guns*, he thought. *And secrets.*

Later they went to get some dinner in Mount Kisco. The TV on the restaurant wall had the latest details about the murder of Christian Chilton and his body's being found in Brad Cowl's pool. The news said nothing with regard to the whereabouts of the missing magnate.

They walked back to the town house to find Jill Tapshaw and Valentine chatting in the kitchen.

"Hello," said Tapshaw to Montgomery. "I'm Jill."

Devine said quickly, "Jill, this is Michelle Montgomery, she's a friend from—"

"—the city," filled in Montgomery. "Nice to meet you."

"Jill founded Hummingbird."

"The dating service? I've been on there. It's really cool."

"*You've* been on a dating site?" said Devine, while Valentine gaped.

Tapshaw frowned. "Dating services, at least the good kind, are for everyone looking for relationships."

"Travis told me that Sara Ewes was on Hummingbird," said Montgomery.

"That's right," said Tapshaw. "She was one of my first hundred subscribers."

Devine stared down at his hands because he didn't want anyone to see his expression. *I don't remember mentioning that to Michelle.*

Later, while Montgomery was in his bathroom, Devine slipped into his room, got his gun, and put it in the back of his waistband, then slid his shirt over the weapon to hide it.

Montgomery came out of the bathroom wearing loose-fitting athletic shorts and a T-shirt.

"You don't have to sleep on the couch, you know." When he shot her a glance she added, "Men and women have been known to sleep in the same bed without having sex."

"Yeah, *married* men and women," Devine quipped. "I'll be safer on the couch."

He fell asleep quickly, but in his dreams he once more saw the dead faces of Blankenship and Hawkins. He tried to say something in his sleep, answer their haunting looks in some way, but he couldn't. Yet it did manage to wake him up.

And he just lay there staring at the ceiling and wondering when this would all be over. And whether he would be there to see it.

*Just like in the Middle East, the odds are not looking to be in my favor.*

## CHAPTER

# 71

At seven o'clock the next morning Devine got a call from Campbell.

"The surveillance camera in Area 51 completely went out last night. We're in the dark now."

"What do you want me to do?"

"Get there and see what you can find out."

Devine went upstairs and knocked on his bedroom door.

"Yes?" said Montgomery.

"Can I come in?"

He heard her feet padding across the floor and the door was unlocked.

Her face was puffy with sleep, and her hair was wonderfully tousled. To Devine, she had never looked more beautiful.

"What?" she said.

"I'm gonna grab a shower and get dressed."

"Where are you going?"

"I'm taking the train in to work. You can come with me if you want."

"I want to go see Poppy."

"Poppy?"

"Yes. His grandson is dead."

"I doubt he'll understand that if you try to tell him. And he has other family, doesn't he?"

"I'm just going to hold his hand and be there for him. And I feel like I *am* family, in a way."

"Okay," he said quietly.

On the train they passed Cowl's place. Devine watched Montgomery's expression as the train stopped. She studied the pool area where yesterday they had pulled out Chilton's body.

She glanced at him. "Different perspective."

"Yeah, I guess so."

She looked at the other passengers, but this wasn't the 6:20, so it wasn't the normal crew for Devine. But several guys were giving Montgomery pathetically lustful glances. She let out a resigned sigh and looked out the window again.

Devine decided to broach the subject he'd been thinking about since last night.

"Funny that you had been on Hummingbird and Sara had been, too. But you knew that already. About Sara being on there."

"Christian told me he was thinking about investing in it. I'd remembered it was a cool site. I went on there and found Sara Ewes."

"You just happened to see her on the site? But last night you told Jill that I had told you."

She glanced at him. "Did I? I don't really remember."

"You did. So why would you do that?"

Her expression tightened. "Does it matter?"

"I don't know, it might."

"Do you have a question you want to ask me, Travis?"

"I don't believe in coincidences. So I'd like to know how you knew Sara was on Hummingbird."

"I told you I saw her on there when I visited the site."

"Out of all the people on there, you saw her?"

"Okay, I did a search for her!"

"Why?"

"If you really want to know, it was because of Christian. I knew he was in the investment business. But I didn't think he invested in things like a dating service. And I knew you suspected him of being involved with the money laundering with Cowl. And that it might be connected to Sara's murder. So I went on Hummingbird and searched for Sara. I thought if she were on the site, *that* might be the connection with Christian. The reason he was interested in investing in it."

"But Sara worked at Cowl. *That's* the connection. Not Hummingbird."

"I was just playing a hunch." She eyed him darkly. "But if you don't trust me, you don't trust me."

His expression softened. "I *do* trust you, Michelle. You saved my ass with Cowl and his phone. I'm sorry. I guess stress is making me see things that aren't there."

"Don't apologize for being human. Personally, my stress level is through the roof. What are you going to do when you get to work?"

"Pay a visit to the fifty-first floor, if I can."

# CHAPTER

# 72

Surprisingly, it seemed business as usual at Cowl and Comely, despite a body's having been found in the pool of the firm's leader. And that leader's still being absent from the scene.

*Money trumps murder*, Devine concluded.

On the way up in the elevator, he pressed the button for Area 51. Stunningly, it lighted up.

*Okay, didn't see that one coming.*

He got off on that floor and looked around. The door was open. He poked his head inside and gaped.

It was empty. Every server, every computer screen was gone. All that was left were the cabinets and the tables. He hurried over to the wall where he had placed the camera. It was gone.

He hurried back down to the lobby, texting Campbell on the way to let him know what he had found.

*Or not found.*

He walked up to Sam the guard and asked him if he knew of any movers coming into the building to take some things out.

He shook his head. "Not while I've been here."

"Can you check with the night guard?"

"Sure, I can try. He's probably asleep by now. What's up?"

"Just wondering about something."

"Hey, I heard on the news about the guy being found in Mr. Cowl's pool. What the hell is that about?"

"Yeah, I was wondering that, too."

"I haven't seen Mr. Cowl for a while. Everything okay with him?"

"That's way above my pay grade, Sam. Any idea where Jerry Myers is?"

"Yeah, third-floor dining hall. Some snafu with an oven."

He found Myers in the kitchen working on one of the ovens, and asked him if he'd seen any moving trucks at the building.

"No, but if it happened last night, I wouldn't know about it. What got moved?"

"I'm not sure."

He next located Wanda Simms and decided to be more direct with her.

"I was on the fifty-first floor this morning, Wanda."

"What?" she said sharply. "You couldn't have been. It's off-limits."

"Come take a ride with me."

They got on the elevator, and he made a theatrical show of hitting the button. When it lighted up, Simms gasped.

When they got to the fifty-first floor and he showed her the vast, empty space, she looked at him suspiciously.

"Why did you come up here in the first place?"

"Do you still think they were running their high-frequency trading platform from here? Because I can tell you for a fact that runs out of a building in Queens."

"Who are you, Travis? I mean, who are you really?"

"Just a guy who stumbled onto something."

"Onto what? Do you mean"—she looked around—"something *criminal*?"

"Why else would this room have been cleared out?"

"So you knew what was in here?"

"Did you know of any moving company coming to do it?"

"No. There was nothing in the office memos. What was in here?"

"I can't tell you. But five people connected to this firm have died."

"Five!"

"A guy named Christian Chilton was part of what was going on in this room."

"I don't know who that is, but the name sounds familiar."

"He was the man who ended up dead in Cowl's pool."

Her hand flew to her mouth. "Oh my God, that's right. I heard his name on the news. Should I start looking for another job? My husband and I just bought a vacation property in Connecticut, and the mortgage payment is a real bitch."

*Well*, thought Devine, *everyone has their priorities*. "If I were you, I'd get my résumé dusted off."

Devine left her and went to his cubicle. By now the other Burners were all there. But he noted that fingers were not flying across the keys. Some of the Burners were actually out of their chairs and talking together in small groups.

The same woman he had argued with before, Lydia White, came over to him. She looked pale and distraught. "What is going on, Travis?"

Though she had angered him before, he now felt sorry for her. For all of them, really. They had busted their humps all this time for maybe nothing.

"Nothing good, that's for sure. Area 51?"

"What about it?"

The other Burners were now gathering around the pair.

"You can go up and see for yourself. It's accessible now."

White said, "But I thought that was where the firm did high-freq—"

Devine interjected, "That's what they wanted everyone to think. The place is cleared out now. It was full of computers and servers and now it's all gone. They emptied it out in the middle of the night."

White said, "So this is all connected with the murders?"

"It's definitely connected to the guy who was found dead in Cowl's pool."

White was fighting back tears. "My father told me to accept the offer I got from JP Morgan. But I thought Cowl would be more exciting."

"I would take boring old JP Morgan over this kind of excitement."

"What should we do?"

"Keep working, make sure your paychecks clear, and get your CVs out to as many other places as you can."

He watched as the Burners scrambled to their computers to do just that.

However, White didn't move. She held her gaze on Devine. "I was wrong about you, obviously. I'm sorry."

"You were naturally suspicious, Lydia. I would have been, too."

"You are clearly here for another reason, correct? Whoever you work for knew something was up and you were placed here to find out?"

He smiled. "You're really smart, and you're going to have a wonderful career wherever you land. Maybe you should steer clear of Wall Street, though, and try something that might have a positive impact on lots of people who actually need the help."

"My older sister is starting a nonprofit to help the homeless in California, which is a big problem there. That's where I'm from. The Bay Area."

"Well, you won't make nearly as much money, but at the end of your days I think you'll have a lot more to smile about."

He rode the elevator down to the lobby and decided to do a direct frontal assault on an entrenched foe. He sent a text to Brad Cowl after taking some time to compose it in his head. Cowl was a transactional guy. So Devine was going to give him an offer he couldn't refuse.

Emptying out Area 51 won't cut it. The feds are closing in. I can make all your problems go away. Just hear me out and we both win. You're a dealmaker, so let's do a deal.

He walked out into the fresh air and kept right on going.

# CHAPTER

# 73

Devine texted Montgomery and told her he would meet her at the assisted living center where Poppy Chilton lived on the Upper East Side.

When he got there, she was waiting outside and looking distraught.

"You okay? What happened?"

"Poppy passed away."

"What? When? Please don't tell me—"

"No, it was natural causes. Well, sort of."

"I'm not following."

"There was a TV. The news was on. He saw—"

"He saw that his grandson was dead, you mean? But I thought he wasn't capable of understanding things like that anymore."

"The doctor I spoke with said you can never tell. There are moments of lucidity. And seeing Christian's name on the TV screen and the fact that he was dead jolted Poppy into one of those moments. He went into cardiac arrest. They couldn't resuscitate him."

"And this happened last night?"

"Yes. They told me when I got here. The family is coming in for...both funerals."

He hugged her tightly while she cried into his shoulder. When she composed herself and stepped back, she said, "We really need to nail these bastards."

He told her about Area 51 and about the text he had sent Cowl.

"Do you think you'll get a response? He might think you're trying to trap him or something."

"It's worth a shot. And I don't have a Plan B."

* * *

Later, they had lunch at a restaurant on the harbor, where Devine took a minute to check in with Campbell.

Campbell said, "We had operatives posted outside the Cowl Building last night. When the moving trucks came, we were naturally suspicious but had no grounds to intervene or get a search warrant. And one of my men checked with the security guard on duty. He said he'd been told they were moving equipment *in*, not out, so we weren't as concerned as we would have been. They went in through the loading dock, so we couldn't gain access to see what was really going on. Burns my ass, though."

Devine put his phone away and looked out at the water. This was where he and Stamos had gone that day. He eyed the Statue of Liberty and looked back to see Montgomery watching him.

"Does it feel cool that you fought to keep that ideal of freedom going?" she asked.

"While you're actually fighting, you don't really dwell on the big-picture stuff. It's just surviving day to day that occupies your mind. But I felt proud to be serving my country. Even if my father didn't see it that way."

"Is that also why you're working with Campbell?"

He eyed her more intently. "Why do you ask?"

"Because you talked to me about baggage. And while I can see you as a soldier, I don't necessarily see you as some sort of federal spy in a suit."

"You're more right about that than you probably know."

"It must have been bad."

"It was bad enough. It sort of ruined everything that came before that."

"That must've been tough to take."

"Tougher than I am, apparently."

They sat in silence for a few moments. Devine finally said, "Chilton was killed because of his connection to Cowl and Area 51."

"But if they killed Christian for confronting Brad, why would they dump his body in Brad's pool? That would lead the police to suspect Brad right off. There were plenty of other ways to get rid of his body."

"Which might mean that Cowl and his partners had a falling-out. They might have done that to incriminate Cowl."

"Does that mean he's already dead? They clear Area 51, get rid of Christian and Brad, and go somewhere else and set up the money-laundering operation?"

Devine's phone buzzed. He answered it and his mouth fell open. He listened for a few moments, said, "I'll be there," and then put the phone down. "Well, Cowl is still alive. That was him, and he wants to meet tonight."

"Where?"

"In his penthouse."

"Do we trust him?"

"Not with either one of our lives."

"So what do we do? Not go? Call in the cavalry?"

"Neither one."

"But we have to have a plan. We just can't waltz in there to get killed."

"Going into battle is the one thing I do really well. And you're not going."

She looked incredulous. "What the hell are you talking about?"

"I'm trained for this stuff, you're not."

"Like you were trained when Brad was about to grab the phone and let you out only it wouldn't have worked the elevator and your cover would have been blown right there? I was the one who stepped in and saved your ass."

Devine drew close to her and started speaking slowly and earnestly. "Listen, I figure I have about a fifty-fifty chance of making it out of there alive. That's good enough for me, but it's not good enough for you. I can't let you do that."

"How about allowing me to make that choice?"

"Jesus, Michelle, can you just trust me on this one?"

"How about *you* trust *me* on this one?"

"What are you talking about?"

"I have a plan that I think will get us in and out alive."

"How could you possibly know that?"

"Because I know Brad, better than you ever will. And you asked me to trust you once, and I did. How about I get the same courtesy?"

They held a stare-off for about five seconds until Devine broke it.

"What's your plan?"

# CHAPTER

# 74

At half past eleven that night Devine used his security card to let himself and Montgomery inside the Cowl Building. The guard wasn't around. Devine looked at his watch. Making rounds, he assumed. Or maybe he was lying dead somewhere. There was a lot of that going around here.

They took the elevator up as high as they could, and the doors opened.

And there was Cowl. He was dressed nattily in a dark suit, white shirt, and no tie. He looked fresh despite the hour and smiled when they climbed off the elevator car.

"Michelle, didn't expect to see you tonight."

"Where the hell have you been, Brad?" exclaimed Montgomery.

"Just taking care of business," said Cowl. He turned to Devine. "I got your message. I have no idea what it means, but I thought I'd have you up for a chat."

"Christian was found dead in your pool," snapped Montgomery. "The police think you killed him."

"Well, I didn't. In fact, I've been out of town, and I have lots of people who can verify that. My attorneys have already been in touch with the police and we are fully cooperating. If Christian got himself killed it's not my problem. In fact, he and Devine here had a real dustup. Maybe Devine went back to finish the job at my place to make it look like I had something to do with it." Cowl gave Devine a smirk. "In fact, we've already let the authorities know all about that. I'm sure they'll be in touch."

"Is that really how you're going to play it, then?" said Devine. "With Stamos's death, too?"

"Let's head up and discuss this." He led them to his private elevator.

When they got to the penthouse, Cowl patted Devine down, checking for weapons. When he turned to Montgomery, she gave him a fierce look and said, "Don't even think about it, Brad."

He grinned and held up his hands in mock surrender. "Okay, babe, okay." He eyed her extremely tight midriff tube top and knee-length flared skirt. "Don't think you have any hiding places on you anyway. But let me see inside your purse."

She did.

"Now, turn your phones off, because I don't like being recorded."

They complied with his order.

"And just so you know, I've got a signal jammer in here in case you're wearing a wire or shit like that. Drink?"

"Not for me," said Devine. Montgomery simply shook her head.

"Hate to drink alone, but oh well." He mixed himself a bourbon and Coke and took a sip. "Let's sit."

Montgomery and Devine sat next to each other on a couch, while Cowl sat across from them.

"Stamos?" said Devine.

"You got a message that night," interjected Montgomery. "And you went to meet someone."

Cowl said, "Okay, I'll give it to you straight. The message *was* from Jenn. She was afraid."

"Afraid of what?"

"She wouldn't tell me on the phone. So I went over there." His face twisted with the memory. "And between the time I got the message and made my way there, someone . . . cut her up really bad."

Devine leaned forward. "And was that someone you?"

"Why would I do that to her? I liked her. A lot."

"Because Sara Ewes knew about the Locust Group owning the Lombard Theater. And she told Stamos to check it out. And maybe she did and realized what was going on. Or maybe you let something slip during pillow talk and she had to be taken care of."

"Jesus, Devine, you're making me out to be some sort of creepy killer."

"Aren't you?"

"I'm a businessman."

"Were you the one to call the cops?"

He hesitated. "Yeah, I called them. But if you tell anyone, I'll deny it." He added, with a disgusted look, "What twisted psycho would do that to a woman? They...mutilated her."

"Did you see or hear anyone while you were there?"

"No. I had a key. I let myself in. I called out to her. No answer. I went back into her bedroom, and bam...there she was, tied up and cut up. The word *bitch* was carved into her stomach. I almost threw up."

He looked like he might throw up now.

"The police said she bled out. It must've taken some time, but you couldn't have missed the killer by much."

"Yeah, I know. I've been thinking that if I got there twenty minutes sooner *I* might've died."

Now Montgomery's face twisted. "Or you might have been able to *save* her, Brad."

He looked surprised by this. "Yeah, that's right, maybe. I didn't think of that."

"Obviously," she said with disgust.

Cowl looked at Devine. "So, you said you want to make a deal? Care to explain?"

"Area 51?"

"Oh, that. We were just doing some crypto-mining there and also some carryover high-frequency trading that our facility in Queens couldn't handle. All totally legit."

"The place has been cleared out," said Devine.

"Yeah, we decided to do some operational consolidation and shifted all of that, plus our Queens operation, to a building in

Jersey. Again, nothing illegal about that." He cocked his head and gave Devine an enigmatic smile. "You trying to shake me down somehow? Now, *that's* illegal."

"Money coming in from all over the world and money going out to the Locust Group, Mayflower Enterprises, thousands of other entities. I don't believe there's enough soap in the world to do that much laundry."

"You're a really funny guy. Where's your proof of anything?"

"I put a camera up there. Now it's gone."

"Oh, right. Illegal search, evidence inadmissible. Thrown out of court or not even filed. In fact, there's no proof of where that camera was or what it was taking pictures of. Let's go down to the fifty-first floor and compare what's on the film to what's in that room. You want to do that?"

"But the optics won't look good when people hear what we know."

"You start spewing lies about me and this firm, I bury you in court for the next twenty years. I bury whoever you're working for, too. And at the end, I'll still be rich, and I don't know what you'll be, but it won't be good. And I've been doing some digging on you, Devine. You left the Army under a cloud. Guy in your unit killed himself by hanging. Left behind a luscious wife. Then another guy you knew ended up dead. My people tell me he might have been banging the bedsprings with the first guy's wife. He might have killed the guy instead of it being a suicide. You knew them both. And they're both dead. And then you dump your career and come into my world. What's that all about? You got some guilty secret hanging out there?"

"This isn't about me."

Cowl eyed Montgomery and held up his phone. "And you helped him plant the camera, sweetie. After all I've done for you. I mean, shit, a guy can't trust women, can he?"

"Like Dominique Deveraux?" she said. "You couldn't trust her, so she took a dive into the East River?"

Cowl stared blankly at her.

"How did you make her death go away?" asked Devine.

"Poor kid. She was all messed up, a druggie. The cops actually thanked me for trying to give her a better life. And she would have had a much better life if she hadn't been so inquisitive."

"And Sara? She knew about the Lombard Theater being owned by Locust Group. She told Stamos. And I think you killed them because they found out what you were doing."

"You got one wild imagination. I already told you I found Jenn. I didn't kill her. And so what about the Lombard Theater? I didn't know it was a crime to own something."

Devine glanced at Montgomery, but didn't respond.

Cowl shook his head, grinning. "You got nothing to deal with and you're sure as hell not getting a dime from me. That's what this is about, right? You shaking me down? Or trying to get a confession? Well, forget it."

"Then I guess we'll be going," said Devine.

Cowl shook his head. "Oh no, that's not how this is ending."

Four men edged from the shadows.

Karl Hancock eyed Devine, his face still battered from being hit with a car tire. He had his pistol out. Two other men had shotguns. The fourth man held an MP5. They had brought a howitzer to a knife fight. But that was okay. Devine didn't have a knife.

Cowl said, "Instead of waiting for you to try and make trouble, we decided to do a preemptive move. You saved us from chasing you down by coming here."

Devine said, "There's an army of people waiting right downstairs. If we don't show, they come up."

Hancock said, "There's no one down there. I'm having the whole block monitored. You came here because you thought you could roll Cowl over. Well, you were wrong."

Cowl said, "I've been playing this game a long time. I've seen it all. And now, so will you."

"Okay, Devine," said Hancock. "You and the lady are going to get jacked. Taken to a really, really bad section of the Bronx, robbed and killed, and your bodies dumped in an alleyway for NYPD to find and lots of forensic evidence that a particularly violent gang did the honors. And the cops will also find evidence tying you to Chilton's murder. He was in love with the lady here, and you cut him out. You and he previously fought over another chick. He tried to get the lady back, and you decided to end it and put him in the pool to try and implicate poor Mr. Cowl here. That was easy enough to do since the lady here has a key to the place and she told the staff to leave. We know you met up with Chilton the night of his death outside the place where his grandfather lives. You made arrangements for him to meet you at Mr. Cowl's home. And he did. And you killed him. All while Mr. Cowl wasn't even in town."

Devine wasn't listening to any of this because it didn't matter. He was focused on the business of combat. In his mind the dimensions of the room shrank down into a close-quarters battle zone.

The four men became numbers in his head. Their positions, the accuracy and potency of their weaponry, their sight lines, the obstacles to getting away, the issue of having Montgomery with him, the proximity and possible use of Brad Cowl were also assigned numbers in his brain. The MP5 he could see was on two-shot selector, not full auto. Shotguns were side by side, not pump action, so twin barrels and two rounds each. Hancock had his Glock, with a standard magazine. Cowl was four feet away, drink in hand, no weapon that he could see. Shooting angles and obstructions thereto were observed and dialed into his combat brain. Possible scenarios were spit out. None of them were good. But they never were.

His battle plan now set, it was time to play a game that was not in any way a game at all. Cowl might be really good at making money illegally. But, courtesy of the United States Army, Devine was maybe one of the absolute best at what was about to go down.

*Three... two... one.*

# CHAPTER 75

Stand up, now!" barked Hancock.

They both stood, but Montgomery started swaying and looked like she might be sick. "Oh my God. Oh my God," she sobbed. "Brad, please don't do this. Please. I'll do anything."

Hancock snapped, "We are way past that, lady."

"Please, Brad, I don't want to die. I won't say anything. I swear."

"Too late, bitch," said Cowl. "You screw me, I screw you right back, only a lot harder."

Montgomery's eyes fluttered and then rolled back into her head. She collapsed in a dead faint against Devine, who grabbed her so she wouldn't hit the floor.

"Oh come on!" barked Cowl. "I don't need this shit." He looked at Hancock. "I got plans tonight."

Devine laid her on the couch, his back to the men. His hand slipped under the woman's skirt. He pulled the palm-sized ten-shot Beretta subcompact that was holstered around Montgomery's thigh and hidden by the flared skirt. In the span of one breath, he whirled and got off two quick shots. MP5 Man was his first take-down because that weapon vanquished all others in close-quarters combat. Shotgun Number One was next because Devine had sized up that guy as more comfortable with that weapon than Shotgun Number Two.

Cowl screamed and tried to jump over his chair but failed. He dropped his drink, slid to the floor on his back, and covered his face with his hands. Montgomery flipped over the back of the couch and lay flat on the floor.

Devine slid between the couch and a chair as Shotgun Number Two finally opened fire. The man had wasted precious seconds trying to fathom what had just happened. In combat, that cost you your life.

The twin blasts tore right into the chair, only Devine wasn't there anymore. And now the idiot had to reload. A five-shot pump in hand, and Devine was dead. It really was all in the details.

And in a fight, you kept moving, even when part of your brain said to hunker down. A moving target drew attention, yes, but also led to poor decisions by those trying to follow the action. An immobile target let the adversary take his time, make better choices, and finish the quarry off.

And stupid Hancock, after being nearly knocked off his feet by the falling MP5 guy, was spraying pistol shots indiscriminately, in a wide arc. That was fine if you had another shooter doing the same from a parallel position. Then the field of fire was overlapping and you got your target nine times out of ten. But the field of fire was not overlapping, and thus the man was screwed.

The CIA apparently needed to train its people better.

Devine curved around the back of the chair and placed a round into Shotgun Number Two's neck, ripping the fat artery there right in two, just as planned. The man screamed, let his weapon fall, and flipped over the chair clutching at a wound that was sending blood streaming out of him like a miniature hose. He had about five seconds to live. Hancock screamed and fell back.

Devine used the cover of that horrific spectacle to place a round into Hancock's left knee, blowing out the cap and all bone and tissue behind it. The man collapsed in bloody agony on what was probably a fifty-thousand-dollar rug.

Devine could have done a kill shot, but he needed one of them alive in addition to Cowl, and Hancock was now the only candidate for the job.

Hancock had dropped his Glock and was, despite his obvious pain, reaching out for it.

Devine had to admire the man's guts. But that was the extent of the admiration. He rushed over, kicked the gun away, and pointed his Beretta at Hancock as Montgomery poked her head over the top of the couch.

Cowl was on the floor screaming bloody murder, with Shotgun Number Two lying pretty much on top of him.

"Shut up!" barked Devine. A bloodied Cowl pushed the dead man off him and skittered over to the couch.

Devine picked up Hancock's gun and thrust it into his waistband, while the man lay on the floor moaning and holding his destroyed knee. Devine glanced over at Cowl, who was staring in disbelief at him.

Hancock glared at Cowl. "You pat down everybody for weapons, you idiot!"

Devine eyed Montgomery. "Nice plan."

"Thanks." Montgomery said to Cowl triumphantly, "You were right, Brad—you just can't trust women, at least this one."

Devine checked Hancock's blood loss. He had seen enough wounded people to be able to gauge whether someone was going to live or not. And Hancock would make it.

He looked at Cowl. "You said you had a signal jammer in here. Where is it?"

"Behind that vase," said Cowl in a shaky voice, the other man's blood all over his expensive suit and shirt.

Devine nodded at Montgomery, who rushed over and found and turned off the device.

"Call an ambulance," said Devine.

Montgomery turned her phone back on and called 911. Devine turned on his phone, texted Campbell about what had happened, and then put the phone away.

"And now, Cowl, sit down, compose yourself, and start talking."

"I'm not telling you shit."

"Okay, but since you just tried to kill us, it doesn't matter how much you gave the mayor and governor for their last elections."

"You came up here and shot the shit out of the place."

"Right, taking on four armed guys in a place that only you have access to."

"Who *are* you?" screamed Cowl.

"Right now, a seriously pissed-off guy." He pointed his gun at Cowl's head, and the man covered his face with his hands.

"Don't, sweet Jesus, don't shoot."

"I'd like to hear about Area 51."

"You say nothing, Cowl!" screamed Hancock.

Devine pointed his gun at him. "Shut up or I'll take out the other knee. Then you bleed out before the EMTs get to you."

Montgomery put her phone way and joined him. She was pale and avoided looking at the dead men.

"Area 51?" said Devine.

"You've seen it, asshole," spat Cowl.

"I'd like to hear your version."

Cowl's tone changed and he spread his hands wide. "Look, I've got people to answer to. We can make a deal."

Hancock shouted, "You say one word, you are dead, Cowl. You know who I'm talking about."

Devine slugged the man on the head with the butt of his gun and Hancock fell unconscious to the floor. Then Devine looked at Cowl. "You were saying?"

"You came here to get rich, right? Well, I can make you so rich you'll never be able to spend it all. You can buy your island and have the bitch there in bikinis twenty-four seven, and ten more like her."

"I never really liked making money," confessed Devine.

"Then what the hell were you doing here?" snapped Cowl.

"Area 51?"

"This is more than me, Devine. It's more than all of us."

"Well, we have to start somewhere. But let me throw you a bone. *Anne Comely* equals *Clean Money*. How's that?"

Cowl looked at him and snorted. "Maybe you *could* have done well here."

"I don't think there's a *here* left, Cowl."

Montgomery used Cowl's phone to let the EMTs in when they arrived minutes later. They confirmed the deaths of the other men, then stabilized the still-unconscious Hancock and took him away. A contingent of federal agents appeared a few minutes later, with Campbell leading them.

He sat down across from Cowl and studied him.

"Who the hell are you?" said Cowl.

"I'm either your worst nightmare or your savior. It all depends on how you want to play this."

"I don't know what you're talking about."

Campbell rose. "Then I'm your worst nightmare. Hope you enjoy prison food."

"Wait a minute, wait a minute."

"I'm listening."

"Any deal I do, my lawyers sign off on it."

He looked at his men. "Take him but don't charge him. Not yet."

They led Cowl away. Campbell looked at him and Montgomery. "I guess you thought you had gotten away from war zones, Captain."

"Maybe you never do," replied Devine.

As Devine and Montgomery left the penthouse, she said, "So, it's finally over?"

He shook his head. "No, not even close."

# CHAPTER 76

THE 6:20 TRAIN.

It was rainy and foggy and chilly, the opposite of what summer should be, thought Devine, but then so was everything else. He was in his normal seat. He was looking out the window. The train slowed and then stopped. There was Cowl's mansion.

Empty.

He was heading to Cowl and *Clean Money*, as he thought of it now. The media hadn't gotten wind of anything that had happened in Cowl's penthouse, which had been walled off and preserved for additional processing. The decision had been made to allow the Cowl firm to stay in business for now. Campbell had texted about the progress so far. It was not encouraging.

We have Cowl and Bartlett, for that is indeed who Karl Hancock is. But there is no electronic trail left from Area 51. It's been NSA-level wiped. What we have on the photos and the camera feed isn't enough. There is no chain of custody. We'll be laughed out of court. But with Cowl cutting a deal we think we can get there in the end.

Devine had gotten that text at one in the morning.

As he neared the city he got a call from Campbell.

"Extremely bad news, Devine. Cowl and Bartlett are both dead. The latter in the hospital. Pillow over his face. Sentry killed, too."

"And Cowl?"

"Shivved in a holding cell. The CCTV was taken offline. We've put a dome of silence over all this. No leaks, no one knows, for now. But that won't last long. Back to square one, unfortunately, but I think we have them on the run. And DOJ and the other agencies are going after them with all they've got, even with the stonewalling going on with some of the politicos."

Devine was not nearly as optimistic as the retired general. He was sure that Area 51 would be set up somewhere else, or consolidated with another ongoing operation. He wondered how much of America others truly owned.

*The world is upside down. Good is bad and bad is deified.*

And his instincts were telling him that a killer was still out there. Four people dead and it had everything to do with Sara Ewes, and not Brad Cowl and Area 51.

*And it somehow has everything to do with me. I got the emails. They were sent to me for a reason. The killer is speaking directly to me. This is as personal as it gets.*

He didn't get much done at work. His brain was in too much of a fog. All the other Burners were in the process of getting interviews at other firms and venting about their problems. He just tried to tune it out.

When he got home from work that night, he found Valentine on the couch, sucking down beer and eating a hot dog instead of pizza.

"Hey, dude, you're early tonight. How goes it? You figure all that shit out?"

"I think so."

"So all is good?"

"I wouldn't go that far."

* * *

The news finally broke about the murder of Brad Cowl while in police custody. The financial press, already reeling from the string of murders connected to the firm, was covering all of this with astonishment mixed with a bit of glee, even as a few rumors started to circulate about possible financial improprieties at Cowl and Comely.

As Devine read through these news accounts on his phone in his room after coming home from work one night, he shook his head.

*Possible financial improprieties? Just wait. This will make Bernie Madoff look like a third-rate grifter if it ever sees the light of day.*

Later, he texted Montgomery and arranged to meet her at a hotel the next day, where she was staying with a security team.

In the city, he cleared her armed guards and knocked on the door of Montgomery's room. She opened it immediately. She had on jeans and a white T-shirt. She looked like she'd been crying.

He closed the door behind him. "What's wrong? Are you okay?"

She dabbed at her eyes and sat on the bed. "My mother called. She heard about Brad and also about Christian. She wanted to know if I was involved somehow. My own mother!"

He perched on a chair opposite her. "That must've been a difficult conversation."

"Well, at least it was a short one, since I hung up on her."

"You've still got your retirement portfolio."

"I'm not sure that's going to be enough, Travis," she said dully. "Apparently I've got a bull's-eye on my back. You too."

"Maybe, maybe not. They probably don't want to make more waves. They know the big guns are out for their blood."

She brushed the hair out of her face. "Do you really think so?"

"I can't guarantee it, but the truth is these guys just care about getting their money clean and using it to buy property and people. And the fact is, we're not that important, Michelle. They go somewhere else and set up shop, and the pipeline opens up again." He sat back. "But that doesn't get us any closer to figuring out who killed four people."

"So, what are you going to do?"

"I was thinking of going back to the scene of Sara's murder."

"Can I come?" she said quickly.

"Why?"

"Because right now I don't want to be alone."

Devine hesitated.

"My ass is on the line too, Travis," she snapped.

"Okay, let me clear it with Campbell before your security team freaks out."

"After seeing what you did in Brad's penthouse I feel safer with you than I do with them."

He got permission from Campbell, and they left the hotel. Devine used his security card to get into the Cowl Building. It being a weekend and the firm probably going under, the place was pretty much empty. They rode the elevator up to the fifty-second floor and got off. Devine led Montgomery over to the storage closet and opened the door.

"That's where she was found?" said Montgomery.

"Yes. By the custodian. She was hanging from that pipe you can see in the ceiling. The chair was knocked over. Her shoes were on the floor. They tried to make it look like suicide but failed."

She glanced nervously at him. "Murder disguised as suicide, like Brad was talking about with you and those men in the Army who died?"

"That's a long story that I hope one day to be able to share with you, but not right now."

"And the guy who found Sara's body?"

"Jerry Myers, the custodian who works here. Freaked him out. There was no one else on the floor because there was an all-hands-on-deck seminar at the Ritz that morning. And the admin folks hadn't arrived yet."

"Is that a coincidence?" said Montgomery. "That her body was found on the morning when no one would be up here?"

"I don't think so. I believe it was planned that way, which smacks of inside information."

"When was Ewes killed again?"

"The previous night, between like midnight and four."

"So whoever killed her was long gone by the next morning. But you got the email in the morning telling you about her being dead."

"That's right."

"Well, I doubt whoever killed her snuck back up in that time window you were talking about to look at the crime scene so they could write you that email. They already knew what it looked like."

Devine thought this over. "You're right about that. But the message did mention that a custodian had found her body. That led me to believe that the person was there that morning, because how else would they know about *who* found the body and when?"

"But why would it be important for you to know *who* found the body? Wasn't it enough to tell you that she was hanging in a storage room?"

Devine started to say something and then stopped. "You're right. I just never thought about that."

"So why wait until the next morning to tell you about it? Why not email you that night, as soon as she was dead? *You* would have called the cops and *they* would have found the body."

"I don't know. The way you set it out, it makes no sense."

"But it does make sense if the killer and email sender were two different people," said Montgomery. "The killer murdered Sara. And told the email sender about it."

"But we get back to the same issue. How would the killer know a *custodian* found the body the next morning? And if he didn't know that, how could the person who sent me the email know about it?"

She looked around the space. "So this guy Myers found her. Why did he come into the storage room in the first place?"

"To get a printer cartridge that someone on the floor told him they—"

Devine stopped and looked around at the supplies on the shelving units before glancing at Montgomery.

She said, "Only you just told me there was no one on this floor on Friday. Then who told Myers to get a printer cartridge?"

"Let's go ask him."

# CHAPTER

# 77

DEVINE GOT MYERS'S HOME ADDRESS from the company database he had previously hacked into. He lived on Staten Island. They cabbed over, and Devine had the driver drop them off about a block from the house. It was situated in a neighborhood of working-class homes.

"He's got a new ride," said Devine, eyeing the silver Ford F-150 pickup truck in the driveway with temporary tags. "Wonder where he got the money for that?"

"I doubt he'll volunteer it," said Montgomery.

"I can be persuasive."

They knocked on the door, but no one answered. They looked in the small backyard. It was empty except for an old pickup truck up on cinder blocks. There was a one-car garage, but the doors were locked. Devine peered in the window but didn't see anything helpful.

"Maybe he has another car," said Montgomery.

"Maybe, but I doubt it. He's not married and lives alone, the security guard at Cowl told me."

"Can I help you?" the voice said.

They looked around to see a woman standing on the front porch of the house next door. She had on leggings and a long T-shirt. She was in her twenties with a baby riding on one hip.

"We were looking for Jerry," said Devine. "We were supposed to meet for a beer, but he didn't show."

She gazed over at the house. "It's funny. He was supposed to help my husband with a project we're doing in the backyard. When he didn't show up this morning we called and went over there, but it's all locked up and Jerry didn't answer his phone."

"Does he have another car?"

"No, he bought that new Ford. It's a beauty. A King Ranch model with lots of bells and whistles. My husband Barry says it musta cost around sixty thousand."

"Wow," said Devine.

"Yeah. He works at some big muckety-muck company in the city. Jerry said they gave out big bonuses to everybody."

"But if this is his only ride, he must be inside. Do you think he's sick or something?"

A large, beefy man came out onto the front porch.

The woman said, "Barry, these people were supposed to meet Jerry for a beer. But no one answered. Now I'm getting worried."

Barry looked over at Myers's house and the truck. He eyed Devine. "Should we call the cops?"

"Maybe we should check first. If he's in there sleeping off a bender the cops will not be happy with us."

"Good point. Jerry likes his beer for sure."

He and Devine went up on Myers's front porch, and Devine studied the door and the glass side panel.

"This is the easiest way." He put his elbow through the glass, cleared out the shards, reached through, and undid the lock.

Barry opened the door and they stepped through.

"Hey, Jer, it's Barry from next door. You okay—" Barry sucked in a breath and blanched.

"What the hell is that smell?"

Devine knew exactly what it was. "Go call the cops, Barry."

"What?"

"The cops. Call them. We have a situation."

"What situation?"

Devine peered around a corner and into the small kitchen. "A dead-body situation."

*Jerry Myers will never get to enjoy his new pickup truck.*

* * *

Two hours later the house was swarming with police and a forensic scrub team. Devine had thought to call Detective Shoemaker. He was off today, but he and Ekman showed up anyway. They met up outside the house.

"The dead guy is Jerry Myers, the custodian at Cowl who found Sara Ewes's body," explained Devine while Montgomery leaned against a patrol car. "Looks like somebody killed him."

The detectives went into the house and came back out thirty minutes later.

Shoemaker said, "The prelim from the ME is some sort of poison. Frothing on the lips, color of the skin. He was on the kitchen floor. There was an open bottle of whisky on the counter and some in a glass. We're having it all analyzed."

"What's the TOD?" asked Devine.

"Prelim is about six thirty last night."

"Did anybody see anything?" asked Montgomery.

"Not so far."

"But why kill the janitor?" asked Ekman.

Devine said, "Because I think *Myers* killed Sara Ewes late on Thursday night. Then, on Friday morning, he 'finds' the body, which makes him pretty much above suspicion."

"Jesus," exclaimed Shoemaker. "We never thought about that angle."

"I wouldn't have either, except for her," said Devine, motioning to Montgomery.

Ekman eyed Montgomery suspiciously. "And how do you figure into this?"

"I was Brad Cowl's girlfriend."

"Oh, you were, were you?"

Devine said, "She's working with us on this. And we came out here because something Myers told me didn't add up."

"Like what?" asked Shoemaker.

Devine told him Myers said he had gone into the storage closet because someone had requested a printer cartridge.

"But there was no one on the floor that morning because of a seminar at the Ritz. So there was no one to ask Myers to get anything. I think they knew about the seminar and picked that day because of it. That way there would be no one on the floor who might find the body. Myers also probably wanted a second chance to go over the crime scene to make sure there was nothing incriminating left there."

"*And* any forensics of his found there would seem innocent since he went in there and found the body," added Ekman.

"Right."

"Pretty slick plan," said Shoemaker. "But why kill Ewes? Were they having an affair? Was he a jealous stalker who wanted to be with Ewes and she rebuffed him? Is it just the old story of a rejected guy?"

"I might think so except for that." Devine pointed at the brand-new F-150.

"*That* was his payoff," said Montgomery.

"And the fact that he was poisoned shows he was working with someone and that someone decided to get rid of that loose end," opined Ekman.

"That the guy ran out and bought a new truck was probably not a good thing. The person who hired him might have been afraid the cops would take a second look at Myers, and he'd fall apart and start pointing fingers," said Devine.

Shoemaker nodded. "We did check on the guy, always do when it's the person who finds the body. You don't need a security card to get in during regular business hours if you come through the front doors. Now, you need your security card at all times if you come in the rear. He said he came in the front doors at eight and left at five the same way, and took the ferry to Staten Island. The guard doesn't remember specifically seeing him that day, but he did confirm that Myers always came and went by the front entrance. We had no reason to suspect him. Myers had no motive or opportunity, at least that we thought."

"What about the building's security cameras showing people coming and leaving?"

"Inconclusive. We checked the footage for that time, but there was a large group of people leaving around five and we couldn't ID everybody, including him."

"I can tell you from experience, Detective, that that footage isn't worth the pixels it's built on."

# CHAPTER

# 78

DEVINE AND MONTGOMERY TOOK THEIR leave from the detectives, and Staten Island.

As they cabbed it back to Manhattan, Montgomery said, "So, Myers killed four people in exchange for a new pickup truck?"

He glanced at her. "I've seen people do it for a lot less than that, Michelle."

They rode the rest of the way in silence.

Devine took the train back out to his house after dropping off Montgomery at her hotel, and walked home from there.

Valentine wasn't on the couch or in the kitchen filling his belly. Overhead, Devine could hear Tapshaw tap-tapping away on her computer, happy as a clam. Helen Speers stood in her doorway and stared at him as he came up the stairs.

"Busy day?" she said.

"Another dead body found."

"Who was it this time?" she asked calmly.

"You're not surprised?"

"What's one more?"

He stood in front of her and shook his head. "I really don't get you."

"You don't have to. Just like I don't have to *get* you. Where's your friend Michelle?"

"In a safe place. So, you like the Glock over the Sig?"

"And you like the Sig Sauer over the Glock, good Army man

that you are. But diversity makes the world go round. I'm living proof of that."

She closed the door.

He knocked on Valentine's door but there was no answer. He tried the knob. It turned and he poked his head in. "Will, you in here eating pizza under the bedcovers?"

But Valentine wasn't there. He'd never been in Valentine's room before. What was astonishing to him was how neat and clean it was. Bed made, desk tidy. Monster computer screens that rivaled Tapshaw's. Some books in Russian were on a shelf. Shoes lined up against one wall. He looked in the closet and saw that the clothes were neatly hung and separated by pants and shirts. His dresser was just as organized.

He had gotten adept at doing searches like this back in the Army. Out on patrols, they would frequently have to work their way through the homes of suspected Taliban and Al-Qaeda allies and informants. And those guys really knew how to hide stuff, he had discovered.

He looked over the desk and saw some Post-it notes affixed to the screen. They were all in Cyrillic. He smiled. Nice little piece of security there. In one desk drawer were some framed photos. They looked to be about twenty years old or so, judging by the clothes the people wore. A man and a woman were holding a baby with a girl around six next to them. Maybe that was Valentine's family back in Mother Russia. He might be the baby boy.

He heard a noise downstairs. Devine put the photo back, closed the door, and left the room. He knocked on Tapshaw's door just as Valentine came up the stairs.

His expression was serious, focused, Devine thought, until he saw Devine. Then Valentine smiled, and said, "Dude."

*Yeah, dude.* "Hey, Will, how goes it?"

Tapshaw opened her door in her fluffy bunny slippers and capri pants with a white top. "Hey, guys. Is this a party or what?"

Speers opened her door and looked out. She eyed everyone and said, "All we do is pass each other every day and night. How about we go out for some beer and chips, roomies? And actually get to *know* each other?"

They crammed into Tapshaw's Mini Cooper and made the short drive to downtown Mount Kisco.

The pub was rocking, but they found an empty table outside and ordered their beers and food. Valentine also had a vodka tonic and a slice of meatball pizza.

Tapshaw took a sip of her beer and said, "I think the Taiwanese are going to invest. Not the full amount I was initially looking for, but at least half."

"That's great, Jill," said Devine. He didn't know if she had heard about Chilton's murder, and he was not going to bring it up.

Speers looked at her and said, "How did you get into the online dating space? I know your background because I googled you. You could be working for NASA or NSA."

"I got offers from both while I was at MIT. But while NASA does many wonderful things, I'd rather focus on this planet. And the NSA? I don't want to spy on people. I want to help them be happy."

Valentine finished his vodka tonic in one impressive gulp. "But people can be happy alone. I am example of this. I do not need nobody to be, as you say, happy. I am happy with me."

"Come on, Will, everyone needs somebody," countered Tapshaw.

Devine eyed him. "How'd you end up in Mount Kisco doing what you do?"

"I can do what I do from anywhere. This is nice place. I move around a lot before, but this is nice place. I stay here."

"Where were you before?" asked Speers.

"In big city of New York. But I did not like it. Too many people. Remind me of Moscow, only in Moscow people either stay home or go to bar. They do not, how you say, wander around. You wander around there, you get shot or arrested."

Tapshaw said, "Well, I like it here, too. But I also like to travel. I did that to learn about what people wanted from each other. That helped me put my platform together. Other sites ask you all these questions to build a profile so they can match you with a person of like interests. And we do some of that, too—but what about the old saying, 'Opposites attract'? A great relationship doesn't mean that the people are carbon copies of each other. Then it's like you're staring in a mirror every day. What about two very different people getting together and learning from each other? Changing what they like and dislike because they have someone who lets them see another slice of life?"

"Me?" said Valentine. "I want another *slice* of pizza. Then I am happy man."

Tapshaw tittered at this, but Devine didn't join in. Speers had eyed Valentine in a way that Devine didn't like. A thought suddenly hit him.

*Did these two know each other before? But if they did, why was she searching his room?*

Then he thought about the picture in Valentine's room. And the girl.

"Hey, Will, do you have family back in Russia? Brother? Sister?"

Valentine finished his beer before answering. "I have nobody, dude. Nobody. Way I like it."

# CHAPTER 79

IT WAS NEARLY FOUR A.M. when Devine rolled over in his bed and coughed. Then he coughed again, harder. The next moment he couldn't catch his breath.

In his murky mind he thought, *Am I having a heart attack?*

He sat up in bed and his head felt like it was underwater. What the hell was going on? He'd had two beers, not ten.

Then he inhaled and the smell answered all his questions.

*Shit!*

He jumped out of bed and almost crashed against the wall. He ripped open the door and gagged. He pulled his T-shirt up over his nose and mouth, went down to his knees, and scuttled across the hall to Speers's room. He tried the knob. It was locked. He rose and put his shoulder to it. It flew open and he saw Speers in the bed. She didn't react to his crashing into her room, which was not a good sign.

He stumbled over and tried to wake her. He checked her pulse. Still there. Barely.

He lifted her up and carried her down the stairs and out the front door. He set her down in the grass and ran back in. He checked Tapshaw's room next. Her door was not locked. She was unconscious on the floor. He confirmed that she was still breathing and carried her outside and set her next to Speers.

He ran back inside and knocked open Valentine's locked door. He wasn't in there. Devine looked wildly around and even checked under the bed, in the closet, and also the bathroom. The man wasn't there.

After grabbing his phone, he ran back outside and called 911 and then the gas company's emergency number. There was a garden hose next to the front door. He turned it on and sprinkled water over the women. Then he patted their faces, turned them on their sides, and applied pressure to their backs to help their lungs expand. Their breaths started getting deeper, and their color finally started returning; Speers even managed to sit up. She looked at Devine.

"Wh-what is . . . what is . . . ?"

"Gas in the house. You're okay now. I called the ambulance. But I can't find Will."

She plopped back down in the grass and threw up.

Tapshaw briefly came to, and Devine told her the same thing.

Then he turned and ran back into the house. He threw open windows everywhere and also the back door. He searched every inch of the space for Valentine, but the Russian was not there.

A minute later two ambulances pulled up. The EMTs jumped out and administered oxygen to both the women and Devine, too. They ran fluids into the women as well, but Devine declined, telling them that he was fine.

"What about the town houses on either side of you?" said one of the EMTs. "The gas might have seeped into them, too, or originated from there."

"They're both empty," said Devine.

After triaging the ladies, the EMTs decided to take them both to the hospital. The ambulances pulled out about the time the gas company showed up. Two men quickly climbed out of the truck, and Devine told them what had happened.

Thirty minutes later they came back out of the house.

"Somebody did it on purpose," said one of the men. "Fiddled with the line going into your town house and then opened up the pilot on the fireplace in the living room. We got safety features for that now, but this is an old house and nobody upgraded it."

"I told the EMTs the homes next door were empty. But they're being renovated and guys might be showing up to work there today. Some of the gas might have gone in there."

"We'll put up signs for them to stay out. Then we'll contact the owner and get the places checked and cleared out if need be."

"Okay, thanks."

"Lucky escape for you," said the other man. "You sure you're okay?"

"I'm fine. Is it safe to go in now?"

"Yeah, it's all aired out, but don't turn on any electrical switches for a while, just to be sure. I'll have a crew out here in an hour to check everything seven ways from Sunday."

"Thanks."

"You got any enemies, buddy?" asked the other man.

Devine looked at him. "Well, I got at least one."

* * *

Another team from the gas company showed up later and gave the house a thorough going-over. They also checked the homes next door after getting in touch with the owner. There was no evidence of gas in either of them.

Devine went back into the house after calling the hospital and checking on Speers and Tapshaw. They were both in the ER and being monitored. Their oxygen levels were still low, and the doctors had decided to keep them in the hospital until they were completely out of danger.

Devine looked around the house once more and found no sign of Valentine. Devine had called and texted him but gotten no reply. He went up to the man's room and found that his bed had not been slept in. They had gotten home around eleven last night, and Devine had fallen asleep pretty much right away. Obviously, Speers and Tapshaw had too.

Nor was Valentine's laptop or phone anywhere to be found.

But a suitcase he had spotted in the closet when he had previously searched Valentine's room was gone, along with what looked to be some clothes.

He went into Tapshaw's room and looked around. Then his gaze froze on her computer screen. Taped to it was a diagram on a piece of paper. He sat down and read quickly through it.

It started off with the oddly numbered email sender addresses that he had given Tapshaw to track down. In a flow sheet structure, it went from that line of numbers to a dozen different configurations, which he supposed were the electronic subterfuges the sender had used to disguise their identity and also to send an email without the requisite internet protocols. When he got to the end of the flow he gaped. There was an email address that he seemed to recognize. And under it, in parentheses, was written a name:

WILL VALENTINE. And next to that: HOLY SHIT.

Devine went back down to the living room and stared at the gas fireplace. There were no signs of forced entry. Whoever had manipulated the gas here had been inside the house last night. Clearly, suspicion fell on the man who had *not* almost died from carbon monoxide poisoning. And who was now AWOL.

Now things started to fall into place for Devine. Valentine was Russian. He had come to the town house about the same time Devine had. A good portion of the money pouring through Cowl and Comely had been identified by Campbell's people as coming from Russia and countries friendly to it. Valentine was a genius with computers, so it would have been easy for him to put together a very difficult email to trace.

*Ironic that I asked him to track an email* he'd *sent. The guy must have laughed his ass off about that one. I was filling him in on an investigation in which he was already a part—only on the opposite side. And he would tell me nothing about Area 51. Of course he wouldn't.*

How could he have been so blind? Valentine also knew about Devine and Sara Ewes dating, the only roommate of Devine's who had before Ewes had been killed.

*That means that the motive for killing them had nothing to do with me. That was just misdirection. It had everything to do with what Sara found out about the Locust Group. And then she told Jennifer Stamos. And Stamos had come here. Valentine had let her in. He might have eavesdropped on their conversation on the front porch. And so Stamos had to die, too. And the Eweses were in their daughter's house. Valentine and company couldn't take the chance that they might find additional evidence their daughter had left behind. Just like I thought before. Always go with your gut.*

The symbolic murders that Devine had theorized about were all bullshit distractions. This was all about two things: money and power. But in reality, they were one and the same.

Devine left the house and went to the hospital.

CHAPTER

# 80

Tapshaw looked weak and shaky. Her eyes fluttered open and then closed.

Devine studied her vitals on the monitor and noted that her oxygen levels were improved, but not nearly back to normal. She was very thin and probably didn't have a lot of robust reserve to overcome this easily.

He sat next to her bed and held her hand and watched her slight chest rise and fall.

"I'm so sorry this happened, Jill," he said. First she had lost the investment from Chilton and Mayflower Enterprises, and now she'd almost died. And it was probably all connected to what Devine was looking into. With Will Valentine as the unknown factor.

"Is . . . o- . . . kay, T-ravis."

"I saw your information on the email, Jill. I saw that you traced it to Will."

"W-Will . . . e-ma. . . ."

It now occurred to Devine that that was the reason Valentine had made a run for it and tried to kill them all. He had somehow discovered that Tapshaw had found him out.

"I'll follow up on that, Jill. Don't worry about that. We'll find him. I promise. But I think I should contact your family. I know your mom lives in California. But what about your dad? And your brother, Dennis? Do you have contact info for them on your phone? Or in your room?"

He knew he couldn't get on her phone or laptop without her passwords.

She mumbled something incoherent and then fell back asleep.

He glanced at her monitor, where everything seemed to be holding its own but didn't seem to be improving. He wished her color looked better.

He left her there and ventured to Helen Speers's room.

Only she wasn't there.

"She checked herself out AMA about two hours ago," the nurse told Devine when he made inquiries.

"'Against medical advice'?"

"Yes, but I think she'll be fine. She was already recovering nicely when she was brought in. She's a very fit young woman. The other woman is a lot frailer and she's also anemic. We're watching her closely."

"Did Speers say where she might be going? We room together."

"She didn't."

He wondered if Speers and Valentine had met up. And if they had, why.

*I might have enemies on both flanks right in my own camp.*

* * *

He went to work the next day and sat beside Burners who were openly weeping in front of their computer screens. Word had obviously gotten around that the firm was going under.

He had contacted Caltech, because he remembered that was where Tapshaw's mother taught, and left a message for her explaining a little of what had happened. He had heard nothing from Speers.

He then received a text from Montgomery, and they arranged to meet later in the city.

When he got to the café in Tribeca she was already waiting. He filled her in on what had happened at his town house.

"Oh my God," she exclaimed.

"So, two of my roomies are now missing. And Valentine wasn't there when the gas got turned on."

"Was he working with the laundering operation? With Cowl?"

"I think so." He went on to explain that Valentine had been the one to send him the emails.

"Then he *must* be working with them."

"And he tried to get rid of me, and my other roommates were collateral damage. But Jill tracked him down online, and Campbell's men have an APB out on him."

"And Speers?"

Devine shook his head. "She checked herself out of the hospital. She hasn't answered my texts or emails or phone calls."

"That is so odd." She reached out and took his hand. "Look, the stuff Brad was talking about. With you and the other soldiers in the Army?"

"What about it?" he said curtly.

"Is that why you left the military?"

"Yes. It ended with both of them dead, and I have a level of guilt from all of it that will haunt me until my dying day."

She sat back and studied him. "Whatever happened there, I believe that you did what you thought was the right thing, the honorable thing."

"Why do you believe that?" he said earnestly.

"Because, despite your best efforts to make yourself out to be a shit, you're actually a really good guy. A really *nice* guy, Travis. I can tell. Trust me. I've seen the whole spectrum of men. And you're definitely one of the good ones."

He took her hand and squeezed it. And she leaned over and kissed him.

"Now what will you do?" she asked.

"The mission's not finished yet."

"I mean after that."

"Not sure. Keep working for Campbell. I don't think I have a choice, really."

"Do you want company?"

"I'm not sure Campbell would go for that. No, I am sure he wouldn't."

"I meant on the personal side."

"You can do a helluva lot better than me, Michelle. While I hope I am a nice, honorable guy, I'm also a washed-up soldier with daddy problems."

She gazed at him. "You're a West Point grad. Army officer. You defended this country in combat. You have an MBA. I have a high school diploma and look great in a bikini and I have serious *mommy* problems. I think you can do a helluva lot better than *me*. But we could make it, if we worked at it."

"What I need to work at is finding out who killed all those people."

She sighed and sat forward. "But I thought Jerry Myers did it."

"I think he killed Sara. But I'm not sure about the others."

"Do you really think it could be your missing roommate?"

"Which one? Valentine or Speers?"

"Could they be working together?"

Devine thought back to the night at the bar, where Speers and Valentine just seemed to have an odd connection. But then she *had* searched his room. And he had left Speers for dead.

"I don't know. I really don't."

"Have the police found out anything more on Jerry Myers?" she asked.

"Detective Shoemaker contacted me. The killer spiked the bottle of whisky with enough cyanide to kill an elephant."

"Wow, taking no chances. But if you think Myers was paid to kill Sara Ewes, why wouldn't the person who killed him have gotten him to kill all the others, too? I know you have your gut feeling on this, but Myers could have killed everybody."

"Sara, I think, had to be hanged. At least in the killer's deranged mind. Sara was about five nine and athletically built. Not so easy to hoist someone like that up on a rope. And then the person had to strangle her first. Myers was my size, big and strong. And he had access to the building. The others? Stamos was drugged and then killed. A knife was used on the Eweses, too. Anyone could have done that. Including a woman."

"A woman?" she exclaimed. "But now I thought you said Valentine was behind this? Although I guess it could be Helen Speers who killed Jennifer Stamos and the Eweses."

He looked at her inscrutably, certain thoughts, uncomfortable thoughts, running through his mind. "I don't think Will would know which end of a knife to stab someone with. And with his big gut he's not crawling through windows. He can barely walk up the stairs. And if he was working with the people behind the money laundering they'd have plenty of skilled foot soldiers to do the deeds. But— "

"But what?"

"Why pay off Myers to kill Sara? Again, why not just use one of your own people, like Hancock?"

"Well, Myers had access to the building, like you said," countered Montgomery.

"So did Brad Cowl," retorted Devine. He fell silent. At first he had thought Cowl had been behind the killings. Then he had changed his mind and thought there was a different killer, who had had a grudge against him and who had sent him the weird emails, and killed his victims symbolically. Then he'd changed his opinion again, and decided it was the people behind Cowl and now Valentine who had done the killings, or at least he was involved, and all the rest was just misdirection.

*But now I'm not sure. Again.*

There was something off here, really off. And he just couldn't figure out what it was.

*But I have to. Eventually. Or else a killer walks free. To kill me.*

# CHAPTER 81

That night, Devine went back to an empty town house. Speers's room held her unused law books, but not the Glock under the mattress. The woman had evidently left the hospital, come back here, and gotten her weapon. He wondered why. And he also wondered where she was now.

They had all returned from the bar and gone to their rooms. At around four a.m. Devine had been awoken by the gas. During that time, Valentine must have messed with the gas lines and fled, leaving them all to die.

Campbell had texted him that their APB had so far turned up no leads on the man.

*Where the hell are you, Will? Back in Moscow getting a medal from Putin?*

He was about to go up to his room when the phone rang. He didn't recognize the number but decided to answer it.

"Hello?"

"Mr. Devine?"

"Yes. Who is this?"

"Emily Spanner."

"I'm afraid I don't— "

"I'm Jill Tapshaw's mother."

"Oh, Mrs. Spanner, I'm sorry. I looked up the faculty at Caltech but didn't see a Tapshaw listed. So I just left a message on the department receptionist's voice mail for Professor Tapshaw."

"It's all right. Spanner is my maiden name. That's happened before and I finally got your message. But what has happened? Is Jill okay?"

"She's fine. There was a gas leak in our town house. I'm one of her roommates. But we all got out okay. They took Jill to the hospital for observation, but the last time I checked she was fine."

"Oh my God, I had no idea. You're sure she's in no danger?"

Devine wasn't quite sure how to answer that, since it was clear someone had tried to kill them. *Or maybe just me.* But he didn't want to unduly worry the woman.

"No, she's fine. Really."

"Do you think I should come out there?"

"From a health perspective I don't think it's necessary, but I'm sure she'd love to see you."

"I'm not too sure about that."

"I don't understand."

"It's just family issues, Mr. Devine. We're all dysfunctional in our own way."

Devine thought of his own family. *Truer words were never spoken.* "I didn't have any contact info on Jill's father, or even his first name."

"George is in Canada. We're divorced."

"And I couldn't find any contact information for your son."

"Dennis?"

"Yes, I thought Jill's twin might want to know about what happened to her, too."

"I'm sure he would have."

"*Would* have?"

"Dennis is dead. He passed away nearly nine months ago."

"Oh my God, I had no idea. Jill never mentioned that."

"Does Jill have her phone with her in the hospital? Can I call her?"

"No, but I can get it and take it to her."

"That would be very nice, thank you. And thank you for contacting me."

"Jill is a really wonderful person. She works really hard."

"Yes, Hummingbird has been her dream for a while now."

"It's been very successful."

"She could be working anywhere, you know, with her skills and mind. She could be teaching at UPenn or Stanford."

"But this makes her happy. Bringing people together."

"Yes, I suppose it does. Well, thank you again for letting me know."

"Sure, thanks for the call back. And I'll get Jill's phone to her."

"I appreciate that. Goodbye."

Devine put his phone back in his pocket. Why hadn't Tapshaw mentioned that her twin was dead? But then again, he hadn't really talked to his roommates about his family. Still, he wondered how Dennis Tapshaw had died.

He climbed the stairs to Tapshaw's room and went inside. A search of her things revealed no phone. He wondered if she had left it at work. He'd noticed that she hadn't had it with her at the bar.

He looked around and saw a set of keys on a brown file folder. He picked them up and saw her car key on there. There was another key on there, too, but he knew it wasn't to the office. She used an electronic security card to get into her space like they did at Cowl and Comely. He knew that because she had taken him for a tour once and had used her security card to get in.

He had a sudden thought and went down to the garage and unlocked her Mini Cooper. He searched through it and found the RFID card in the console. This should get him into the office okay. He decided he might as well drive her car the short distance to the office rather than firing up his motorcycle. He also searched the car to make sure she hadn't left the phone in here. But he didn't find it. He called the phone to see if it had perhaps slipped down between the seat and the console, but he heard no ringing or vibrating.

There were some stains on the front seat that he wiped away with his hand. Tapshaw was not the cleanest or most organized person in the world. When they had ridden over to the bar in her car, he had been in the backseat with Valentine. His feet had been resting on top of mountains of old fast-food containers and used Starbucks coffee cups. And her car's interior smelled like a Dumpster.

He drove over to the strip of shops where Hummingbird was headquartered. The RFID card did its magic and the door unlocked. He went inside and flicked on the lights. Since Tapshaw had given him a tour through the office he knew the layout.

There was a large, open work area with a dozen computer screens flashing the Hummingbird home page, smartboards on the walls, desks and iPads and stacks of papers and marketing materials and files, copier machines, a water dispenser, a small kitchen and bathroom, and everything else one would normally see in an office.

He knew the cloud that ran the Hummingbird platform was housed elsewhere, because Tapshaw had told him.

Tapshaw's office was in the back corner. He tried the door, but it was locked. Then he saw the reader port and waved the RFID card in front of it, and the door clicked open.

He turned on the light and looked around at the messy space.

He again had the idea of calling her phone to see if it would ring somewhere in the mounds of all the stuff in here, but it didn't. She might have it on silent. But he didn't hear vibrating anywhere, either. The battery might have died for all he knew.

He started to slowly search the space. The woman's workload was immense, if all the docs he was looking at were an indicator. It was no wonder she looked tired all the time.

He looked through all the file cabinets until he came to one that was locked.

He hesitated and then decided to see if the other key on the ring would open it. He didn't know why she would lock her phone up in there, but he had seen her rushing around enough times trying to find stuff at the town house. Her car keys had once ended up in the refrigerator for some odd reason.

The key worked and he slid the drawer open. There was a mass of papers in here and some colored files. He moved them out of the way to see if perhaps the phone had slipped down to the bottom when he saw the red file. He slowly pulled it out.

It was from the doctor's office of Jonathan Wyman, more specifically his clinic for women wanting to undergo artificial insemination.

A stunned Devine slowly opened it and started to read what was inside.

The patient's name was Sara Elise Ewes.

The procedure was artificial insemination using donor sperm.

Then, written on a Post-it note, was a name: *Sperm donor: Dennis Tapshaw.*

*Jill's twin brother was the sperm donor for Sara Ewes's pregnancy?*

Devine was so overwhelmed by these revelations that he could barely think.

He turned when he heard the noise behind him.

Jill Tapshaw was standing in the doorway, pointing Devine's Sig at its owner.

# CHAPTER 82

WHAT ARE YOU DOING HERE, Travis?" she demanded.

He let the file drop to the desk. "Looking for your phone. Your mother called. She wanted to reach you. I knew you didn't have your phone with you at the hospital. I was trying to find it. It wasn't at—"

She held up her hand. "Just stop, okay? Please, just stop. Who cares about a phone or my mother?" She glanced down at what he had been holding. "Wonderful Dr. Wyman."

"Who?"

"Don't pull the stupid act, okay? I'm really tired from sucking in all that gas."

"Okay. Then let's talk about this, but not with the gun pointed at me."

"I told you to drop the stupid act. The gun is going nowhere."

She seemed like a totally different person now. He also had the impression that perhaps the Jill Tapshaw he thought he knew *was* an act. Maybe this was the real version.

He picked up the file. "You and Sara were having a baby together?"

"That was the plan. It didn't end well. But you know that, right?"

"And your brother was the sperm donor?"

"Why not? He was perfect."

"I also understand that he's dead."

By the look on her face, Devine wished he hadn't mentioned that.

"Who told you he was dead?" she said quietly.

"Your mother. I mentioned that I wanted to let him know about your being in the hospital, and that's when she told me he died." He paused. "Only she didn't tell me how he died."

Tapshaw held up the gun. "He put one of these in his mouth and pulled the fucking trigger."

"Why would he do that? You said he had everything going for him."

"Because Dennis desperately wanted to transition to being a woman, and my 'brilliant' father couldn't accept that. That's why my parents finally divorced. He was awful to Dennis. Never one minute's peace, never any support. He drove him to suicide. I wanted to kill him, but he ran away to Canada, and nobody knows where he is."

"Wyman said he didn't know who the sperm donor was."

"He didn't. Neither did Sara, at first."

"So you and Sara were in love and were having a baby? Why didn't anyone know about that?"

"You met her parents, so do you really have to ask the question? Sara wasn't about to tell them about me. And it's not like my father would have been thrilled with *two*, as he would see it, *alien* children."

"But no one even knew you and Sara were dating? That's hard to believe."

"Sara wanted it that way. She wanted to move up in her field."

"There are lots of gay people in the world of finance."

"Not that many gay women." She bit her lip and looked unsure for a moment. "And Sara was...confused, it seemed to me, about her sexuality." Tapshaw's face twisted angrily. "She needed to make up her mind, so we kept things quiet. Very quiet."

"So you two broke up? And she terminated the pregnancy. Why?"

She motioned with the gun to the file drawer that Devine had been looking through.

"Her diary is in there. In a yellow folder. Read it for yourself."

Devine slowly pulled the folder out and found a black journal inside. He flipped through the pages.

"The entry for December fourth," Tapshaw said.

Devine found it and read through Ewes's notes. He finished and looked up. "She was afraid of you? She was afraid you were unbalanced? That you were obsessed with your brother?"

"He had recently killed himself. I was distraught."

"She wrote that you had a shrine to him in your room. That you were too emotional, too over-the-top. Too controlling. And that this was before he killed himself. In her diary she wrote that after that you really lost it."

Tapshaw said in a strident tone, "She had no reason to be afraid of me. I loved her. And so what if I idolized my brother? Is that a crime?"

"You said she didn't know he was the sperm donor until later?"

In a calmer voice, Tapshaw said, "She... she found out. I don't know how. It was supposed to be anonymous, but I arranged for Dennis to donate the sperm."

"Is that why she terminated the pregnancy? She didn't want to carry your brother's baby?"

"It wasn't *his* baby; it was *my* baby. We were twins. If we were the same gender we'd have the same fucking DNA! Dennis got the Y chromosome, but he didn't want it. And she killed my baby. She might as well have put a bullet in *my* mouth."

"And when you found out, you decided to kill her?"

"No, I didn't. I was still dealing with Dennis's death." Her face twisted in anger at him. "But then I found out you two were seeing each other. She moved to her new place. But I found out. I saw you there with her. I know you slept with her. When a room became available at the town house where you lived, I grabbed it."

"Why?"

"I needed to watch you. I needed to know if you were going to be a good *match* for Sara."

"Match? Did you meet her through Hummingbird? She was one of your earliest subscribers, you said."

Tapshaw nodded and moved closer to Devine. "We were perfectly aligned in every way. The algorithm said we would be happy forever. It was love at first sight, the way it sometimes happens." She moved closer. "But then she abandoned me, terminated our child, and hooked up with you. And then she dumped you. I didn't know who she was seeing for a while. I thought it must be another man. I could understand and accept that she might like men and not women. I could have lived with that. I really could have. But then I saw her one night with a woman. They were kissing. They... were very close. They... were in love, obviously."

"Jennifer Stamos."

"I didn't know her name until I overheard you talking to her outside the town house."

*Shit*, thought Devine. *Her room overlooks the front of the house. She heard everything. And that conversation signed Stamos's death warrant.*

"The night she died you were up early. You said you had a Zoom interview with a magazine in the Netherlands."

"There was no interview. But I had just gotten *back* from killing her and you caught me, so I had to come up with something."

"You didn't have any blood on you or anything."

"I wore scrubs over my clothes and booties on my feet and then got rid of them in a Dumpster."

"You mutilated her body, Jill."

"She took Sara from me. So I had to take something from her."

"You were also probably worried that Sara had told Stamos about you. But I never mentioned you to Sara or Jenn; there would have been no reason to. But you couldn't chance that. Jenn was smart. She might put two and two together. And I got the emails telling me of their deaths. That was you, right? The untraceable emails."

"I wanted you to know. I wanted you to feel guilt that you

helped cause Sara's death. And the others', too. And making those emails work the way I did was a challenge. I enjoyed it. These internet assholes think they control everything. Well, I just blew that up, didn't I? A little old girl."

"And you went out the night that the Eweses were killed. You stabbed them in the heart."

"Yes, while you were probably screwing Speers. I know you two were lusting after each other."

"Do you have any idea where she is? Did you kill her, too?"

"I had no reason to kill *her*."

"But you hired Jerry Myers to kill Sara. How did you and Myers hook up?"

"He was Hummingbird subscriber seven thousand nine hundred and four. Lonely man with several bad relationships and one lousy marriage behind him looking for warmth, humor, and female companionship. New York Giants and New York Mets fans and beer drinkers particularly welcome," she said, apparently reciting his profile from memory.

"But how did you get him to do it?"

"He had been to prison. I found that out. It wasn't in his profile. He did it because I paid him and paid him well. He was just that sort of guy."

"But then he bought the truck?"

"It wasn't just that. He came back to me for more money. I paid him. He came back again for more. He left me no other choice. I don't like people who break their word."

"How did he get Sara alone?"

"I sent an email to Sara that she thought was from Brad Cowl basically ordering her to pull an all-nighter to meet a deadline. I later deleted it completely. And I mean completely. I know how. The NSA desperately wanted me to work for them, and I *did* for a year, which I never told anyone about. The NSA usually signs you to five-year deals. They don't like turnover for obvious reasons. But what were they going to do to me? They could keep me from getting another government job, but I didn't want that. So they had no leverage. But the bottom line is that I know how to wipe things *clean*. Jerry had never left the building. He hid in the storage closet where Sara was found. He waited until very late to make sure no one was around, went to her office, strangled her, and then strung her up."

"Hanged her for, what, being a traitor? To you?"

"To me and our baby. I had earlier hacked into the firm's calendar and found out about the M and A seminar the next day. That made it perfect for Jerry to kill her the night before. I told him no one would suspect him if he was the one to find the body. And you don't need your card to enter or leave the building during normal business hours. And Jerry had ridden up on the elevator to the fifty-second floor with some other people he knew worked on that floor, so he didn't have to use his card. After he killed Sara he slept in a spare office and showed up for work in his uniform."

"But he would need his security card to take the elevator down from the fifty-second."

"No, he just used the stairs. There are so many people coming in during the morning that there was no way to say for sure he wasn't in one of those groups. And while he was doing some work in the lobby the day before, Jerry shifted the camera positions just a bit to make it pretty much impossible to verify who came and went through each day. And the guard isn't there every minute. Then Jerry took the elevator up using his card the next morning and started his duties. On the fifty-second floor."

"To 'find' Sara?"

"That's right."

"Even more reason to have cameras on all the floors and the stairwells, not just the front and rear entrances."

She smiled. "From what I heard about Brad Cowl from Jerry, I don't think he would have liked cameras everywhere."

"And my security card being on the log the night Sara died? And my video?"

"I cloned your card while you were at the high school working out. It was easy."

"It's a one twenty-five piece of shit," said Devine dully.

"Yes, it is."

"And the video?"

"I took a film editing class in college. I had started thinking about doing something online, and I thought that skill would come in handy. And it did because I use it on Hummingbird. I took photos and video of you coming and going from the town house, Travis. And Jerry was your height and build. I took video of him going in and out of your building. Then I just digitally sliced and diced and put the appropriate clothes on you. Your head on his body. From a distance, it was close enough for the cops to nail you on it."

"And Stamos?"

"After I found out who she was, I got her address, broke into her place, drugged her, and did what I went there to do."

"Like carve *bitch* into her skin?"

"That was exactly what she was."

"No, she was the woman that Sara loved. And you couldn't live with that. And I was the one who told you about Fred and Ellen Ewes and her attitude toward Sara. So, in a way, I'm the reason they were killed. Stabbed through the heart because they, at least in your mind, had no hearts, or at least you implied that in your email to me. And then you manipulated the entry logs to show my card going in at the requisite time to kill Sara, and then you added a video image of me, too, like you just said. Only that didn't jibe with what the night security guard saw. I guess you didn't know when the guard made his rounds. And Jerry isn't there at night, so he wouldn't know, either. That one little oversight blew up your plan."

Her face crinkled and she gave him a weak smile that showed a bit of the innocent, kindhearted woman he thought he knew. "You're a smart person, Travis. And I do like you. I really do. You've always been so nice to me. You remind me a little of Dennis, actually." She stared off for a moment and her look hardened once more. "But when I found out that witch had killed our baby *and* was now with another *woman*? Well, I had to do something."

"But why send me the emails? Why set me up to take the fall, Jill?"

"You were the perfect choice, Travis. I did all the analysis. You're an Army Ranger, so you know how to kill people. You slept with Sara. You wanted a relationship with her and she rejected you. No one could really be certain you weren't the father. Those are motives to kill. I tried to be very logical in choosing you. But the main thing was you loved the woman I loved. In a way you took her away from me."

"I didn't even know you two were seeing each other."

"It doesn't matter," she snapped. "Okay?" She aimed the gun more rigidly at him.

She glanced over at the large computer where the Hummingbird logo was prominently displayed. "Now *Hummingbird* is my *baby*."

"Yeah, I remember you saying that to me. The only baby left to you."

She said absently, "I liked Will, too. It was a shame."

"What do you mean?" he said sharply. In the face of all this he had forgotten all about Valentine.

"When we got back from the bar? He came to my room later. He was really good at hacking. Better than I thought he was."

Understanding filtered through Devine's expression. "*He* finally traced the emails I got. And he traced them back to *you*. I found the information taped to your computer screen where you showed it was *Will* who sent them. But that was obviously all a lie."

"He was good, despite being a pig. And I hated the way he always used the word *dude*. I mean, it was like a bad 1980s movie or something."

"And when Will found out it was you?"

"He wanted an explanation. I told him I would give him one. At my office, where I told him I had documents that would explain all. I think I convinced him that *you* had killed those people and were trying to use both of us to cover up your crimes."

"You told him I had asked you to track the emails as well?"

"I did. And I intimated that you were working with people that could set us both up as being involved in all this. He wasn't a US citizen yet. So he was terrified of being deported. Before we left, I did as much as I could on the computer to turn the tables on him and show he was the source of the emails, and not me. I taped up that piece of paper on my computer for people to find."

"And then what happened?"

"On the drive over I asked him to get something out of the glove box. While he was doing that, I injected him in the neck with the same sedative I used on Stamos. I drove him to the lake near the town house. I stabbed him in the chest and tied a heavy rock to him. Then I threw his laptop and phone in the lake, too, after I rolled him into the water. Will was very heavy, but I was very determined. When I was throwing his stuff in, my phone fell out of my pocket and went into the water. I had some blood on me from stabbing him. I cleaned it up as best as I could, but I probably missed some."

Devine glanced down at his hand where he had rubbed off the stains from her car seat. *Will's blood?* "And the gas in the house? That was you?"

"I had to come up with a reason for Will's disappearance, namely, that he tried to kill all of us and then disappeared. I went back to the town house, packed some clothes in his suitcase, and tossed it in a Dumpster in the downtown area. Then I came back and fiddled with the gas."

"But weren't you afraid of dying from the gas? I mean, you were really close to it, Jill, when I carried you out of the house."

She looked at him calmly, with an utterly uninterested expression, which, under the tense standoff, was terrifying. "You should have just let me die, Travis. It would have been much better for me and certainly much better for *you*."

"Meaning now it's my turn? Is this what Dennis would have wanted?"

"Dennis never had a chance to know what he really wanted. But for what it's worth, I'm very sorry, Travis."

She fired the gun and the bullet slammed into his right shoulder. He fell back against the file cabinet and then dropped to the floor. The blood spurted down his front, and he desperately tried to use his shirt to stanch the bleeding.

She moved closer and aimed the gun at his head for the kill shot.

"I'm sorry, I meant to shoot you in the chest. I don't have really good aim. But it won't hurt anymore in a second, Travis. I promise. I never wanted any of this to happen."

A second shot rang out.

Devine watched Tapshaw stiffen as a bullet went into her back, traversed her thin torso, and exited out her chest. In his wounded, muddled state, Devine thought he could see the bullet in midair. The round smacked into the wall and stayed there.

Tapshaw swayed on her feet for a moment. Then the Sig fell from her hand. And she followed along with it, hitting the hard floor face-first and not moving again, except for one last involuntary twitch as life quickly transitioned to death.

A bleeding and rapidly weakening Devine swiveled his head to the doorway.

Helen Speers stood there with her Glock still pointing at where Tapshaw had been standing a moment before. She looked down at Devine and started to run toward him, her phone coming out as she tapped in 911.

"Travis!" she cried out.

Right as Devine's eyes closed.

# CHAPTER 83

DEVINE LAY IN A HOSPITAL bed, but his mind was elsewhere.

The *thump-thump* beats of the chopper blades, the swirl of heated desert air, the taste of red sand in his mouth along with the biting fumes of aviation fuel in his bloody nostrils. None of those things should happen while you're dying, because dying was enough of a bitch.

Ass over elbows, the IED had taken Devine, a 225-pound man, loaded down with fifty more pounds of gear, and launched him like a human cannonball across a rut-filled road fifty clicks outside of Kandahar. He hit the dirt unconscious. He woke up to a morphine-inspired fog. He endured multiple surgeries and a skin graft and did it all over again two years later when a badly aimed sniper round went through a defect in his body armor and ripped his shoulder apart instead of his brain.

Only this time it was the other shoulder, and he was nowhere near Kandahar.

Devine blinked himself awake and stared around the antiseptic confines of his hospital room. Just beneath the intoxicating shimmer of the morphine drip, he felt both the snakelike bite of the Sig Sauer nine-millimeter round and the surgery that had followed. Without painkillers he knew he would be shrieking in agony right now.

He flitted across time and space, and then his gaze lingered and stopped on twin figures.

Emerson Campbell was in a suit but without a tie.

Helen Speers was in a dark blue jacket and skirt with a red scarf around her neck. For a moment the drugged-up Devine thought she was an airline flight attendant.

"How is consciousness treating you, Devine?" asked Campbell.

Devine tried to form the words, but his mouth, along with his brain, was not entirely under his command.

Speers sat down next to him and took his hand, squeezing it in a firm grip. "I'm sorry, I should have been there sooner. I'm so sorry."

And she *did* look sorry, Devine had to admit. Very sorry indeed. He thought he saw tears bubbling at the edges of those beautiful eyes. But perhaps that was the morphine talking.

"Who are...?" That was all he could accomplish.

Campbell stepped forward. "She's with us, Devine. Special Agent Helen Speers. She fired the shot on the football field that allowed you to escape from Eric Bartlett and company that morning. Of course, she would have further intervened if you had needed her assistance. However, with Ms. Tapshaw, she couldn't take any chances."

"D-dead?" said Devine.

Speers slowly nodded. "Yes. It was either her or you." She glanced at Campbell. "Can you give us a minute, sir?"

Campbell nodded and stepped from the room.

Speers pulled her chair even closer and looked deeply at Devine.

"So...you were my g-guardian angel?" he said.

"I was supposed to be. When Campbell was thinking of recruiting you, he had me get a room at the town house."

"Do...you sleep with all your...?"

"No, I don't. I made an exception with you." Her face crinkled into a smile even as her eyes filled with tears. "I made some mistakes in my earlier career, Travis. I guess you did, too. I don't know if you know this, but Campbell collects people like you and me. We're sort of like the misfit toys on that island in *Rudolph the Red-Nosed Reindeer*. Damaged but capable of—"

"—re-redemption," he finished for her.

"Yes, redemption."

"So, you slept with me to show you were my ally?" he mumbled.

She stared at him for a long moment, something building in her expression that Devine's drug-induced thoughts could not readily interpret.

"I slept with you, Travis, because I wanted to sleep with you."

"W-why did you s-search Will's r-room?"

"I was suspicious and there seemed to be things hitting too close to that town house. I wanted to find out if we had enemies in our own camp." She reached down and stroked his cheek, and it felt so good.

Devine nodded and closed his eyes as the morphine flowed into him, engaging in a pitched battle with the pain ebbing just below the surface of his punctured shoulder.

When he awoke again, he was feeling better, and time apparently had marched on. It had been dark when Campbell and Speers had been there. It was daylight now, and he sensed that multiple days had passed. Nurses walked in and walked out after checking on him. Doctors and specialists examined him constantly.

He eyed his vitals on the monitor. They looked closer to normal than he probably deserved.

Campbell visited him regularly, and then walked in one morning and sat down next to him. "You look much better today," he said.

Devine managed to inch up a bit on his pillow before hitting the bed control to raise himself up more. "I think I've rounded the corner."

"Good."

"Jill Tapshaw?"

"Her mother came to claim her body. We gave her a full briefing. Well, as full as we could."

"How did you know what to tell her about Jill? I haven't been able to tell you anything."

"She left a full written confession in her room," said Campbell. "I think when she went to her office that night, she intended to kill herself using your gun. But she found you there instead. Worse luck for you. If she had killed you, she probably would have turned the gun on herself. Her poor mother was...devastated. She's lost both her children."

"Jill was a brilliant person. She did a lot to help people. And could have done a lot more."

"She did a lot to *hurt* people, too," countered Campbell.

"What about Cowl and Comely?"

"Shut down. The people behind Area 51 are still out there. But you disrupted their operations to a considerable extent."

"But how much damage have they already done?"

"We reviewed the report your friend Valentine cobbled together. That was hardly all of it, and we're working on finding out more. From what we can make out, foreign interests who are no friend of the United States own more of this country than most people, myself included, can even comprehend. And a lot of politicians across the country have received dark money from these same groups."

"What will happen to them?"

"Probably nothing. They'll shout to the heavens that they didn't know, or it's all fake, or entrapment, or a political hit job. And they'll keep their positions and go on doing exactly what they were doing and sucking on the same dark-money teat."

"That is some sick shit," Devine said wearily.

"But we have to keep this on the QT, Devine."

"What, why?"

"International relations, key alliances, not wanting to rock the boat too much, disrupt political arenas and financial markets, that sort of thing."

"That is total bullshit."

"I agree, it is," Campbell conceded.

Devine looked out the window at the sunny day. "So, I didn't really complete my mission, then. And you don't give out participation trophies. Am I headed to USDB?"

"I think you're well on your way to a second chance, Devine. If you want it."

The two former soldiers stared at each other.

"I want it," Devine finally said.

"And *that's* a good reason to get out of bed every day."

Devine looked around the room. "Is...have you heard from Michelle Montgomery?"

"She's left the country."

Devine nodded, looking and feeling disappointed. "Okay."

"She didn't really have a choice."

Devine glanced back at him. "What?"

"She wanted to visit you here many times, but that would not have been a good thing, so I put the kibosh on that. We arranged for a safe place for her to live abroad."

Campbell pulled an envelope from his pocket. "But she asked me to give you this."

Devine took the envelope. Without another word, Campbell left.

Devine slowly opened the envelope and slipped a single page and two photos out. He glanced down the paper and began to read:

*Dear Travis, what a ride! I've never been more scared and more excited in my life. Not sure what that says about me, but just being honest. I guess the general has told you what happened. I didn't want to leave you, but he didn't give me a choice. I can say I will miss you, and I will. But I'm convinced we will see each other again. And while the general won't like it, you can reach me at this phone number.*

Devine eyed the international phone number with the country code for Italy.

He read the rest of the letter.

*I won't call you because I don't want to put pressure on you. But you can call me. I'm so sorry about what happened to you. I never would have guessed that that sweet-looking girl who founded a dating service to help people find love would have been so screwed up. I hope you recover quickly. Even though I couldn't visit you in the hospital, I was thinking about you, all the time. And remember, while we both have baggage, it can't last forever. And even if it does, life must go on. And I don't think you or I need a dating service to find the person just right for us.*

*I'll Always Love You,*
*Michelle*

*P.S. The man in that photo is a keeper. The one of me is so you won't forget.*

Devine next looked at the photos. The one of him was the same photo she'd taken on the rooftop of her building: the troubled man with baggage. The one of her did not have her in a bikini but, rather, jeans and a T-shirt. With the loveliest smile he had ever seen.

He reluctantly set her picture aside and stared at the ceiling.

He had never suspected Jill Tapshaw. He had trusted her and then nearly been killed by her.

He had not trusted Helen Speers, and she had been the one to save his life.

He had suspected Will Valentine of wrongdoing, and the man had done nothing but be his friend and help him. And his payment for that had been the loss of his life.

During an earlier visit, Campbell had told him that Valentine's family back in Russia had been taken away by the state. The infant Valentine had been left alone and then whisked out of the country by family friends.

But with Michelle Montgomery, in the end, he had trusted her. And that trust had been amply rewarded.

*So maybe my instincts aren't all bad. But one out of four isn't going to cut it while working for Campbell.*

He turned to the window and lay there, staring at the rising sun of a new day.

CHAPTER

# 84

It was three weeks later, at precisely 6:20 in the morning.

Devine, his arm in a sling, stepped onto the train. He was leaving the area the next day. But he wanted to take one more trip on the 6:20. He wasn't sure why, but then again, maybe he was.

The train started to fill, station after station, with the young gladiators in their suits and skirts, their laptops and clouds fired up and gestating future wealth for those with already too much of it. Later, the train climbed the little knoll, slowed, and then stopped, like a thirsty animal does at creekside for a drink.

The Cowl palace was for sale. There was no Michelle Montgomery in her Morse code bikini. No swaggering billionaire in his natural habitat of unparalleled luxuriousness. Devine looked around the train car and saw all gazes stuck to computer screens.

He took out his laptop and looked over the email he had crafted along with a large attachment. It documented everything he had found out about Cowl and Comely. He hit the Send key, and off it flew to one Elaine Nestor, the tarred-and-feathered journalist.

*Go and win a Pulitzer, Elaine. And screw the powers that be and the dark money they suck on.*

Devine found himself staring out the window and conjuring up images that bordered partly on nostalgia and partly on necessity. His need to feel something. To regret things. To sense guilt and loss and other things he couldn't readily identify right now. Figuring out the inexplicable was never easy.

Sara Ewes and Jenn Stamos dead. Jill Tapshaw, too. Three remarkable women who could have done a lot of good in the world, given the chance.

But Tapshaw hadn't given the other two the opportunity. In her brilliant, twisted mind they needed to be punished and removed from the living.

And Will Valentine, his beer-guzzling friend with more optimism than any person Devine had ever met, and who loved his adopted country more than some native-born citizens, was also dead.

But Michelle Montgomery was still alive, though denied a place at whatever table Devine would be heading to, alone.

*But I have her phone number. And a letter from her in which she says she'll always love me. Right now that is enough.*

The train started up again with a jolt.

He turned away from the glass and stared straight ahead.

The only direction he could now see himself heading.

What lay there for him could be bullets or bombs once more. Or the more subtle entanglements that happened all over the world outside combat zones.

He didn't know which was more dangerous, or whether it would end up being a tie.

He only hoped that he was up to the task.

Ranger tabbed and Ranger scrolled. And a seasoned financial analyst to boot.

Devine would probably need all of it and a little bit more to survive. Along with luck.

A good soldier never discounted the intervention of well-timed luck.

Redemption, a second shot, a new lease on life.

Maybe this was all of those things.

*You'll never know until you try, soldier.*

He sat back, closed his eyes, and let the 6:20 train take him somewhere, one more time.

# ACKNOWLEDGMENTS

To Michelle, thanks for the early read and great comments on this one.

To Michael Pietsch, Ben Sevier, Elizabeth Kulhanek, Jonathan Valuckas, Matthew Ballast, Beth de Guzman, Anthony Goff, Rena Kornbluh, Karen Kosztolnyik, Brian McLendon, Albert Tang, Andy Dodds, Ivy Cheng, Joseph Benincase, Alexis Gilbert, Andrew Duncan, Morgan Martinez, Bob Castillo, Kristen Lemire, Briana Loewen, Mark Steven Long, Marie Mundaca, Lynn von Hassel, Rachael Kelly, Kirsiah McNamara, Lisa Cahn, John Colucci, Megan Fitzpatrick, Nita Basu, Alison Lazarus, Barry Broadhead, Martha Bucci, Ali Cutrone, Raylan Davis, Tracy Dowd, Melanie Freedman, Elizabeth Blue Guess, Linda Jamison, John Leary, John Lefler, Rachel Hairston, Tishana Knight, Jennifer Kosek, Suzanne Marx, Derek Meehan, Christopher Murphy, Donna Nopper, Rob Philpott, Barbara Slavin, Karen Torres, Rich Tullis, Mary Urban, Tracy Williams, Julie Hernandez, Laura Shepherd, Maritza Lumpris, Jeff Shay, Carla Stockalper, Ky'ron Fitzgerald, and everyone at Grand Central Publishing. As my readers can see from the long list of folks, it does take an army!

To Aaron and Arleen Priest, Lucy Childs, Lisa Erbach Vance, Frances Jalet-Miller, and Kristen Pini, for being such great partners.

To Mitch Hoffman, for continuing to be an amazing editor and friend.

To Jeremy Trevathan, Lucy Hale, Trisha Jackson, Stuart Dwyer,

Leanne Williams, Alex Saunders, Sara Lloyd, Claire Evans, Eleanor Bailey, Laura Sherlock, Jonathan Atkins, Christine Jones, Andy Joannou, Charlotte Williams, Rebecca Kellaway, Charlotte Cross, Lucy Grainger, Lucy Jones, and Neil Lang at Pan Macmillan, for continuing to amaze me with your creativity and dedication.

To Praveen Naidoo and the wonderful team at Pan Macmillan in Australia. Praveen, great to finally see you, albeit in a Zoom.

To Blake Smith and Thomas Dearden, for able assistance on the technology material.

To Caspian Dennis and Sandy Violette, for being far more than agents: for being dear friends.

To the charity auction winner, Paul Ekman (James V. Brown Library), thanks for supporting such a great institution. I hope you enjoyed your namesake in the story.

To Chuck Betack, for all matters military. Thanks for making me look good.

To Tom DePont, for making me look smart in financial matters, and providing me inspiration for monetary skullduggery!

And to Kristen White and Michelle Butler, who keep everything rolling along!